A CENTURY
OF STORIES
NEW HANOVER COUNTY PUBLIC LIBRARY
1906-2006

Hominids

Books by Robert J. Sawyer

NOVELS
Golden Fleece*
End of an Era*
The Terminal Experiment
Starplex
Frameshift*
Illegal Alien
Factoring Humanity*
Flashforward*
Calculating God*
Hominids*

THE QUINTAGLIO ASCENSION
Far-Seer
Fossil Hunter
Foreigner

SHORT-STORY COLLECTION
Iterations and Other Stories

ANTHOLOGIES
Tesseracts 6 *(with Carolyn Clink)*
Crossing the Line *(with David Skene-Melvin)*
Over the Edge *(with Peter Sellers)*

*published by Tor Books
(Readers' group guides available at www.sfwriter.com)

Hominids

Robert J. Sawyer

A Tom Doherty Associates Book

HOMINIDS

This novel was serialized in the January through April 2002 issues of *Analog Science Fiction and Fact* magazine.

This book is printed on acid-free paper.

Edited by David G. Hartwell

Book design by Angela Arapovic

A Tor Book
Published by Tom Doherty Associates, LLC
175 Fifth Avenue
New York, NY 10010

www.tor.com

Tor® is a registered trademark of Tom Doherty Associates, LLC.

Library of Congress Cataloging-in-Publication Data

Sawyer, Robert J.
    Hominids / Robert J. Sawyer.—1st ed.
        p. cm.
    "A Tom Doherty Associates book."
    ISBN 0-312-87692-0 (acid-free paper)
    1. Neanderthals—Fiction. 2. Prehistoric peoples—Fiction. I. Title

PO9199.3.S2533 H66 2022
813'.54—dc21

                                                                    2001059650

First Edition: May 2002

Printed in the United States of America

0 9 8 7 6 5 4 3 2 1

For
Marcel Gagné
and
Sally Tomasevic

Dude
and
The Other Dude

Great People,
Great Friends

Acknowledgments

For anthropological and paleontological advice, I thank: Jim Ahren, Ph.D., University of Wyoming; Shara E. Bailey, Arizona State University; Miguel Bombin, M.D., Ph.D., Laurentian University; Michael K. Brett-Surman, Ph.D., and Rick Potts, Ph.D., both of the National Museum of Natural History, Smithsonian Institution; John D. Hawks, Ph.D., University of Utah; Christopher Kuzawa, Emory University; Philip Lieberman, Ph.D., Brown University; Jakov Radovcic, Ph.D., Croatian Natural History Museum; Robin Ridington, Ph.D., Professor Emeritus, University of British Columbia; Gary J. Sawyer [no relation] and Ian Tattersall, Ph.D., both of the American Museum of Natural History; Anne-marie Tillier, Ph.D., Université de Bordeaux; Erik Trinkaus, Ph.D., Washington University in St. Louis; and Milford H. Wolpoff, Ph.D., University of Michigan.

Special thanks to: Art McDonald, Ph.D., Director, Sudbury Neutrino Observatory Institute, and J. Duncan Hepburn, Ph.D., site manager, Sudbury Neutrino Observatory; David Gotlib, M.D., Medical Director, Crisis Team, St. Joseph's Health Centre, Toronto; the Rev. Paul Fayter, historian of science and theology, York University, Toronto; and Andrew Stok, Photonics Group, University of Toronto.

Acknowledgments

Huge thanks to my lovely wife, Carolyn Clink; my editor, David G. Hartwell, and his associate, Moshe Feder; my agent, Ralph Vicinanza, and his associates, Christopher Lotts and Vince Gerardis; Tom Doherty, Linda Quinton, Jennifer Marcus, Aimee Crump, and everyone else at Tor Books; Harold and Sylvia Fenn, Robert Howard, Heidi Winter, and everyone else at H. B. Fenn and Company; Dr. Stanley Schmidt, Sheila Williams, Trevor Quachri, and Brian Bieniowski of *Analog Science Fiction and Fact*; Melissa Beckett; Megan Beckett; Marv Gold; Terence M. Green; Andrew Zimmerman Jones; Joe and Sharon Karpierz; Chris and Donna Krejlgaard; Donald Maass; Pete Rawlik; Joyce Schmidt; Tim Slater; and David G. Smith.

As always, I'm grateful to those friends and colleagues who commented on this book's manuscript: Asbed Bedrossian, Ted Bleaney, Michael A. Burstein, David Livingstone Clink, John Douglas, Marcel Gagné, James Alan Gardner, Richard Gotlib, Peter Halasz, Howard Miller, Laura Osborn, Dr. Ariel Reich, Alan B. Sawyer, Sally Tomasevic, Edo van Belkom, Andrew Weiner, and David Widdicombe.

Some of this novel was written while I was Writer-in-Residence at the Richmond Hill (Ontario) Public Library. Sincere thanks to librarian extraordinaire Cameron Knight, the Richmond Hill Public Library Board, and the Canada Council for the Arts.

Parts of this book were written at John A. Sawyer's vacation home on Canandaigua Lake, New York; at Mary Stanton's vacation home in West Palm Beach, Florida; and at Robin and Jillian Ridington's guest cottage on Retreat Island, British Columbia. I thank them all for their extraordinary generosity and hospitality.

Author's Note: A -Tal Tale

So is it *Neanderthal* or *Neandertal?*

Both spellings are correct, and both are in common usage, even among paleoanthropologists.

The fossil this type of hominid is named for was found in 1856, in a valley near Düsseldorf. The place was then called *Neanderthal*—*thal* meaning "valley," and "Neander" being a Greek version of "Neumann," the surname of the fellow after whom the valley was named.

Early in the twentieth century, the German government regularized spelling across all parts of their nation, and "thal" and "tal," both of which were in use up to that time in various parts of the country, became just "tal." So it's clear that the place that used to be called *Neanderthal* is now only correctly spelled *Neandertal.*

But what about the fossil hominid? Should we therefore rename it *Neandertal,* as well?

Some say yes. But there's a problem: scientific names are cast in stone once coined and, for all time, this type of hominid will be known in technical literature with a "th" spelling, either as *Homo neanderthalensis* or *Homo sapiens neanderthalensis* (depending on whether one classifies it as a separate species from us, or merely a subspecies). It does seem awkward to spell the "neanderthal" part differently in the scientific and English names.

Meanwhile, those who favor the use of the spelling "Neandertal man" are notably silent when the topic of Peking man comes up; there's no movement to change that name to "Beijing man," even though the city's name is always spelled Beijing in English these days.

I checked the latest editions of six major English-language dictionaries: *The American Heritage English Dictionary*, *The Encarta World English Dictionary*, *Merriam-Webster's Collegiate Dictionary* (Tor's house standard), *The Oxford English Dictionary*, *Random House Webster's Unabridged Dictionary*, and *Webster's New World Dictionary*. All accept both spellings.

And what about pronunciation? Some purists contend that regardless of whether you spell it *-tal* or *-thal*, you should pronounce it with a hard-T sound, since both *t* and *th* have always denoted that in German.

Maybe so, but I've heard many paleoanthropologists say it with an English *th* sound (as in *thought*). And of the six dictionaries I checked, all of them except the *OED* allow both pronunciations (with the *OED* accepting only *-tal*). The argument that English speakers should pronounce it the way German speakers do seems to imply that we should also call the capital of France "par-ee," rather than "pair-is," and yet doing so would be considered pretentious in most contexts.

Ultimately, it comes down to personal choice. In the extensive collection of research materials I consulted in creating this book, the *-thal* spelling outnumbers the *-tal* by better than two-to-one (even in recent technical literature), so I've settled on the original spelling, *Neanderthal*— which you may pronounce whichever way you wish.

The southern forests provide the message that it didn't have to be this way, that there is room on the earth for a species biologically committed to the moral aspects of what, ironically, we like to call "humanity": respect for others, personal restraint, and turning aside from violence as a solution to conflicting interests. The appearance of these traits in bonobos hints at what might have been among Homo sapiens, *if evolutionary history had been just slightly different.*

—RICHARD WRANGHAM AND DALE PETERSON
Demonic Males: Apes and the Origins of Human Violence

You have zero privacy anyway. Get over it.

—SCOTT MCNEALY
Chief Executive Officer
Sun Microsystems

Chapter One

The blackness was absolute.

Watching over it was Louise Benoît, twenty-eight, a statuesque postdoc from Montreal with a mane of thick brown hair stuffed, as required here, into a hair net. She kept her vigil in a cramped control room, buried two kilometers—"a mile an' a quarder," as she sometimes explained for American visitors in an accent that charmed them—beneath the Earth's surface.

The control room was next to the deck above the vast, unilluminated cavern housing the Sudbury Neutrino Observatory. Suspended in the center of that cavern was the world's largest acrylic sphere, twelve meters—"almost fordy feet"—across. The sphere was filled with eleven hundred tonnes of heavy water on loan from Atomic Energy of Canada Limited.

Enveloping that transparent globe was a geodesic array of stainless-steel struts, supporting 9,600 photomultiplier tubes, each cupped in a reflective parabola, each aimed in toward the sphere. All of this—the heavy water, the acrylic globe that contained it, and the enveloping geodesic shell—was housed in a ten-story-tall barrel-shaped cavern, excavated from the surrounding norite rock. And that gargantuan cavern was filled almost to the top with ultrapure regular water.

The two kilometers of Canadian shield overhead, Louise knew, protected the heavy water from cosmic rays. And the shell of regular water absorbed the natural background radiation from the small quantities of uranium and thorium in the surrounding rock, preventing that, too, from reaching the heavy water. Indeed, nothing could penetrate into the heavy water except neutrinos, those infinitesimal subatomic particles that were the subject of Louise's research. Trillions of neutrinos passed right through the Earth every second; in fact, a neutrino could travel through a block of lead a light-year thick with only a fifty-percent chance of hitting something.

Still, neutrinos poured out of the sun in such vast profusion that collisions did occasionally occur—and heavy water was an ideal target for such collisions. The hydrogen nuclei in heavy water each contain a proton—the normal constituent of a hydrogen nucleus—plus a neutron, as well. And when a neutrino did chance to hit a neutron, the neutron decayed, releasing a proton of its own, an electron, and a flash of light that could be detected by the photomultiplier tubes.

At first, Louise's dark, arching eyebrows did not rise when she heard the neutrino-detection alarm go *ping*; the alarm sounded briefly about a dozen times a day, and although it was normally the most exciting thing to happen down here, it still didn't merit looking up from her copy of *Cosmopolitan*.

But then the alarm sounded again, and yet again, and

then it stayed on, a solid, unending electric bleep like a dying man's EKG.

Louise got up from her desk and walked over to the detector console. On top of it was a framed picture of Stephen Hawking—not signed, of course. Hawking had visited the Sudbury Neutrino Observatory for its grand opening a few years ago, in 1998. Louise tapped on the alarm's speaker, in case it was on the fritz, but the keening continued.

Paul Kiriyama, a scrawny grad student, dashed into the control room, arriving from elsewhere in the vast, underground facility. Paul was, Louise knew, usually quite flustered around her, but this time he wasn't at a loss for words. "What the heck's going on?" he asked. There was a grid of ninety-eight by ninety-eight LEDs on the detector panel, representing the 9,600 photomultiplier tubes; every one of them was illuminated.

"Maybe someone accidentally turned on the lights in the cavern," said Louise, sounding dubious even to herself.

The prolonged bleep finally stopped. Paul pressed a couple of buttons, activating five TV monitors slaved to five underwater cameras inside the observatory chamber. Their screens were perfectly black rectangles. "Well, if the lights *were* on," he said, "they're off now. I wonder what—"

"A supernova!" declared Louise, clapping her long-fingered hands together. "We should contact the Central Bureau for Astronomical Telegrams; establish our priority." Although SNO had been built to study neutrinos from the sun, it could detect them from anywhere in the universe.

Paul nodded and plunked himself down in front of a

Web browser, clicking on the bookmark for the Bureau's site. It was worth reporting the event, Louise knew, even if they weren't yet sure.

A new series of pings sounded from the detector panel. Louise looked at the LED board; several hundred lights were illuminated all over the grid. Strange, she thought. A supernova should register as a *directional* source . . .

"Maybe something's wrong with the equipment?" said Paul, clearly reaching the same conclusion. "Or maybe the connection to one of the photomultipliers is shorting out, and the others are picking up the arc."

The air split with a creaking, groaning sound, coming from next door—from the deck atop the giant detector chamber itself. "Perhaps we should turn on the chamber lights," said Louise. The groaning continued, a subterranean beast prowling in the dark.

"But what if it *is* a supernova?" said Paul. "The detector is useless with the lights on, and—"

Another loud cracking, like a hockey player making a slap shot. "Turn on the lights!"

Paul lifted the protective cover on the switch and pressed it. The images on the TV monitors flared then settled down, showing—

"*Mon dieu,*" declared Louise.

"There's something inside the heavy-water tank!" said Paul. "But how could—?"

"Did you see that?" said Louise. "It's moving, and— good Lord, it's a man!"

The cracking and groaning sounds continued, and then—

They could see it on the monitors and hear it coming through the walls.

The giant acrylic sphere burst apart along several of the seams that held its component pieces together. "*Tabernacle*," Louise swore, realizing the heavy water must now be mixing with the regular H_2O inside the barrel-shaped chamber. Her heart was jackhammering. For half a second, she didn't know whether to be more concerned about the destruction of the detector or about the man who was obviously drowning inside it.

"Come on!" said Paul, heading for the door leading to the deck above the observatory chamber. The cameras were slaved to VCRs; nothing would be missed.

"*Un moment,*" said Louise. She dashed across the control room, grabbed a telephone handset, and pounded out an extension from the list taped to the wall.

The phone rang twice. "Dr. Montego?" said Louise, when the Jamaican-accented voice of the mine-site physician came on. "Louise Benoît here, at SNO. We need you right away down at the neutrino observatory. There's a man drowning in the detector chamber."

"A man drowning?" said Montego. "But how could he possibly get in there?"

"We don't know. Hurry!"

"I'm on my way," said the doctor. Louise replaced the handset and ran toward the same blue door Paul had gone through earlier, which had since swung shut. She knew the signs on it by heart:

Keep Door Closed
Danger: High Voltage Cables
No Unauthorized Electronic Equipment Beyond This Point
Air Quality Checked—Cleared for Entry

Louise grabbed the handle, pulling the door open, and hurried onto the wide expanse of the metal deck.

There was a trapdoor off to one side leading down to the actual detector chamber; the final construction worker had exited through it, and had sealed it shut behind him. To Louise's astonishment, the trapdoor was still sealed by forty separate bolts—of course, it was *supposed* to be sealed, but there was no way a man could have gotten inside except through that trapdoor . . .

The walls surrounding the deck were covered with dark green plastic sheeting to keep rock dust out. Dozens of conduits and polypropylene pipes hung from the ceiling, and steel girders sketched out the shape of the room. Computing equipment lined some walls; others had shelves. Paul was over by one of the latter, desperately rummaging around, presumably for pliers strong enough to crank the bolts free.

Metal screamed in anguish. Louise ran toward the trapdoor—not that there was anything she could do to unseal it with her bare hands. Her heart leapt; a sound like machine-gun fire erupted into the room as the restraining bolts shot into the air. The trapdoor burst open, slapping back on its hinges and hitting the deck with a reverberating clang. Louise had jumped out of the way, but a geyser of cold water leapt up through the opening, soaking her.

The very top of the detector chamber was filled with nitrogen gas, which Louise knew must be venting now. The water spout quickly subsided. She moved toward the opening in the deck and looked down, trying not to breathe. The interior was illuminated by the floodlights Paul had turned on, and the water was absolutely pure; Louise could see all the way to the bottom, thirty meters below.

She could just make out the giant curving sections of the acrylic sphere; the acrylic's index of refraction was almost identical to that of water, making it hard to see. The sections, separated from each other now, were anchored to the roof by synthetic-fiber cables; otherwise, they would have already sunk to the bottom of the surrounding geodesic shell. The trapdoor's opening gave only a limited perspective, and Louise couldn't yet see the drowning man.

"*Merde!*" The lights inside the chamber had gone off. "Paul!" Louise shouted. "What are you doing?"

Paul's voice—now coming from back in the control room—was barely audible above the air-conditioning equipment and the sloshing of the water in the huge cavern beneath Louise's feet. "If that man's still alive," he shouted, "he'll see the lights up on the deck through the trapdoor."

Louise nodded. The only thing the man would now be seeing was a single illuminated square, a meter on a side, in what, to him, would be a vast, dark ceiling.

A moment later, Paul returned to the deck. Louise looked at him, then back down at the open trapdoor. There was still no sign of the man. "One of us should go in," said Louise.

Paul's almond-shaped eyes went wide. "But . . . the heavy water—"

"There's nothing else to do," said Louise. "How good a swimmer are you?"

Paul looked embarrassed; the last thing he ever wanted to do, Louise knew, was look bad in her eyes, but . . . "Not very," he said, dropping his gaze.

It was already awkward enough down here with Paul mooning over her all the time, but Louise couldn't very well swim in her SNO-issue blue-nylon jumpsuit. Underneath, though, like almost everyone else who worked at SNO, she only had on her underwear; the temperature was a tropical 40.6 Celsius this far beneath Earth's surface. She yanked off her shoes, then pulled on the zipper that ran down the front of the jumpsuit; thank God she'd worn a bra today—although she wished now that it hadn't been as lacy.

"Turn the lights back on down there," said Louise. To his credit, Paul didn't tarry. Before he'd returned, Louise had slipped through the trapdoor into the cold water; the water was chilled to ten degrees Celsius to discourage biological growth and to reduce the spontaneous noise rate of the photomultiplier tubes.

She felt a rush of panic, a sudden feeling of being a long way up with nothing supporting her; the bottom was far, far below. She was treading water, her head and shoulders sticking up through the open trapdoor into the air, waiting for her panic to subside. When it did, she took three deep breaths, closed her mouth tight, and dived beneath the surface.

Louise could see clearly, and her eyes didn't sting at all. She looked around, trying to spot the man, but there were so many pieces of acrylic, and—

There he was.

He had indeed floated up, and there was a small gap—

maybe fifteen centimeters—between the top of the water and the deck above. Normally it was filled with ultrapure nitrogen. The poor guy *must* be dead; three breaths of that would be fatal. A sad irony: he probably fought his way to the surface, thinking he could find air, only to be killed by the gas he inhaled there. Breathable air from the open trapdoor must now be mixing with the nitrogen, but presumably it was too late to help him.

Louise pushed her own head and shoulders up through the trapdoor again. She could see Paul, desperately waiting for her to say something—anything. But there was no time for that. She gulped more air, filling her lungs as much as she could, then dived under. There wasn't enough room for her to keep her nose above water without constantly banging her head into the metal roof as she swam. The man was about ten meters away. Louise kicked her feet, covering the distance as quickly as she could, and—

A cloud in the water. Something dark.

Mon dieu!

It was blood.

The cloud surrounded the man's head, obscuring his features. He wasn't moving at all; if he were still alive, he was surely unconscious.

Louise craned to get her mouth and nose into the air gap. She took one tentative breath—but there was plenty of breathable air there now—then grabbed the man's arm. Louise rolled the fellow over—he'd been floating face-down—so that his nose was sticking up into the air gap, but it seemed to make no difference. There was no spluttering from him, no sign that he was still breathing.

Louise dragged him through the water. It was tough work: the man was quite stocky, and he was fully dressed; his clothes were waterlogged. Louise didn't have time to notice much, but it did register on her that the man *wasn't* wearing coveralls or safety boots. He couldn't possibly be one of the nickel miners, and although Louise had only gotten a fleeting glimpse of the man's face—a white guy, blond beard—he wasn't from SNO, either.

Paul must have been crouching on the deck above. Louise could see his head sticking into the water; he was watching as Louise and the man came closer. Under other circumstances, Louise would have gotten the injured person out of the water before she herself left it, but the trapdoor was only big enough for one of them to go through at a time, and it would take both her and Paul to drag this large man out.

Louise let go of the man's arm and stuck her head up through the trapdoor, Paul having now backed off from it. She took a moment just to breathe; she was exhausted from pulling the man through the water. And then she put her palms flat on the wet deck and began to lift herself up and out. Paul crouched down again and helped Louise onto the deck, then they turned back to the man.

He had started to drift away, but Louise managed to grab his arm and drag him back under the opening. Louise and Paul then struggled to get him out, finally succeeding in lifting him onto the deck. He was still bleeding; the injury was clearly to the side of his head.

Paul immediately knelt next to the man and began administering mouth-to-mouth resuscitation, his cheek getting slick with blood each time he turned to see if the man's broad chest was rising.

Louise, meanwhile, found the man's right wrist and searched for a pulse. There didn't—no, no, wait! There was! There *was* a pulse.

Paul continued to blow air into the man's mouth, over and over again, and finally the man began to gasp on his own. Water and vomit came pouring out of him. Paul turned his head sideways, and the liquid he was ejecting mixed with the blood on the deck, washing some of it away.

The man still seemed to be unconscious, though. Louise, soaking wet, almost naked, and still chilled from the water, was starting to feel quite self-conscious. She struggled back into her jumpsuit and zipped it up—Paul watching her, she knew, even while he pretended not to.

It would still be a while before Dr. Montego arrived. SNO wasn't just two kilometers down; it was also a kilometer and a quarter horizontally from the nearest elevator, at mineshaft number nine. Even if the lift cage had been at the top—and there was no guarantee it would have been—it would still take Montego twenty-odd minutes to get here.

Louise thought she should get the man out of his wet clothes. She reached for the front of his charcoal gray shirt, but—

But there were no buttons—and no zipper. It didn't appear to be a pullover, even though it was collarless, and—

Ah, there they were! Hidden snaps running along the tops of the broad shoulders. Louise tried to undo them, but they didn't budge. She glanced down at the man's pants. They seemed to be dark olive green, although they might have been much lighter if dry. But there was no belt; instead, a series of snaps and folds encircled the waist.

It suddenly occurred to Louise that the man might be suffering from the bends. The detector chamber was thirty meters deep; who knew how far down he'd gone or how quickly he'd come up? Air pressure this much below Earth's surface was 130 percent of normal. At that moment, Louise couldn't figure out how that would affect whether someone got the bends, but it did mean the man would now be receiving a higher concentration of oxygen than he would have up top, and that surely must be to the good.

There was nothing to do now but wait; the man was breathing, and his pulse had strengthened. Louise finally had a chance to really look at the stranger's face. It was broad but not flat; rather, the cheekbones trailed back at an angle. And his nose was gargantuan, almost the size of a clenched fist. The man's lower jaw was covered by a thick, dark blond beard, and straight blond hair was plastered across his forehead. His facial features were vaguely Eastern European, but with Scandinavian rather than olive coloring. The wide-spaced eyes were closed.

"Where could he possibly have come from?" asked Paul, now sitting cross-legged on the deck next to the man. "No one should have been able to get down here, and—"

Louise nodded. "And even if he could, how would he get inside the sealed detector chamber?" She paused and brushed hair out of her eyes—realizing for the first time that she'd lost her hair net while swimming in the tank.

"You know, the heavy water is ruined. If he survives this stunt, he'll face one heck of a lawsuit."

Louise found herself shaking her head. Who could this man be, anyway? Maybe a Native Canadian zealot—an Indian who felt the mining was interfering with sacred ground. But the man's hair was blond, rare among Natives. Nor was this a youthful prank gone bad; the guy looked to be about thirty-five.

It was possible he was a terrorist or an antinuclear protester. But although Atomic Energy of Canada Limited had indeed supplied the heavy water, there was no nuclear work done at this site.

Whoever he was, Louise reflected, if he did finally die from his injuries, he'd be a prime candidate for the Darwin Awards. This was classic evolution-in-action stuff: a person who did something so incredibly stupid it cost him his own life.

Chapter Two

Louise Benoît heard the sound of the opening door; someone was coming out onto the deck above the detector
chamber. "Yoo-hoo!" she called, getting Dr. Montego's attention. "Over here!"

Reuben Montego, a Jamaican-Canadian in his midthir-
ties, hurried over to them. He shaved his head completely
bald—meaning he was the only person allowed into SNO
without a hair net—but, like everyone else, he still had to
wear a hardhat. The doctor crouched down, rotated the
injured man's left wrist, and—

"What the heck is that?" said Reuben, in his accented
voice.

Louise saw it, too: something set, apparently, into the
skin of the man's wrist, a high-contrast, matte-finish rectangular screen about eight centimeters long and two
across. It was displaying a string of symbols, the leftmost of
which was changing about once per second. Six small
beads, each a different color, formed a line beneath the
display, and something—maybe a lens—was positioned at
the end of the device farthest up the man's arm.

"Some kind of fancy watch?" said Louise.

Reuben clearly decided to ignore this mystery for the

moment; he placed his index and middle fingers over the man's radial artery. "He's got a decent pulse," he announced. He then lightly slapped one of the man's cheeks, then the other, seeing if he could bring him to consciousness. "Come on," he said in an encouraging tone. "Come on. Wake up."

At last the man did stir. He coughed violently, and more water spilled from his mouth. Then his eyes fluttered open. His irises were an arresting golden brown, unlike any Louise had ever seen before. It seemed to take a second or two for them to focus, then they went wide. The man looked absolutely astonished by the sight of Reuben. He turned his head and saw Louise and Paul, and his expression continued to be one of shock. He moved a bit, as if trying perhaps to get away from them.

"Who are you?" asked Louise.

The man looked at her blankly.

"Who are you?" Louise repeated. "What were you trying to do?"

"*Dar*," said the man, his deep voice rising as if asking a question.

"I need to get him to the hospital," said Reuben. "He obviously took a nasty hit to the head; we'll need skull x-rays."

The man was looking around the metal deck, as if he couldn't believe what he was seeing. "*Dar barta dulb tinta?*" he said. "*Dar hoolb ka tapar?*"

"What language is that?" Paul asked Louise.

Louise shrugged. "Ojibwa?" she said. There was an Ojibwa reserve not far from the mine.

"No," Reuben said, shaking his head.

"*Monta has palap ko,*" said the man.

"We don't understand you," said Louise to the stranger. "Do you speak English?" Nothing. "*Parlez-vous français?*" Still nothing.

Paul said "*Nihongo ga dekimasu ka?*" which Louise assumed meant, "Do you speak Japanese?"

The man looked at each of them in turn, eyes still wide, but he made no reply.

Reuben rose, then extended a hand down toward the man. He stared at it for a second, then took it in his own, which was huge, with fingers like sausages and an extraordinarily long thumb. He let Reuben pull him to his feet. Reuben then put an arm around the man's broad back, helping to hold him up. The man must have outweighed Reuben by thirty kilos, all of it muscle. Paul moved to the man's other side and used an arm to help support the stranger as well. Louise went ahead of the three of them, holding open the door to the control room, which had closed automatically after Reuben had entered.

Inside the control room, Louise put on her safety boots and hardhat, and Paul did the same; the hats had built-in lamps and hearing-protection cups that could be swung down when needed. They also put on safety glasses. Reuben was still wearing his own hardhat. Paul found another one on top of a metal locker and proffered it to the injured man, but before he could respond the doctor waved the hat away. "I don't want any pressure on his skull until we've done those x-rays," he said. "All right, let's get him up to the surface. I called for an ambulance on my way over."

The four of them left the control room, headed down

a corridor, and walked into the arrival area for the SNO facility. SNO maintained clean-room conditions—not that it mattered much anymore, Louise thought ruefully. They walked past the vacuuming chamber, a shower stall–like affair that sucked dust and dirt off those entering SNO. Then they passed a row of real shower stalls; everyone had to wash before entering SNO, but that, too, wasn't necessary on the way out. There was a first-aid station here, and Louise saw Reuben looking briefly at the locker labeled "Stretcher." But the man was walking well enough, so the doctor motioned for them to continue out into the drift.

They turned on their hardhat lights and began trudging the kilometer and a quarter down the dim dirt-floored tunnel. The rough-hewn walls were peppered with steel rods and covered over with wire mesh; this far beneath Earth's surface, with the weight of two kilometers of crust pressing down on them, unreinforced rock walls would burst into any open space.

As they walked along the drift, occasionally coming across muddy patches, the man began to take more of his own weight; he was clearly recovering from his ordeal.

Paul and Dr. Montego were engaged in an animated discussion about how this man could have possibly gotten into the sealed chamber. For her part, Louise was lost in thought about the ruined neutrino detector—and what that was going to do to her research funding. Air blew into their faces all the way along the drift; giant fans constantly pumped atmosphere down from the surface.

Finally, they reached the elevator station. Reuben had ordered the lift cage locked off here, on the 6,800-foot level—the mine's signage predated Canada's switch to the metric system. It was still waiting for them, no doubt to the chagrin of miners who wanted to come down or go up.

They entered the cage, and Reuben repeatedly activated the buzzer that would let the hoist operator on the surface know it was time to start the winch. The lift shuddered into motion. The cage had no internal lighting, and Reuben, Louise, and Paul had turned off their hardhat lamps rather than blind each other with their glare. The only illumination came in flashes from fixtures in the tunnels they passed every 200 feet, visible through the open front of the cage. In the weird, strobing light, Louise caught repeated glimpses of the strange man's angular features and his deep-set eyes.

As they went higher and higher, Louise felt her ears pop several times. They soon passed the 4,600-foot level, Louise's favorite. Inco grew trees there for reforestation projects around Sudbury. The temperature was a constant twenty degrees; adding artificial light turned it into a fabulous greenhouse.

Crazy thoughts occurred to Louise, weird *X-Files* notions about how the man could have gotten inside the sphere with the trapdoor still bolted shut. But she kept them to herself; if Paul and Reuben were having similar flights of fancy, they were also too embarrassed to give them voice. There *had* to be a rational explanation, Louise told herself. There had to be.

The cage continued its long ascent, and the man seemed to take stock of himself. His strange clothes were still somewhat wet, although the blowing air in the tunnels had done much to dry them. He tried wringing out his shirt, a few drops falling on the yellow-painted metal floor of the elevator cage. He then used his large hand to brush his wet hair off his forehead revealing, to Louise's astonishment—she gasped, although the sound surely was inaudible over the clanging of the rising car—a prodigious ridge arching above each eye, like a squashed version of the McDonald's logo.

At last the elevator shuddered to a halt. Paul, Louise, Dr. Montego, and the stranger disembarked, passing a small group of perplexed and irritated miners who were waiting to go down. The four of them headed up the ramp into the large room where workers hung their outdoor clothes each day, swapping them for coveralls. Two ambulance attendants were waiting. "I'm Reuben Montego," said Reuben, "the mine-site doctor. This man nearly drowned, and he's suffered a cranial trauma . . ." The two attendants and the doctor continued to discuss the man's condition as they hustled him out of the building and into the hot summer day.

Paul and Louise followed, watching as the doctor, the injured man, and the attendants entered the ambulance and sped away on the gravel road.

"Now what?" said Paul.

Louise frowned. "I have to call Dr. Mah," she said. Bonnie Jean Mah was SNO's director. Her office was at Carleton University in Ottawa, almost 500 kilometers away. She was rarely seen at the actual observatory site; the day-to-day operations were left to postdocs and grad students, like Louise and Paul.

"What are you going to tell her?" asked Paul.

Louise looked in the direction of the departing ambulance, with its impossible passenger. "*Je ne sais pas,*" she said, shaking her head slowly.

Chapter Three

It had started *much* more serenely. "Healthy day," Ponter Boddit had said softly, propping his jaw up with a crooked arm as he looked over at Adikor Huld, who was standing by the washbasin.

"Hey, sleepyhead," said Adikor, turning now and leaning his muscular back against the scratching post. He shimmied left and right. "Healthy day."

Ponter smiled back at Adikor. He liked watching Adikor move, liked watching the muscles in his chest work. Ponter didn't know how he would have survived the loss of his woman-mate Klast without Adikor's support—although there were still some lonely times. When Two became One—the latest occurrence of which had just ended—Adikor went in to be with his own woman-mate and their child. But Ponter's daughters were getting older, and he'd hardly seen them this time. Of course, there were plenty of elderly women whose men had died, but women so full of experience and wisdom—women old enough to vote!—would want nothing to do with one as young as Ponter, who had seen only 447 moons.

Still, even if they didn't have much time for him, Ponter had enjoyed seeing his daughters, although—

It depended on the light. But sometimes, when the sun was behind her, and she tilted her head just so, Jasmel was the absolute image of her mother. It took Ponter's breath away; he missed Klast more than he could say.

Across the room, Adikor was now filling the pool. He was bent over, operating the nozzle, his back to Ponter. Ponter lowered his head onto the disk-shaped pillow and watched.

Some people had cautioned Ponter against moving in with Adikor, and, Ponter was sure, a few of Adikor's friends had probably expressed a similar concern to him. It had nothing to do with what had transpired at the Academy; it was simply that working *and* living together could be an awkward combination. But although Saldak was a large city (its population was over twenty-five thousand, split between Rim and Center), there were only six physicists in it, and three of those were female. Ponter and Adikor both enjoyed talking about their work and debating new theories, and both appreciated having someone who really understood what they were saying.

Besides, they made a good pair in other ways. Adikor was a morning person; he hit the day running and enjoyed drawing the bath. Ponter rallied as the day progressed; he always looked after preparing the evening meal.

Water continued to spray from the nozzle; Ponter liked the sound, a raucous white noise. He let out a contented sigh and climbed out of the bed, the moss growing on the floor tickling his feet. He stepped over to the window and grasped the handles attached to the sheet-metal panel, pulling the shutter off the magnetic window frame. He then reached over his head, placing the shutter in its daytime position, adhering to a metal panel set in the ceiling.

The sun was rising through the trees; it stung Ponter's eyes, and he tilted his head down, bringing the front of his jaw to his chest, letting his browridge shade his vision. Outside, a deer was drinking from the brook three hundred paces away. Ponter hunted occasionally, but never in the residential areas; these deer knew they had nothing to fear—not here, not from any of the humans. Off in the distance, Ponter could see the glint of the solar panels spread along the ground by the next house.

Ponter spoke into the air. "Hak," he said, calling his Companion implant by the name he'd given it, "what's the forecast?"

"Quite lovely," said the Companion. "The high today: sixteen degrees; the low tonight, nine." The Companion used a feminine voice. Ponter had recently—and, he now realized, stupidly—reprogrammed it to use recordings of Klast's voice, taken from her alibi archive, as the basis for the way it spoke. He'd thought hearing the sound of her voice would make him feel less lonely, but instead it tugged at his heart every time his implant talked to him.

"No chance of rain," continued his Companion. "Winds from twenty-percent deasil, at eighteen thousand paces per daytenth."

Ponter nodded; the implant's scanners could easily detect him doing that.

"Bath's ready," said Adikor from behind him. Ponter turned and saw Adikor slipping into the circular pool recessed into the floor. He started the agitator, and the water roiled around him. Ponter—naked, like Adikor—walked over to the pool and slipped in as well. Adikor preferred his water warmer than Ponter did; they'd eventually settled on a compromise temperature of thirty-seven degrees—the same as body temperature.

Ponter used a *golbas* brush and his hands to clean the parts of Adikor that Adikor himself couldn't reach, or preferred to have Ponter do. Then Adikor helped clean Ponter.

There was much moisture in the air; Ponter breathed deeply, letting it humidify his sinus cavities. Pabo, Ponter's large reddish brown dog, came into the room. She didn't like to get wet, so she stayed several paces from the pool. But she clearly wanted to be fed.

Ponter gave Adikor a "what can you do?" look and hauled himself out of the bath, dripping on the blanket of moss. "All right, girl," he said. "Just let me get dressed."

Satisfied that her message had been delivered, Pabo padded out of the bedroom. Ponter moved over to the washbasin and selected a drying cord. He gripped the two handles and rolled it from side to side across his back; he then chomped down on one of the cord's handles while he dried off his arms and legs. Ponter looked at himself in the square mirror above the washbasin, and used splayed fingers to make sure his hair was deployed properly on either side of his central part.

There was a pile of clean clothes in a corner of the room. Ponter walked over and surveyed the selection. He normally didn't think much about clothing, but if Adikor and he were successful today, one of the Exhibitionists might come look at them. He picked out a charcoal gray shirt, pulled it on, and did up the clasps at the tops of the shoulders, closing the wide gaps. This shirt was a good choice, he thought—it had been a gift from Klast.

He selected a pant and put it on, slipping his feet into the baggy pouches at the end of each leg. He then cinched the leather ankle and instep ties, producing a comfortable snugness.

Adikor was getting out of the pool now. Ponter glanced at him, then looked down at the display on his own Companion. They really did have to get going; the hover-bus would be along shortly.

Ponter headed out into the main room of the house. Pabo immediately bounded over to him. Ponter reached down and scratched the top of the dog's head. "Don't worry, girl," he said. "I haven't forgotten you."

He opened the vacuum box and pulled out a large, meaty bison bone, saved from last night's dinner. He then set it on the floor—the moss overlain with glass sheets here to make cleanups easier—and Pabo began to gnaw at it. Adikor joined Ponter in the kitchen and set about fixing breakfast. He took two slabs of elk meat out of the vacuum box and put them in the laser cooker, which filled with steam to remoisturize the meat. Ponter glanced over, looking through the cooker's window, watching the ruby beams crisscrossing in intricate patterns, perfectly grilling every part of the steaks. Adikor filled a bowl with pine nuts and set out mugs of diluted maple syrup, then fetched the now-done steaks.

Ponter turned on the Voyeur, the square wall-mounted panel springing instantly to life. The screen was divided into four smaller squares, one showing transmissions from Hawst's enhanced Companion; another, those from Talok's; the lower-left, pictures of Gawlt's life; and the lower-right, images of Lulasm's. Adikor, Ponter knew, was a Hawst fan, so he told the Voyeur to expand that image to fill the entire screen. Ponter had to admit that Hawst was always up to something interesting—this morning, he'd headed to the outskirts of Saldak where five people had been buried alive by a rockslide. Still, if an Exhibitionist did come by the mineshaft entrance today, Ponter hoped it would be Lulasm; Ponter thought she usually asked the most insightful questions.

Ponter and Adikor both sat and put on dining gloves. Adikor scooped up some pine nuts from the bowl and sprinkled them over his steak, then pounded them into the meat with the palm of his gloved hand. Ponter smiled; it was one of Adikor's endearing quirks—he'd never met anyone else who did that.

Ponter picked up his own steak, still sizzling slightly, and bit a hunk off. It had that sharp tang one only tasted in meat that had never been frozen; how had anyone survived before vacuum storage had been invented?

A short time later, Ponter saw the hover-bus settle to the ground outside the house. He told the Voyeur to shut off, they tossed their dining gloves in the sonic cleanser, Ponter patted Pabo on the head, and he and Adikor went out the door, leaving it open so that Pabo could come and go as she pleased. They entered the hover-bus, greeting the seven other passengers already on board, and headed off to work as if it were just another ordinary day.

Chapter Four

Ponter Boddit had grown up in this part of the world; he'd been aware of the nickel mine his whole life. Still, he'd never met anyone who had visited its depths; the mining was done exclusively by robots. But when Klast had been diagnosed with leukemia, Ponter and she had begun to meet with others suffering from cancers—for support, for companionship, and to share information. They met in a *kobalant* facility, which, of course, was vacant in the evenings.

Ponter had expected several of the others who were afflicted to have visited the mine. After all, by going deep in the rocks, they surely would have been exposed to abnormally high radioactivity.

But no one who had gone down into the mine was part of their group. Ponter started asking around and discovered that this was a very unusual nickel mine; the background radiation levels in its ancient granites were extraordinarily low.

And, because of that, an idea occurred to him. He was a physicist, working with Adikor Huld on building quantum computers. But the quantum registers were enormously sensitive to outside disturbances; they'd had a real problem with cosmic rays provoking decoherence.

The solution, it seemed, was right beneath their feet. With a thousand armspans of rock over their heads, cosmic rays would no longer pose a problem. At that depth, nothing short of neutrinos could penetrate, and they wouldn't affect the experiments Ponter and Adikor wanted to run.

Delag Bowst was Saldak's chief administrator; the position had been forced upon him by the Grays. But, of course, it was always that way with administrators: no one who would choose such a contribution was suited to make it.

Ponter had presented his proposal to Bowst: let him build a quantum-computing facility deep inside the mine. And Bowst had convinced the Grays to agree. A technological civilization could not exist without metals, after all, but the mine had not always been friendly to the environment. Any opportunity to do something positive was welcomed.

And so the computing facility had been built. Ponter and Adikor were still having problems with an unexpected source of decoherence: piezoelectric discharges caused by the stresses on the rocks at such great depths. But Adikor felt he'd now solved that problem, and today they would try again, factoring a number bigger than any ever done before.

The hover-bus dropped Ponter and Adikor off at the entrance to the mine. It was a beautiful summer day, with a bright blue sky, just as Ponter's Companion implant had promised. Ponter could smell pollens in the air and hear the plaintive calls of loons on the lake. He picked up a head protector from the storage shed and attached it to his shoulders, the two struts holding a flat shelf above his skull; Adikor put on his own head protector.

The elevator at the mine entrance was cylindrical. The two physicists got into the car, and Ponter tapped the activation switch with his foot.

The lift started its long descent.

Ponter and Adikor left the elevator and headed down the lengthy drift toward the quantum-computing lab; naturally, it had been built in a part of the mine that had yielded no valuable ores. They walked in silence, the easy, companionable silence of two men who had known each other for ages.

Finally, they reached the quantum-computing facility. It consisted of four rooms. The first was a tiny cubicle for eating; it wasn't worth taking the time to ride the elevator all the way back up to the surface for meals. The second was a dry toilet facility; there was no plumbing down here, so the waste had to be hauled out at the end of each day. The third was the control room, containing instrument clusters and worktables. And the fourth, the only large room, was the giant computing chamber, bigger than all the rooms combined in the house that Ponter and Adikor shared.

The usual goal in building computers was to make them as small as possible: that kept delays caused by the speed of light to a minimum. But Ponter and Adikor's quantum-computer array was based on using quantally entangled protons as registers, and there had to be a way to distinguish between reactions that were occurring simultaneously, because of the entanglement, and those that were ·occurring as a result of normal speed-of-light communication between two protons. And the simplest way to do that was by putting some distance between each register, so that the time it would take for light to travel between two registers was easily measurable. The protons were therefore held in place inside magnetic-containment columns spaced throughout the chamber.

Ponter and Adikor removed their head protectors and entered the control room. Adikor was the practical one; he found ways to implement Ponter's ideas in software and hardware. He settled in at a console and began going through the routines required to initialize the quantum-computing array. "How long until we're ready?" asked Ponter.

"Another half-tenth," said Adikor. "I'm still having trouble stabilizing register 69."

"Do you think it's going to work?" asked Ponter.

"Me?" said Adikor. "Sure." He smiled. "Of course, I said that yesterday and the day before and the day before that."

"The perpetual optimist," said Ponter.

"Hey," said Adikor, "when you're this far down, there's nowhere to go but up."

Ponter laughed, then walked through the archway into the eating room to get a squeeze tube of water. He hoped the experiment would indeed succeed today. The next Gray Council was coming up soon, and he and Adikor would have to explain again what they were giving back to the community through their work. Scientists usually got their proposals approved—everyone could clearly see how science had bettered their lives—but, still, it was always more satisfying to report positive results.

Ponter used his teeth to pull open the plastic tab on the tube of water, and gulped some of the cool liquid. He then moved back into the control room, sat at his desk, and started reading through a fan of pale green sheets of square plastic, reviewing the notes from their last attempt, occasionally taking sips of his water. Ponter's back was to Adikor, who was fiddling with controls on the opposite side of the small room. The main wall of the room was mostly glass, a big window looking out over the large computing chamber, which had both a higher ceiling and a lower floor than the other rooms.

They'd already had considerable success with their quantum computer. Last tenmonth, they had factored a number that required 10^{73} hydrogen atoms as registers— a quantity vastly greater than all the hydrogen in all the stars in this entire galaxy, and sixty-odd orders of magnitude greater than the capacity of the entire computing chamber, even if it had been filled entirely with hydrogen. The *only* way they could have succeeded was if they really were getting true quantum-computing effects—having their limited number of physical registers existing simultaneously in multiple states superimposed one upon the other.

In a way, this next experiment was merely incremental: it was an attempt to factor an even bigger number. But the number in question was one of the vastly huge ones that Digandal's Theorem said should be prime. No conventional computer could test that, but their quantum computer should be able to do so.

Ponter checked a few more pages of the printout, then went over to another control cluster and pulled some operational buds, adjusting parts of the recording system. He wanted to make sure that every facet of the run would be recorded, so that there could be no doubt afterward about the result. If they could just—

"Ready," said Adikor.

Ponter felt his heart begin to race. He so much wanted it to work—both for his own sake, and for Adikor's, too. Ponter had had much luck early in his career; his was a respected name in physics circles. Even if he were to die today, he would be long remembered. Adikor hadn't been as successful, Ponter knew, although he surely deserved to be. How wonderful it would be for both of them if they could prove—or disprove; either result would be significant—Digandal's Theorem.

There were two control clusters to be operated, one on each side of the small room. Ponter stayed at the one he was now at, next to the arch leading to the eating room; Adikor moved over to the other one on the opposite side of the room. All the controls should have been localized in one place, but this setup had saved almost thirty arm-spans' worth of the expensive quantally transductive cable used to link the registers. Each control cluster was mounted on a wall. Adikor stood next to his and pulled the buds that needed pulling. Ponter, meanwhile, was operating the appropriate controls on his own cluster.

"All set?" asked Adikor.

Ponter looked at the series of indicator lights on his board; they were all red, the color of blood, the color of health. "Yes."

Adikor nodded. "Ten beats," he said, starting the

countdown. "Nine. Eight. Seven. Six. Five. Four. Three. Two. One. Zero."

Several lights flashed on Ponter's board, showing that the registers were working. In theory, over the span of a fraction of a beat, all the possible factors had been tried, and the results had already been received as a series of interference patterns on photographic film. It would take the conventional computer that decoded the interference patterns a while to compose the list of factors—which, if Digandal was wrong and this number wasn't prime, could be a very large list indeed.

Ponter left his console and moved to sit down. Adikor paced back and forth, looking out the window at the rows of register tanks, each a sealed glass-and-steel column containing a specific amount of hydrogen.

Finally, the conventional computer made a *plunk* sound, signaling that it had finished.

There was a monitor square in the center of Ponter's control cluster; the results appeared on it in black glyphs on a yellow background. And the results were—

"*Gristle!*" swore Adikor, standing behind Ponter, a hand on his shoulder.

The display read: "Error in register 69; factoring aborted."

"We have *got* to get that one replaced," said Ponter. "It's given us nothing but trouble."

"It's not the register," said Adikor. "It's the base that holds it to the floor. But it'll take tendays to get a new one made."

"So we can't do anything before the Gray Council?"

asked Ponter. He didn't look forward to facing the elder
citizens and saying that nothing had been added to our
knowledge since the last Council session.

"Not unless . . ." Adikor trailed off.

"What?"

"Well, the problem with 69 is that it tends to vibrate
on its base; the attachment clamps weren't machined quite
right. If we could find something to anchor it with . . ."

Ponter scanned the room. There was nothing that
looked suitable. "How about if I just go out on the computing floor and lean on it? You know, press down with all
my weight. Wouldn't that keep it from vibrating?"

Adikor frowned. "You'd have to hold it very steady. The
equipment can tolerate some movement, of course,
but . . ."

"I can do it," said Ponter. "But—but will my presence
on the computing floor promote decoherence?"

Adikor shook his head. "No. The register columns are
heavily shielded; it would take something a lot more radi-
oactive or electrically noisy than a human body to upset
the contents."

"Well, then?"

Adikor frowned again. "It's hardly an elegant solution
to the problem."

"But it might work."

Adikor nodded. "I suppose it's worth a try. Better than
going to Council empty-handed."

"All right!" said Ponter, decisively. "Let's do it." Adikor
nodded, and Ponter opened the door that separated the
other three rooms from the large chamber containing
the register tanks. He then walked down the steps to the

room's polished granite floor, which had been leveled with laser beams. Ponter moved carefully along it; he'd slipped once before while crossing. When he got to cylinder 69, he placed one hand on its curved top, covered that with his other hand, and then pressed down with all his strength. "Any time you're ready," Ponter shouted.

"Ten," Adikor shouted back. "Nine. Eight. Seven."

Ponter fought to keep his hands steady. As far as he could tell, the cylinder wasn't vibrating at all.

"Six. Five. Four."

Ponter took a deep breath, trying to calm himself. He held it in.

"Three. Two. One."

Here we go, thought Ponter.

"Zero!"

Adikor heard the glass rattle fiercely in the window looking over the computing floor. "Ponter!" he shouted. Adikor hurried to the window. "P-Ponter?"

But there was no sign of him.

Adikor pulled the grip that unlatched the door, and—

Whoosh!

The door swung forward, flying open, the grip wrenched from Adikor's hand as a great rush of air from the control room flew past him out into the computing chamber; it was almost enough to tumble Adikor face first down the small staircase. Air was rushing *into* the computing chamber from the control room and the mine beyond as if—as if somehow the air that had been in there earlier had all been sucked away. Adikor's ears popped repeatedly.

"Ponter!" he called again once the wind had died down, but although the room was large, the register tanks, arrayed in a vast grid, were all narrow columns; there was no way Ponter could be concealed behind one of them.

What could have happened? If a rock wall elsewhere in the mine had collapsed, and behind it had been an area of low pressure, maybe . . .

But there were seismic sensors throughout the mining complex, and they'd have triggered the release of warning smells here in the computing lab if there had been any such disturbance.

Adikor hurried across the granite floor. "Ponter!" he called again. "Ponter?"

There was no fissure in the flooring; he couldn't have been swallowed up by the ground. Adikor could see register tank 69, the one Ponter had been working on, at the far end of the room. Ponter obviously wasn't there, but Adikor ran over to the register, anyway, looking for any clue, and—

Gristle!

Adikor found his feet going out from under him, and he came slamming down on his back on the granite floor. The surface was covered with water—lots of water. Where had it come from? Ponter had been drinking from a tube earlier, but Adikor was sure he'd finished it upstairs. And besides, there was much more here than could have fit in a tube; there were buckets of it, spreading out in a wide puddle.

The water—if that's what it was—looked clean, clear. Adikor brought his wet palm up to his face, sniffed. No odor.

A tentative lick.

No taste at all.

It *was* pure, apparently. Pure, clean water.

Heart pounding, head racing, Adikor went to get some containers to collect it in; it was the only clue he had.

Where had the water possibly come from?

And where on Earth had Ponter gone?

Chapter Five

What the—?

Absolute blackness.

And—water! Ponter Boddit's legs were wet, and—

And he was sinking, water up to his waist, his chest, the bottom of his jaw.

Ponter kicked violently.

His eyes were indeed wide open, but there was nothing—absolutely nothing—to be seen.

He flailed with his arms while treading water. He gulped in air.

What had happened? Where could he be?

One moment he'd been standing in the quantum-computing facility, and the next—

Darkness—so unrelentingly dark, Ponter thought perhaps he was blind. An explosion could have done that; rock bursts were always a danger this far underground, and—

And an influx of subterranean water *was* possible. He swung his arms some more, then stretched out his toes, trying to feel for the bottom, but—

But there was nothing, nothing at all. Just more water. He could be a handspan from the bottom, or a thousand times that much. He thought about diving down to find out, but in the dark, floating freely, with no light at all, he might lose track of which way was up and not make it back to the surface in time.

He'd taken in a mouthful of water as he'd felt for the bottom. It was utterly free of taste; he'd have expected a subterranean river to be brackish, but this seemed as pure as meltwater.

He continued to gulp air. His heart was racing, and—

And he wanted to swim toward the edge, wherever that—

A groaning sound, low, deep, from all around him.

Again, like an animal awakening, like . . .

Like something under great stress?

He finally had enough air in his lungs to manage a shout. "Help!" Ponter called. "Help!"

The sound echoed weirdly, as if he were in an enclosed space. Could he still be in the computing room? But, if he were, why wasn't Adikor responding to his calls?

He couldn't just stay there. Although he wasn't exhausted yet, he soon would be. He needed to find a surface to clamber onto, or something in the water with him that he could use as a flotation aid, and—

The groaning again, louder, more insistent.

Ponter started to dog paddle. If only there were some light—any light. He swam for what seemed a short distance, and—

Agony! Ponter banged his head into something hard. He switched back to treading water, his limbs beginning to ache, and he reached out with one hand, fingers splayed, palm forward. Whatever he had hit was hard and warm—

not metal or glass, then. And it was absolutely smooth, maybe slightly concave, and—

Another groan, coming from—

His heart fluttered; he felt his eyes go wide, but they saw nothing at all in the blackness.

—coming from the hard wall in front of him.

He began to swim in the opposite direction, the noise now growing to earsplitting proportions.

Where was he? Where was he?

The volume continued to increase. He swam farther and—

Ouch! That hurt!

He'd slammed into another hard, smooth wall. These certainly weren't the walls in the quantum-computing chamber; those were covered with soft sound-deadening fabric.

Whooooooshhhh!

Suddenly, the water around Ponter was moving, rushing, roaring, and he was caught up in it, as if he were in a raging river. Ponter took a huge breath, drawing some water in with the air, and then—

And then he felt something hard smash into the side of his head, and, for the first time since this madness began, he saw light: stars before his eyes.

And then, the blackness again, and silence, and—

Nothing more.

Adikor Huld walked back up to the control room, shaking his head in astonishment, in disbelief.

Ponter and he had been friends for ages; they were

both 145s, and had first met as students at the Science Academy. But in all that time, he'd never known Ponter to be given to practical jokes. And, besides, there was no place he could be hiding. Fire safety required multiple exits from a room on the surface, but down here practicality made that impossible. The only way out was by walking through the control room. Some computing facilities had false floors to conceal cabling, but here the cabling was out in the open, and the floor was ancient granite, polished smooth.

Adikor had been watching the controls; he hadn't been looking out the window at the computing chamber. Still, there had been no flash of light to catch his eye. If Ponter had been—well, what? Vaporized? If he'd been vaporized, surely there should have been a smell of smoke or a tinge of ozone in the air. But there was nothing. He was simply *gone.*

Adikor collapsed into a chair—Ponter's chair—stunned.

He didn't know what to do next; he literally had no idea. It took several beats for him to focus his thoughts. He should notify the town's administrative office that Ponter was missing; get them to organize a search. It was conceivable—barely—that the ground had opened up, and Ponter had fallen through, maybe into another drift, another level of the mine. In which case he might be injured.

Adikor got to his feet.

Dr. Reuben Montego, the two ambulance attendants, and the injured man entered through the sliding glass doors to Emergency Admitting at St. Joseph's Health Centre, part of the Sudbury Regional Hospital.

The E.R.'s casualty officer turned out to be a Sikh in his midfifties with a jade green turban. "What is it that is wrong?" he asked.

Reuben glanced down at the man's nametag, which read N. SINGH, M.D. "Dr. Singh," he said, "I'm Reuben Montego, the site doctor at the Creighton Mine. This man here almost drowned in a tank of heavy water, and, as you can see, he's suffered a cranial trauma."

"Heavy water?" said Singh. "Where would you—"

"At the neutrino observatory," said Reuben.

"Ah, yes," replied Singh. He turned and called for a wheelchair, then looked back at the man and started making notes on a clipboard. "Unusual body form," he said. "Pronounced supraorbital ridge. Very muscular, very broad shouldered. Short limbs. And—hello!—what is this, then?"

Reuben shook his head. "I don't know. It seems to be implanted in his skin."

"Very strange," said Singh. He looked at the man's face. "How do you feel?"

"He doesn't speak English," said Reuben.

"Ah," said the Sikh. "Well, his bones will talk for him. Let's get him into Radiology."

Reuben Montego paced back and forth in the emergency department, occasionally speaking to a passing doctor he happened to know. At last, Singh got word that the x-rays were ready. Reuben was hoping to be invited along, out of professional courtesy, and Singh did indeed beckon for him to follow.

The injured man was still in the x-ray room, presumably in case Singh decided to order more pictures. He was seated now in his wheelchair, looking more frightened, Reuben thought, than even a small child usually did in a hospital. The radiology technician had clipped the man's x-rays—a front view and a lateral shot—to a lighted wall panel, and Singh and Reuben moved over to examine them.

"Will you look at that?" said Reuben softly.

"Remarkable," said Singh. "Remarkable."

The skull was long—much longer than a normal skull, with a rounded protrusion at the back, almost like a hair bun. The doubly arched browridge was prominent and the forehead low. The nasal cavity was gigantic, with strange triangular projections pointing into it from either side. The huge mandible, visible at the bottom of the frame, revealed what the beard had hidden: the complete lack of a chin. It also showed a gap between the last molar and the rest of the jaw.

"I've never seen anything like it," said Reuben.

Singh's brown eyes were wide. "I have," he said. "I have." He turned to look at the man, who was still sitting in the wheelchair, babbling gibberish. Then Singh consulted the ghostly gray images again. "It is impossible," said the Sikh. "Impossible."

"What?"

"It cannot be . . ."

"What? Dr. Singh, for God's sake—"

Singh raised his hand. "I do not know how it can be thus, but . . ."

"Yes? Yes?"

"This patient of yours," said Singh, in a voice full of wonder, "appears to be a Neanderthal."

Chapter Six

"Good night, Professor Vaughan."

"Good night, Daria. See you tomorrow." Mary Vaughan glanced at the clock; it was now 8:55 P.M. "Be careful."

The young grad student smiled. "I will." And she headed out of the lab.

Mary watched her go, remembering wistfully when her own figure had been as slim as Daria's. Mary was thirty-eight, childless, and long separated from her husband.

She went back to poring over the autoradiograph film, reading off nucleotide after nucleotide. The DNA she was studying had been recovered from a passenger pigeon mounted at the Field Museum of Natural History; it had been sent here, to York University, to see whether it could be completely sequenced. Previous attempts had been made, but the DNA had always been too degraded. But Mary's lab had had unprecedented success reconstructing DNA that other facilities couldn't read.

Sadly, though, the sequence broke down; there was no way to determine from this sample what string of nucleotides had originally been present. Mary rubbed the bridge of her nose. She would have to extract some more DNA from the pigeon specimen, but she was too tired to do that tonight. She looked at the wall clock; it was now 9:25.

That wasn't too late; many of the university's summer evening classes got out at 9:00, so there should still be lots of people milling about. If she worked past 10:00 P.M., she usually called for someone from the campus walking service to escort her to her car. But, well, it didn't really seem necessary this early in the evening. Mary removed her pale green lab coat and hung it on the rack by the door. It was August; the lab was air conditioned, but it was surely still quite warm out. Another sticky, uncomfortable night lay ahead.

Mary shut off the lights in the lab; one of the fluorescents strobed a bit as it died. She then locked the door and made her way down the second-floor corridor, past the Pepsi machine (Pepsi had paid York University two million dollars to become the exclusive soft-drink vendor on campus).

The corridor was lined with the usual bulletin boards, announcing faculty openings, classroom assignments, club meetings, come-ons for cheap credit cards and magazine subscriptions, and all sorts of items for sale by students and faculty, including one poor clown hoping to get someone to pay him money for an old electric typewriter.

Mary continued down the corridor, her heels clicking against the tiles. No one else was in the hallway. She did hear the sound of the urinals flushing as she passed the men's room, but that happened automatically, governed by a timer.

The door to the stairwell had safety-glass windows, with wire mesh embedded in them. Mary pushed open the door and headed down the four flights of concrete steps, each flight taking her a half story lower. On the ground floor she left the stairwell and continued a short distance down another corridor, this one also empty except for a janitor working at the far end. She walked into the entryway, passing distribution boxes for the campus paper, *The Excalibur*, and, at last, headed out through the double doors into the warm night air.

The moon wasn't up yet. Mary headed along the sidewalk, passing a few students as she did so, although none she recognized. She swatted at the occasional insect, and—

A hand clamped down over her mouth, and she felt something cold and sharp against her throat. "Don't make a sound," said a deep, raspy voice, pulling her backward.

"Please—" said Mary.

"Be quiet," the man said. He was continuing to pull her back, the knife pressing sharply into her throat. Mary's heart pounded violently. The hand over her mouth came off, and she felt it again a moment later on her left breast, squeezing roughly, painfully.

He'd pulled her into a small alcove, two concrete walls meeting at a right angle, a large pine blocking most of the view. He then spun her around, pinning her arms against the wall, his left hand still holding the knife even as it also gripped her wrist. She could see him now. He was wearing a black balaclava, but he was clearly a white man—rings of his skin were visible around his blue eyes. Mary tried to bring her knee up into his groin, but he arched backward, and all she managed was a glancing contact.

"Don't fight me," said the voice. She smelled tobacco on his breath, and could feel that his palms were sweaty against her wrists. The man pulled his arm away from the wall, yanking Mary's with it, then he slammed both their arms back against the concrete so that the knife was closer to Mary's face. His other hand found the front of his own pants, and Mary could hear the sound of a zipper. She felt acid at the back of her throat.

"I've—I've got AIDS," said Mary, scrunching her eyes closed, trying to shut everything out.

The man laughed, a sandpapery, humorless sound. "That makes two of us," he said. Mary's heart skipped, but he was probably lying, too. How many women had he done this to? How many had tried the same desperate gambit?

There was a hand now on the waist of her pants, pulling down. Mary felt her zipper parting, and her pants coming down around her hips, and his pelvis and his rock-hard erection grinding against her panties. She let out a yelp and the man's hand was suddenly on her throat, squeezing, nails biting into her flesh. "*Quiet, bitch.*"

Why didn't someone come by? Why was there no one around? God, why did—

She felt a hand yank down her panties, then felt his penis against her labia. He rammed it into her vagina. The pain was excruciating; it felt as though things were ripping down there.

It's not about sex, thought Mary, even as tears welled from the corners of her eyes. *It's a crime of violence.* The small of her back slammed against the concrete wall, as the man smashed his body against hers, ramming himself deep into her, again and again and again, his animal grunts growing louder with each thrust.

And then, at last, it was over. He pulled out. Mary knew she should look down, look for any identifying details, look even to see whether he was circumcised, anything that might help convict the bastard, but she couldn't bear to look at it, at him. She tilted her head up at the dark sky, everything blurred through stinging tears.

"Now, you just stay here," said the man, tapping her cheek with a flat side of the knife. "You don't say a word, and you stay here for fifteen minutes." And then she heard the sound of a zipper going up, and the man's footfalls as he ran away across the grass-covered ground.

Mary leaned back against the wall and slid down to the concrete sidewalk, her knees coming up to her chin. She hated herself for the wracking sobs that escaped from her.

After a while, she put a hand down between her legs, then pulled it away and looked at it to see if she was bleeding; she wasn't, thank God.

She waited for her breathing to calm down, and for her stomach to settle enough that she thought she could rise to her feet without vomiting. And then she did get up, painfully, slowly. She could hear voices—women's voices— off in the distance, two students chatting and laughing as they went along. Part of her wanted to call out to them, but she couldn't force the sound out of her throat.

She knew it was maybe twenty-five Celsius out, but she felt cold, colder than she'd ever been in her life. She rubbed her arms, warming herself.

It took—who knew? Five minutes? Five hours?—for her to recover her wits. She should find a phone, dial 911, call the Toronto police . . . or the campus police, or—she knew about it, had read about it in campus handbooks—the York University rape-crisis center, but . . .

But she didn't want to talk to anyone, to see anyone— to . . . to have anyone see her like this.

Mary closed her pants, took a deep breath, and started walking. It was a few moments before she was conscious of the fact that she wasn't heading on toward her car, but rather was going back toward the Farquharson Life Sciences Building.

Once she got there, she held the banister all the way up the four half flights of stairs, afraid of letting go, afraid of losing her balance. Fortunately, the corridor was just as deserted as it had been before. She made it back into her lab without being seen by anyone, the fluorescents sputtering to life.

She didn't have to worry about being pregnant. She'd been on the Pill—not a sin in her view, but certainly one in her mother's—ever since she'd married Colm, and, well, after the separation, she'd kept it up, although there had turned out to be little reason. But she *would* find a clinic and get an AIDS test, just to be on the safe side.

Mary wasn't going to report it; she had already made up her mind about that. How many times had she cursed those she'd read about who had failed to report a rape? They were betraying other women, letting a monster get away, giving him a chance to do it again to someone else, to—to *her*, now, but—

But it was easy to curse when it wasn't you, when you hadn't been there.

She knew what happened to women who accused men of rape; she'd seen it on TV countless times. They'd try to establish that it was *her* fault, that she wasn't a credible witness, that somehow she had consented, that her morals were loose. "*So, you say you're a good Catholic, Mrs. O'Casey— oh, I'm sorry, you don't go by that name anymore, do you? Not since you left your husband Colm. No, it's* Ms. *Vaughan now, isn't it? But you and Professor O'Casey are still legally married, aren't you? Tell the court, please, have you slept with other men since you abandoned your husband?"*

Justice, she knew, was rarely found in a courtroom. She would be torn apart and reassembled into someone she herself wouldn't recognize.

And, in the end, nothing would likely change. The monster would get away.

Mary took a deep breath. Maybe she'd change her mind at some point. But the only thing that was really important right now was the physical evidence, and she, Professor Mary Vaughan, was at least as competent as any policewoman with a rape kit at collecting that.

The door to her lab had a window in it; she moved so that she couldn't possibly be seen by anyone passing by in the corridor. And then she undid her pants, the sound of her own zipper causing her heart to jump. She then got a glass specimen container and some cotton swabs, and, blinking back tears, she collected the filth that was within her.

When she was done, she sealed the specimen jar, wrote the date on it in red ink, and labeled it "Vaughan 666," her name and the appropriate number for such a monster. She then sealed her panties in an opaque specimen container, labeled it with the same date and designation, and put both containers in the fridge in which biological specimens were stored, placing them alongside DNA taken from a passenger pigeon and an Egyptian mummy and a woolly mammoth.

Chapter Seven

"Where am I?" Ponter knew his voice sounded panicky, but, try as he might, he couldn't control it. He was still seated in the odd chair that rolled on hoops, which was a good thing, because he doubted he'd be very steady on his feet.

"Calm down, Ponter," said his Companion implant. " Your pulse is up to—"

"Calm down!" snapped Ponter, as if Hak had suggested a ridiculous impossibility. "*Where am I?*"

"I'm not sure," said the Companion. "I'm picking up no signals from the positioning towers. In addition, I'm cut off entirely from the planetary information network, and am receiving no acknowledgment from the alibi archives."

"You're not malfunctioning?"

"No."

"Then—then this can't be Earth, can it? You'd be getting signals if—"

"I'm sure it *is* Earth," said Hak. "Did you notice the sun while they brought you over to that white vehicle?"

"What about it?"

"Its color temperature was 5,200 degrees, and it subtended one-seven-hundredth of the celestial sphere—just like Sol as seen from Earth's orbit. Also, I recognized most of the trees and plants I saw. No, this is clearly the surface of the Earth."

"But the stench! The air is foul!"

"I'll have to take your word for that," said Hak.

"Could we have—could we have traveled in time?"

"That seems unlikely," replied the Companion. "But if I can see the constellations tonight, I will be able to tell if we've moved forward or backward an appreciable amount. And if I can spot some of the other planets and the phase of the moon, I should be able to figure the exact date."

"But how do we get back home? How do we—"

"Again, Ponter, I must exhort you to calm down. You are close to hyperventilating. Take a deep breath. There. Now let it out slowly. That's right. Relax. Another breath—"

"What are those *creatures?*" Ponter asked, waving a hand at the scrawny figure with dark brown skin and no hair and the other scrawny figure with lighter skin and a wrapping of fabric around his head.

"My best guess?" said Hak. "They are Gliksins."

"*Gliksins!*" exclaimed Ponter, loud enough that the two strange figures turned to look at him. He lowered his voice. "Gliksins? Oh, come *on . . .*"

"Look at those skull images over there." Hak was speaking to Ponter through a pair of cochlear implants, but by changing the left-right balance of his voice he could indicate a direction as surely as if he had pointed. Ponter got up—shakily—and crossed the room, heading away from the strange beings and approaching an illuminated panel like the one they were looking at, with several deepviews of skulls clipped to it.

"Green meat!" said Ponter, looking at the strange skulls. "They *are* Gliksins—aren't they?"

"I would say so. No other primate has that lack of brow-ridge, or that projection from the front of the lower jaw."

"Gliksins! But they've been extinct for—well, for how long?"

"Perhaps 400,000 months," said Hak.

"But this *can't* possibly be Earth of that long ago," said Ponter. "I mean, there's no way the civilization we've seen would have failed to leave traces in the archeological record. At best, Gliksins chipped stone into crude choppers, right?"

"Yes."

Ponter tried to keep from sounding hysterical. "So, again, where *are* we?"

Reuben Montego looked agape at the casualty officer, Dr. Singh. "What do you mean, 'He appears to be a Neander-thal'?"

"The skull features are absolutely diagnostic," said Singh. "Believe me: I've got a degree in craniology."

"But how can that be, Dr. Singh? Neanderthals have been extinct for millions of years."

"Actually, only for 27,000 years or so," said Singh, "if you accept the validity of some recent finds. If those finds prove spurious, then they died out 35,000 years ago."

"But then how . . ."

"That I do not know." Singh waved his hand at the

x-rays clipped to the illuminated panel. "But the suite of characters visible here is unmistakable. One or two might happen in any given modern *Homo sapiens* skull. But all of them? Never."

"What characters?" asked Reuben.

"The browridge, obviously," said Singh. "Note that it is unlike other primate browridges: it is doubly arched, and has a sulcus behind it. The way the face is drawn forward. The prognathism—just look at that jaw jut out! The lack of a chin. The retromolar gap"—he pointed to the space behind the last tooth. "And see those triangular projections into the nasal cavity? Those are found in no other mammal, let alone any other primate." He tapped the image of the skull's rear. "And see this rounded projection at the back? That is called the *occipital bun*; again, it's distinctly Neanderthaloid."

"You're pulling my leg," said Reuben.

"This is something I would never do."

Reuben looked back at the stranger, who had gotten up out of the wheelchair and was now staring, with astonishment, at a couple of skull x-rays on the other side of the room. Reuben then looked again at the x-ray film in front of him. Both he and Singh had been out of the room when the technician had taken the pictures; it was possible that, for whatever reason, someone had substituted different shots, although—

Although these *were* real x-rays, and they were x-rays of a living head, not a fossil: nasal cartilage and the outline of flesh were clearly visible. Still, there was something very strange about the lower jaw. Parts of it showed as a much lighter shade of gray in the x-ray, as if they were made of a less-dense material. And those parts were smooth, featureless, as though the material was uniform in composition.

"It's a fake," said Reuben, pointing to the anomalous part of the jaw. "I mean—*he's* a fake; he's had plastic surgery to make himself look Neanderthal."

Singh squinted at the x-ray. "There is reconstructive work here, yes—but only in the mandible. The cranial features all seem to be natural."

Reuben glanced at the injured man, who was still looking at other skull x-rays while babbling to himself. The doctor tried to imagine the stranger's skull beneath his skin. Would it have looked like the one Singh was now showing him?

"He has several artificial teeth," said Singh, still studying the x-ray. "But they're all attached to the section of jaw that has been reconstructed. As for the rest of the teeth, they seem natural, although the roots are taurodontid— another Neanderthaloid trait."

Reuben turned back to the x-ray. "No cavities," he said, absently.

"That is right," said Singh. He took a moment to assess the x-rays. "In any event, he seems to have no subdural hematoma, nor any skull fracture. There is no reason to keep him in hospital."

Reuben looked at the stranger. Who the hell could he be? He babbled in some strange tongue, and he'd had extensive reconstructive surgery. Could he be a member of some bizarre cult? Was that why he'd broken into the neutrino observatory? It made a certain amount of sense, but—

But Singh *was* right; except for the mandibular restoration, what they were seeing in the x-ray was a natural skull. Reuben Montego crossed the room slowly, warily, as if—Reuben realized within a few moments what he was doing: he was approaching the stranger not as one would approach another human being, but rather as one might come near a wild animal. And yet there had been nothing in his manner so far to suggest anything except civility.

The man clearly heard Reuben approaching. He took his attention away from the x-rays he'd been captivated by and turned to face the doctor.

Reuben stared at the man. He had noted earlier that his face was strange. The browridge, arching above each eye, was obvious. His hair was parted precisely in the middle, not at either side, and it looked like that was the natural part, not some affectation. And the nose: the nose was huge—but it wasn't the least bit aquiline. In fact, it wasn't quite like any other nose Reuben had ever seen before; it completely lacked a bridge.

Reuben lifted his right hand slowly, fingers gently spread, making sure the gesture looked tentative, not threatening. "May I?" he said, moving his hand closer to the stranger's face.

The man might not have understood the words, but the intent of the gesture was obvious. He tilted his head forward, inviting the touch. Reuben ran his fingers along the browridge, over his forehead, along the length of the skull from front to back, feeling the—what had Singh called it?—the occipital bun at the rear, a hard dome of bone beneath the skin. There was no doubt at all: the skull shown in the x-rays belonged to this person.

"Reuben," said Dr. Montego, touching his own chest. "Roo-ben." He then gestured at the stranger with an up-turned palm.

"Ponter," said the stranger, in a deep, sonorous voice.

Of course, the stranger might be taking "Reuben" to be the term for Montego's kind of humanity, and "Ponter" might be the stranger's word for Neanderthal.

Singh moved over to join them. "Naonihal," he said—revealing what the *N* stood for on his nametag. "My name is Naonihal."

"Ponter," repeated the stranger. Other interpretations were still possible, thought Reuben, but it did seem likely that was the man's name.

Reuben nodded at the Sikh. "Thank you for your help." He then turned to Ponter and motioned for him to follow. "Come on."

The man moved toward the wheelchair.

"No," said Reuben. "No, you're fine."

He gestured again for him to follow, and the man did so, on foot. Singh unclipped the x-rays, put them in a large envelope, and walked out with them, heading back to Emergency Admitting.

Frosted glass doors blocked the way ahead. As Singh stepped on the rubber mat in front of the doors, they slid aside, and—

Electronic flashes exploded in their faces.

"Is this the guy who blew up SNO?" called a male voice.

"What charges are Inco going to lay?" asked a female one.

"Is he injured?" called another male.

It took a few moments for Reuben to digest the scene.

He recognized one man as a correspondent for the local CBC station, and another was the mining-affairs reporter for the *Sudbury Star*. The dozen other people crowding around he didn't know, but they were shoving microphones forward that bore the logos of Global Television, CTV, and Newsworld, and the call letters of local radio stations. Reuben looked at Singh and sighed, but he supposed this had been inevitable.

"What's the suspect's name?" shouted another reporter.

"Does he have any prior record?"

The reporters continued to snap pictures of Ponter, who was making no effort to hide his face. At that moment, two RCMP officers entered from outside, wearing dark blue police uniforms. "Is this the terrorist?"

"Terrorist?" said Reuben. "There's no evidence of that."

"You're the mine-site doctor, aren't you?" said one of the cops.

Reuben nodded. "Reuben Montego. But I don't believe this man is a terrorist."

"But he blew up the neutrino observatory!" declared a reporter.

"The observatory was damaged, yes," said Reuben, "and he was there when it happened, but I don't believe he intended it. After all, he almost drowned himself."

"Irregardless," said the cop, causing Montego to immediately lower his opinion of him, "he will have to come with us."

Reuben looked at Ponter, at the reporters, then back at Singh. "You know what happens in cases like this," he said softly to the Sikh. "If the authorities take Ponter away, no one will ever see him again."

Singh nodded slowly. "So one might assume."

Reuben chewed his lower lip, thinking. Then he took a deep breath and spoke loudly. "I don't know where he came from," said Reuben, putting an arm now around Ponter's massive shoulders, "and I'm not sure how he got here, but this man's name is Ponter, and—"

Reuben stopped. Singh looked at him. Reuben knew he could conclude with that; yes, the man's name was known. He didn't have to say anything more. He could stop now, and no one would think him crazy. But if he went on—

If he went on, all hell would break loose.

"Can you spell that?" called a reporter.

Reuben closed his eyes, summoning strength from within. "Only phonetically," he said, now looking at the journalist. "P-O-N-T-E-R. But whichever of you jotted that down the fastest is, I'm sure, the first person ever to render that name in the English alphabet." He paused again, looked once more at Singh for encouragement, then pressed on. "This gentleman here, we are beginning to suspect, is not *Homo sapiens sapiens*. He may be—well, I think anthropologists are still arguing about what the proper designation for this kind of hominid is, aren't they? He seems to be what they call either *Homo neanderthalensis* or *Homo sapiens neanderthalensis*—at any rate, he's apparently a Neanderthal."

"What?" said one of the reporters.

Another just snorted derisively.

And a third—the mining reporter from the *Sudbury*

Star—pursed his lips. Reuben knew that reporter had a bachelor's in geology; doubtless he'd taken a paleo course or two as part of his studies. "What makes you say that?" he asked skeptically.

"I've seen x-rays of his skull. Dr. Singh here was quite sure of the identification."

"What does a Neanderthal have to do with the destruction of SNO?" asked a reporter.

Reuben shrugged, acknowledging that that was a very good question. "We don't know."

"This has got to be a hoax," said the mining reporter. "It's *got* to be."

"If it is, I've been hoodwinked, and so has Dr. Singh."

"Dr. Singh," called a reporter, "is this—this person here—is he a caveman?"

"I'm sorry," said Singh, "but I cannot discuss a patient except with other involved physicians."

Reuben looked at Singh, agog. "Dr. Singh, please . . ."

"No," said Singh. "There are rules . . ."

Reuben looked down for a moment, thinking. He then turned to Ponter with pleading eyes. "It's up to you," he said.

Ponter surely didn't understand the words, but apparently he grasped the significance of the situation. Indeed, it occurred to Reuben that Ponter might have a good shot at making a run for it, if he were so inclined; although not particularly tall, he was burlier by far than either of the cops. But Ponter's eyes soon swung in the direction of Singh—and, as Reuben followed the Neanderthal's line of sight, he realized that Ponter was actually looking at the manila envelope Singh was clutching tightly.

Ponter strode over to Singh. Reuben saw one of the cops put his hand on his holster; he evidently assumed Ponter was going to attack the doctor. But Ponter stopped short, right in front of Singh, and held out a beefy hand, palm up, in a gesture that transcended cultures.

Singh seemed to hesitate for a second, then he relinquished the envelope. There was no illuminated viewing plate in the room, and it was now well after dark. But there was a large window, with light from a lamp in the parking lot streaming in. Ponter moved to the window; he perhaps knew that the cops would have tried to restrain him if he'd gone instead for the glass doors leading outside. He then held one of the x-rays, the side view, up against the glass so that everyone could see it. Camcorders were instantly trained on it, and more still pictures were taken. Ponter then gestured for Singh to come over. The Sikh did so, and Reuben followed. Ponter tapped on the x-ray, then pointed at Singh. He repeated the sequence two or three times, and then opened and closed his left hand with fingers held straight, the—apparently universal—gesture for "talk."

Dr. Singh cleared his throat, looked around the lobby surveying the faces, then shrugged a little. "It, ah, it seems I have my patient's permission to discuss his x-rays." He pulled a pen out of his lab coat's breast pocket and used it as a pointer. "Do you all see this rounded protrusion at the back of the skull? Paleoanthropologists call that the occipital bun . . ."

Chapter Eight

Mary Vaughan had slowly driven the ten kilometers to her apartment in Richmond Hill. She lived on Observatory Lane, near the David Dunlap Observatory, once—briefly, and a long time ago—home of the world's largest optical telescope, now reduced to little more than a teaching facility because of the lights from Toronto.

Mary had bought the condominium here in part because of its security. As she drove up the driveway, the guard in the gatehouse waved at her, although Mary couldn't meet his—or anyone's—eyes yet. She drove along, past the manicured lawn and large pines, around back, and down into the underground garage. Her parking spot was a long walk from the elevators, but she'd never felt unsafe doing it, no matter how late it was. Cameras hung from the ceiling, between the sewer and water pipes and the sprinklers poking down like the snouts of star-nosed moles. She was watched every step of the way to the elevators, although tonight—this one hellish night—she wished that no one could see her.

Was she betraying anything by how she walked? By the quickness of her step? By her bowed head, by the way she clutched the front of her jacket as though the buttons were somehow failing to provide enough security, enough closure?

Closure. No, there was surely no way she could ever have that.

She entered the P2 elevator lobby, pushing first one door then the other open in front of her. She then pressed the single call button—there was nowhere to go from here but up—and waited for one of the three cars to come. Normally, when she waited, she looked at the various notices put up by management or other residents. But tonight Mary kept her eyes firmly on the floor, on the scuffed, stippled tiles. There were no floor-number indicators to watch above the closed doors, as there were two levels up in the main lobby, and although the UP button would go dark a few seconds before one of the doors would rumble open, she chose not to watch for that, either. Oh, she was eager to be home, but after one initial glance, she couldn't bring herself to look at the glowing upward-pointing arrow . . .

Finally, the farthest of the doors yawned. She entered and pushed the button for the fourteenth floor—really the thirteenth, of course, but that designation was considered unlucky. Above the panel of numbers was a glass frame that contained a laser-printed notice saying, "Have a Nice Day— From Your Board of Directors."

The elevator made its ascent. When it stopped, the door shuddered to one side, and Mary headed down the corridor—recently recarpeted by order of the same Board of Directors in a hideous cream-of-tomato-soup shade— and came to her apartment door. She fished in her purse for her keys, found them, pulled them out, and—

—and stared at them, tears welling in her eyes, vision blurring, her heart pounding again.

She had a small key chain, and on its end, a gift a dozen years ago from her ever-practical then-mother-in-law, was a yellow plastic rape whistle.

There had never been a chance to use it—not until it was too late. Oh, she could have blown it after the attack, but . . .

. . . but rape was a crime of violence, and she had survived it. A knife had been held to her throat, been pressed against her cheek, and yet she hadn't been cut, hadn't been disfigured. But if she'd sounded the alarm, he might have come back, might have killed her.

There was a gentle chime; another elevator had arrived. One of her neighbors would be in the corridor within a second. Mary fumbled the key into the lock, the whistle dangling, and quickly entered her dark apartment.

She hit the switch, the lights came on, and she turned around and closed the door, cranking over the lever that caused the deadbolt to clunk into place.

Mary removed her shoes and passed through the living room, with its peach-colored walls, noting, but not caring, that the red eye on the answering machine was winking at her. She entered her bedroom and took off her clothes— clothes that she knew she would throw out, clothes that she could never wear again, clothes that could never come clean no matter how many times they were washed. She then entered the *en suite* bathroom, but didn't turn on the light in there; she made do with the illumination spilling in from the Tiffany lamps on her night tables. She climbed into the shower and, in the semidarkness, she scrubbed and scrubbed and scrubbed until her skin felt raw, and then she got out her heavy flannel pajamas—the ones she saved for the coldest winter nights, the ones that covered her most completely—and she put them on, and she crawled into bed, hugging herself and shivering and crying some more and finally, finally, finally, after hours of trying, falling into a fitful sleep punctuated by dreams of being chased and dreams of fighting and dreams of being cut with knives.

Reuben Montego had never met his ultimate boss, the president of Inco, and the doctor was actually surprised to find he had a listed number. With considerable trepidation, Reuben called him.

Reuben was proud of his employer. Inco had started, like so many Canadian companies, as a subsidiary of an American firm: in 1916, it had been created as the Canadian arm of the International Nickel Company, a New Jersey mining concern. But twelve years later, in 1928, the Canadian subsidiary became the parent company through an exchange of shares.

Inco's principal mining operations were in and around the meteor crater here in Sudbury where, 1.8 billion years ago, an asteroid between one and three kilometers wide had slammed into the ground at fifteen klicks per second.

Inco's fortunes rose and fell along with the worldwide demand for nickel; the company provided a third of the world's supply. But during it all, Inco really did strive to be a good corporate citizen. And when Herbert Chen of the University of California had proposed, in 1984, that the depth of Inco's Creighton Mine, its low natural radio-activity, and the availability of large amounts of heavy water stockpiled for use in Canada's CANDU reactors, made Sudbury the ideal location for the world's most advanced neutrino detector, Inco had enthusiastically agreed to make the site available for free, and to do the additional excavation for the ten-story-tall detector chamber, and the 1,200-meter drift leading to it, at cost.

And although the Sudbury Neutrino Observatory was a joint project of five Canadian universities, two American ones, Oxford, and America's Los Alamos, Lawrence Berkeley, and Brookhaven National Laboratories, any trespassing charges against this Neanderthal, this Ponter, would have to be laid by the site's owner. And that was Inco.

"Hello, sir," Reuben said, when the president answered the phone. "Please forgive me for disturbing you at home. This is Reuben Montego. I'm the site doc—"

"I know who you are," said the cultured, deep voice.

That flustered Reuben, but he pressed on. "Sir, I'd like you to call the RCMP and tell them that Inco is not going to press any charges against the man found inside the Sudbury Neutrino Observatory."

"I'm listening."

"I've managed to convince the hospital not to discharge the man. Massive heavy-water ingestion can be fatal, according to the Material Safety Data Sheet. It upsets the osmotic pressure across cell boundaries. Now, the man couldn't possibly have taken in enough to do real damage, but we're using that as a pretext to keep him from being discharged. Otherwise, he'd be in the slammer right now."

" 'The slammer,' " repeated the president, sounding amused.

Reuben felt even more discombobulated. "Anyway, like I said, I don't think he belongs in prison."

"Tell me why," said the voice.

And Reuben did just that.

The president of Inco was a decisive man. "I'll make the call," he said.

Ponter was lying on a—well, it was a bed, he supposed, but it wasn't recessed to be flush with the floor; instead it was raised up by a harsh-looking metal frame. And the pillow was an amorphous bag stuffed with—he wasn't sure what, but it certainly wasn't dried pine nuts, like his pillow back home.

The bald man—Ponter had now seen that there was a stubble against his dark scalp, so the baldness must be an affectation, not a congenital condition—had left the room. Ponter had interlaced his fingers behind his own head, giving some firmer support for his skull. It wasn't rude to Hak. His Companion's scanners perceived everything within a couple of paces; it only needed its directional lens uncovered when looking at an object outside its scanning range.

"It's clearly nighttime," said Ponter, into the air.

"Yes," said Hak. Ponter could feel the cochlear implants vibrate slightly as his head pressed back against his arms.

"But it's not dark out. There's a window in this room,

but they seem to have flooded the outdoors with artificial light."

"I wonder why?" said Hak.

Ponter got up—so strange to dangle one's feet over the side of the bed in order to rise—and hurried to the window. It was too bright to see stars, but—

"It's there," said Ponter, facing his wrist out through the glass so Hak could see.

"That's Earth's moon, all right," said Hak. "And its phase—a waning crescent—is exactly right for today's date of 148/118/24."

Ponter shook his head and moved back to the strange, elevated bed. He sat on the edge of it; it was uncomfortable to do so, what with no back support. He then touched the side of his head, which had been bandaged by the man with the wrapped head; Ponter wondered if that man's bandages were because of a massive head wound of his own. "I hurt my head," Ponter said, into the air.

"Yes," replied Hak, "but you saw the deepviews they took of you; there was no serious damage done."

"But I almost drowned, too."

"That's certainly true."

"So . . . so maybe my brain was injured. Anoxia, and all that . . ."

"You think you're hallucinating?" asked Hak.

"Well," said Ponter, lifting his right arm, and gesturing at the bizarre room around him, "how else to explain all this?"

Hak was silent for a moment. "If you *are* hallucinating," the Companion said, "then my telling you that you are not could just be part of that hallucination. So there's really no point in me trying to disabuse you of that notion, is there?"

Ponter lay back down on the bed and stared up at the ceiling, which was devoid of timepieces and artwork.

"You really should try to get some sleep," said Hak. "Maybe things will make more sense in the morning."

Ponter nodded slightly. "White noise," he said. Hak complied, playing a soft, soothing hiss through the cochlear implants, but still it seemed to Ponter to be a long time before he fell asleep.

Chapter Nine

Adikor Huld couldn't take being inside the house. Everything there reminded him of poor, vanished Ponter. Ponter's favorite chair, his datapad, the sculptures Ponter had selected—everything. And so he'd gone out back, to sit on the deck, to stare sadly at the countryside. Pabo came out and looked at Adikor for a time; Pabo had been Ponter's dog—he'd had her long before Adikor and Ponter had begun living together. Adikor would keep her—if only so the house would not be so lonely. Pabo went back inside. She'd be going to the front door, Adikor knew, looking out there to see if Ponter were returning. She'd trekked back and forth, looking through both doors, ever since Adikor had come home yesterday. Adikor had never returned from work without Ponter before; poor Pabo was baffled and clearly very sad.

Adikor was hugely sad, too. He'd been crying off and on for most of the morning. Not blubbering, not wailing—just crying, sometimes even unaware of it himself until a fat drop splashed down onto his arm or hand.

Rescue teams had searched exhaustively in the mine, but they'd found no sign of Ponter. They'd used portable equipment to scan for his Companion, but had been unable to detect its transmissions. Humans and dogs had passed through drift after drift, trying to catch the odor of a man who might be unconscious, lying hidden from view.

But there was nothing. Ponter had vanished utterly and completely, without a trace.

Adikor shifted his weight in his chair. The chair was made of pine boards with a back that flared out and arms that had wide, flat rests on which a drinking tube could easily be balanced. There was no doubt the chair was useful. Its maker—Adikor forgot the woman's name, but it was branded on the back of the chair—doubtless felt she contributed sufficiently to society. People needed furniture; Adikor had a table and two cabinets made by the same carpenter.

But what would Adikor's contribution be, now that Ponter was gone? Ponter had been the brilliant one of the pair; Adikor recognized that and had accepted it. But how would he contribute now, without Ponter, dear, dear Ponter?

The quantum-computing work was dead, as far as Adikor could see. With Ponter gone, it couldn't go on. Others—there was that female group across the ocean in Evsoy, and another male one on the west coast of this continent—would continue work along related lines. He wished them luck, he supposed, but although he would read their reports with interest, part of him would always regret that it was not Ponter and him making the breakthroughs.

Aspens and birches formed a shady canopy around the deck, and white trilliums bloomed at the trees' mossy bases. A chipmunk scurried by, and Adikor could hear a woodpecker tapping away at a trunk. He breathed deeply, inhaling pollens and the smells of mulch and soil.

There was a sound of something moving; occasionally, a large animal would wander this close to a home during the day, and—

Suddenly, Pabo came tearing out of the back door. She'd detected the arrival, too. Adikor flared his nostrils. It was a person—a man—coming.

Could it be—?

Pabo let out a plaintive whimper. The man came into view.

Not Ponter. Of course not.

Adikor's heart hurt. Pabo made her way back into the house, back to the front, to continue her vigil.

"Healthy day," said Adikor to the man now coming up on the deck. It was no one he'd ever seen before: a stocky fellow, with reddish hair. He wore a loose-fitting dark blue shirt and a gray pant.

"Is your name Adikor Huld, and do you reside here in Saldak Rim?"

"Yes to the former," said Adikor, "and obviously to the latter."

The man held up his left arm, with the inside of his wrist facing Adikor; he clearly wanted to transfer something to Adikor's Companion.

Adikor nodded and pulled a control bud on his Companion. He watched the little screen on his unit flash as it received data. He expected it to be a letter of introduction: this perhaps was a relative visiting the area, or maybe a tradesperson looking for work, transferring his credentials. Adikor could erase the information easily enough if it were of no interest.

"Adikor Huld," said the man, "it is my duty to inform you that Daklar Bolbay, acting as *tabant* of the minor children Jasmel Ket and Megameg Bek, is accusing you of the murder of their father, Ponter Boddit."

"What?" said Adikor, looking up. "You're joking."

"No, I'm not."

"But Daklar is—was—Klast's woman-mate. She's known me for ages."

"Nonetheless," said the man. "Please show me your wrist so that I can confirm that the appropriate documents have been transferred."

Adikor, stunned, did just that. The man merely glanced at the display—it said "Bolbay charging Huld, transfer complete"—then he looked back at Adikor. "There will be a *dooslarm basadlarm*"—an old phrase that literally meant "asking small before asking large"—"to determine if you should face a full tribunal for this crime."

"There's been no crime!" said Adikor, fury growing within him. "Ponter is missing. He may be dead—I grant you that—but if so, it was an accident."

The man ignored him. "You are free to choose any one person to speak on your behalf. The *dooslarm basadlarm* has been scheduled for tomorrow morning."

"Tomorrow!" Adikor felt his fist clenching. "That's ridiculous!"

"Justice postponed is no justice at all," said the man as he walked away.

Chapter Ten

Mary needed coffee. She rolled out of her single bed, made her way to the kitchen, and set the coffeemaker to its task. She then stepped into the living room and pushed the play button on her answering machine, an old, reliable silver-and-black Panasonic that made loud clunkings when it started and stopped rewinding its tape.

"Four new messages," announced the cold, emotionless male voice, and then they began to play.

"Howdy, Sis, it's Christine. I just *have* to tell you about this new guy I'm seeing—I met him at work. Yeah, I know, I know, you always say never get involved with anyone at the office, but, really, he is so cute, and so nice, and so funny. Honest to God, Sis, he's a real find!"

A real find, thought Mary. *Good grief, another real find.*

The mechanical voice again: "Friday, 9:04 P.M." That was just after six Sacramento time; Christine must have called as soon as she'd gotten home from the office.

"Hey, Mary, it's Rose. Haven't seen you for ages. Let's do lunch, eh? Don't they have a Blueberry Hill up at York? I'll come up there, and we'll go—they closed the one near me. Anyway, I guess you're out right now—hope you're having a great time, whatever you're doing. Give me a call."

The machine's voice: "Friday, 9:33 P.M."

Christ, thought Mary. Good Christ. That would have been precisely when . . . when . . .

She closed her eyes.

And then the next message played: "Professor Vaughan?" said a voice with a Jamaican accent. "Is this the home of Professor Mary Vaughan, the geneticist? I'm sorry if it isn't—and I hate to be calling so late; I tried the York campus, on the off chance that you were still there, but only got your voice mail. I had directory assistance give me the numbers for every M. Vaughan in Richmond Hill— that's where an article I found about you on the Web said you live." Mary's outgoing message said only, "This is Mary," but the caller had presumably been buoyed by that. "Anyway—God, I hope I don't get cut off here—look, my name is Reuben Montego, and I'm an M.D.; the camp doctor up at Inco's Creighton Mine in Sudbury. I don't know if you've seen the news reports on this yet, but we've found a . . ." He paused, and Mary wondered why; he'd been burbling to this point. "Well, look, if you haven't seen the reports, let's just say we've found what we believe to be a Neanderthal specimen in, ah, remarkable condition."

Mary shook her head. There were no Neanderthal fossils from anywhere in North America; the guy must have some old Native Canadian material . . .

"Anyway, I did a Web search on 'Neanderthal' and 'DNA,' and your name kept coming up. Can you—"

Beep. The guy had indeed exceeded the maximum message length.

"Friday, 10:20 P.M.," reported the robotic voice.

"Damn, I hate these things," said Dr. Montego, coming

on again. "Look, what I was saying was, we'd really like you to authenticate what we've got here. Give me a call—anytime, day or night, on my cell phone at . . ."

She didn't have time for this. Not today, not anytime soon. Still, Neanderthals weren't her only interest; if it was a well-preserved ancient Native bone, that would be intriguing, too—but the preservation would have to be remarkable indeed for the DNA to have not deteriorated, and—

Sudbury. That was in Northern Ontario. Could they have—?

That would be fabulous. Another ice man, frozen solid, maybe found buried deep in a mine.

But, sweet Jesus, she didn't want to think about that right now; she didn't want to think about anything.

Mary went back into the kitchen and filled a mug with the now-ready coffee, which she poured a little chocolate milk into from a half-liter carton—she didn't know anyone else who did that, and she had given up trying to get it in restaurants. She then returned to the living room and put on the TV, a fourteen-inch set that normally didn't get much use; Mary preferred to curl up with a John Grisham novel, or, occasionally, a Harlequin romance, when she was home in the evenings.

She used the remote to select CablePulse 24, a twenty-four-hour news channel that devoted only part of its screen to the newscast; the right-hand side showed weather and financial information, and the bottom flashed headlines from *The National Post*. Mary wanted to see what today's high would be, and if it was going to finally rain, taking some of the awful humidity out of the air, and—

"—the destruction of the Sudbury Neutrino Observatory yesterday," said the Skunk Woman; Mary could never remember her name, but she had an incongruous white streak in her otherwise dark hair. "Few details are yet known, but the facility, buried more than two kilometers underground, apparently suffered a major accident at about 3:30 P.M. No one was hurt, but the 73-million-dollar lab is currently shut down. The detector, which made headlines around the world last year by solving the so-called Solar Neutrino Problem, probes the mysteries of the universe. It opened with great fanfare in 1998, with a visit by renowned physicist Stephen Hawking." File footage of Hawking in his wheelchair going down a mineshaft elevator ran behind the Skunk Woman's words.

"And speaking of mysteries, there are claims from a hospital in Sudbury that a *living* Neanderthal was found inside the mine. We have a report from Don Wright. Don?"

Mary watched, absolutely stunned, as a Native Canadian journalist gave a brief report. The guy they were showing on screen did indeed have browridges, and—

—God, the skull, glimpsed briefly in an x-ray that someone was holding up against a window . . .

It *did* look Neanderthal, but . . .

But how could that be? How could that possibly be? For Pete's sake, the guy was clearly not a wild man, and he had a funky haircut. Mary watched CablePulse 24 often enough; she knew they weren't above occasionally airing stories that amounted to little more than thinly disguised promos for current movies, but . . .

But Mary subscribed to the hominid listserv; there was enough idle chatter on it that there was no way she could have failed to have heard if a movie about Neanderthals was going to be made here in Ontario.

Sudbury . . . She'd never been to Sudbury, and—

And, Christ, yes, it would do her some good to just get the hell away for a while. She pushed the backward-review button on her phone's caller-ID display; a number with a 705 area code was the first to appear. She hit the dial button, and settled back into her Morticia seat, a high-backed wicker chair that was her favorite. After three rings, the voice she'd already heard answered. "Montego."

"Dr. Montego, this is Mary Vaughan."

"Professor Vaughan! Thank you for calling back. We've got . . ."

"Dr. Montego, look—you have no idea how . . . how . . . *swamped* I am right now. If this is a joke, or—"

"It's no joke, Professor, but we don't want to take Ponter anywhere yet. Can you come up here to Sudbury?"

"You're absolutely sure you've got something real?"

"I don't know; that's what we want you to tell us. Look, we're also trying to reach Norman Thierry at UCLA, but it's not even 8:00 A.M. there yet, and—"

Jesus, she didn't want Thierry to get this; if this was for real—although, God, how could it be?—it would be absolutely huge.

"Why do you need me to come up there?" asked Mary.

"I want you to take the DNA specimens directly; I want there to be no question about their authenticity or where they came from."

"It would take—God, I don't know, maybe four hours to drive to Sudbury from here."

"Don't worry about that," said Montego. "We've had a

corporate jet standing by at Pearson since last night, in case you did call. Grab a cab, get over to the airport, and we can have you up here before noon. Don't worry; Inco will reimburse all your expenses."

Mary looked around her apartment, with its white bookcases and wicker furniture, her collection of Royal Doulton figurines, the framed Renoir prints. She could drop by York University to pick up the appropriate primers, but . . .

No. No, she didn't want to go back there. Not yet, not today—maybe not until September, when she had to start teaching again.

But she *would* need the primers. And it was day now, and she could park over in Lot DD, approaching the Farquharson Building from a completely different direction, not going anywhere near where . . .

Where . . .

She closed her eyes. "I'll have to go by York to get some things, but . . . yes, all right, I'll do it."

Chapter Eleven

It was twenty-four days until Two would next become One, that fabulous four-day holiday Adikor Huld so looked forward to each month. But, despite propriety, he certainly couldn't wait until then to talk with the person he hoped would speak on his behalf at the *dooslarm basadlarm*. He could have called her with voice communication, but so much was lost when only words, without gestures or pheromones, were exchanged. No, this was going to be very delicate; it clearly merited a trip into the Center.

Adikor used his Companion to call for a travel cube and driver. The community had over three thousand cars; he shouldn't have to wait long for one to come and get him.

His Companion spoke to him. "You know it's Last Five, don't you?"

Gristle! He'd forgotten that. The effect would be in full swing. He'd only twice before gone into the Center during Last Five; he'd known men who had never done it, and he had teased them, saying he'd barely gotten out with his life.

Still, it was probably a wise precaution to slip into the

pool again before going in, to cut down on his own pheromones. He went and did precisely that.

Once done, he dried off with a cord, then dressed in a dark brown shirt and a light brown pant. No sooner had he finished than the travel cube settled to the ground outside the house. Pabo, still looking for Ponter, ran out to see who had arrived. Adikor walked out more slowly.

The cube was the latest version, mostly transparent, with two ground-effect motors underneath and chairs at each of its corners, one of which was occupied by the driver. Adikor got in, folding himself against the heavily padded saddle-seat next to the driver.

"You're going into the Center?" said the driver, a 143 with a bald stripe running back over his head, where his part had widened.

"Yes."

"You know it's Last Five?"

"I do."

The driver chuckled. "Well, I won't be waiting around for you."

"I know," said Adikor. "Let's go."

The driver nodded and operated the controls. The cube had good sound-deadening; Adikor could barely hear the fans. He settled in for the ride. They passed a couple of other cubes, both of which had male passengers. Adikor thought that drivers probably felt quite useful; he himself had never operated a travel cube, but maybe *that* was a job he'd enjoy . . .

"What's your contribution?" asked the driver in an easy tone, making conversation.

Adikor continued to look out the cube's walls at the scenery going by. "I'm a physicist."

"Here?" said the driver, sounding incredulous.

"We have a facility down in one of the mineshafts."

"Oh, yeah," replied the driver. "I've heard about that. Fancy computers, right?"

A goose was flying by overhead, its white cheeks stark against its black neck and head. Adikor tracked it with his eyes. "Right."

"How's that going?"

Being accused of a crime changed your perspective on everything, Adikor realized. Under normal circumstances, he might have just said "Fine," rather than go into the whole sorry mess. But even the driver might be called for questioning at some point: "Yes, Adjudicator, I drove Scholar Huld, and when I asked him how things were going at his computing facility, he said 'fine.' Ponter Boddit was dead, but he didn't show any remorse at all."

Adikor took a deep breath, then measured his words carefully. "There was an accident yesterday. My partner was killed."

"Oh," said the driver. "I'm sorry to hear that."

The landscape was barren at this point: ancient granite outcrops and low brush. "Me, too," Adikor said.

They continued on in silence. There was no way he could be found guilty of murder; surely the adjudicator would rule that if there was no body, there was no proof that Ponter was dead, let alone that he had fallen victim to foul play.

But if—

If he were convicted of murder, then—

Then what? Certainly he'd be stripped of his property, and all of it would be given to Ponter's woman-mate and children, but . . . but, no, no, Klast had been dead for twenty months now.

But beyond taking his property, what else?

Surely . . . surely not *that*.

And yet, for murder, what other penalty could they prescribe? It seemed inhumane, but it had been invoked whenever necessary since the first generation.

Surely, though, he was worrying for nothing. Daklar Bolbay was obviously inconsolable over the loss of Ponter— for Ponter had been the man-mate of Daklar's own woman-mate; they had both been bonded to Klast, and her death must have hit Bolbay as hard as it had Ponter. And now she had lost Ponter as well! Yes, Adikor could see how her mental state might be temporarily unbalanced by this double loss. Doubtless after a day or two, Bolbay would come to her senses, withdrawing the accusation and offering an apology.

And Adikor would graciously accept the apology; what else could he do?

But if she *didn't* drop the charge? If Adikor had to proceed with this nonsense all the way to a full tribunal? What then? Why, he'd have to—

The driver broke Adikor's contemplation by speaking again. "We're almost to the Center. Do you have an exact address?"

"North side, Milbon Square."

Adikor could see the driver's head move up and down as he nodded acknowledgment.

They were indeed approaching the Center: the open lands were giving way to stands of aspen and birch, and clusters of buildings made of cultured trees and gray brick. It was almost noon, and the clouds of earlier in the day had vanished.

As they continued in, Adikor saw first one, and then another, and then several more, walking along: the most beautiful creatures in all the world.

One of a pair of them caught sight of the travel cube, and pointed at Adikor. It wasn't all that unusual for a man to be coming into the Center at sometime other than the four days during which Two became One, but it *was* noteworthy during Last Five, the final days of the month.

Adikor tried to ignore the stares of the women as the driver took him in deeper.

No, he thought. No, they couldn't find him guilty. There was no body!

And yet, if they did . . .

Adikor squirmed in his seat as the cube flew on. He could feel his scrotum contracting, as if its contents wanted to climb into his torso, out of harm's way.

Chapter Twelve

Reuben Montego was delighted that Mary Vaughan was on her way up from Toronto. Part of him was hoping that she could prove genetically that Ponter *wasn't* a Neanderthal, that she could show he was just a plain old garden-variety human being. That would restore some rationality to the situation; after a fitful night's sleep, Reuben realized that it really was easier to swallow the idea that some nut had had himself altered to look like a Neanderthal, rather than that he actually *was* one. Perhaps Ponter was indeed a member of some weird cult, as Reuben had first thought. If he'd worn a series of tight helmets while growing up, each of which had their interiors sculpted to look like a Neanderthal head, his own skull could have grown into that shape. And at some point, he'd obviously had that submaxillary surgery to give his lower jaw the same pre-historic cast . . .

Yes, it *could* have happened that way, thought Reuben.

There was no point going directly to the Sudbury airport; it would still be a couple of hours before Professor Vaughan arrived. Reuben headed to St. Joseph's Health Centre to see how Ponter was doing.

The first thing he noticed when he entered the hospital room were the dark semicircles beneath Ponter's deep-set eyes. Reuben was delighted that he himself was not subject to such signs of fatigue. His parents, back in Kingston (Jamaica, that is, not Ontario—although he'd lived briefly for a time there, too) hadn't been able to tell when he'd stayed up half the night reading comic books.

Perhaps, thought Reuben, Dr. Singh should have prescribed a sedative for Ponter. Even if he really was a Neanderthal, almost certainly any that worked on regular humans would be effective on him, too. But, then again, if it had been his call to make, Reuben might have erred on the side of caution himself.

In any event, Ponter was now sitting up in bed, eating a late breakfast a nurse had just brought him. He had looked at the tray for a time after its arrival, as though something was missing. He'd finally wrapped his right hand in the white linen napkin, and was using that covered hand to eat with, picking up strips of bacon one at a time. He only used cutlery for the scrambled eggs, and for those he employed the spoon rather than the fork.

Ponter set the toast back down after sniffing it. He also disdained the contents of the little box of Kellogg's Corn Flakes, although he did seem to enjoy puzzling out the complex perforations to open it up into a self-contained bowl. After a tentative sip, he drained the small plastic cup of orange juice in a single gulp, but he seemed to want nothing to do with either the coffee or the 250-milliliter carton of partially skimmed milk.

Reuben went to the bathroom to get Ponter a cup of water—and he stopped dead in his tracks.

Ponter *was* from somewhere else. He had to be. Oh, it was common enough for a person to forget to flush the toilet, but . . .

But Ponter not only hadn't flushed—he had wiped himself with the long, thin "Sanitized for Your Protection" loop, instead of with the toilet paper. No one from anywhere in the developed world could possibly make that mistake. And Ponter *was* indeed from a technological culture; there was that intriguing implant on the inside of his left wrist.

Well, thought Reuben, the best way to find out about this man was by talking with him. He clearly didn't—or wouldn't—speak English, but, as Reuben's old grandmother used to say, there be nine and sixty ways to skin a cat.

"Ponter," said Reuben, using the one word he'd picked up the previous night.

The man was silent for a moment too long, and he tilted his head slightly. Then he nodded, as if acknowledging someone other than Reuben. "Reuben," said the man.

Reuben smiled. "That's right. My name is Reuben." He spoke slowly. "And your name is Ponter."

"Ponter, *ka*," said Ponter.

Reuben pointed at the implant on Ponter's left wrist. "What's that?" he said.

Ponter lifted his arm. "*Pasalab*," he said. Then he repeated it slowly, syllable by syllable, presumably understanding that a language lesson had begun: "*Pas-a-lab*."

And with that, Reuben realized he'd made a mistake; there was no corresponding English word he could now supply. Oh, perhaps "implant," but that seemed such a generic term. He decided to try something different. He held up one finger. "One," he said.

"*Kolb,*" said Ponter.

He made a peace sign. "Two."

"*Dak,*" said Ponter.

Scout's honor. "Three."

"*Narb.*"

Four fingers. "Four."

"*Dost.*"

A full hand, digits splayed. "Five."

"*Alm.*"

Reuben continued, adding a finger at a time from his left hand until he had heard numerals from one to ten. He then tried the numbers out of sequence, to see if Ponter would always give the same word in response, or was just making it up as he went along. As far as Reuben could tell—he was having trouble keeping track of these strange words himself—Ponter never slipped up. It wasn't just a stunt; it seemed to be a real language.

Reuben next started indicating parts of his own body. He pointed an index finger at his shaved head. "Head," he said.

Ponter pointed at his own head. "*Kadun,*" he said.

Next, Reuben indicated his left eye. "Eye."

And then, Ponter did something astonishing. He lifted his right hand, palm out, as if asking Reuben to hold on for a minute, and then he began talking rapidly in his own language, with his head slightly lowered and cocked, as if speaking to somebody over an invisible telephone.

"This is pathetic!" said Hak, through Ponter's cochlear implants.

"Yeah?" replied Ponter. "We're not all like you, you know; we can't just download information."

"More's the pity," said Hak, "but, really, Ponter, if you'd been paying attention to what they'd been saying to each other and to you since we got here, you'd already have picked up a lot more of their language than a simple list of nouns. I have cataloged with high confidence 116 words in their language, and with reasonable confidence guessed at another 240, based on the context in which they have been used."

"Well," said Ponter, somewhat miffed, "if you think you can do a better job than me . . ."

"With all due respect, a chimpanzee could do a better job than you at learning language."

"Fine!" said Ponter. He reached down and pulled out the control bud on his Companion that turned on the external speaker. "You do it!"

"My pleasure," said Hak, through the cochlear implants, then, switching to the speaker—

"Hello," said a female voice. Reuben's heart jumped. "Yoo-hoo! Over here."

Reuben looked down. The voice was coming from the strange implant on Ponter's left wrist. "Talk to the hand," the implant said.

"Umm," said Reuben. And then, "Hello."

"Hello, Reuben," replied the female voice. "My name is Hak."

"Hak," repeated Reuben, shaking his head slightly. "Where are you?"

"I am here."

"No, I mean *where* are you? I get that that thingamajig is some kind of cell phone—say, you know, you're not supposed to use those in hospitals; they can interfere with monitoring equipment. Could we call you back—"

Bleep!

Reuben stopped talking. The bleep had come from the implant.

"Language learning," said Hak. "Follow."

"Learning? But . . ."

"*Follow,*" repeated Hak.

"Um, yes, all right. Okay."

Suddenly, Ponter nodded, as if he'd heard a request that Reuben hadn't. He pointed at the door to the room.

"That?" said Reuben. "Oh, that's a door."

"Too much words," said Hak.

Reuben nodded. "Door," he said. "Door."

Ponter got up out of the bed and walked toward the door. He put his large hand on the handle, and pulled the door open.

"Um," said Reuben. Then: "Oh! Open. Open."

Ponter closed the door.

"Close."

Ponter then swung the door repeatedly open and closed.

Reuben frowned, then, getting it: "Opening. You're

opening the door. Or closing it. Opening. Closing. Opening. Closing."

Ponter walked over to the window. He indicated it with a sweep of both hands.

"Window," said Reuben.

He tapped on the glass.

"Glass," Reuben supplied.

The female voice again, as Ponter lifted the window up in its frame, exposing the screen: "I am opening the window."

"Yes!" said Reuben. "Opening the window! Yes."

Ponter pulled the window down. "I am closing the window," said the female voice.

"Yes!" said Reuben. "Yes, indeed!"

Chapter Thirteen

Adikor Huld had forgotten what Last Five was like. He could smell them, smell all the women. They weren't menstruating—not quite yet. The beginning of that, coinciding with the new moon, would mark the end of Last Five, the end of the current month and the start of the next. But they all would be menstruating soon; he could tell by the pheromones wafting on the air.

Well, not *all* of them, of course. The prepubescent ones—members of generation 148—wouldn't, and neither would the postmenopausal ones—most members of generation 144, and just about everyone from earlier generations. And if any of them had been pregnant or lactating, they wouldn't menstruate, either. But generation 149 wasn't due for many months, and generation 148 had long since been weaned. Of course, there were a few who, usually through no fault of their own, were sterile. But the rest, all living together in the Center, all easily smelling each other's pheromones, all synchronized in their cycles: they were all about to begin their periods.

Adikor understood well that it was hormonal changes that made so many of them testy at the end of each month, and why his male ancestors, long before they'd started numbering generations, had headed for the hills during this time.

The driver had dropped Adikor off near the home he had been looking for, a simple rectangular building, half grown by arboriculture, half built with bricks and mortar, with solar panels on its roof. Adikor took a deep breath through his mouth—a calming breath, bypassing his sinuses and his sense of smell. He let the air out slowly and walked along the small path through the arrangement of rocks and flowers and grasses and shrubs that covered the area in front of the house. When he got to the door—which was ajar—he called out, "Hello! Anybody home?"

A moment later, Jasmel Ket appeared. She was tall, lithe, and just past her 250th moon, the age of majority. Adikor could see Ponter in her face, and Klast, too; lucky Jasmel had inherited his eyes and her cheeks, instead of the other way around.

"W-w-what—" stammered Jasmel. She fought to compose herself, then tried again. "What are you doing here?"

"Healthy day, Jasmel," said Adikor. "It's been a long time."

"You've got a lot of neck muscle coming here—and during Last Five besides!"

"I didn't kill your father," said Adikor. "Honestly, I did not."

"He's gone, isn't he? If he's alive, where is he?"

"If he's dead, where is his body?" asked Adikor.

"I don't know. Daklar says you disposed of it."

"Is Daklar here?"

"No, she's gone to the skills exchange."

"May I come in?"

Jasmel glanced down at her Companion implant, as if to make sure it was still functioning. "I—I guess so," she said.

"Thanks." She stepped aside, and Adikor walked into the house. The interior was cool, a welcome relief from the summer heat. A household robot was puttering along in the background, lifting up knickknacks with its insect-like arms and sucking dust off them with a small vacuum.

"Where's your sister?" asked Adikor.

"*Megameg*," said Jasmel, emphasizing the name, as if it were a slight that Adikor had apparently forgotten it. "Megameg is playing *barstalk* with friends."

Adikor wondered whether to demonstrate that he did know all about Megameg; after all, Ponter talked of her and Jasmel constantly. Had this been just a social call, he'd perhaps have let it go. But it was more than that; much more. "Megameg," repeated Adikor. "Yes, Megameg Bek. A 148, isn't she? A little small for her age, but feisty. She wants to be a surgeon when she grows up, I believe."

Jasmel said nothing.

"And you," said Adikor, driving the point home, "Jasmel Ket, are studying to be a historian. Your particular interest is pre-generation-one Evsoy, but you also have a fondness for generations thirty through forty here on this continent, and—"

"All right," said Jasmel, cutting him off.

"Your father spoke of you often—and with great pride and love."

Jasmel raised her eyebrow slightly, clearly both surprised and pleased.

"I did not kill him," said Adikor again. "Believe me, I

miss him more than I can say. It—" He stopped himself; he'd been about to point out that there hadn't yet been a Two becoming One since Ponter's disappearance; Jasmel hadn't really had to face his absence yet. Indeed, it would have been unusual for her to have seen her father in the past three days, since Two last ceased being One. But Adikor had had to deal with the reality of Ponter's absence, with the emptiness of their home, every waking moment since he'd disappeared. Still, it was pointless to argue whose grief was the greater; Adikor recognized, after all, for all that he loved Ponter, Ponter and his daughter Jasmel were genetically related.

Perhaps Jasmel had been thinking the same thing, though. "I miss him, too. Already. I—" She looked away. "I didn't spend much time with him when Two last became One. There's this boy, you see, who . . ."

Adikor nodded. He wasn't quite sure what it was like for a father of a young woman. He himself had no child from generation 147; oh, he'd been paired to Lurt back when that generation was conceived, but somehow she hadn't become pregnant—and, yes, they had endured the requisite jokes about a physicist and a chemist failing to understand biology. Adikor's offspring from generation 148 was Dab, a small boy still living with his mother, and Dab wanted to spend every possible moment with his father when they got together each month.

But Adikor had heard Ponter's—well, not complaints, really. He'd understood it was the natural way of things. But, still, that Jasmel had so little time for him when Two became One had saddened Ponter, Adikor knew. And now, it seemed, Jasmel was coming to grips with the fact that her father wouldn't be there ever again, that she'd missed out on time she could have spent with him, and now there was no way to make amends, no way to catch up, no way she would ever be hugged by him again, ever hear his voice praising her or telling her a joke or asking her how things were going.

Adikor looked around the room and helped himself to a seat. The chair was wooden, made by the same carpenter who supplied the ones he and Ponter had had on their deck; the woman had been an acquaintance of Klast.

Jasmel sat on the opposite side of the room. Behind her, the cleaning robot left, heading into another part of the house.

"Do you know what will happen if I'm found guilty?" asked Adikor.

Jasmel closed her eyes, perhaps to forestall them making a quick glance down. "Yes," she said softly. But then, as if it were a defense: "What difference does it make, though? You've already reproduced; you've got two children."

"No, I don't," said Adikor. "I have only one, a 148."

"Oh," said Jasmel softly, perhaps embarrassed that she knew less about her father's partner than Adikor did about his partner's daughters.

"And, besides, it's not just me. My son Dab will be sterilized, too, and my sister Kelon—everyone who shares fifty percent of my genetic material."

Of course, these were no longer the barbaric days of yore; this was the era of genetic testing. Normally, if Kelon or Dab could show that they hadn't inherited Adikor's aberrant genes, they would have been entitled to be spared an operation. But although some crimes had single genetic causes that were well understood, a murderous trait had no such simple markers. And, besides, murder was a crime so heinous, no possibility, however remote, of its predisposition being further passed on could be allowed.

"I'm sorry about that," said Jasmel. "But . . ."

"There are no buts," said Adikor. "I am innocent."

"Then the adjudicator will find you so."

Ah, the artlessness of youth, thought Adikor. It would almost be endearing, if it weren't for what he had on the line. "This is a most unusual case," Adikor said. "Even I admit that. But there is no reason I would have killed the man I love."

"Daklar says it was difficult for you to always be downwind of my father."

Adikor felt his back stiffen. "I wouldn't say that."

"I would," said Jasmel. "My father—let's be honest—was more intelligent than you. You didn't like being an adjunct to his genius."

" 'We contribute as best we can,' " said Adikor, quoting the *Code of Civilization*.

"Indeed we do," said Jasmel. "And you wanted your contribution to be the principal one. But in your collaboration, it was Ponter's ideas that were being tested."

"That's no reason to kill him," snapped Adikor.

"Isn't it? My father is gone, and you were the only one with him when he disappeared."

"Yes, he's gone. He's gone, and—" Adikor felt tears welling at the corners of his eyes, tears of sadness and tears of frustration. "I miss him so much. I say this with my head tilted back: I did not do this. I couldn't have."

Jasmel looked at Adikor. He could see her nostrils dilating, taking in his scent, his pheromones. "Why should I believe you?" she said, crossing her arms in front of her chest.

Adikor frowned. He'd made his grief plain; he'd tried arguing emotions. But this girl had more than Ponter's eyes; she had his mind, too—a keen, analytical mind, a mind that prized logic and rationality.

"All right," said Adikor. "Consider this: if I am guilty of murdering your father, I will be sentenced. I will lose not just my ability to reproduce, but my position and my holdings. I will be unable to continue my work; the Gray Council will surely demand a more direct and tangible contribution from a convicted killer if I am to remain part of society."

"And well they should," said Jasmel.

"Ah, but if I'm *not* guilty—if *no one* is guilty, if your father is missing, if he's lost, he needs help. He needs *my* help; I'm the only one who might be able to . . . to *retrieve* him. Without me, your father is gone for sure." He looked at her golden eyes. "Don't you see? The sensible position is to believe me: if I am lying, and I did murder Ponter—well, no punishment will bring him back. But if I am telling the truth, and Ponter was not murdered, then the only hope he has is if I can continue to search for him."

"The mine *has* been searched," said Jasmel, flatly.

"The mine, yes, but—" Did he dare tell her? It sounded crazy when the words echoed inside his head; he could only imagine how insane they would seem when given voice. "We were working with parallel universes," said Adikor. "It's possible—remotely possible, I know, but I refuse to give up on him, on the man who is so very important to both you and me—that he has, well, *slipped*, somehow, into another of those universes." He looked at her, imploring. "You must know something of your father's work. Even if you made little time for him"—he saw those words cut deep—"he must have told you about our work, about his theories."

Jasmel nodded. "He told me, yes."

"Well, then, there might—just might—be a chance. But I need to get this reeking *dooslarm basadlarm* over with; I need to get back to work."

Jasmel said nothing for a long time. Adikor knew from his own occasional arguments with her father that just letting her consider quietly would be more effective than pressing his point, but he couldn't help himself. "Please, Jasmel. Please. It's the only sensible wager to make: assume that I'm not guilty, and there's a chance that we might get Ponter back. Assume that I am guilty, and he is surely gone for good."

Jasmel was silent a while longer, then: "What do you want from me?"

Adikor blinked. "I, ah, I should have thought it was obvious," he said. "I want you to speak on my behalf at the *dooslarm basadlarm*."

"Me?" exclaimed Jasmel. "But I'm one of those accusing you of murder!"

Adikor held up his left wrist. "I've carefully reviewed the documents I was given. My accuser is your mother's woman-mate, Daklar Bolbay, acting on behalf of your mother's children: you, and Megameg Bek."

"Exactly."

"But she *cannot* act on your behalf. You've seen 250 moons now; you're an adult. Yes, you can't vote yet—neither can I, of course—but you *are* responsible for yourself. Daklar is still the *tabant* of young Megameg, but not of you."

Jasmel frowned. "I—I hadn't thought of that. I've gotten so used to Daklar looking after my sister and me . . ."

"You are your own person under the law now. And no one could better persuade an adjudicator that I did not murder Ponter than his own daughter."

Jasmel closed her eyes, took a deep breath, and let it out slowly in a long, shuddery sigh. "All right," she said at last. "All right. If there's a chance, any chance at all, that my father still lives, I have to pursue it. I have to." She nodded once. "Yes, I'll be the one to speak on your behalf."

Chapter Fourteen

The conference room at the Creighton Mine had wall diagrams showing the network of tunnels and drifts. A hunk of nickel ore sat as a centerpiece on a long wooden table. A Canadian flag stood at one end of the room; the other had a large window overlooking the parking lot and the rough countryside beyond.

At the head of the table was Bonnie Jean Mah—a white woman with lots of brown hair who was married to a Chinese-Canadian, hence her last name. She was the director of the Sudbury Neutrino Observatory, and had just flown in from Ottawa.

Along one side of the table sat Louise Benoît, the tall, beautiful postdoc who'd been down in the SNO control room when the disaster had occurred. And on the other side sat Scott Naylor, an engineer from the company that had manufactured the acrylic sphere at the heart of SNO. Next to him was Albert Shawwanossoway, Inco's top expert on rock mechanics.

"All right," said Bonnie Jean. "Just to bring everyone up to date, they've started draining the SNO chamber, before the heavy water gets any more polluted. AECL is going to try to separate the heavy water from the regular water, and, in theory, we should be able to reassemble the sphere and load it up with the recovered heavy water, getting SNO back on-line." She looked at the faces in the room. "But I'd still like to know exactly what caused the accident."

Naylor, a balding, tubby white man, said, "I'd say the sphere containing the heavy water burst apart because of pressure from the inside."

"Could the displacement caused by a man entering the sphere have done that?" asked Bonnie Jean.

Naylor shook his head. "The sphere held 1,100 tonnes of heavy water; you add a human being, weighing a hundred kilos—one-tenth of a tonne—and you've only increased the mass by one ten-thousandth. Human beings have about the same density as water, so the displacement increase would only be about one ten-thousandth, as well. The acrylic could easily handle that."

"Then he must have used an explosive of some sort," said Shawwanossoway, an Ojibwa of about fifty, with long, black hair.

Naylor shook his head. "We've done assays on the water recovered from the tank. There's no evidence of any explosive—and there aren't that many that would work soaking wet, anyway."

"Then what?" asked Bonnie Jean. "Could there have been, I don't know, a magma incursion or something, and the water boiled?"

Shawwanossoway shook his head. "The temperature of SNO, and the whole mine complex, is closely monitored; there was no change. In the observatory cavern, it held steady at its normal value of 105 degrees—Fahrenheit, that is; forty-one Celsius. Hot, but nowhere near boiling. Remember, too, that the mine is a mile and a quarter underground, meaning the air pressure is about thirteen hundred millibars—30 percent above that at sea level. And at higher pressures, of course, the boiling point goes *up*, not down."

"What about the flip side?" asked Bonnie Jean. "What if the heavy water froze?"

"Well, it would indeed have expanded, just like regular water," said Naylor. He frowned. "Yes, that would have burst the sphere. But heavy water freezes at 3.82 Celsius. It just couldn't possibly get that cold that far down."

Louise Benoît joined the conversation. "What if more than just the man entered the sphere? How much material would have to be added before it would burst?"

Naylor thought for a moment. "I'm not sure; it was never specced for that. We always knew exactly how much heavy water AECL was going to loan us." He paused. "Maybe . . . I don't know, maybe 10 percent. A hundred cubic meters, or so."

"Which is what?" asked Louise. She looked around the conference room. "This room's about six meters on a side, isn't it?"

"Twenty feet?" said Naylor. "Yeah, I guess."

"And it's got ten-foot ceilings—that's three meters," continued Louise. "So you're talking about a volume of material as big as the contents of this room."

"More or less, I suppose."

"That's ridiculous, Louise," said Bonnie Jean. "All you found down there was one man."

Louise nodded, conceding that, but then she lifted her arched eyebrows. "What about *air*? What if a hundred cubic meters of air were pumped into the sphere?"

Naylor nodded. "I'd thought about that. I thought maybe a belch of gas had somehow welled up into the sphere, although how it would get inside I have no idea. The water samples we took were somewhat aerated, but . . ."

"But what?" asked Louise.

"Well, they were indeed aerated, with nitrogen, oxygen, and some CO_2, as well as some gabbroic rock dust and pollen. In other words, just regular mine air."

"Then it couldn't have come from the SNO facility," said Bonnie Jean.

"That's right, ma'am," said Naylor. "That air is all filtered; it's free of rock dust and other pollutants."

"But the only parts of the mine connecting to the detector chamber are in the SNO facility," said Louise.

Naylor and Shawwanossoway both nodded.

"Okay, okay," said Bonnie Jean, steepling her fingers in front of her. "What have we got? The volume of material inside the sphere was increased by, at a guess, 10 percent or more. That might have been caused by an infusion of a hundred cubic meters or more of unfiltered air—although unless the air was pumped in very rapidly, it would have been compressed by the weight of the water, no? And, in any event, we don't know where the air came from—it certainly wasn't from SNO—or how it was conveyed into the sphere, right?"

"That's about the size of it, ma'am," said Shawwanossoway.

"And this man—we don't know how he got into the sphere, either?" asked Bonnie Jean.

"No," said Louise. "The access hatch between the inner heavy-water sphere and the outer regular-water containment tank was sealed tight even after the sphere broke apart."

"All right," said Bonnie Jean, "do we know how this—this Neanderthal, they're calling him—even got down into the mine?"

Shawwanossoway was the only one present who actually worked for Inco. He spread his arms. "The mine-security people have reviewed the security-camera tapes and access logs for the forty-eight hours prior to the incident," he said. "Caprini—that's our head of security—swears that heads will roll when he finds out who screwed up by letting that guy in, and he says even worse will happen when he finds out who's been trying to hide it."

"What if no one is lying?" said Louise.

"That's just not possible, Miss Benoît," said Shawwanossoway. "No one could get down to SNO without it being recorded."

"No one could if he came down by the elevator," said Louise. "But what if he didn't come that way?"

"You think maybe he climbed down two kilometers of vertical air shafts?" said Shawwanossoway, scowling. "Even if he could do that—and it would take nerves of steel—security cameras still would have recorded him."

"That's my point," said Louise. "He obviously didn't go down into the mine. As Professor Mah said, they're calling him a Neanderthal—but he's a Neanderthal with some sort of high-tech implant on his wrist; I saw that with my own eyes."

"So?" said Bonnie Jean.

"Please!" exclaimed Louise. "You all must be thinking the same things *I'm* thinking. He didn't take the elevator. He didn't go down the ventilation shafts. He *materialized* inside the sphere—him, and a roomful of air."

Naylor whistled the opening notes of the original *Star Trek* theme.

Everyone laughed.

"Come on," said Bonnie Jean. "Yes, this is a crazy situation, and it might be tempting to jump to crazy conclusions, but let's stay down to earth."

Shawwanossoway could whistle, too. He did the theme to *The Twilight Zone.*

"Stop that!" snapped Bonnie Jean.

Chapter Fifteen

Mary Vaughan was the only passenger on the Inco Learjet flying from Toronto to Sudbury; she'd noted on boarding that the plane, painted with dark green sides, was labeled "The Nickel Pickle" on its bow.

Mary used the brief flight time to review research notes on her notebook computer; it had been years since she'd published her study of Neanderthal DNA in *Science*. As she read through her notes, she twirled the gold chain that held the small, plain cross she always wore around her neck.

In 1994, Mary had made a name for herself recovering genetic material from a 30,000-year-old bear found frozen in Yukon permafrost. And so, two years later, when the *Rheinisches Amt für Bodendenkmalpflege*—the agency responsible for archeology in the Rhineland—decided it was time to see whether any DNA could be extracted from the most famous fossil of all, the original Neanderthal man, they called on Mary. She'd been dubious: that specimen was desiccated, having never been frozen, and—opinions varied—it might be as old as 100,000 years, three times the age of the bear. Still, the challenge was irresistible. In June 1996, she'd flown to Bonn, then headed to the *Rheinisches*

Landesmuseum, where the specimen was housed.

The best-known part—the browridged skullcap—was on public display, but the rest of the bones were kept in a steel box, within a steel cabinet, inside a room-sized steel vault. Mary was led into the safe by a German bone pre-parator named Hans. They wore protective plastic suits and surgeons' masks; every precaution had to be taken against contaminating the bones with their own modern DNA. Yes, the original discoverers had doubtless contaminated the bones—but after a century and a half, their unprotected DNA on the surface should have degraded completely.

Mary could only take a very small piece of bone; the priests at Turin guarded their shroud with equal jealousy. Still, it was extraordinarily difficult for both her and Hans—like desecrating a great work of art. Mary found herself wiping away tears as Hans used a goldsmith's saw to cut a semicircular chunk, just a centimeter wide and weighing only three grams, from the right humerus, the best preserved of all the bones.

Fortunately, the hard calcium carbonate in the outer layers of the bone should have afforded some protection for any of the original DNA within. Mary took the speci-men back to her lab in Toronto and drilled tiny pieces out of it.

It took five months of painstaking work to extract a 379-nucleotide snippet from the control region of the Ne-anderthal's mitochondrial DNA. Mary used the polymerase chain reaction to reproduce millions of copies of the re-covered DNA, and she carefully sequenced it. She then checked the corresponding bit of mitochondrial DNA in 1,600 modern humans: Native Canadians, Polynesians,

Australians, Africans, Asians, and Europeans. Every one of those 1,600 people had at least 371 nucleotides out of those 379 the same; the maximum deviation was just eight nucleotides.

But the Neanderthal DNA had an average of only 352 nucleotides in common with the modern specimens; it deviated by a whopping twenty-seven bases. Mary concluded that her kind of human and Neanderthals must have diverged from each other between 550,000 and 690,000 years ago for their DNA to be so different. In contrast, all modern humans probably shared a common ancestor 150,000 or 200,000 years in the past. Although the half-million-year-plus date for the Neanderthal/modern divergence was much more recent than the split between genus *Homo* and its closest relatives, the chimps and bonobos, which occurred five to eight million years ago, it was still far enough back that Mary felt Neanderthals were probably a fully separate species from modern humans, not just a subspecies: *Homo neanderthalensis*, not *Homo sapiens neanderthalensis*.

Others disagreed. Milford Wolpoff of the University of Michigan was sure that Neanderthal genes had been fully co-opted into modern Europeans; he felt any test strand that showed something different was, therefore, an aberrant sequence or a misinterpretation.

But many paleoanthropologists agreed with Mary's analysis, although everyone—Mary included—said that further studies needed to be done to be sure . . . if only more Neanderthal DNA could be found.

And now, maybe, just maybe, more *had* been found. There was no way this Neanderthal man could be real, thought Mary, but if it were . . .

Mary closed her laptop and looked out the window. Northern Ontario spread out below her, with Canadian Shield rocks exposed in many places and aspen and birch dotting the landscape. The plane was beginning its descent.

Reuben Montego had no idea what Mary Vaughan looked like, but since there were no other passengers aboard the Inco jet, he didn't have any trouble spotting her. She turned out to be white, in her late thirties, with honey-blond hair showing darker roots. She was perhaps ten pounds overweight, and, as she came closer, Reuben could see that she clearly hadn't gotten much sleep the night before.

"Professor Vaughan," Reuben said, offering his hand. "I'm Reuben Montego, the M.D. at the Creighton Mine. Thank you so very much for coming up." He indicated the young woman he'd picked up on the way to the Sudbury airport. "This is Gillian Ricci, the press officer for Inco; she's going to look after you."

Reuben thought Mary looked inordinately pleased to see the attractive young woman who was accompanying him; maybe the professor was a lesbian. He reached out to take the suitcase Mary was holding. "Here, let me help you."

Mary relinquished the bag, but she fell in beside Gillian, rather than Reuben, as they walked across the tarmac, the summer sun beating down. Reuben and Gillian were both wearing sunglasses; Mary was squinting against the brightness, evidently having forgotten to bring a pair.

When they arrived at Reuben's wine-colored Ford Explorer, Gillian politely began to get in the backseat, but Mary spoke up. "No, I'll sit there," she said. "I—ah—I want to stretch out."

Her odd statement hung between them for a second, and then Reuben saw Gillian shrug a little and move up to the front passenger's seat.

They drove directly to St. Joseph's Health Centre, on Paris Street, just past the snowflake-shaped museum Science North. Along the way, Reuben briefed Mary about the accident at SNO and the strange man who had been found.

As they pulled into the hospital parking lot, Reuben saw three vans from local TV stations. Surely hospital security was keeping reporters away from Ponter, but, just as surely, the journalists would be following this story closely.

When they arrived at Room 3-G, Ponter was standing up, looking out the window, his broad back to them. He was waving—and Reuben realized that TV cameras must be trained up at his window. *A cooperative celebrity*, thought Reuben. *The media are going to love this guy.*

Reuben coughed politely, and Ponter turned around. He was backlit by the window and still hard to make out. But as he stepped forward, the doctor enjoyed watching Mary's jaw drop when she got her first good look at the Neanderthal. She'd briefly seen Ponter on TV, she'd said, but that seemingly hadn't prepared her for the reality.

"So much for Carleton Coon," Mary said, after apparently recovering her wits.

"Say what?" said Reuben sharply.

Mary looked puzzled, then flustered. "Oh, my, no.

Carleton Coon. He was an American anthropologist. He's
the guy who said if you dressed a Neanderthal up in a
Brooks Brothers suit, he'd have no trouble passing for a
regular human."

Reuben nodded. "Ah," he said. Then: "Professor Mary
Vaughan, I'd like you to meet Ponter."

"Hello," said the female voice from Ponter's implant.

Reuben saw Mary's eyes go wide. "Yes," he said, nodding. "That thing on his wrist is talking."

"What is it?" asked Mary. "A talking watch?"

"Much more."

Mary leaned in for a look. "I don't recognize those
numerals, if that's what they are," she said. "And—say—
aren't they changing too fast for seconds?"

"You've got a good eye," said Reuben. "Yeah, they are.
The display uses ten distinct numerals, although none of
them look like any I've ever seen. And I timed it: it incre-
ments every 0.86 seconds, which, if you work it out, is exactly one one-hundred-thousandth of a day. In other
words, it's a decimal-counting Earth-based time display.
And, as you can see, it's a very sophisticated device. That's
not an LCD; I don't know what it is, but it's readable no
matter what angle you look at it or how much light is falling on it."

"My name is Hak," said the implant on the strange
man's left wrist. "I am Ponter's Companion."

"Ah," said Mary, straightening up. "Um, glad to know
you."

Ponter made a series of deep sounds that Mary
couldn't understand. Hak said, "Ponter is glad to know
you, too."

"We spent the morning having a language lesson," said Reuben, looking now at Mary. "As you can see, we've made some real progress."

"Apparently," said Mary, astonished.

"Hak, Ponter," said Reuben. "This is Gillian."

"Hello," said Hak. Ponter nodded in agreement.

"Hello," said Gillian, trying, Reuben thought, to remain composed.

"Hak is—well, I guess 'computer' is the right term. A talking, portable computer." Reuben smiled. "Beats all hell out of my Palm Pilot."

"Does—does *anyone* make a device like that?" asked Gillian.

"Not as far as I know," said Reuben. "But she—Hak—has an apparently perfect memory. Tell her a word once, and she's got it for good."

"And this man, this Ponter, he really doesn't speak English?" asked Mary.

"No," said Reuben.

"Incredible," said Mary. "Incredible."

Ponter's implant bleeped.

"Incredible," repeated Reuben, turning to Ponter. "It means not believable"—another *bleep*—"not true." He faced Mary again. "We worked out the concepts of *true* and *false* using some simple math, but, as you can see, we've still got a ways to go. For one thing, although it clearly seems easier for Hak, with her perfect memory, to learn English, than for us to learn her language, neither she nor Ponter can make the *ee* sound, and—"

"Really?" said Mary. She looked quite earnest, Reuben thought. He nodded.

"Your name is Mare," said Hak, demonstrating the point. "Her name is Gill'an."

"That's—that's amazing," said Mary.

"Is it?" said Reuben. "Why?"

Mary took a deep breath. "There's been a lot of debate over the years about whether Neanderthals could speak, and, if they could, what range of sounds they could have made."

"And?" said Reuben.

"Some linguists think they couldn't have made the *ee* phoneme, because their mouths would have been much longer than ours."

"So he *is* a Neanderthal!" declared Reuben.

Mary took another breath, then let it slowly out. "Well, that's what I'm here to find out, isn't it?" She set down the small bag she'd been carrying and opened it up. She then pulled out a pair of latex gloves and snapped them on. Next, she removed a plastic jar full of cotton swabs and extracted one.

"I need you to get him to open his mouth," said Mary.

Reuben nodded. "That one's easy." He turned to Ponter. "Ponter, open mouth."

There was a second's lag—Hak, Reuben had learned, could convey the translation to Ponter without the others hearing it. Ponter rolled his continuous blond eyebrow up his browridge—quite a startling sight—as if surprised by the request, but did as he was asked.

Reuben was astonished. He'd had a friend in high school who could stuff his own fist all the way into his mouth. But Ponter's mouth went back so far and was so capacious, he probably could have stuffed in not just his fist but a third of his forearm as well.

Mary moved in tentatively and reached her swab into Ponter's mouth, swiping it across the inside of his long, angled cheek. "Cells in the mouth slough off easily," she said, by way of explanation, apparently noting Gillian's quizzical expression. "It's the simplest way to take a DNA specimen." She pulled out the swab, immediately transferred it to a sterile container, sealed, then labeled the container, and said, "Okay, that's all I need."

Reuben smiled at Gillian, then at Mary. "Great," he said. "When will we know for sure?"

"Well, I've got to get back to Toronto, and—"

"Of course, if you want," said Reuben, "but, well, I called a friend of mine in Laurentian's Department of Chemistry and Biochemistry. Laurentian's a tiny university, but they've got a great lab that does contract DNA forensics work for the RCMP and the OPP. You could do your work there."

"Inco will certainly put you up at the Ramada," added Gillian.

Mary was clearly taken aback. "I . . ." But then she seemed to reconsider. "Sure," she said. "Sure, why not?"

Chapter Sixteen

Now that Jasmel had agreed to speak on Adikor's behalf, the next step should have been for him to take her out to the Rim and show her the scene of the so-called crime. But Adikor begged Jasmel's indulgence for a daytenth or so, saying there was one more errand he had to run here in the Center.

Ponter, of course, had had Klast as his woman-mate; Adikor remembered her fondly, and had been very sad when she'd died. But Adikor had a woman of his own, and she, wonderfully, was still very much alive. Adikor had known the lovely Lurt Fradlo as long as he'd known Ponter, and he and Lurt had one son, Dab, a 148. Still, despite knowing her that long, Adikor had only occasionally been to Lurt's chemistry lab; after all, when Two became One, it was a holiday and nobody went to work. Fortunately, his Companion knew the way, and it directed him there.

Lurt's lab was made entirely of stone; although there was only a small chance of an explosion in any chemistry lab, safety dictated making the structure out of something that could contain blasts and fires.

The front door to the lab building was open. Adikor walked in.

"Healthy day," said a woman, doing, Adikor thought, an admirable job of hiding her surprise at seeing a man here at this time of month.

"Healthy day," replied Adikor. "I'm looking for Lurt Fradlo."

"She's down that hall."

Adikor smiled and headed along the corridor. "Healthy day," he called, as he stuck his head in the door to Lurt's lab.

Lurt turned around, a big grin on her lovely face. "Adikor!" She closed the distance between them and gave him a hug. "What a pleasant surprise!"

Adikor couldn't remember ever seeing Lurt during Last Five before. She seemed perfectly sane and rational—and so had Jasmel, for that matter. Maybe this whole Last Five thing was overblown in men's minds . . .

"Hello, beautiful," said Adikor, squeezing her again. "It's good to see you."

But Lurt knew her man well. "Something's wrong," she said, releasing him. "What is it?"

Adikor looked back over his shoulder, making sure they were alone. He then took Lurt's hand and led her across the room to a couple of lab chairs next to a chart of the periodic table; the only other animate entities in the lab were a pair of spindly robots, one pouring liquid between beakers; another assembling a structure out of pipes and glassware. Adikor sat down, and Lurt took the seat next to him.

"I've been accused of murdering Ponter," he said.

Lurt's eyes went wide. "Ponter is dead?"

"I don't know. He's been missing since yesterday afternoon."

"I was at a flensing party last night," said Lurt. "I hadn't heard."

He told her the whole story. She was sympathetic, and never expressed disbelief in Adikor's innocence; Lurt's trust in him was something Adikor could always count on.

"Would you like me to speak for you?" asked Lurt.

Adikor looked away. "Well, that's the thing. You see, I've already asked Jasmel."

Lurt nodded. "Ponter's daughter. Yes, that would impress an adjudicator, I should think."

"That was my thought. I hope you don't feel slighted."

She smiled. "No, no, of course not. But, look, if there's anything else I can do to help . . ."

"Well, there is one thing," said Adikor. He pulled a small vial out of his hip pouch. "This is a sample of a liquid I collected at the site of Ponter's disappearance; there were buckets of it on the floor. Could you do an assay on it for me?"

Lurt took the vial and held it up to the light. "Sure," she said. "And if there's anything else I can do, just ask."

Ponter's daughter Jasmel accompanied Adikor back to the Rim. They went straight to the nickel mine; Adikor wanted to show Jasmel exactly where her father had disappeared. But when they got to the mineshaft-elevator station, Jasmel looked hesitant.

"What's wrong?" asked Adikor.

"I—um, I've got claustrophobia."

Adikor shook his head, confused. "No, you don't. Ponter told me how when you were little, you liked to hide inside *dobalak* cubes. And he took you caving last tenmonth."

"Well, um . . ." Jasmel trailed off.

"Oh," said Adikor, nodding his head, getting it. "You don't trust me, do you?"

"It's just that . . . well, my father *was* the last person to go down there with you. And he never came back up."

Adikor sighed, but he could see her point. Somebody—some private citizen—had to accuse Adikor of the crime, or the legal proceedings could not continue. Why, if he now got rid of Jasmel and Megameg and Bolbay, perhaps there would be no one left to press the accusation . . .

"We can get someone to go down with us," said Adikor.

Jasmel considered, but she, too, must have been thinking about how everything took on new significance during a time like this. Yes, she could ask for an escort—someone she really knew, someone she trusted implicitly. But that person might be called for questioning, too, if this went to a full tribunal. "Yes, adjudicators, I know that Jasmel is speaking on behalf of Adikor, but even she was too frightened of him to go down into the mine alone with him. And can you blame her? After what he did to her father?"

Finally, though, she managed a small smile—a smile that reminded Adikor a bit of Ponter's own. "No," she said. "No, of course not. I'm just edgy, I guess." She smiled more, making light of it. "It *is* that time of month, after all."

But as they approached the elevator station, a particularly burly man emerged from behind it. "Stop right there, Scholar Huld," he said.

Adikor felt sure he'd never seen the man before in his life. "Yes?"

"You're thinking of going down to your lab?"

"I am, yes. Who are you?"

"Gaskdol Dut," said the man. "My contribution is enforcement."

"Enforcement? Of what?"

"Of your judicial scrutiny. I can't let you go underground."

"Judicial scrutiny?" said Jasmel. "What's that?"

"It means," said Dut, "that the transmissions from Scholar Huld's Companion are being monitored directly by a living, breathing human being as they are received at the alibi-archive pavilion—and they will be so, ten tenths a day, twenty-nine days a month, until if and when his innocence is proven."

"I didn't know you were allowed to do that," said Adikor, shocked.

"Oh, yes, indeed," said Dut. "The moment Daklar Bolbay lodged her complaint against you, an adjudicator ordered you placed under judicial scrutiny."

"Why?" said Adikor, trying to control his anger.

"Didn't Bolbay transfer a document to you explaining this?" asked Dut. "An oversight, if she didn't. Anyway, judicial scrutiny ensures that you don't attempt to leave this jurisdiction, tamper with potential evidence, and so forth."

"But I'm not trying to do any of those things," said Adikor. "Why won't you let me go down to my lab?"

Dut looked at Adikor as if he couldn't believe the question. "Why not? Because your Companion's signals won't be detectable from down there; we wouldn't be able to keep you under scrutiny."

"Marrowless bone," said Adikor, softly.

Jasmel crossed her arms in front of her chest. "I'm Jasmel Ket, and—"

"I know who you are," said the enforcer.

"Well, then, you know that Ponter Boddit was my father."

The enforcer nodded.

"This man is trying to rescue him. You *have* to let him go down to his lab."

Dut shook his head in astonishment. "This man is accused of killing your father."

"But it's possible he didn't," said Jasmel. "My father might still be alive. The only way to find out is to repeat the quantum-computing experiment."

"I don't know anything about quantum experiments," said Dut.

"Why doesn't that surprise me?" said Adikor.

"My, you *are* a mouthy one, aren't you?" said Dut, looking Adikor up and down. "Anyway, my orders are simple. Keep you from leaving Saldak, and keep you from going to your lab. And I received a call from the alibi-archive pavilion saying you were heading off to do precisely that."

"I have to go down there," said Adikor.

"Sorry," said Dut, crossing his own massive arms in front of his massive chest. "Not only can't you be monitored from down there, but you might try to get rid of evidence that hasn't yet been found."

Jasmel did indeed have her father's quickness of mind.

"There's nothing preventing *me* from going down to the lab, is there? I'm not under judicial scrutiny."

Dut considered this. "No, I suppose not."

"All right," said Jasmel, turning now to Adikor. "Tell me what to do to try to bring my father back."

Adikor shook his head. "It's not that easy. The equipment is very complex, and, since Ponter and I assembled it ourselves, half the control buds aren't even labeled."

Jasmel was clearly frustrated. She looked at the big man. "Well, what if you went down with us? You'd be able to see what Adikor was doing."

"Go down there?" Dut laughed. "You want me to go to the one place my Companion can't be monitored—and to do so with a person who may well have committed murder there previously? You're ruffling my back hair."

"You *have* to let him go down there," Jasmel said.

But Dut just shook his head. "No. What I have to do is *keep* him from going down there."

Adikor thrust out his jaw. "How?" he said.

"I—I beg your pardon?" replied Dut.

"How? How are you going to keep me from going down there?"

"By whatever means necessary," said Dut, his tone even.

"All right, then," said Adikor. He stood motionlessly for a moment, as if thinking about whether he really wanted to try this. "All right, then," he said again, and started walking purposefully toward the entrance to the elevator.

"Stop," said Dut, with no particular force to the word.

"Or what?" said Adikor, without looking back. He tried to sound fearless, but his voice cracked, which didn't really give the effect he wanted. "Are you going to stave in my skull?" Despite himself, his neck muscles contracted, already preparing for the blow.

"Hardly," said Dut. "I'll just put you to sleep with a tranquilizer dart."

Adikor stopped walking and turned around. "Oh." Well, he'd never run up against the law before—nor had he known anyone who ever had. He supposed it made sense that they had a way to stop people without actually hurting them.

Jasmel interposed herself between Dut's dart launcher, which was now in his hand, and Adikor. "You'll have to shoot me first," she said. "He's going down there."

"If you like. But I should warn you: you'll wake up with an awful headache."

"Please!" said Jasmel. "He's trying to save my father—don't you understand?"

For once Dut's voice had some warmth in it. "You're clutching at smoke. I know it must be very hard to deal with, but you *have* to face reality." He gestured with his launcher for the two of them to start walking away from the mine. "I'm sorry, but your father is dead."

Chapter Seventeen

The genetics lab at Laurentian didn't have the special equipment for extracting degraded DNA from old specimens that Mary's lab at York did. But none of that would be needed. It was a straightforward matter to take the cells from Ponter's mouth and extract DNA from one of the mitochondria; any genetics facility in the world could have done it.

Mary introduced two primers—small pieces of mitochondrial DNA that matched the beginning of the sequence that she had identified years ago in the German Neanderthal fossil. She then added the enzyme DNA-polymerase, triggering the polymerase chain reaction, which would cause the section she was interested in to be amplified, reproducing itself over and over again, doubling the quantity each time. She would soon have millions of copies of the string to analyze.

As Reuben Montego had said, the Laurentian lab did a lot of forensic work, and so had sealing tape that could be applied to the glassware. The tape was used so that geneticists could truthfully testify that there was no way the contents of a vial could have been tampered with while out of their sight. Mary sealed the container in which the PCR amplification was happening and wrote her signature on the seal.

She then used a web terminal in the lab to access her e-mail at York. She'd received more e-mails in the last day than she had in the preceding month, and many of them were from Neanderthal experts around the world who had somehow gotten wind of the fact that she was now in Sudbury. There were messages from Washington University, the University of Michigan, UCB, UCLA, Brown, SUNY Stony Brook, Stanford, Cambridge, Britain's Natural History Museum, France's Institute of Quaternary Prehistory and Geology, her old friends at the *Rheinisches Landesmuseum*, and more—all asking for samples of the Neanderthal DNA while, at the same time, making a joke of it, as if, of course, this *couldn't* really be happening.

She ignored all those messages, but she did feel a need to send a note to her grad student back at York:

Daria:

Sorry to leave you in the lurch, but I know you can handle things. I'm sure you've seen the reports in the press, and all I can say is, yes, there really does seem to be a chance that he might be a Neanderthal. I'm running DNA tests right now to find out for sure.

I don't know when I'll be back. I'll probably stay here a few more days at least. But I wanted to tell you ... to warn you really ... that I think a man was trying to follow me when I left the lab on Friday night. Be careful ... if you are going to work late, have your boyfriend come and meet you at the end of the day or call for a walking companion to escort you back to the residence.

Take care.

MNV

Mary read the note over a couple of times, then clicked "Send Now."

She then simply sat, staring at the screen for a long, long time.

Damn it.

Damn it. Damn it. Damn it.

She couldn't get it out of her head—not for five minutes. She guessed that fully half her waking thoughts today had been devoted to the horrible events of—*My God, was it really only yesterday?* It seemed so much longer ago than that, although the memories of the horrible things he'd done to her were still scalpel sharp.

Had she been down in Toronto, she might have talked it over with her mother, but—

But her mother was a good Catholic, and there was no way to avoid unpleasant issues when discussing a rape. Mom would be worried about whether Mary might be pregnant—not that she'd ever countenance an abortion; Mary and she had argued about John Paul's edict that raped nuns in Bosnia had to bring their children to term. And telling her mother that there was nothing to worry about because Mary was on the Pill would hardly be better. As far as Mary's parents had been concerned, the rhythm

method was the only acceptable form of birth control—
Mary thought it was a miracle that she only had three siblings instead of a dozen.

And, indeed, she *could* speak to her siblings, but . . .
but . . . but there was no way she could talk to a man—*any*
man—about this. That left out her brothers Bill and John.
And her one sister, Christine, had moved to Sacramento,
and somehow this didn't seem to be the sort of thing she
wanted to talk about over the phone.

And yet, she had to speak to someone. Someone in
person.

Someone *here*.

There was a copy of the Laurentian calendar sitting on
a table in the lab; Mary found the campus map in it, and
located what she was looking for. She got up and made
her way down the corridor to the stairs, crossed over from
Science One to the Classroom Building, then headed
down to what she'd learned Laurentian students called
"the bowling alley"—the long ground-floor glass corridor
that ran between the Classroom Building and the Great
Hall. She walked down its length, afternoon sun streaming
in, past a Tim Hortons donut stand and a few kiosks devoted to student activities. She finally turned left at the
bowling alley's far end, going past the liaison office, up the
stairs, past the campus bookstore, and down a short corridor.

Going to the rape-crisis center at York University would
have been out of the question. The counselors there were
volunteers mostly, and, although they all were doubtless
supposed to keep things confidential, the gossip that a faculty member had been attacked might prove irresistible.
Plus, she might be seen entering or leaving the facility.

But Laurentian University, small as it was, had a rape-crisis center, too. The sad truth was that *every* university needed to have one; she'd heard there was even one at Oral Roberts University. Nobody here knew Mary, and she hadn't yet been interviewed on TV, although she doubtless would be once she had results of Ponter's DNA tests. So, if she wanted any anonymity at all, this couldn't wait.

The door was open. Mary entered the small reception area. "Hello," said the young black woman behind the desk. She stood up and walked over to Mary. "Come in, come in." Mary understood her solicitousness. Many women probably made it to the threshold, but then scurried away, unable to give voice to what had happened to them.

Still, the woman could probably tell that if Mary were a rape victim, it hadn't just happened. Mary's clothes weren't disheveled, and her makeup and hair were all fine. And the center must get visitors who weren't victims: people coming in to volunteer, to do research, to service the photocopier.

"Have you been hurt?" asked the woman.

Hurt. Yes, that was the right approach. It was easier to admit you'd been hurt than to accept the R-word.

Mary nodded.

"I have to ask," said the woman. She had large brown eyes, and a small jeweled stud in her nose. "Did it happen today?"

Mary shook her head.

For half a second, the woman looked—well, disappointed would be the wrong word, Mary thought, but things were doubtless much more interesting if it had just occurred, if the rape kit was to be employed to gather evidence, if . . .

"Yesterday," said Mary, speaking for the first time. "Last night."

"Was it—was it someone you know?"

"No," said Mary . . . but then she paused. Actually, she wasn't sure of the answer to that question. The monster had worn a ski mask. It could have been anyone: a student she'd taught; another faculty member; someone from the support staff; a punk from the Driftwood corridor. Anyone. "I don't know. He—he had a mask on."

"I know he hurt you," said the young woman, putting an arm through Mary's and leading her farther inside, "but did he *injure* you? Do you need to see a doctor?" The woman held up a hand. "We've got an excellent female doctor on call."

Mary shook her head again. "No," she said. "He had a—" Mary's voice broke, surprising herself. She tried again. "He had a knife, but he didn't use it."

"Animal," said the woman.

Mary nodded in agreement.

They moved into an inner room, with walls painted a soft pink. There were two chairs, but no couch—even here, even in this sanctuary, the sight of a couch might be too much. The woman gestured for Mary to take one of the chairs—a padded easy chair—and she took the other one, sitting opposite her, but reaching over and gently taking Mary's left hand.

"Would you like to tell me your name?" asked the woman.

Mary thought about giving a fake name, or maybe—

she didn't want to lie to this sweet young person who was trying so hard to help; maybe she'd tell the woman her middle name, Nicole—that wouldn't really be a lie, then, but it would still conceal her identity. But when she opened her mouth, "Mary" came out. "Mary Vaughan."

"Mary, my name is Keisha."

Mary looked at her. "How old are you?" she asked.

"Nineteen," said Keisha.

So young. "Were you . . . were you ever . . . ?"

Keisha pressed her lips together and nodded.

"When?"

"Three years ago."

Mary felt her own eyes go wide. She would have been just sixteen then; it might—my God, her first time might have been a rape. "I'm so sorry," said Mary.

Keisha tilted her head, accepting the comment. "I won't tell you you'll get over it, Mary, but you *can* survive it. And we'll help you to do just that."

Mary closed her eyes and took a deep breath, then let it out slowly. She could feel Keisha gently squeezing her hand, transfusing strength into her. At last, Mary spoke again. "I *hate* him," she said. She opened her eyes. Keisha's face was concerned, supportive. "And . . ." said Mary, slowly, softly, "I hate myself for letting it happen."

Keisha nodded and reached over with her other arm, taking and gently holding Mary's right hand, as well.

Chapter Eighteen

Adikor and Jasmel walked back from the mine to Adikor's home, the house he'd shared with Ponter. The lighting ribs came on in response to Adikor's spoken request, and Jasmel looked around with interest.

This was Jasmel's first time visiting what had been her father's residence; Two always became One by the men coming into the Center, rather than the women going out to the Rim.

Jasmel was fascinated in a melancholy sort of way as she poked about the house, looking at Ponter's collection of sculptures. She'd known he liked stone rodents, and had indeed made a habit of giving him such carvings every time there was a lunar eclipse. Jasmel knew Ponter particularly liked rodents made of minerals that weren't indigenous to the animal's own area—his pride and joy, judging by its place next to the *wadlak* slab—was a half-size beaver, a local animal, molded from malachite imported from central Evsoy.

While she continued to putter around, Adikor's Companion made a *plunk* sound. "Healthy day," he said into it. "Oh, wonderful, love. Great news! Be patient a beat . . ." He turned to Jasmel. "You'll want to hear this; it's my woman-mate, Lurt. She's got an analysis of that liquid I found in the quantum-computing lab after your father disappeared." Adikor pulled out a control bud on his Companion, activating the external speaker.

"Jasmel Ket—Ponter's daughter—is with me now," said Adikor. "Go ahead."

"Healthy day, Jasmel," said Lurt.

"And to you," said Jasmel.

"All right," continued Lurt, "This should surprise you. Do you know what the liquid you brought me is?"

"Water, I'd thought," said Adikor. "Isn't it?"

"Sort of. It's in fact *heavy* water."

Jasmel raised her eyebrow.

"Really?" said Adikor.

"Yes," said Lurt. "Pure heavy water. Of course, heavy-water molecules *do* occur in nature; they make up about point-zero-one percent of normal rainwater, for instance. But to get a concentration like this—well, I'm not sure how it would be done. I suppose you could devise a technique to fractionate naturally occurring water, based on the fact that heavy water is indeed about ten percent heavier, but you'd have to process an enormous amount of water to separate out the amount you said you found. I don't know of any facility that can do that, and I can't think of any reason *why* someone would want to do it."

Adikor looked at Jasmel, then back at his wrist. "There's no way it's naturally occurring? No way it could have welled up from the rocks?"

"Not a chance," said Lurt's voice. "It *was* slightly contaminated with what I eventually realized was the cleaning solution used on the floors of your lab; there must have been a dried residue of it that dissolved in the water. But otherwise it was absolutely pure. Ground water would have minerals dissolved in it; this was *manufactured*. By whom, I don't know, and how, I'm not sure—but it absolutely isn't something that occurred naturally."

"Fascinating," said Adikor. "And there was no trace of Ponter's DNA?"

"No. There was a little of your own—doubtless you sloughed off some cells while mopping up the water—but none of anyone else's. No traces of blood plasma or anything else that might have come from him, either."

"All right. Many thanks!"

"Healthy day, my dear," said Lurt's voice.

"Healthy day," repeated Adikor, and he pulled the control bud that broke the connection.

"What is heavy water?" asked Jasmel.

Adikor explained, then: "It must be the key," he said.

"You're telling the truth about the source of the heavy water?" asked Jasmel.

"Yes, of course," Adikor said. "I collected it from the floor of the computing chamber after Ponter disappeared."

"It's not poisonous, is it?"

"Heavy water? I can't imagine why it would be."

"What uses does it have?"

"None that I know of."

"There's no way my father's body could have been—I don't know—*converted* somehow into heavy water?"

"I highly doubt it," said Adikor. "And there's no trace of the chemicals that made up his body. He didn't disintegrate or spontaneously combust; he simply disappeared."

Adikor shook his head. "Maybe tomorrow, at the *dooslarm basadlarm*, we can explain to the adjudicator why we need to go down to the lab. Until then, I hope Ponter is all right, wherever he might be."

After getting Mary Vaughan set up in the genetics lab at Laurentian, Reuben Montego grabbed some lunch at a Taco Bell, then headed back to St. Joseph's Health Centre. In the lobby he saw Louise Benoît, that beautiful French-Canadian postdoctoral student from SNO. She was arguing with someone who appeared to be from the hospital's security department.

"But I saved his life!" Reuben heard Louise exclaim. "He'd certainly want to see me!"

Reuben walked up to the young woman. "Hello," he said. "What's the problem?"

The woman turned her lovely face toward him, her brown eyes going wide with gratitude. "Oh, Dr. Montego!" she said. "Thank God you're here. I came to see how our friend is doing, but they won't let me go up to his floor."

"I'm Reuben Montego," said Reuben to the security man, a muscular fellow with red hair. "I'm Mr. Ponter's . . ." *Well, why not?* ". . . general practitioner; you can confirm that with Dr. Singh."

"I know who you are," said the security man. "And, yes, you're on the approved list."

"Well, this young lady is with me. She did indeed save Ponter's life at the Sudbury Neutrino Observatory."

"Very well," said the man. "Sorry to be a pain, but we've

got reporters and curious members of the public trying to sneak in all the time, and—"

At that moment, Dr. Naonihal Singh walked by, sporting a dark brown turban. "Dr. Singh!" called Reuben.

"Hello," said Singh, coming over and shaking Reuben's hand. "Escaping from the telephone, are we? Mine has been ringing off the hook."

Reuben smiled. "Mine, too. Everybody wants to know about our Mr. Ponter, it seems."

"You know I'm delighted that he is well," said Singh, "but, really, I would like to discharge him. We don't have enough hospital beds as it is, thanks to Mike Harris."

Reuben nodded sympathetically. The tightwad former premier of Ontario had closed or amalgamated many hospitals across the province.

"And," continued Singh, "not putting too fine a point on it, but if he could be gone from here, perhaps I would stop being pestered by the media."

"Where should we take him?" asked Reuben.

"That I am not knowing," replied Singh. "But if he is well, he does not belong in a hospital."

Reuben nodded. "All right, okay. We'll take him with us when we leave. Is there a way to sneak him out without the press seeing?"

"The whole idea," said Singh, "is for the press to *know* he is gone."

"Yes, yes," said Reuben. "But we'd like to get him somewhere safe *before* they realize."

"I see," said Singh. "Take him out via the underground garage. Park in there; take the staff elevator down to B2, and exit through the corridor there. As long as Ponter keeps his head down in your car, no one will see him departing."

"Excellent," said Reuben.

"Please to take him today," said Singh.

Reuben nodded. "I will."

"Thank you," said Singh.

Reuben and Louise headed upstairs.

"Hello, Ponter," said Reuben, as he came into the hospital room. Ponter was sitting up on the bed, wearing the same clothes he'd been found in.

At first Reuben thought Ponter had been watching TV, but then the doctor noticed the way he was holding up his left arm, with Hak's glass eye faced toward the monitor. More likely, the Companion had been listening to further language samples, trying to pick up more words from context.

"Hello, Reuben," said Hak, presumably on behalf of Ponter. Ponter turned to look at Louise. Reuben noted that he didn't react the way a normal human male might; there was no smile of delight at the unexpected visit from a gorgeous young woman.

"Louise," said Reuben. "Meet Ponter."

Louise stepped forward. "Hello, Ponter!" she said. "I'm Louise Benoît."

"Louise pulled you out of the water," Reuben said.

Ponter now did smile warmly; perhaps everyone here looked the same to him, thought Reuben. "Lou—" said Hak's voice. Ponter shrugged apologetically.

"He can't make the *ee* sound in your name," said Reuben.

Louise smiled. "That's fine. You can call me Lou; lots of my friends do."

"Lou," repeated Ponter, speaking for himself in his deep voice. "I—you—I . . ."

Reuben looked at Louise. "We're still building up his vocabulary. I'm afraid we haven't gotten to social niceties yet. I'm sure he's trying to say thank you for saving his life."

"My pleasure," said Louise. "I'm glad you're all right."

Reuben nodded. "And speaking of being all right," he said, "Ponter, you from here go."

Ponter's one continuous eyebrow rolled up his brow-ridge. "Yes!" said Hak, speaking again for him. "Where? Where go?"

Reuben scratched the side of his shaved head. "That's a good question."

"Far," said Hak. "Far."

"You want to go far away?" said Reuben. "Why?"

"The—the . . ." Hak trailed off, but Ponter moved a hand up, covering his giant nose—perhaps the Neanderthal equivalent of pinching one's nostrils.

"The smell?" said Reuben. He nodded and turned to Louise. "With a honker like that, I'm not surprised that he's got a keen sense of smell. I hate the smell of hospitals myself, and I spend a lot of time in them."

Louise looked at Ponter, but spoke to Reuben. "You still have no idea where he's from?"

"No."

"I'm thinking parallel world," said Louise, simply.

"What?" said Reuben. "Oh, come on!"

Louise shrugged. "Where else could he be from?"

"Well, that's a good question, but . . ."

"And if he is from a parallel world," said Louise, "suppose that world doesn't have internal-combustion engines, or any of the other things that pollute our air. If you really did have a very sensitive nose, you'd never adopt stinking technologies."

"Perhaps, but that hardly means he's from another universe."

"Either way," said Louise, brushing her long, brown hair out of her eyes, "he probably wants to go somewhere away from civilization. Somewhere where it doesn't smell as bad."

"Well, I can get a leave from Inco," said Reuben. "The beauty of being the staff physician is that you get to write your own leave authorizations. I'd really like to keep working with him."

"I've got nothing to do, either," said Louise, "while they're draining the SNO facility."

Reuben felt his heart pound. Damn, he was still a hound dog! But surely Louise was thinking of coming with them because of her scientific interest in Ponter. Still, it would be lovely to spend more time with her; her accent was incredibly sexy.

"I wonder if the authorities will try to take him again," said Reuben.

"It's only been a day since he got here," said Louise, "and I bet no one in Ottawa is really taking it seriously yet. It's just another crazy *National Enquirer*–type story. Federal agents and military types don't show up every time someone claims a UFO has been sighted. I'm sure they haven't even begun to think this might be real."

The smells are indeed awful, thought Ponter, as he looked at Lou and Reuben. They made a stark contrast: him with dark skin and completely bald, and her with skin even paler than Ponter's own, and with thick, brown hair cascading past her narrow shoulders.

Ponter was still frightened and confused, but Hak whispered soothing words into his cochlear implants whenever the Companion detected that Ponter's vital signs were getting too agitated. Without Hak's aid, Ponter felt sure he would have already gone mad.

So much had happened in such a short time! Just yesterday, he had awoken in his own bed with Adikor, had fed his dog, had gone to work . . .

And now he was *here*, wherever here might be. Hak was right; this *must* be Earth. Ponter rather suspected there were other habitable planets in the infinite reaches of space, but he seemed to weigh the same here as he had at home, and the air was breathable—breathable, in the way that his beloved Adikor's cooking might be said to be edible! There were foul aromas, gaseous smells, fruity smells, chemical smells, smells he couldn't even begin to identify. But, he had to admit, the air did sustain him, and the food they had given him was (mostly!) chemically compatible with his digestive system.

So: Earth. And surely not Earth of the past. There were parts of modern Earth, especially in equatorial regions, that were little explored, but, as Hak had pointed out, the vegetation here was largely the same as that in Saldak, meaning it was unlikely that he was on another continent, or in the southern hemisphere. And although it was warm, many of the trees he'd seen were deciduous; this couldn't be an equatorial area.

The future, then? But no. If humanity faded from existence, for some unfathomable reason, it wouldn't be Gliksins that rose to take its place. Gliksins were *extinct*; a revival of them would be as unlikely as one of dinosaurs.

If this was not just Earth, but in fact the same *part* of Earth Ponter himself had come from, then where were the vast clouds of passenger pigeons? He'd seen not a single one since arriving here. Maybe, thought Ponter, the nauseating smells drove them away.

But no.

No.

This was neither the future, nor the past. It was the *present*—a parallel world, a world where, incredibly, despite their innate stupidity, the Gliksins had not gone extinct.

"Ponter," said Reuben.

Ponter looked up, a vaguely lost expression on his face, as if a reverie had been broken. "Yes?" he said.

"Ponter, we will take you somewhere else. I'm not sure where. But, well, for starters, we'll get you out of here. You, um, you can come stay with me."

Ponter tipped his head, listening to Hak's translation, no doubt. He looked puzzled at a few points; presumably Hak wasn't quite sure how to render some of the words Reuben had used.

"Yes," said Ponter, at last. "Yes. We go from here."

Reuben gestured for Ponter to take the lead.

"Open door," said Ponter, speaking on his own behalf, with evident delight, as he pulled open the hospital room's door. "Go through door," he said, following the words with the appropriate deed. He then waited for Louise and Reuben to exit as well. "Close door," he said, shutting the door behind them. And then he smiled broadly, and when Ponter smiled broadly, it measured almost a foot from edge to edge. "Ponter out!"

Chapter Nineteen

Following Dr. Singh's instructions, Reuben Montego, Louise Benoît, and Ponter made it safely down to Reuben's car, which he'd moved to the staff garage. Reuben had a wine-colored SUV, the paint chipped from the gravel roads at the Inco site. Ponter got into the backseat and lay down, covering his head with an opened section of today's *Sudbury Star*. Louise—who had walked to the hospital—sat up front with Reuben. She'd accepted Reuben's invitation to join him and Ponter at his place for dinner; he'd said he'd give her a lift back home later in the evening.

They drove along, CJMX-FM playing softly on the car's stereo; the current song was Geri Halliwell's rendition of "It's Raining Men." "So," said Reuben, looking over at Louise, "make me a believer. Why do you think Ponter came from a parallel universe?"

Louise pursed her full lips for a moment—God, thought Reuben, she really *is* lovely—then: "How much physics do you know?"

"Me?" said Reuben. "Stuff from high school. Oh, and I bought a copy of *A Brief History of Time* when Stephen Hawking came to Sudbury, but I didn't get very far into it."

"All right," said Louise, as Reuben made a right-hand turn. "let me ask you a question. If you shoot a single photon at a barrier with two vertical slits in it, and a piece of photographic paper on the other side shows interference patterns, what happened?"

"I don't know," said Reuben, truthfully.

"Well," Louise said, "one interpretation is that the single photon turned into a wave of energy, and, as it hit the wall with the slits, each slit created a new wave front, and you got classical interference, with crests and troughs either amplifying each other or canceling each other out."

Her words rang a vague bell in Reuben's mind. "All right."

"Well, as I said, that's one interpretation. Another is that the universe actually *splits*, briefly becoming two universes. In one, the photon—still a particle—went through the left slit, and in the other, the photon went through the right slit. And, because it doesn't make any conceivable difference which slit the photon went through in this or the other universe, the two universes collapse back into one, with the interference pattern being the result of the universes rejoining."

Reuben nodded, but only because that seemed the right thing to do.

"So," said Louise, "we have an experimental physical basis for possibly believing in the temporary existence of parallel universes—those interference patterns really do show up, even if you only send one photon toward a pair of slits. But what if the two universes *didn't* collapse back into one? What if, after splitting, they continued to go their separate ways?"

"Yes?" said Reuben, trying to follow.

"Well," said Louise, "imagine the universe splitting into two, who knows, tens of thousands of years ago, back when there were two species of humanity living side by side: our ancestors, which were the Cro-Magnons" (Reuben noted she pronounced it just as a French-speaker should, with no *g* sound), "and Ponter's ancestors, ancient Neanderthals. I don't know how long the two kinds coexisted, but—"

"From 100,000 years ago until maybe 27,000 years ago," said Reuben.

Louise made an impressed face, clearly surprised that Reuben had this tidbit at hand.

Reuben shrugged. "We've got a geneticist up from Toronto named Mary Vaughan. She told me."

"Ah. Okay, well, at some point during that time, perhaps a split occurred, and the two universes continued to diverge. In one, our ancestors became dominant. And in the other, Neanderthals went on to become dominant, creating their own civilization and language."

Reuben felt his head swimming. "But . . . but then how did the two universes come back into contact?"

"*Je ne sais pas,*" said Louise, shaking her head.

They exited Sudbury, heading down a country road to the misnamed town of Lively, near where the mine was actually located.

"Ponter," said Reuben. "You can probably get up now; we won't be stuck in traffic anymore."

Ponter didn't move.

Reuben realized he'd been too complex. "Ponter, up," he said.

He heard the sound of newspaper rustling and saw

Ponter's massive head emerge in the rearview mirror. "Up," confirmed Ponter.

"Tonight," said Reuben, "you will stay at my house, understand?"

After a pause, presumably in which a translation was rendered, Ponter said, "Yes."

Hak spoke up. "Ponter must have food."

"Yes," said Reuben. "Yes, we eat soon."

They continued to Reuben's home, arriving there about twenty minutes later. It was a modern two-story house on a couple of acres of land just outside Lively. Ponter, Louise, and Reuben headed indoors, with Ponter watching in fascination as Reuben unlocked the front door then bolted and chained it shut from the inside once they were within.

Ponter smiled. "Cool," he said, with delight.

At first, Reuben thought he was complimenting him on his decor, but then he realized Ponter meant it literally. He was evidently quite pleased to find Reuben's house to be air conditioned.

"Well," said Reuben, smiling at Louise and Ponter, "welcome to my humble abode. Make yourselves comfortable."

Louise looked around. "You're not married?" she asked.

Reuben wondered at the question; the first, best interpretation was that she was checking on his availability. The second, more likely, interpretation was she had suddenly realized that she had gone out into the country with a man she hardly knew, and was now alone with him and a Neanderthal in an empty house. And the third interpretation, Reuben realized, as he took stock of his own messy living room, with magazines scattered here and there and a plate with the remnants of a pizza crust sitting on the coffee table, was that *obviously* Reuben lived alone; no woman would have put up with such a mess.

"No," said Reuben. "I was, but . . ."

Louise nodded. "You've got good taste," she said, looking at the furnishings, a mixture of Caribbean and Canadian, with lots of dark stained wood.

"My wife did," said Reuben. "I haven't changed it much since we split."

"Ah," said Louise. "Can I help you with dinner?"

"No, I thought I'd just put on some steaks. I've got a barbecue out back."

"I'm a vegetarian," said Louise.

"Oh. Um, I could grill you some vegetables—and, um, a potato?"

"That would be great," said Louise.

"Okay," said Reuben. "You keep Ponter company." He headed off to the bathroom to wash his hands.

Working on the deck behind the house, Reuben could see Louise and Ponter having an increasingly animated conversation. Presumably, Hak was picking up more words as they went along. Finally, when the steaks were done, Reuben tapped on the glass to get Louise's and Ponter's attention, and waved for them to come on out.

A moment later, they did so. "Dr. Montego," said Louise, excitedly, "Ponter is a physicist!"

"He is?" said Reuben.

"Yes. Yes, indeed. I haven't got all the details yet, but he's definitely a physicist—and, I think, actually a *quantum* physicist."

"How did you determine that?" asked Reuben.

"He said he thinks about the way things work, and I said—guessing he might be an engineer—did he mean big things, and he said, no, no, little things, things too small to be seen. And I drew some diagrams—basic physics stuff—and he recognized them, and said that's what he did."

Reuben looked at Ponter with renewed admiration. The low forehead and the prominent browridge made him look, well, a little dim, but—a physicist! A scientist! "Well, well, well," said Reuben. He motioned for them to sit at a circular deck table with an umbrella, and he transferred steaks and grilled veggies he'd wrapped in aluminum foil to plates and set them on the table.

Ponter smiled his wide smile. This, clearly, was real food to him! But then he looked around again, just as Reuben had seen him do this morning, as if something were missing.

Reuben used his knife to slice a piece off his steak, and brought it to his mouth.

Ponter, awkwardly, mimicked what Reuben had done, although he sliced off a much bigger piece.

After Ponter had finished chewing, he made some sounds that must have been words in his language. They were immediately followed by a male voice Reuben hadn't heard before. "Good," it said. "Good food." The voice seemed to have come from Ponter's implant.

Reuben raised his eyebrows in surprise, and Louise explained. "I was getting confused talking to them, trying to keep straight what was the implant speaking on its own, and what was the implant translating for Ponter. It's now using a male voice for Ponter's translated words, and a female voice for its own words."

"Simpler this way," said Hak's familiar female voice.

"Yes," said Reuben, "it certainly is."

Louise gingerly used her long fingers to unwrap the foil around her grilled veggies. "Well," she said, "let's see what else we can find out."

And for the next hour Reuben and Louise talked with Ponter and Hak. But by then, the mosquitoes were out in abundance. Reuben lit a citronella candle to drive them away, but the smell made Ponter gag. Reuben extinguished the candle, and they went back into his living room, Ponter sitting in a big easy chair, Louise at one end of the couch with her long legs tucked underneath her body, and Reuben at the other end.

They continued talking for another three hours, slowly piecing together what had happened. And, once the full story had emerged, Reuben sank back into the couch, absolutely amazed.

Chapter Twenty

NEWS SEARCH

Keyword(s): *Neanderthal*

Word this morning from Sudbury, Canada, is that marriage proposals are outnumbering death threats two-to-one for the Neanderthal visitor. Twenty-eight women have sent letters or e-mails c/o this newspaper proposing to him, while Sudbury police and the RCMP have recorded only thirteen threats against his life . . .

USA TODAY POLL:

•Percentage who believe the so-called Neanderthal is a fake: 54.

•Who believe he's really a Neanderthal, but came from somewhere on this Earth: 26.

•Who believe he came from outer space: 11.

•Who believe he came from a parallel world: 9.

Police today defused a bomb left at the entrance to the mineshaft elevator leading down to the cavern containing the Sudbury Neutrino Observatory, where the so-called Neanderthal first appeared . . .

A religious sect in Baton Rouge, Louisiana, is hailing the arrival of the Neanderthal in Canada as the Second Coming of Christ. "Of

course he looks like an ancient human," said the Rev. Hooley
Gordwell. "The world is 6,000 years old, and Christ first came
among us fully a third of that span ago. We've changed a bit,
perhaps due to better nutrition, but he hasn't." The group is
planning a pilgrimage to the mining town of Sudbury, Ontario,
where the Neanderthal is currently living.

Early the next morning, after taking care not to be
seen *en route*, Ponter and Dr. Montego rendezvoused with
Mary in the lab at Laurentian. It was time to analyze Ponter's DNA, to answer the big question.

Sequencing 379 nucleotides took meticulous work.
Mary sat hunched over a milky white plastic desktop, the
surface illuminated by fluorescent tubes beneath it. She'd
placed the autorad film on the desktop and, with a felt-tip
marker, wrote out the letters of the genetic alphabet for
the string in question: G-G-C—one of the triplets that
coded for the amino acid glycine; T-A-T, the code for ty-
rosine; A-T-A, which in mitochondrial DNA, as opposed to
nuclear DNA, specified methionine; A-A-A, the recipe for
lysine . . .

At last she was done: all 379 bases from a specific part
of Ponter's control region were identified. Mary's notebook computer had a little DNA-analysis program on it.
She started by typing in the 379 letters she'd just written
on the film, and then she asked Reuben to type them in
again, just to make sure they'd been entered correctly.

The computer immediately reported three differences
between what Mary had entered and what Reuben had,
noting—it was an intelligent little program—a frameshift
caused by Mary accidentally leaving off a T at one point;
the other two errors were typos by Reuben. When she was

sure they had all 379 letters entered correctly, she had the program compare Ponter's sequence to the one she'd extracted from the Neanderthal type specimen at the *Rheinisches Landesmuseum.*

"Well?" said Reuben. "What's the verdict?"

Mary leaned back in her chair, astonished. "The DNA I took from Ponter," she said, "differs in seven places from the DNA recovered from the Neanderthal fossil." She raised a hand. "Now, some individual variation was to be expected, and naturally there'd be some genetic drift over time, but . . ."

"Yes?" said Reuben.

Mary lifted her shoulders. "He's a Neanderthal, all right."

"Wow," said Reuben, looking at Ponter as if seeing him for the first time. "Wow. A living Neanderthal."

Ponter spoke a bit in his own language, and his implant interpreted: "My kind gone?" said the male voice.

"From here?" asked Mary. "Yes, your kind is gone from here—for at least 27,000 years."

Ponter lowered his head, contemplating this.

Mary contemplated it, too. Until Ponter had shown up, the nearest living relatives *Homo sapiens* had were the two members of genus *Pan:* the chimpanzee and the bonobo. Both were equally closely related to humans, sharing about 98.5 percent of humanity's DNA. Mary was nowhere near finished with her studies on Ponter's DNA, but she guessed he shared as much as 99.5 percent with her kind of *H. sapiens.*

And that 0.5 percent accounted for all the differences. If he was a typical Neanderthal, his braincase probably was larger than a normal man's. And he was better muscled than just about any human Mary had ever met: his arms were as thick around as most men's thighs. Plus, his eyes were an incredible golden brown; she wondered if there was any eye-color variation among his kind.

He was also quite hairy, although it seemed less so because of its light color. His forearms, and, she presumed, his back and chest, were well thatched. And he had a beard, and a full head of hair, parted in the center.

It hit her then: where she'd seen that sort of part before. Bonobos, those lithe apes sometimes called pygmy chimpanzees, all sported the same 'do. Fascinating. She wondered whether all his people had hair like that or if it was just a style he cultivated.

Ponter spoke again in his own language, his voice low, perhaps really just talking to himself, but the implant rendered the words in English anyway: "My kind gone."

Mary made her tone as gentle as she could. "Yes. I'm sorry."

More syllables spilled from Ponter's lips, and his Companion said, "I . . . no others. I . . . all . . ." He shook his head, and spoke again. The Companion switched to its female voice, speaking for itself. "I do not have the vocabulary to translate what Ponter is saying."

Mary nodded slowly, sadly. "The word you're looking for," she said gently, "is 'alone.' "

Adikor Huld's *dooslarm basadlarm* was held in the Gray Council building, on the periphery of the Center. Males could get to it without crossing deep into female territory;

females could enter it without technically leaving their land. Adikor wasn't sure what having the preliminary inquiry during Last Five would do for his chances, but the adjudicator, a woman named Komel Sard, looked to be from generation 142, and so would be long past menopause.

Adikor's accuser, Daklar Bolbay, was now holding forth in the large square chamber. Fans blew air from the chamber's north side to its south, and Adjudicator Sard sat at the south end, watching the action unfold with a neutral expression on her lined, wise face. The blowing air served a double purpose: it brought pheromones to her from the accused, which could often convey as much meaning as the words being spoken, and it kept her own pheromones—which might have betrayed which arguments were impressing her—from being detectable by the accuser or the accused, both of whom were positioned on the north side.

Adikor had met Klast many times, and had always gotten along well with her; her man-mate, after all, had been Ponter. But Bolbay, who had been Klast's woman-mate, seemed to have none of Klast's warmth or easy humor.

Bolbay was wearing a dark orange pant and a dark orange top; orange had always been the color of the accuser. For his part, Adikor wore blue, the color of the accused. Hundreds of spectators, equally split between male and female, sat on either side of the room; a *dooslarm basadlarm* for murder was clearly considered well worth seeing. Jasmel Ket was there, as was her young sister, Megameg Bek. Adikor's own woman-mate, Lurt, was present as well; she'd given him a big hug when she'd arrived. Seated next to

Lurt was Adikor's son Dab, the same age as little Megameg.

And, of course, almost all of Saldak's Exhibitionists were present; there was no more interesting event going on right now than this hearing. Despite his current situation, Adikor was pleased to see Hawst in the flesh, having used his Voyeur to look in on so much of his life in the past. He also recognized Lulasm, who had been Ponter's favorite, and Gawlt and Talok and Repeth and a couple of others. The Exhibitionists were easy to spot: they had to wear silver clothes, signaling to everyone around them that their implant broadcasts were publicly accessible.

Adikor was sitting on a stool; there was plenty of room on all sides of it for Bolbay to circle him as she spoke, and she did so with great theatrical relish: "So tell us, Scholar Huld, did your experiment succeed? Did you successfully factor your target number?"

Adikor shook his head. "No."

"So doing it beneath the surface did not help," said Bolbay. "Whose idea was it to perform this factoring experiment far underground?" Her voice was low for a female's, a deep rumbling sound.

"Ponter and I jointly agreed to it."

"Yes, yes, but who initially suggested the idea? You, or Scholar Boddit?"

"I'm not sure."

"It was you, wasn't it?"

Adikor shrugged. "It might have been."

Bolbay was now in front of him; Adikor refused to acknowledge her presence by shifting his gaze to her. "Now, Scholar Huld, tell us all why you chose this location."

"I didn't say I chose it. I said I *might* have."

"Fine. Tell us, then, why this location was selected for your work."

Adikor frowned, thinking about how much detail was appropriate. "Earth," he said at last, "is constantly bombarded by cosmic rays."

"Which are?"

"Ionizing radiation coming from outer space. A stream of protons, helium nuclei, and other nuclei. When they collide with nuclei in our atmosphere, they produce secondary radiation—mostly pions, muons, electrons, and *dutar* rays."

"And these are dangerous?"

"Not really—at least, not in the small quantities produced by cosmic rays. But they do interfere with delicate instruments, and so we wanted to set up our equipment somewhere that was shielded from them. And, well, the Debral nickel mine *was* nearby."

"Couldn't you have used another facility?"

"Conceivably, I suppose. But Debral is unique not only for its depth—it is the deepest mine in the world—but also for the low background radiation of its rocks. The uranium and other radioactives present in many other mines give off charged particles that would have impaired our instruments."

"So you were well shielded down there?"

"Yes—from everything except neutrinos, I suppose." Adikor caught the expression on Adjudicator Sard's face. "Minuscule particles that stream right through solid matter; nothing can shield against them."

"Now, weren't you also shielded against something else down there?" asked Bolbay.

"I don't understand," said Adikor

"A thousand armspans of rock between you and the surface. No radiation—not even cosmic-ray particles that had traveled unimpeded for huge distances—could get down to you."

"Correct."

"And no radiation could make it up from the surface to where you were working, isn't that right?"

"How do you mean?"

"I mean," said Bolbay, "that the signals from your Companions—yours, and Scholar Boddit's—could not be transmitted out of there to the surface."

"Yes, that's true, although I hadn't really given it any thought until an enforcer mentioned it to me yesterday."

"Hadn't given it much thought?" Bolbay's tone was one of incredulity. "Since the day you were born, you've had a personal recording cube in the alibi-archive pavilion adjacent to this very Council building. And it has recorded everything you've done, every moment of your life, as transmitted by your Companion. Every moment of your life, that is, except the time you spent far, far below Earth's surface."

"I'm no expert on such matters," said Adikor, somewhat disingenuously. "I really don't know much about the transmission of data from a Companion."

"Come now, Scholar Huld. A moment ago you were regaling us with stories of muons and pions, and now you expect us to believe you don't understand simple radio broadcasting?"

"I didn't say I don't understand it," said Adikor. "It's

just that I've never thought about the issue that's been raised."

Bolbay was behind him again. "Never thought about the fact, that, while down there, for the first time since your birth, there would be no record available of what you were doing?"

"Look," said Adikor, speaking directly to the adjudicator, before the orbiting Bolbay blocked his line of sight again. "I haven't had cause to access my own alibi archive for countless months. Sure, the fact that my actions are normally being recorded is something I'm aware of, in an abstract sense, but I just don't think about it every day."

"And yet," said Bolbay, "every day of your life, you enjoy the peace and safety made possible by that very recording." She looked at the adjudicator. "You know that as you walk at night, the chances of you being the victim of robbery or murder or *lasagklat* are almost zero, because there's no way to get away with such a crime. If you charged that— well, say, that *I* had attacked you in Peslar Square, and you could convince an adjudicator that your charge was reasonable, the adjudicator could order your alibi archive or mine unlocked for the time span in question, which would prove that I am innocent. But the fact that a crime cannot be committed without a record of it being made lets us all relax."

Adikor said nothing.

"Except," said Bolbay, "when someone contrives a situation to secrete himself and his victim in a place—practically the *only* place—in which no record of what happens between them could have been made."

"That's preposterous," said Adikor.

"Is it? The mine was dug long before the beginning of the Companion Era, and, of course, we've used robots to do the mining for ages now. It's almost unheard of for a human to have to go down into that mine, which is why we've never addressed the problem of lack of communication between Companions there and the alibi-archive pavilion. But you set up a situation in which you and Scholar Boddit would be in this subterranean hideaway for great spans of time."

"We didn't even think about that."

"No?" said Bolbay. "Do you recognize the name Kobast Gant?"

Adikor's heart pounded, and his mouth went dry. "He's an artificial-intelligence researcher."

"Indeed he is. And he will state that seven months ago he upgraded both your Companion and Scholar Boddit's, adding sophisticated artificial-intelligence components to them."

"Yes," said Adikor. "He did that."

"Why?"

"Well, um . . ."

"Why?"

"Because Ponter hadn't liked being out of touch with the planetary information network. With our Companions cut off from the network down there, he thought it would be handy to have a lot more processing power localized in them, so that they could help us more with our work."

"And you somehow forgot this?" said Bolbay.

"As you said," replied Adikor, his tone sharp, "it was done months ago. I'd gotten quite used to having a Companion that was more chatty than usual. After all, I'm sure Kobast Gant will also state that, although these were early versions of his companionable artificial-intelligence software, his intention was to make it available for all those who wanted it. He expected people to find it quite helpful, even if they are never cut off from the network—and he felt people would get used to it quickly, so that it would soon be as natural to them as having a dumber Companion." Adikor folded his hands in his lap. "Well, I rapidly got used to mine, and, as I said at the outset, I didn't give much thought to it, or to why it had originally been necessary . . . but . . . wait! Wait!"

"Yes?" said Bolbay.

Adikor looked directly at Adjudicator Sard, seated across the room. "My Companion could tell you what happened down there!"

The adjudicator leveled a steady stare at Adikor. "What is your contribution, Scholar Huld?" she asked.

"Me? I'm a physicist."

"*And* a computer programmer, is that not so?" said the adjudicator. "Indeed, you and Scholar Boddit were working on complex computers."

"Yes, but—"

"So," said the adjudicator, "I hardly think we can trust anything your Companion might say. It would be a trivial enough matter for one of your expertise to program it to tell us whatever you wanted it to."

"But I—"

"Thank you, Adjudicator Sard," said Bolbay. "Now, tell us, Scholar Huld, how many people are normally involved in a scientific experiment?"

"That's a meaningless question," said Adikor. "Some projects are undertaken by a single individual, and—"

"—and some are undertaken by tens of researchers, isn't that true?"

"Sometimes, yes."

"But your experiment involved just two researchers."

"That's not correct," said Adikor. "Four other people worked on various stages of our project."

"But none of them were invited down into the mineshaft. Only the two of you—Ponter Boddit and Adikor Huld—went down there, isn't that right?"

Adikor nodded.

"And only one of you returned to the surface."

Adikor was impassive.

"Isn't that right, Scholar Huld? Only one of you returned to the surface."

"Yes," he said, "but, as I've explained, Scholar Boddit disappeared."

"Disappeared," said Bolbay, as if she'd never heard the word before, as if she were struggling to comprehend its meaning. "You mean he vanished?"

"Yes."

"Into thin air."

"That's right."

"But there's absolutely no record of this disappearance."

Adikor shook his head slightly. Why was Bolbay pursuing him so? He'd never been unpleasant to her, and he couldn't imagine that Ponter had ever presented him to Bolbay in unfavorable terms. What was motivating her?

"You've found no body," said Adikor, defiantly. "You've found no body because there *is* no body."

"That's your position, Scholar Huld. But a thousand armspans underground, you could have disposed of the body in any number of places: putting it in an airtight bag to keep its smell from escaping, then throwing it down a fissure, burying it under loose rock, or tossing it into a rock-grinding machine. The mine complex is huge, after all, with tens of thousands of paces' worth of tunnels and drifts. Surely you could have gotten rid of the body down there."

"*But I didn't.*"

"So you say."

"Yes," said Adikor, forcing calmness into his tone, "so I say."

The previous night, at Reuben's, Louise and Ponter had tried to devise an experiment that could prove to others whether what Ponter had claimed was true: that he came from a parallel world.

Chemical analysis of his clothing fibers might do it. They were synthetic, Ponter had said, and presumably didn't match any known polymer. Likewise, some of the components of Ponter's strange Companion implant would almost certainly prove unknown to this world's science.

A dentist might be able to show that Ponter had never been exposed to fluoridated water. It might even be possible to prove that he'd lived in a world without nuclear weapons, dioxins, or internal-combustion engines.

But, as Reuben had pointed out, all those things would simply demonstrate that Ponter didn't come from this Earth, not that he came from *another* Earth. He could, after all, be an alien.

Louise had argued that there was no way life from any other planet would so closely resemble the random results evolution had produced here, but she conceded that for some, the idea of aliens was more acceptable, and certainly more familiar, than the notion of parallel universes—a comment that prompted Reuben to say something about Kira Nerys looking better in leather.

Finally, Ponter himself had come up with a suitable test. His implant, he said, contained complete maps of the nickel mine that was supposedly located near here in his version of Earth; after all, this had been the site of the facility where he worked, too. Of course, most of the major ore bodies had been found by both his people and the Inco staff, but, by comparing the Companion's maps to detailed ones on the Inco web site, Ponter's implant identified a spot it said contained a rich copper deposit that had eluded Inco's detection. If true, it was precisely the sort of information that only someone from a parallel universe might have.

So now Ponter Boddit—they had learned his full name—Louise Benoît, Bonnie Jean Mah, Reuben Montego, and a woman Louise was meeting for the first time, a geneticist named Mary Vaughan, were all standing in the middle of dense woods precisely 372 meters away from the SNO surface building. With them were two Inco geologists, who were operating a core-sampling drill. One of them insisted Ponter could not be right about there being copper at this spot.

They drilled down 9.3 meters, just as Hak had said they should, and the sampling tube was drawn back up. Louise was relieved when the diamond-tipped drill finally shut off; the grinding sound had given her a headache.

The group took the wrapped core back to the parking lot, everyone holding on to it at some point along its length. And there, where there was room to do so, the geologists removed its opaque outer membrane. At the core's top, of course, was humus, and, beneath that, a glacial till of clay, sand, gravel, and pebbles. Below that, said one of the geologists, was Precambrian norite rock.

And beneath that, at precisely the depth Hak had said it would be found at, was—

Louise clapped her hands together in excitement. Reuben Montego was grinning from ear to ear. The doubting geologist was muttering to himself. Professor Mah was shaking her head slowly back and forth in astonishment. And the geneticist, Dr. Vaughan, was staring at Ponter with wide eyes.

It *was* there, precisely where he said it would be: native copper, twisted and bulbous, dull but clearly metallic.

Louise smiled at Ponter as she thought about the verdant, unspoiled world he had described to her the night before. "Pennies from heaven," she said softly.

Professor Mah came over to Ponter and took his giant hand in hers, shaking it firmly. "I wouldn't have believed it," she said, "but welcome to our version of Earth."

Chapter Twenty-one

Everyone except the geologists adjourned to a conference room at the Creighton Mine: Mary Vaughan, the geneticist who'd come up from Toronto; Reuben Montego, the Inco doctor; Louise Benoît, the SNO postdoc who had been on hand when the detector had been destroyed; Bonnie Jean Mah, director of the SNO project; and, most important of all, Ponter Boddit, physicist from a parallel world, the only living Neanderthal to be seen on this Earth since at least 27,000 years ago.

Mary had chosen to sit beside Bonnie Jean Mah, the only woman in the room who'd had an empty chair next to her. Holding forth, standing at the front of the room, was Reuben Montego. "Question," he said in that Jamaican accent Mary found delightful. "Why is there a mining operation on this site?"

Mary herself had no clue, and none of those who obviously did know looked inclined to play games, but at last Bonnie Jean Mah replied. "Because 1.8 billion years ago," she said, "an asteroid hit here, resulting in huge deposits of nickel."

"Exactly," said Reuben. "An event that happened long before there was any multicellular life on Earth, an event both Ponter's world and ours share in their common pasts." He looked from face to face, coming at last to Mary's own. "One has little choice in where mines will be built," Reuben said. "You put them where the ores are. But what about SNO? Why was it built here?"

"Because," said Mah, "the two kilometers of rock over top of the mine provide an excellent shield against cosmic rays, making it an ideal location for a neutrino detector."

"But it's not just that, is it, ma'am?" said Reuben, who, Mary assumed, had become quite the expert thanks to the help of Louise. "There are deep mines elsewhere on the planet. But this mine also has very low background radiation, right? In fact, this site is uniquely qualified for housing instruments that would be adversely affected by natural radiation."

This sounded reasonable to Mary, and she noted that Professor Mah nodded once. But then Mah added, "So?"

"So," said Reuben, "in Ponter's universe a deep mine was also built on this very spot, to excavate the same nickel deposits. And eventually he himself recognized the value of the site and convinced his government to set up a physics facility underground here."

"So he would have us believe that there's a neutrino detector at the same place in the other universe?" asked Mah.

Reuben shook his head. "No," he said. "No, there isn't. Remember, the choice of using this facility for a neutrino observatory also had to do with a historical accident: that Canada's nuclear reactors, unlike those of the U.S. or the U.K. or Japan or Russia, happen to use heavy water as a moderator. That set of circumstances isn't duplicated in

Ponter's world—in fact, they don't seem to use nuclear power. But this underground facility is equally good for another very delicate kind of instrument." He paused and looked from face to face, then he said, "Ponter, where do you work?"

Ponter replied, "*Dusble korbul to kalbtadu.*"

And the implant, using its male voice, provided the translation: "In a quantum-computing facility."

"Quantum computing?" repeated Mary, but feeling uncomfortable doing so; she wasn't used to being the most ignorant one in the room.

"That's right," said Reuben, grinning. "Dr. Benoît?"

Louise got up and nodded at the M.D. "Quantum computing is something we're just starting to play with ourselves," she said, pushing hair out of her eyes. "A regular computer can determine the factors of a given number by trying one possible factor to see if it works, then another, then another, then another: brute-force calculation. But if you used a conventional computer to factor a big number—say, one with 512 digits, like those used to encrypt credit-card transactions on the World Wide Web—it would take countless centuries to try all the possible factors one at a time."

She, too, looked from face to face, making sure she hadn't lost her audience. "But a quantum computer uses superposition of quantum states to check multiple possible factors simultaneously," said Louise. "That is, in essence, new short-lived duplicate universes are spun off specifically to do the quantum calculation, and, once the factoring is complete—which would be virtually instantaneously—all those universes collapse back down into one again, since, except for the candidate number they tested to see if it was a factor, they're otherwise identical. And so, in the time it takes to try just one factor, you actually get them *all* tried simultaneously, and you solve a previously intractable problem." She paused. "At least, until now, that's how we've believed quantum computing works—relying on the momentary superposition of quantum states effectively creating different universes."

Mary nodded, trying to follow along.

"But suppose that isn't how it really happens," said Louise. "Suppose that rather than creating temporary universes for a fraction of a second, a quantum computer instead accesses *already existing* parallel universes—other versions of reality in which the quantum computer also exists."

"There's no theoretical basis for believing that," said Bonnie Jean, sounding annoyed. "And, besides, there's no quantum computer at this location, in the only universe that we know *does* exist."

"Exactly!" said Louise. "What I propose is this: Dr. Boddit and his colleague were trying to factor a number so large that to check every possible factor of it required more versions of the quantum computer than there were in separate already existing long-term universes. Do you see? It reached into thousands—millions!—of existing ones. And in each of those parallel universes, the quantum computer found a duplicate of itself, and that duplicate tried a different potential factor. Right? But what if you were factoring a huge number, a gigantic number, a number with more possible factors than there are parallel universes in which the quantum-computing facility already exists? What then? Well, I think that's what happened here: Dr. Boddit and his partner were factoring a gigantic number, the quantum computer found its siblings in all—every single one—of the parallel universes in which it already existed, but it still needed more copies of itself, and so it went looking in *other* parallel universes, including ones in which the quantum-computing facility had never been built—such as *our* universe. And when it reached one of those, it was like hitting a wall, causing the factoring experiment to abort. And that crash caused a large part of Ponter's computing facility to be transferred into this universe."

Mary noted that Dr. Mah was nodding. "The air that accompanied Ponter."

"Exactly," said Louise. "As we'd guessed, it *was* mostly just air transferred to this universe—enough air to burst open the acrylic sphere. But, in addition to the air, one person, who happened to be standing in the quantum-computing facility, was transferred, as well."

"So he didn't know he was going to come here?" asked Mah.

"No," said Reuben Montego, "he didn't. If you think we were shocked, imagine how shocked *he* was. The poor guy instantly found himself submerged in water, in absolute darkness. If there hadn't been that massive bubble of air transferred with him, he would have drowned for sure."

Your whole world turned inside out, thought Mary. She looked at the Neanderthal. He was certainly doing a good job of hiding the disorientation and fear he must feel, but the shock surely had been enormous.

Mary gave him a small, empathetic smile.

Chapter Twenty-two

Adikor Huld's *dooslarm basadlarm* continued. Adjudicator Sard still sat at the south end, and Adikor remained in the hot seat, with Daklar Bolbay stalking around him in circles.

"Has a crime really been committed?" asked Bolbay, looking now at Adjudicator Sard. "No dead body has been found, and so one might argue that this is simply a case of a missing individual, no matter how improbable such a circumstance seems today. But we have searched the mine with portable signal detectors, and so we know that Ponter's implant is not transmitting. If he were injured, it *would* be transmitting. Even if he were dead by natural causes, it would continue to transmit, using stored power, for days after Ponter's own biochemical processes ceased. Nothing short of violent action can account for the disappearance of Ponter and the silence of his Companion."

Adikor felt his stomach knotting. Bolbay was right, as far as her reasoning went: the Companions were designed to be foolproof. Before they existed, people did sometimes just go missing, and only after many months were they declared dead, usually simply for lack of a better explanation. But Lonwis Trob had promised his Companions would change that, and they had. No one just disappeared anymore.

Sard obviously agreed. "I'm satisfied," she said, "that the lack both of a body and of Companion transmissions suggests criminal activity. Let's get on with it."

"Very well," said Bolbay. She looked briefly at Adikor, then turned back to the adjudicator. "Murder," Bolbay said, "has never been common. To end the life of another—to put a complete and utter stop to someone's existence—is heinous beyond compare. But, still, there are cases known, most, I grant you, from before the time of the Companions and the alibi-archive recorders. And in previous cases, the tribunals asked for three things to be shown to support a charge of murder.

"The first is a chance to commit the crime—and this Adikor Huld had in a way that no one else on this planet did, for he was beyond the capabilities of his Companion to transmit his actions.

"The second is a technique, a way in which the crime might have been committed. Without a body, we can only speculate on how it might have been done, although, as you will see later, one method is particularly likely.

"And, finally, one needs to show a reason, a rationale for the crime, something that would cause one to commit so awful, so permanent an act. And it's that question of reason I'd like to explore now, Adjudicator."

The old female nodded. "I'm listening."

Bolbay swung to face Adikor. "You and Ponter Boddit lived together, isn't that true?"

Adikor nodded. "For six tenmonths."

"Did you love him?"

"Yes. Very much indeed."

"But his woman-mate had died recently."

"She was also *your* woman-mate," said Adikor, taking the opportunity to emphasize Bolbay's conflict of interest.

But Bolbay was up to the occasion. "Yes. Klast, my beloved. She is no longer alive, and for that I feel great sorrow. But I blame no one; there is no one to blame. Illness happens, and the life-prolongers did all they could to make her final months comfortable. But for the death of Ponter Boddit, there *is* someone to blame."

"Be cautious, Daklar Bolbay," said Adjudicator Sard. "You haven't proven that Scholar Boddit is dead. Until I rule on that, you may speak of that possibility only in hypothetical terms."

Bolbay turned toward Sard and bowed. "Apologies, Adjudicator." She faced Adikor again. "We were discussing another death, one about which no doubt exists: that of Klast, who was Ponter's—and my own—woman-mate." Bolbay closed her eyes. "My own grief is too great for expression, and I will not parade it for anyone. And Ponter's grief, I'm sure, was equally large. Klast often spoke of him; I know how much she loved Ponter, and how much he loved her." Bolbay was silent for a moment, perhaps composing herself. "Given this recent tragedy, though, we must raise another possibility about Ponter's disappearance. Could he have taken his own life, despondent over the death of Klast?" She looked at Adikor. "What is your opinion, Scholar Huld?"

"He was very sad at the loss, but the loss was also some time ago. Had Ponter been suicidal, I'm sure I would have known."

Bolbay nodded reasonably. "I won't pretend to say I knew Scholar Boddit anywhere near as well as you did, Scholar Huld, but I do share your assessment. Still, could there have been any other reasons for him to commit suicide?"

Adikor was taken aback. "Such as?"

"Well, your work—do forgive me, Scholar Huld, but I see no gentle way to phrase this: your work was a failure. A Gray Council session was imminent, at which you and he would have had to discuss your contributions to society. Could he have so feared that your work might be terminated that, well, that he chose to terminate himself?"

"No," said Adikor, stunned by the suggestion. "No, in fact, if anyone were to smell bad at Council, it would have been I, not he."

Bolbay let this comment sink in, then: "Would you be so kind as to elaborate on that thought?"

"Ponter was the theoretician," said Adikor. "His theories had been neither proven nor disproven, so there was still valid work to be done related to them. But I was the engineer: it was I who was supposed to build experimental apparatus to check Ponter's ideas. And it was that apparatus—our prototype quantum computer—that had failed. Council might have found my contribution inadequate, but they certainly wouldn't have judged Ponter's to be so."

"So Ponter's death could not possibly have been a suicide," said Bolbay.

"Again," said Sard, "you will speak of Scholar Boddit as if he is alive, until if or when I rule to the contrary."

Bolbay bowed again to the adjudicator. "Once again,

my apologies." She returned to Adikor. "If Ponter wanted to kill himself, is it fair to say, Scholar Huld, that he would not have taken his life in a way that might implicate you?"

"The suggestion that he would take his own life at all is so improbable . . ." began Adikor.

"Yes, we agree on that," said Bolbay, calmly, "but, hypothetically, if he were to do so, he would surely not choose to do it in a way that would leave a suspicion of nefarious action, don't you agree?"

"Yes, I do," said Adikor.

"Thank you," said Bolbay. "Now, to this matter you raised about your own contribution perhaps being inadequate . . ."

Adikor shifted on the stool. "Yes?"

"Well, I, of course, had no intention of raising this," Bolbay said. Adikor thought he caught a whiff of dishonesty from her. "But since you have brought it up, we should perhaps explore this matter—just to dispel it, you understand."

Adikor said nothing, and, after a time, Bolbay continued. "How," she asked gently, "did it feel, living downwind of him?"

"I—I beg your pardon?"

"Well, you just said his contribution wasn't likely to be questioned, but your own might be."

"At the particular Council that's coming up," said Adikor, "yes. But in general . . ."

"In general," said Bolbay, a slickness to her deep voice, "you must admit that your own contribution was a fraction of his, anyway. Isn't that true?"

"Is this germane?" interjected Sard.

"Actually, Adjudicator, I do believe that it is," said Bolbay.

Sard looked dubious, but nodded for Bolbay to continue. She did so. "Surely, Scholar Huld, you must know that when generations yet to be born study physics and computing, Ponter's name will be mentioned often, while yours will be uttered rarely, if at all?"

Adikor could feel his pulse increasing. "I have never considered such issues," he said.

"Oh, come now," said Bolbay, as if they both knew better. "The disparity in your contributions was obvious."

"I caution you again, Daklar Bolbay," said the adjudicator. "I see no reason to humiliate the accused."

"I'm merely trying to explore his mental state," replied Bolbay, bowing yet again. Without waiting for Sard to respond, Bolbay turned back to Adikor. "So, Scholar Huld, do tell us: how did it feel to be making the lesser contribution?"

Adikor took a deep breath. "It is not my place to weigh our relative worth."

"Of course not, but the difference between yours and his is not in question," said Bolbay, as if Adikor were obsessing on some minor detail, instead of seeing the big picture. "It's well-known that Ponter was the brilliant one." Bolbay smiled solicitously. "So, again, please do tell us how knowing that felt."

"It feels," Adikor said, trying to keep his tone even, "exactly the same today as it did before Ponter went missing. The only thing that has changed is that I am now sad beyond words for the loss of my very best friend."

Bolbay had circled behind him now. The stool had a swivel seat; Adikor could have followed her as she walked, but he chose not to. "Your best friend?" said Bolbay, as if this were a startling admission. "Your best friend, is it? And how did you commemorate this friendship once he was gone? By announcing that it was your software and equipment, not his theorems, that your experiments were all about."

Adikor's jaw dropped. "I—I didn't say that. I told an Exhibitionist I would comment only on the role of software and hardware, because they had been my responsibility."

"Exactly! From the moment he was gone, you were downplaying Ponter's contributions."

"Daklar Bolbay!" snapped Sard. "You will treat Scholar Huld with suitable respect."

"Respect?" sneered Bolbay. "Like that which he showed Ponter once he was gone?"

Adikor's head was spinning. "We can access my alibi archive, or the Exhibitionist's," he said. He indicated Sard, as if they were long-time allies. "The adjudicator can hear the exact words I used."

Bolbay waved her arm, dismissing this suggestion as if it were the utmost craziness. "It doesn't matter precisely what words you said; what matters is what they tell us about what you were feeling. And what you were feeling was relief that your rival was gone—"

"No," said Adikor sharply.

"I'm warning you, Daklar Bolbay," said Sard, sharply.

"Relief that you would no longer be eclipsed by another," continued Bolbay.

"No!" said Adikor, fury growing within him.

"Relief," continued Bolbay, her voice rising, "that you could now begin claiming as your sole contribution everything you had jointly done."

"Desist, Bolbay!" barked Sard, slapping the arm of her chair with the flat of her hand.

"Relief," shouted Bolbay, "that your rival was dead!"

Adikor rose to his feet and turned to face Bolbay. He contracted his fingers into a fist and pulled back his arm.

"*Scholar Huld!*" Adjudicator Sard's voice thundered in the chamber.

Adikor froze. His heart was pounding. Bolbay, he'd noted, had wisely moved downwind of him, so that the fans were no longer blowing her pheromones his way. He looked at his own clenched fist—a fist that could have shattered Bolbay's skull with a single punch, a fist that could have crushed her chest, splintered her ribs, ruptured her heart with one good impact. It was as if it were something foreign to him, no longer a part of his body. Adikor lowered his arm, but there was still so much anger in him, so much indignation, that for several beats he was unable to unclench his fingers. He turned to face Sard, his tone imploring. "I—Adjudicator, surely you understand . . . I—I *couldn't* have . . ." He shook his head. "You heard what she said to me. I—no one could . . ."

Adjudicator Sard's violet eyes were wide in shock as she looked at Adikor. "I've never seen such a display, inside or outside a legal proceeding," she said. "Scholar Huld, what is *wrong* with you?"

Adikor was still seething. Bolbay *must* know the history; of course she must. She was Klast's woman-mate, and Ponter had been with Klast even back in those days. But . . .

but . . . was *that* why Bolbay was pursuing him with such vengeance? Was that *her* motive? Surely she must know that Ponter would never have wanted this.

Adikor had undergone much therapy for his problem with controlling anger. Dear Ponter had recognized it was a sickness, a chemical imbalance, and—to his credit, that wonderful man—had stood by Adikor through his treatment.

But now . . . now Bolbay had *goaded* him, had provoked him, had pushed him over the edge, for all to see.

"Worthy Adjudicator," said Adikor, trying—trying, *trying!*—to sound calm. Should he explain? Could he? Adikor lowered his head. "I apologize for my outburst."

Sard still had an astonished quaver in her voice. "Do you have any more evidence supporting your accusation, Daklar Bolbay?"

Bolbay, clearly having achieved precisely the effect she'd wanted, had reverted to the very picture of reasonableness. "If I may be allowed, Adjudicator, there is one more small thing . . ."

Chapter Twenty-three

At the end of the meeting in the Inco conference room, Reuben Montego invited everyone back to his place for another barbecue. Ponter smiled broadly; he'd obviously quite enjoyed the previous night's meal. Louise accepted the invitation as well, reiterating that, with SNO in ruins, there wasn't much for her to be doing these days anyway. Mary also accepted—it sounded like fun, and beat another evening alone, staring at the ceiling in her hotel room. But Professor Mah begged off. She needed to get back to Ottawa: she had a 10:00 P.M. appointment at 24 Sussex Drive, where she would brief the Prime Minister.

The problem now was shaking the media, who, according to the Inco security guards, were waiting just outside the gates of the Creighton mine site. But Reuben and Louise quickly came up with a plan, which they immediately put into action.

Mary had a rental car now, courtesy of Inco—a red Dodge Neon. (When she'd picked it up, Mary had asked the rental clerk if it ran on noble gas; all she'd gotten was a blank stare in return.)

Mary left her Neon at the mine, and instead got into the passenger seat of Louise's black Ford Explorer, sporting a white-and-blue vanity plate that read "D2O"—which, after a moment, Mary realized was the chemical formula for heavy water. Louise got a blanket out of her car's trunk—sensible drivers in both Ontario and Quebec carried blankets or sleeping bags, in case of winter accidents—and she draped the blanket over Mary.

Mary found it awfully hot at first, but, fortunately, Louise's car was air conditioned; few grad students could afford that, but Mary rather suspected Louise had no trouble getting good deals wherever she went.

Louise drove down the winding gravel road to the mine-site entrance, and Mary, under the blanket, did the best job she could of looking both animate and bulky. After a bit, Louise started to speed, as if trying to get away.

"We're just passing the gate now," said Louise to Mary, who couldn't see anything. "And it's working! People are pointing at us and starting to follow."

Louise led them all the way back into Sudbury. If everything was going according to plan, Reuben would have waited until the reporters had taken off after the Explorer, then driven Ponter to his house just outside Lively.

Louise drove to the small apartment building she lived in, parking in the outdoor lot. Mary could hear other cars pulling up near them, some screeching their tires dramatically. Louise got out of the driver's seat and came over to the passenger door. "Okay," she said to Mary, after opening the door, "you can get out now."

Mary did so, and she could hear other doors slamming shut as their drivers presumably disembarked. Louise shouted "*Voilà!*" as she helped pull the blanket off Mary, and Mary grinned sheepishly at the reporters.

"Oh, crap!" said one of the journalists, and "Damn!" said another.

But a third—there were perhaps a dozen present—was more savvy. "You're Dr. Vaughan, aren't you?" she called. "The geneticist?"

Mary nodded.

"Well," demanded the reporter, "is he or isn't he a Neanderthal?"

It took forty-five minutes for Mary and Louise to extricate themselves from the journalists, who, although disappointed not to have found Ponter, were delighted to hear the results of Mary's DNA tests. Finally, though, Mary and Louise made it into Louise's apartment building and up to her small unit on the third floor. They waited until all the journalists had left the parking lot—clearly visible from Louise's bedroom window—then Louise got a couple of bottles of wine from her fridge, and she and Mary went back down to her car and drove out to Lively.

They got to Reuben's house just before 6:00 P.M. Reuben and Ponter had wisely not started making dinner, being unsure when Louise and Mary would arrive. Ponter actually had been lying down on Reuben's living-room couch; Mary thought perhaps he was feeling a little under the weather—not surprising, after all he'd been through.

Louise announced that she had to help make dinner. Mary learned she was a vegetarian, and had apparently felt bad about putting Reuben to extra effort the night before. Reuben, Mary noted, quickly accepted the offer of Louise's aid—what straight male wouldn't?

"Mary, Ponter," said Reuben, "make yourselves at home. Louise and I will get the barbecue going."

Mary felt her heart begin to race, and her mouth went dry. She hadn't been alone with any man since—since—

But it was only early evening now, and—

And Ponter wasn't—

It was a cliché, but it was also true, truer than it had ever been.

Ponter wasn't like other men.

Surely it would be all right; after all, Reuben and Louise wouldn't be far away. Mary took a deep breath, trying to calm herself. "Sure," she said, softly. "Of course."

"Great," said Reuben. "There's pop and beer in the fridge; we'll open Louise's wine with dinner." He and Louise went into the kitchen, then, a couple of minutes later, headed out to the backyard. Mary found herself sucking in air as Reuben closed the glass door leading to the deck, but he didn't want to air-condition the great outdoors. Still, with the door closed and the hum of the air-conditioning equipment, she doubted Reuben and Louise could hear her now.

Mary turned her head to look at Ponter, who had risen to his feet. She managed a weak smile.

Ponter smiled back.

He wasn't ugly; really, he wasn't. But his face was quite unusual: like someone had grabbed a clay model of a normal human face and pulled it forward.

"Hello," said Ponter, speaking for himself.

"Hi," said Mary.

"Awkward," said Ponter.

Mary remembered her trip to Germany. She'd hated being unable to make herself understood, hated struggling to read the directions on a pay phone, trying to order in a restaurant, attempting to ask directions. How awful it must be for Ponter—a scientist, an intellectual!—to be reduced to communicating at a child's level.

Ponter's emotions were obvious: he smiled, he frowned, he raised his blond eyebrow, he laughed; she hadn't seen him cry, but assumed he could. They didn't yet have the vocabulary to really discuss how he felt about being here; it had been easier to talk about quantum mechanics than about feelings.

Mary nodded sympathetically. "Yes," she said, "it must be very awkward, not being able to communicate."

Ponter tipped his head a bit. Perhaps he'd understood; perhaps he hadn't. He looked around Reuben's living room, as if something were missing. "Your rooms do not have . . ." He frowned, clearly frustrated, apparently wanting to convey an idea for which neither he nor his implant yet had the vocabulary. Finally, he moved over to the end of a row of heavy built-in bookcases, filled with mystery novels, DVDs, and small Jamaican carvings. Ponter turned around and began to rub his back from side to side against the last bookcase's edge.

Mary was astonished at first, then she realized what he was doing: Ponter was using the bookcase as a scratching post. An image of a contented Baloo from Disney's *Jungle Book* came to her mind. She tried to suppress a grin. Her own back itched often enough—and, she thought briefly, it had been a long time since she'd had anyone to scratch it for her. If Ponter's back was indeed hairy, it probably itched with great regularity. Apparently, rooms in his world had dedicated scratching devices of some sort.

She wondered if it would be polite to offer to scratch

his back for him—and that thought made her pause. She'd assumed she'd never want to touch, or be touched, by a man again. There was nothing necessarily sexual about back scratching, but, then again, the literature Keisha had given her confirmed what she already knew: that there was nothing sexual about rape, either. Still, she had no idea what constituted appropriate behavior between a man and a woman in Ponter's society; she might offend him greatly, or . . .

Get over yourself, girl.

Doubtless she no more appeared attractive to Ponter than Ponter did to her. He scratched for a few moments longer, then stepped away from the massive bookcase. He gestured with an open palm at it, as if inviting Mary to take a turn.

She worried about damaging the wood or knocking stuff off the shelves, but everything seemed to have survived Ponter's vigorous movements.

"Thanks," said Mary. She crossed the room, moving behind a glass-topped coffee table, and placed her back against the bookcase's corner. She shimmied a bit against the wood. It actually did feel nice, although the clasp of her bra kept catching as it passed over the angle.

"Good, yes?" said Ponter.

Mary smiled. "Yes."

Just then, the phone rang. Ponter looked at it, and so did Mary. It rang again. "Certain not for I," said Ponter.

Mary laughed and moved over to an end table, which had a teal one-piece phone sitting on it. She picked it up. "Montego residence."

"Is Professor Mary Vaughan there, by any chance?" said a man's voice.

"Um, speaking."

"Great! My name is Sanjit. I'm a producer for *@discovery.ca*, the nightly science-news program on Discovery Channel Canada."

"Wow," said Mary. "That's a great show."

"Thanks. We've been following this stuff about a Neanderthal turning up in Sudbury. Frankly, we didn't believe it at first, but, well, a wire-service report just came through that you had authenticated the specimen's DNA."

"Yes," said Mary. "He does indeed have Neanderthal DNA."

"What about the—the man himself? He's not a fake?"

"No," said Mary. "He's the genuine article."

"Wow. Well, look, we'd love to have you on the show tomorrow. We're owned by CTV, so we can send someone over from our local affiliate and do an interview between you up there and Jay Ingram, one of our hosts, down here in Toronto."

"Um," said Mary, "well, sure. I guess."

"Great," said Sanjit. "Now, let me just take you through what we'd like to talk about."

Mary turned and looked out the living-room window; she could see Louise and Reuben fussing over the barbecue. "All right."

"First, let me see if I've got your own history right. You're a full professor at York, right?"

"Yes, in genetics."

"Tenured?"

"Yes."

"And your Ph.D. is in . . . ?"

"Molecular biology, actually."

"Now, in 1996, you went to Germany to collect DNA from the Neanderthal type specimen there, is that correct?"

Mary glanced over at Ponter, to see if he was offended that she was talking on the phone. He gave her an indulgent smile, so she continued. "Yes."

"Tell me about that," said Sanjit.

In all, the pre-interview must have taken twenty minutes. She heard Louise and Reuben pop in and out of the kitchen a couple of times, and Reuben stuck his head in the living room at one point to see whether Mary was okay; she held her hand over the phone's microphone and told him what was going on. He smiled and went back to his cooking. At last Sanjit finished with his questions, and they finalized the arrangements for taping the interview. Mary put down the phone and turned back to Ponter. "Sorry about that," she said.

But Ponter was lurching toward her, one arm outstretched. She realized in an instant what an idiot she'd been; he'd maneuvered her over here, next to the bookcases, away from the door. With one shove from that massive arm, she'd be away from the window, too, invisible to Reuben and Louise outside.

"Please," said Mary. "Please. I'll scream . . ."

Ponter took another shuddering step forward, and then—

And then—

And then Mary did scream. "*Help! Help!*"

Ponter was now slumping to the carpeted floor. His brow above the ridge was slick with perspiration, and his skin had turned an ashen color. Mary knelt down next to him. His chest was moving up and down rapidly, and he'd started to gasp.

"*Help!*" she yelled again.

She heard the glass door sliding open. Reuben dashed in. "What's—oh, God!"

He hurried over to the downed Ponter. Louise arrived a few seconds later. Reuben felt Ponter's pulse.

"Ponter is sick," said Hak, using its female voice.

"Yes," said Reuben, nodding. "Do you know what's wrong with him?"

"No," said Hak. "His pulse is elevated, his breathing shallow. His body temperature is 39."

Mary was startled for a moment to hear the implant citing what she presumed was a Celsius figure, in which case it was in the fever range—but, then again, it *was* a logical temperature scale for any ten-fingered being to develop.

"Does he have allergies?" asked Reuben.

Hak bleeped.

"Allergies," said Reuben. "Foods or things in the environment that normal people are unaffected by, but cause sickness in him."

"No," said Hak.

"Was he ill before he left your world?"

"Ill?" repeated Hak.

"Sick. Not well."

"No."

Reuben looked at an intricately carved wooden clock,

siting on one of his bookshelves. "It's been about fifty-one hours since he arrived here. Christ, Christ, Christ."

"What is it?" asked Mary.

"God, I am an idiot," said Reuben, rising. He hurried off to another room in the house and returned with a worn brown-leather medical bag, which he opened up. He extracted a wooden tongue depressor and a small flashlight. "Ponter," he said firmly, "open mouth."

Ponter's golden eyes were half-covered by his lids now, but he did what Reuben asked. Evidently, Ponter had never been examined in quite this way before; he resisted the placing of the wooden spatula on his tongue. But, perhaps calmed by some words from Hak that only he could hear, he soon stopped struggling, and Reuben shined the light inside the Neanderthal's cavernous mouth.

"His tonsils and other tissues are highly inflamed," said Reuben. He looked at Mary, then at Louise. "It's an infection of some sort."

"But either you, Professor Vaughan, or I have been with him just about all the time he's been here," said Louise, "and we're not sick."

"*Exactly*," snapped Reuben. "Whatever he's got, he probably got here—and it's something the three of us have natural immunity to, but he doesn't." The doctor rummaged in his case, found a vial of pills. "Louise," he said, without turning around, "get a glass of water, please."

Louise hurried off to the kitchen.

"I'm going to give him some industrial-strength aspirin," said Reuben to Hak, or to Mary—she wasn't sure which. "It should bring down his fever."

Louise returned with a tumbler full of water. Reuben

took it from her. He pushed two pills past Ponter's lips. "Hak, tell him to swallow the pills."

Mary was unsure whether the Companion understood Reuben's words, or merely guessed at his intention, but a moment later Ponter did indeed swallow the tablets, and, with his own large hand steadied by Reuben's, managed to chase them down with some water, although much of it ran down his chinless jaw, dampening his blond beard.

But he didn't splutter at all, Mary noted. A Neanderthal couldn't choke; that was the plus side of not being able to make as many sounds. The mouth cavity was laid out so that neither liquid nor food could go down the wrong way. Reuben helped pour more water into Ponter, emptying the glass.

Damn it, thought Mary. *God damn it.*

How could they have been so stupid? When Cortez and his conquistadors had come to Central America, they'd brought diseases to which the Aztecs had no immunity—and yet the Aztecs and the Spaniards had only been separated for a few thousand years, time enough for pathogens to develop in one part of the planet that those in the other couldn't defend against. Ponter's world had been separated from this one for at least twenty-seven thousand years; diseases *had* to have evolved here that he would have no resistance to.

And . . . and . . . and . . .

Mary shuddered.

And vice versa, too, of course.

The same thought had clearly occurred to Reuben. He hurried to his feet, crossed the room, and picked up the teal one-piece phone Mary had used earlier.

"Hello, operator," he said into the phone. "My name is Dr. Reuben K. Montego, and this is a medical emergency. I need you to connect me with the Laboratory Centre for Disease Control at Health Canada in Ottawa. Yes, that's right—whoever's in charge of infectious-disease control there . . ."

Chapter Twenty-four

Adikor Huld's *dooslarm basadlarm* was temporarily halted, ostensibly for the evening meal, but also because Adjudicator Sard clearly wanted to give him a chance to calm down, to regain composure, and to consult with others about how he might undo the damage of his violent outburst earlier in the day.

When the *dooslarm basadlarm* started back up, Adikor sat again on the stool. He wondered what genius had thought of having the accused sit on a stool while others circled about him? Perhaps Jasmel knew; she was studying history, after all, and such proceedings were ancient in their origins.

Bolbay strode into the center of the chamber. "I now wish for us to move to the alibi-archive pavilion," she said, facing the adjudicator.

Sard glanced at the timepiece mounted on the ceiling, clearly concerned about how long all this was taking. "You've already established that Scholar Huld's alibi archive can't possibly show anything leading up to Ponter Boddit's disappearance." She scowled. "I'm *sure*"—she said this in a tone that would brook no argument—"that Scholar Huld and whoever is going to speak on his behalf will agree that this is true without you having to drag us over there to prove it."

Bolbay nodded respectfully. "Indeed, Adjudicator. But it isn't Scholar Huld's alibi cube I wish to have unlocked. It is Ponter Boddit's."

"It won't show anything of his disappearance, either," said Sard, sounding exasperated, "and for the same reason: the thousand armspans of rock blocking its transmissions."

"Quite true, Adjudicator," said Bolbay. "But it is not Scholar Boddit's disappearance that I wish to review. Rather, I want to show you events dating from 254 months ago."

"Two hundred and fifty-four!" exclaimed the adjudicator. "How could something that long past possibly be germane to these proceedings?"

"If you will indulge me," said Bolbay, "I think you will see that it has great bearing."

Adikor was tapping above his browridge with a cocked thumb, thinking. Two-and-a-half hundredmonths: that was a little over nineteen years. He'd known Ponter back then; they were both 145s, and had entered the Academy simultaneously. But what event from that far back could—

Adikor found himself on his feet. "Worthy Adjudicator, I object to this."

Sard looked at him. "Object?" she said, startled to hear such a thing during a legal proceeding. "On what basis? Bolbay isn't proposing to unlock your alibi archive—only Scholar Boddit's. And since he *is* missing, then opening his archive is something Bolbay, as *tabant* of his closest living relatives, has a right to request."

Adikor was angry with himself. Sard might have indeed

denied Bolbay's request, if he'd just kept his mouth shut. But now she was no doubt curious about what it was that Adikor wanted to keep hidden.

"Very well," said Sard, making her decision. She looked out at the crowd of spectators. "You people will have to stay here, until I decide whether this is something that needs to be seen publicly." She shifted her gaze. "Scholar Boddit's immediate family, Scholar Huld, and whoever will be speaking on behalf of him may join us, assuming none of them are Exhibitionists." And, at last, her eyes fell on Bolbay. "All right, Bolbay. This better be worth my time."

Sard, Bolbay, Adikor, Jasmel, and Megameg, holding Jasmel's hand, made their way down the wide, moss-covered corridor to the alibi pavilion. Bolbay apparently couldn't resist a dig at Adikor as they walked along. "No one to speak on your behalf, eh?" she said.

For once, Adikor did manage to keep his mouth shut.

There weren't many people still alive who had been born before the introduction of the Companions: those few from generation 140 and even fewer from 139 who hadn't yet died. For everyone else, a Companion had been part of their lives since just after birth, when the initial infant-sized implant was installed. The celebration of the thousandth month since the beginning of the Alibi Era would happen shortly; great festivities were planned worldwide.

Even just here in Saldak, there were tens of thousands who had been born and had already died since the first Companion was installed; that initial implant had been put into the forearm of its own creator, Lonwis Trob. The great alibi-archive pavilion, here, next to the Gray Council building, was divided into two wings. The one on the south abutted an outcropping of ancient rock; it would be extraordinarily difficult to expand that wing, and so it was used to store the active alibi cubes of those now alive, a number that was pretty much a constant. The north wing, although currently no bigger than the south, could expand for a great distance, as required; when someone died, his or her alibi cube was disconnected from the receiver array and brought there.

Adikor wondered which wing Ponter's cube was being stored in now. Technically, the adjudicator had yet to rule that murder had occurred. He hoped it was the wing of the living; he wasn't sure if he could maintain his composure if he had to face Ponter's cube on the other side.

Adikor had been to the archives before. The north wing, the wing of the dead, had a separate room, with an open archway leading into it, for each generation. The first one was tiny, holding a single cube, that of Walder Shar, the only member of generation 131 to still be alive in Saldak when the Companions were introduced. The next four rooms were successively bigger, housing cubes from members of generations 132, 133, 134, and 135, each ten years older than its predecessor. Starting with generation 136, all the rooms were the same size, although very few cubes had yet been transferred over from generations after 144, almost all of whose members were still alive.

The south wing had but a single room, with 30,000 receptacles for alibi cubes. Although originally there had been great order in the south wing, with the initial collection of cubes sorted by generation and, within each generation, subdivided by sex, much of that had been lost over time. Children were all born in orderly lots, but people died at a wide range of ages, and so cubes from subsequent generations had been plugged into vacant receptacles wherever they happened to be.

That made finding a particular cube out of more than 25,000—the population of Saldak—impossible without a directory. Adjudicator Sard presented herself to the Keeper of Alibis, a portly woman of generation 143.

"Healthy day, Adjudicator," said the woman, sitting on a saddle-seat behind a kidney-shaped table.

"Healthy day," said Sard. "I wish to access the alibi archive of Ponter Boddit, a physicist from generation 145."

The woman nodded and spoke into a computer. The machine's square screen displayed a series of numbers. "Follow me," she said. Sard and the others did just that.

For all her bulk, the keeper had a sprightly step. She led them down a series of corridors, the walls of which were lined with niches, each containing an alibi cube, a block of reconstituted granite about the size of a person's head. "Here we are," said the woman. "Receptacle number 16,321: Ponter Boddit."

The adjudicator nodded, then turned her wrinkled wrist with its own Companion to face the glowing blue eye on Ponter's cube. "I, Komel Sard, adjudicator, hereby order the unlocking of alibi receptacle 16,321, for just and appropriate legal inquiries. Timestamp."

The eye on the receptacle turned yellow. The adjudicator stepped out of the way, and the archivist held up her Companion. "I, Mabla Dabdalb, Keeper of Alibis, hereby concur with the unlocking of receptacle 16,321, for just and appropriate legal inquiries. Timestamp." The eye turned red, and a tone sounded.

"There you are, Adjudicator. You can use the projector in room twelve."

"Thank you," said Sard, and they marched back up to the front. Dabdalb pointed out the room she'd assigned them, and Sard, Bolbay, Adikor, Jasmel, and Megameg walked over to it and went inside.

The room was large and square, with a small gallery of saddle-seats against one wall. Everyone sat down, except for Bolbay, who moved over to the wall-mounted control console. It was only within this building that the alibi archives could be accessed; to protect against unauthorized viewing, the archive pavilion was completely isolated from the planetary information network, and had no outside telecommunications lines. Although it was sometimes inconvenient to have to physically come to the archives to access one's own recordings, the isolation was considered an appropriate safeguard.

Bolbay looked at the small group that had assembled here. "All right," she said. "I'm going to call up the events of 146/128/11."

Adikor nodded in resignation. He wasn't sure about the eleventh day, but the 128th moon since the birth of generation 146 sounded right.

The room darkened and an almost invisible sphere, like a soap bubble, appeared to float in front of them. Bolbay evidently felt the default size wasn't dramatic enough for her purposes: Adikor could hear her snapping control buds out, and the sphere's diameter grew until it was more than an armspan across. She plucked more controls, and the sphere filled with three smaller spheres packed together, each tinged with a slightly different color. Then those spheres subdivided into three more each, and those ones subdivided again, and on and on, like sped-up video of some alien cell undergoing mitosis. As the overall sphere filled with progressively smaller and smaller spheres, those smaller spheres took on more and more colors, until, finally, the process stopped, and an image of a young man standing in a positive-pressure thinking room at the Science Academy filled the viewing sphere, as though it were a three-dimensional sculpture made of beads.

Adikor nodded; this recording was made long enough ago that the new resolution enhancements weren't available. Still, it was eminently watchable.

Bolbay was evidently operating more controls. The bubble spun around so that everyone could see the face of the person being depicted. It was Ponter Boddit. Adikor had forgotten how young Ponter had looked back then. He glanced at Jasmel, sitting next to him. Her eyes were wide in wonder. It probably wasn't lost on her that here was her father at just about the age she was now; indeed, Klast had already been pregnant with Jasmel at the time these images were recorded.

"That, of course, is Ponter Boddit," said Bolbay. "At half his current age—or what would be his current age, if he were still alive." She quickly pushed on before the adjudicator could berate her. "Now, I'm going to fast-forward . . ."

The image of Ponter walked, sat, stood, puttered around the room, consulted a datapad, shimmied against a scratching pole, all at frenetic speed. And then the air-lock door to the room opened—the positive pressure kept out pheromones that might distract one's studying—and a young Adikor Huld entered.

"Pause," said Adjudicator Sard. Bolbay froze the image. "Scholar Huld, will you confirm that that is indeed you?"

Adikor was somewhat mortified to see his own face; he'd forgotten that for a brief time he'd adopted the affectation of shaving off his beard. Ah, but if that were the only folly from his youth that had been recorded . . . "Yes, Adjudicator," said Adikor, softly. "That's me."

"All right," said Sard. "Continue."

The image in the bubble started running forward again at high speed. Adikor moved around the room, as did Ponter—although the image of Ponter always stayed in the center of the sphere; it was the space around him that shifted.

Adikor and Ponter seemed to be talking amiably . . .

And then talking less amiably . . .

Bolbay slowed the playback to normal speed.

Ponter and Adikor were arguing by this point.

And then—

And then—

And then—

Adikor wanted to close his eyes. His own memories of this event were vivid enough. But he'd never seen it from this perspective, never seen the expression that had been on his face . . .

And so he watched.

Watched as he clenched his fingers . . .

Watched as he pulled back his arm, biceps bulging . . .

Watched as he propelled his arm forward . . .

Watched as Ponter lifted his head just in time . . .

Watched as his fist connected with Ponter's jaw . . .

Watched as Ponter's jaw snapped sideways . . .

Watched as Ponter staggered backward, blood spurting from his mouth . . .

Watched as Ponter spit out teeth.

Bolbay froze the image again. Yes, to his credit, the expression now on the young Adikor's face was one of shock and great remorse. Yes, he was bending over to help Ponter up. Yes, he clearly regretted what he'd done, which of course had been . . .

. . . had been coming within a hair's-breadth of killing Ponter Boddit, staving in the front of his skull with a punch backed by all of Adikor's strength.

Megameg was crying now. Jasmel had shifted in her chair, moving away from Adikor. Adjudicator Sard was shaking her head slowly back and forth in disbelief. And Bolbay—

Bolbay was standing, arms crossed in front of her chest.

"So, Adikor," said Bolbay, "should I play the whole thing back with the sound on, or would you like to save us all some time and tell us what you and Ponter were fighting about?"

Adikor felt nauseous. "This isn't fair," he said softly. "This isn't fair. I've undergone treatments to help me control my temper—adjustments to neurotransmitter levels; my personality sculptor will confirm that. I'd never hit anyone before in my life, and I never have since."

"You didn't answer my question," said Bolbay. "What were you fighting about?"

Adikor was silent, slowly shaking his head back and forth.

"Well, Scholar Huld?" demanded the adjudicator.

"It was trivial," said Adikor, looking down at the moss-covered floor now. "It was . . ." He took a deep breath, then let it out slowly. "It was a philosophical point, related to quantum physics. There have been many interpretations of quantum phenomena, but Ponter was clinging to what he knew full well was an incorrect model. I—I know now he was just goading me, but . . ."

"But it proved too much for you," said Bolbay. "You let a simple discussion of science—*science!*—get out of hand, and you got so angry that you lashed out in a way that might have cost Ponter his life had you hit him just a fraction of a handspan higher."

"This isn't fair," Adikor repeated, looking now at the adjudicator. "Ponter forgave me. He never brought a public accusation; without a victim's accusation, by definition no crime has been committed." His tone was pleading now. "*That's the law.*"

"We saw this morning in the Council chamber just how well Adikor Huld controls his temper these days," said Bolbay. "And you've now seen that he tried once before to kill Ponter Boddit. He failed that time, but I believe there's every reason to think he recently succeeded, down in the quantum-computing facility deep beneath the Earth." Bolbay paused, then looked at Sard. "I think," she said, her voice smug, "we've established the facts sufficiently to merit you sending this matter on to a full tribunal."

Chapter Twenty-five

Mary went to the front window of Reuben's house and looked outside. Even though it was after 6:00 P.M., there would still be light for another couple of hours at this time of year, and—

Good God! The producer for Discovery Channel wasn't the only one who had figured out where they were. Two TV vans with microwave antennas on their roofs, and three cars decorated with radio-station logos were outside as well, plus a beat-up Honda with one fender a different color than the rest of the car; it presumably belonged to a print journalist. Once the wire-service piece had gone out about her authenticating Ponter's DNA, apparently everyone had started taking this seemingly impossible story seriously.

Reuben finally got off the phone. Mary turned to look at him.

"I'm not really set up for guests," said the doctor, "but . . ."

"What?" said Louise, surprised.

But Mary had already figured it out. "We're not going anywhere, are we?" she said.

Reuben shook his head. "The LCDC has ordered a

quarantine on this building. Nobody goes in or out."

"For how long?" said Louise, her brown eyes wide.

"That's up to the government," replied Reuben. "Several days, at least."

"Days!" exclaimed Louise. "But . . . but . . ."

Reuben spread his hands. "I'm sorry, but there's no telling what's floating around in Ponter's bloodstream."

"What was it that wiped out the Aztecs?" asked Mary.

"Smallpox, mostly," said Reuben.

"But smallpox . . ." said Louise. "If he had that, shouldn't he have lesions on his face?"

"Those come two days after the onset of fever," said Reuben.

"But, anyway," said Louise, "smallpox has been eradicated."

"In this universe, yes," said Mary. "And so we don't vaccinate for it anymore. But it's possible—"

Louise nodded, getting it. "It's possible it hasn't been wiped out in *his* universe."

"Exactly," said Reuben. "And, even if it has been, there could be countless pathogens that have evolved in his world to which we have no immunity."

Louise took a deep breath, presumably trying to stay calm. "But I feel fine," she said.

"So do I," said Reuben. "Mary?"

"Fine, yes."

Reuben shook his head. "We can't take any chances, though. They've got samples of Ponter's blood over at St. Joseph's; the woman I'm dealing with at the LCDC says she'll speak to their head of pathology and run smears for everything they can think of."

"Do we have enough food?" asked Louise.

"No," said Reuben. "But they'll bring us more, and—"
Ding-dong!

"Oh, Kee-ryst!" said Reuben.

"There's somebody at the door!" declared Louise, looking out the front window.

"A reporter," said Mary, seeing the man.

Reuben ran upstairs. For half a second, Mary thought he was going to get a shotgun, but then she heard him shouting, presumably through a window he'd opened up there. "Go away! This house is quarantined!"

Mary saw the reporter step back a few paces and tip his head up, looking at Reuben. "I'd like to ask you a few questions, Dr. Montego," he called.

"Go away!" Reuben shouted back. "The Neanderthal is sick, and this place has been quarantined by the order of Health Canada." Mary became aware of more vehicles arriving on the country road, and red-and-yellow lights starting to sweep across the scene.

"Come on, Doctor," the reporter replied. "Just a few questions."

"I'm serious," Reuben called. "We are containing an infectious disease here."

"I understand Professor Vaughan is in there, as well," shouted the reporter. "Can she comment on the Neanderthal's DNA?"

"Go away! For God's sake, man, go away!"

"Professor Vaughan, are you in there? Stan Tinbergen, *Sudbury Star*. I'd like—"

"*Mon dieu!*" exclaimed Louise, pointing out toward the street. "That man has a rifle!"

Mary looked where Louise was pointing. There was indeed someone there, aiming a long gun right at the house from maybe thirty meters away. A second later, a man standing next to him raised a megaphone to his mouth. "*This is the RCMP,*" said the man's amplified, reverberating voice. "*Move away from the house.*"

Tinbergen turned around. "This is private property," he shouted back. "No one has committed a crime, and—"

"*MOVE AWAY,*" bellowed the Mountie, who was clad in plain clothes, although Mary saw that his white car was indeed marked with the letters RCMP and the French equivalent, GRC.

"If Dr. Montego or Professor Vaughan will just answer a few questions," said Tinbergen, "I'll—"

"Last warning!" said the Mountie through the bullhorn. "My partner will try only to wound you, but . . ."

Tinbergen obviously wanted his story. "I've got a right to ask questions!"

"*Five seconds,*" thundered the RCMP officer's voice.

Tinbergen stood his ground.

"*Four!*"

"The public has a right to know!" the reporter shouted.

"*Three!*"

Tinbergen turned around again, apparently determined to get in at least one question. "Dr. Montego," he shouted, looking up, "does this disease pose any risk to the public?"

"*Two!*"

"I'll answer all your questions," Reuben shouted back. "But not like this. Move away!"

"*ONE!*"

Tinbergen swiveled around, holding his hands up at midchest height. "All right already!" He began walking slowly away from the house.

No sooner had the reporter reached the far end of the driveway than the telephone rang inside Reuben's house. Mary moved across the living room and picked up the teal one-piece, but Reuben must have already answered on an extension upstairs. "Dr. Montego," she heard a man's voice say, "this is Inspector Matthews, RCMP."

Normally, Mary would have put down the phone, but she was dying of curiosity.

"Hello, Inspector," said Reuben's voice.

"Doctor, we've been asked by Health Canada to render any assistance you might require." The man's voice sounded thin; Mary presumed he was calling from a cellular phone. She craned her neck to see out the front window; the man who'd been using the bullhorn earlier was indeed now standing next to his white car and talking into a cell phone. "How many people are inside your house?"

"Four," said Reuben. "Myself, the Neanderthal, and two women: Professor Mary Vaughan from York University, and Louise Benoît, a physics postdoctoral student associated with the Sudbury Neutrino Observatory."

"I understand one of them is sick," said Matthews.

"Yes, the Neanderthal. He's running a high fever."

"Let me give you my cell-phone number," said the Mountie. He read off a string of digits.

"Got it," said Reuben.

"I'm going to be out here until my relief arrives at 2300," said Matthews. "The relief will be on the same phone; call if you need anything."

"I need antibiotics for Ponter. Penicillin, erythromycin—a slew of others."

"Do you have e-mail access in there?" asked Matthews.

"Yes."

"Do up the list. Send it to Robert Matthews—two T's—at rcmp-grc.gc.ca. Got that?"

"Yes," said Reuben. "I'll need those as soon as humanly possible."

"We'll get them here tonight, if they are things a regular pharmacy or St. Joseph's will have on hand."

"We're going to need more food, too," said Reuben.

"We'll get you whatever you want. E-mail me a list of food, toiletries, clothes, whatever you need."

"Great," said Reuben. "And I should collect blood samples from all of us, and have you get them over to St. Joseph's and other labs."

"Fine," said Matthews.

They agreed to call each other immediately if there were any changes in circumstances, and Reuben clicked off. Mary heard him coming down the stairs.

"Well?" said Louise—giving away that Mary had been listening, Mary thought, by looking in equal turns at her and at Reuben.

Reuben summarized the call, then: "I'm sorry about this; I really am."

"What about the others?" said Mary. "The other people who were exposed to Ponter?"

Reuben nodded. "I'll get Inspector Matthews to have the RCMP round them up; they'll probably quarantine them at St. Joseph's rather than here." He went into the kitchen and returned with a pad and a stubby pencil that looked like they were normally used for recording shop-ping lists. "All right, who else was exposed to Ponter?"

"A grad student who was working with me," said Lou-ise. "Paul Kiriyama."

"Dr. Mah, of course," said Mary, "and—my God—she's already on her way back to Ottawa. We better stop her from meeting with the Prime Minister tonight!"

"There were also a bunch of people from St. Joseph's," said Reuben. "Ambulance attendants, Dr. Singh, a radiol-ogist, nurses . . ."

They continued to draw up the list.

Ponter was still lying on Reuben's champagne-colored carpet through all this. He seemed to be unconscious now; Mary could see his massive chest rising and falling. His sloped brow was still slick with sweat, and his eyes were moving beneath their lids, subterranean animals at the bot-toms of burrows.

"All right," said Reuben. "I think that's everyone." He looked at Mary, then at Louise, then at the ailing Ponter. "I've got to write up a list of drugs I need to treat Ponter. If we're lucky . . ."

Mary nodded, and looked at Ponter, too. *If we're lucky,* she thought, *none of us are going to die.*

Chapter Twenty-six

NEWS SEARCH

Keyword(s): *Neanderthal*

"Did Ponter Boddit gain legal entry into Canada? That question continues to bother immigration experts at home and abroad. Our guest tonight is Professor Simon Cohen, who teaches citizenship law at McGill University in Montreal . . ."

Top Ten reasons why we know that Ponter Boddit must be a real Neanderthal . . .

•Number ten: When he met his first human female, he hit her with a club and dragged her away by her hair.

•Number nine: Mistaken in dim light for Leonid Brezhnev.

•Number eight: When Arnold Schwarzenegger dropped by for a visit, Boddit said, "Who's the scrawny kid?"

•Number seven: Watches nothing but Fox.

•Number six: McDonald's sign now says, "Billions and billions of *Homo sapiens* served—plus one Neanderthal."

•Number five: Called Tom Arnold "a hunk."

•Number four: When shown rare rock specimen at the Smithsonian, chipped it into a perfect spearhead.

•Number three: Wears Fossil watch and drinks Really, Really, Really Old Milwaukee.

•Number two: Now collecting royalties on fire.

•And the number one reason we know that Ponter Boddit must be a Neanderthal? Hairy cheeks—all four of them.

John Pearce, director of international acquisitions for Random House Canada, has offered Ponter Boddit the largest advance in Canadian publishing history for world rights to his authorized biography, reports the trade journal *Quill & Quire* . . .

The Pentagon is rumored to be interested in speaking with Ponter Boddit. The military implications of the way in which he supposedly arrived here have caught the attention of at least one five-star general . . .

Now, thought Adikor Huld, as he took his seat on the stool in the Council chamber, *we'll see if I've made the biggest mistake of my life.*

"Who speaks on behalf of the accused?" asked Adjudicator Sard.

Nobody moved. Adikor's heart jumped. Had Jasmel Ket decided to forsake him? After all, who could blame her? She'd seen yesterday with her own eyes that once—granted, a long time ago—Adikor had apparently tried to kill her father.

The room was quiet, although one of the spectators, presumably making the same assumption Bolbay had earlier, let out a short, derisive laugh: *no one* was going to speak on behalf of Adikor.

But then, at last, Jasmel did rise to her feet. "I do," she said. "I speak for Adikor Huld."

There were gasps from many in the audience.

Daklar Bolbay, who was sitting on the sidelines, rose as

well, her face agog. "Adjudicator, this isn't right. The girl is one of the accusers."

Adjudicator Sard tipped her wrinkled head forward, looking out at Jasmel from under her browridge. "Is this true?"

"No," said Jasmel. "Daklar Bolbay was my mother's woman-mate; she was appointed my *tabant* when my mother died. But I have now seen 250 moons, and I claim the rights of majority."

"You're a 147?" asked Sard.

"Yes, Adjudicator."

Sard turned to Bolbay, who was still standing. "All 147s gained personal responsibility two months ago. Unless you are contending that your ward is mentally incompetent, your guardianship of her ended automatically. Is she, in fact, mentally incompetent?"

Bolbay was seething. She opened her mouth, clearly to make a remark, but thought better of it. She looked down and said, "No, Adjudicator."

"All right, then," said Sard. "Take your seat, Daklar Bolbay."

"Thank you, Adjudicator," said Jasmel. "Now, if I may—"

"Just a moment, 147," said Sard. "It would have been polite to tell your *tabant* that you were going to oppose her case."

Adikor understood why Jasmel had remained silent. Had she forewarned Bolbay, Bolbay would have done everything she could to dissuade her. But Jasmel had her father's charm. "You speak wisely, Adjudicator. I shall keep your advice behind my browridge."

Sard nodded, satisfied, and motioned for Jasmel to proceed.

Jasmel walked into the center of the chamber. "Adjudicator Sard, you've heard much innuendo from Daklar Bolbay. Innuendo, and baseless attacks on Adikor Huld's character. But she hardly knows the man. Adikor was my father's man-mate; granted, I saw Adikor only briefly whenever Two became One—he has his own son, young Dab there, here in this chamber, and his woman, Lurt, seated next to Dab. But, still, we met frequently—much more frequently than Daklar and he did."

She moved next to Adikor and placed a hand on his shoulder. "I stand here, the daughter of the man Adikor is accused of killing, and say to you that I do not think he did it." She paused, looked briefly down at Adikor, then met Adjudicator Sard's gaze from across the room.

"You *saw* the alibi recording," prodded Bolbay, still straddling her saddle-seat at the side of the room, in the first row of spectators. Sard shushed her.

"Yes," said Jasmel. "Yes, I did. I knew that my father had a damaged jaw. It pained him occasionally, especially on cold mornings. I hadn't known who had caused the damage—he never said. But he did say that it was long ago, that the person who had done it was extremely contrite, and that he'd forgiven the individual." She paused. "My father was good at gauging character. He would not have partnered with Adikor had he thought there was the slightest possibility that Adikor would repeat his actions." She looked at Adikor, then back at the Adjudicator. "Yes, my father is missing. But I don't think he was murdered.

If he *is* dead, it was because of an accident. And if he is not—"

"Do you think him injured?" asked Adjudicator Sard. Jasmel was taken aback; it was unusual for the adjudicator to ask direct questions.

"He might be, Adjudicator."

But Sard shook her head. "Child, I sympathize with you. I really do. I know all too well what it's like to lose a parent. But what you're saying makes no sense. Men searched the mines for your father. Women were called in to search as well, even though it was Last Five. Dogs were brought in to search, too."

"But if he were dead," said Jasmel, "his Companion would have broadcast a locator signal, at least for a while. They scanned for it with portable equipment, and found nothing."

"True," said Sard. "But if his Companion had been deliberately disabled or destroyed, there would be no signal."

"But there's no evidence—"

"Child," said the adjudicator, "men have been known to disappear before. If circumstances are untenable in their personal lives, some have gouged out their own implants and headed into the wilderness. They shed all trappings of advanced civilization and join one of the communities that choose to live by traditional means, or they simply fend for themselves and live a nomadic life. Is there anything that might have made your father wish to disappear?"

"Nothing," said Jasmel. "I saw him when Two last become One, and he was fine."

"Briefly," said the adjudicator.

"Pardon?"

"You saw him briefly." Sard evidently noted Jasmel's eyebrow going up. "No, I haven't looked at your alibi archive; you've been accused of no crime, after all. But I did make some inquiries; it's prudent for an adjudicator to do so in a case as unusual as this. So I ask again, was there any reason your father would choose to disappear? He could simply have eluded Adikor down in the mine, after all, then waited until none of the mining robots were about and gone up the elevator."

"No, Adjudicator," said Jasmel. "I saw no evidence of mental instability, no sign that he wasn't happy—well, as happy as one who had lost a mate could be."

"I'll vouch for that," said Adikor, speaking directly to the adjudicator. "Ponter and I were very happy together."

"Your word is somewhat suspect, given the present circumstances," said Sard. "But, again, I have made my own inquires, and they confirm what you have said. Ponter had no debts he could not handle, no enemies, no *nadalp*—no reason to leave behind a family and a career."

"Exactly," said Adikor, knowing that yet again he should be quiet but being unable to control himself.

"So," said Adjudicator Sard, "if he had no reason to wish to disappear, and no mental instability, then we return to Bolbay's assertion. If Ponter Boddit were merely injured, or dead by natural causes, the search teams would have found him."

"But—" said Jasmel.

"Child," said, Sard, "if you have some proof—not simple assertions on your part, but actual evidence—that Adikor Huld is not guilty, let's have it."

Jasmel looked at Adikor. Adikor looked at Jasmel. Except for the odd person coughing or shifting in his or her chair, the giant hall was quiet.

"Well?" said the adjudicator. "I'm waiting."

Adikor shrugged at Jasmel; he had no idea whether presenting this would be the right thing to do. Jasmel cleared her throat. "Yes, adjudicator, there is one other possibility . . ."

Chapter Twenty-seven

It had been an uncomfortable night for Mary.

Reuben Montego had wind chimes in his backyard; Mary thought all people with wind chimes should be shot, but, well, given that Reuben did have a couple of acres of land, normally they probably didn't disturb anyone else. Still, the constant tinkling had made it hard for her to get to sleep.

There'd been much discussion of sleeping arrangements. Reuben had a queen-size bed in his bedroom, a couch upstairs in his office, and another down in the living room. Unfortunately, neither of the couches folded out into beds. Ultimately, they agreed to give Ponter the bed; he needed it more than anyone else. Reuben took the upstairs couch, Louise had the downstairs couch for the first night, and Mary slept in a La-Z-Boy, also in the living room.

Ponter was indeed sick—but Hak wasn't. Mary, Reuben, and Louise had agreed to take turns giving further language lessons to the implant. Louise said she was a night person, anyway, so Hak could be taught pretty much around the clock now. And Louise had indeed disappeared into Ponter's room a little before 10:00 P.M., not coming down to the living room again until after 2:00 A.M. Mary wasn't sure if it was the sound of Louise's arrival that woke her, or whether she had really already been awake, but she knew she had to go up now and help Hak learn more English.

Speaking to the Companion *was* uncomfortable for Mary, not because she was unnerved talking to a computer—far from it; she was fascinated—but because she had to go alone into Ponter's upstairs bedroom, and because she had to close the door behind her, lest the noise of her conversations with the Companion disturb Reuben sleeping next door.

She was astonished by how much more fluent Hak had become in the hours the Companion had spent talking with Louise.

Fortunately, Ponter slept right through the language lesson, although Mary did have a brief moment of panic when he suddenly moved, rolling over on his side. If Mary understood what Hak was trying to convey, the Companion was pumping white noise through Ponter's auditory implants so that the quiet conversations Hak was having wouldn't disturb Ponter.

Mary only managed about an hour of naming nouns and acting out verbs for Hak before she was too tired to go on. She excused herself and went back downstairs. Louise had stripped down to her bra and panties and was lying on the couch, partly covered by an afghan.

Mary leaned back in the recliner, and this time, out of sheer exhaustion, fell quickly to sleep.

By morning, Ponter's fever had apparently broken; perhaps the aspirin and antibiotics Reuben had given him were helping. The Neanderthal got out of bed and came downstairs—and, to Mary's shock, he was absolutely naked. Louise was still asleep, and Mary, curled up in the recliner, had only recently awoken. For half a second, she was afraid Ponter had come down looking for her or—no, doubtless, if he were interested in anyone, it was surely the young, beautiful French-Canadian.

But although he glanced briefly at both Louise and Mary, it turned out he was really heading for the kitchen. He apparently hadn't noticed that Mary's eyes were open.

She was going to speak up, objecting to his nudity, but, well . . .

My goodness, Mary thought, as he crossed through the living room. *My goodness.* He might not be much to look at above the neck, but . . .

She swiveled her head to watch his buns as he disappeared into the kitchen, and she watched again as he re-emerged, holding one of Reuben's cans of Coke; Reuben had a whole shelf of his fridge devoted to the stuff. The scientist in Mary was fascinated to see a Neanderthal in the flesh, and—

And the woman in her simply enjoyed watching Ponter's muscular body move.

Mary allowed herself a little smile. She'd thought, perhaps, that she'd never be able to look at a man in that way again.

It was nice to know she still could.

Mary, Reuben, and Louise had been repeatedly interviewed by phone now, and Reuben, with Inco's permission, had organized a press conference—all three of them standing around a speakerphone in a conference call to journalists, who were shooting the proceedings through the living-room window with zoom lenses.

Meanwhile, tests were being done for smallpox, bubonic plague, and a range of other diseases. Blood samples had been flown in Canadian Forces jets to the Centers for Disease Control and Prevention in Atlanta and to the level-four hot lab at the Canadian Science Centre for Human and Animal Health in Winnipeg. The results from the first round of cultures came in at 11:14 A.M. No pathogens had been found in Ponter's blood yet, and no one else who had been with him—including all the others now quarantined at St. Joseph's—were showing any signs of illness. While other cultures were being tested, the microbiologists were also looking at blood samples for unknown pathogens—cells or other inclusions of kinds they'd never seen before.

"It's a pity he's a physicist rather than a physician," said Reuben to Mary, after the press conference.

"Why?" asked Mary.

"Well, we're lucky we have any useful antibiotics left to offer him. Bacteria build up immunity over time; I usually give my patients erythromycin, because penicillin is so ineffective these days, but I actually gave Ponter penicillin first. It's based on bread mold, of course, and if Ponter's people don't make bread, then they may never have stumbled on to it, so it might be very effective against any bacteriological infection he brought with him from his world. Then I gave him erythromycin, and a bunch of others, to combat anything he caught here. Still, Ponter's people probably have antibiotics of their own, but they're likely different from those we've discovered. If he could tell us what they use, we'd have a new weapon in the war on disease—one that our bacteria don't yet have any resistance to."

Mary nodded. "Interesting," she said. "It's too bad the gateway between his world and ours closed almost immediately. There are probably lots of fascinating trade possibilities between two versions of Earth. Pharmaceuticals are surely just the tip of the iceberg. Most of the foods we eat don't occur in the wild. He may not care for wheat products, but the modern potato and tomato, corn, the domestic chicken and pig and cow—all of them are forms of life we essentially created through selective breeding. We could trade those for whatever foodstuffs they've got."

Reuben nodded. "And that's just for starters. There's doubtless lots more to be done in terms of trading mining sites. I bet we know where all sorts of valuable minerals, fossils, and so on are that they haven't found, and vice versa."

Mary realized he was probably right. "Anything natural that's older than a few tens of thousands of years would be present in both worlds, wouldn't it? Another Lucy, another *Tyrannosaurus* Sue, another set of Burgess Shale fossils, another Hope diamond—at least, the original uncut stone." She paused, considering it all.

By the middle of the day, Ponter was clearly feeling much better. Mary and Louise both looked in at him, covered by a blanket, lying on the bed, as he slept quietly. "I'm glad he doesn't snore," said Louise. "With a nose that big . . ."

"Actually," said Mary, softly, "that's probably *why* he doesn't snore; he's getting plenty of airflow."

Ponter rolled over on the bed.

Louise looked at him for a moment, then turned back to Mary. "I'm going to have a shower," she said.

Mary's period had begun that morning; she'd certainly like a shower herself. "I'll have one after you."

Louise headed into the bathroom, closing the door behind her.

Ponter stirred again, then woke. "Mare," he said softly. He slept with his mouth closed, and his voice on waking didn't sound at all raw.

"Hello, Ponter. Did you sleep well?"

He raised his long, blond eyebrow—Mary still hadn't gotten used to the sight of it rolling up his browridge—as if he thought it a preposterous question.

He cocked his head; Louise had started the shower. And then he flared his nostrils, each the diameter of a twenty-five-cent piece, and looked at Mary.

And suddenly she realized what was happening, and she felt enormously embarrassed and uncomfortable. He could smell that she was menstruating. Mary backed across the room; she could hardly wait for her turn at the shower.

Ponter's expression was neutral. "Moon," he said.

Yes, thought Mary, *it's that time of the month.* But she certainly didn't want to talk about it. She hurried back downstairs.

Chapter Twenty-eight

Adjudicator Sard had an expression on her lined, wise face that conveyed, "This had *better* be good." "All right, child," she said to Jasmel, who was still standing next to Adikor in the Council chamber. "What other explanation, besides violent action, is there for your father's disappearance?"

Jasmel was quiet for a moment. "I would gladly tell you, Adjudicator, but . . ."

Sard was growing more impatient than usual. "Yes?"

"But, well, Scholar Huld could explain it much better than I."

"Scholar Huld!" exclaimed the adjudicator. "You propose the *accused* should speak on his own behalf?" Sard shook her head in astonishment.

"No," said Jasmel quickly, clearly realizing Sard was about to prohibit this outlandish notion. "No, nothing like that. He would simply address some points of technical information: information about quantum physics, and—"

"Quantum physics!" said Sard. "What bearing could quantum physics possibly have on this case?"

"It may in fact be the key," said Jasmel. "And Scholar Huld can present the information much more eloquently . . ." she saw Sard frowning ". . . and *succinctly* than could I."

"Is there no one else who could provide the same information?" asked the adjudicator.

"No, Adjudicator," said Jasmel. "Well, there *is* a group of females in Evsoy engaged in similar research, but—"

"Evsoy!" exclaimed Sard, as if Jasmel had named the far side of the moon. She shook her head again. "Oh, all right." She fixed a predator's gaze on Adikor. "Do be brief, Scholar Huld."

Adikor wasn't sure if he should rise, but he was getting tired of sitting on the stool, and so he did. "Thank you, Adjudicator," he said. "I, ah, I appreciate you allowing me to speak other than simply in response to questions posed."

"Don't make me regret my indulgence," said Sard. "Get on with it."

"Yes, of course," said Adikor. "The work Ponter Boddit and I were doing involved quantum computing. Now, what quantum computing does—at least in one interpretation—is reach into countless parallel universes in which identical quantum computers also exist. And all these quantum computers simultaneously tackle different portions of a complex mathematical problem. By pooling their capabilities, they get the work done much more quickly."

"Fascinating, I'm sure," said Sard. "But what has this to do with Ponter's alleged death?"

"It is, ah, my belief, Worthy Adjudicator, that when we were last running our quantum-computing experiment, a . . . a macroscopic passage of some sort . . . might have opened up into another one of these universes, and Ponter fell through that, so—"

Daklar Bolbay snorted derisively; others in the audience followed her lead. Sard was once again shaking her head in disbelief. "You expect me to believe that Scholar Boddit vanished into *another universe?*"

Now that the crowd knew which way the adjudicator's sentiments were leaning, they felt no need to hold back. There was out-and-out laughter emanating from many seats.

Adikor felt his pulse quickening, and his fists clenching—which was the last thing he should be doing, he knew. He couldn't do anything about the tachycardia, but he slowly managed to force his hands to open. "Adjudicator," he said, managing as deferential a tone as he could, "the existence of parallel universes underlines much theoretical thought in quantum physics these days, and—"

"*Silence!*" shouted Sard, her deep voice thundering in the hall. Some audience members gasped at her volume. "Scholar Huld, in all my hundreds of months as an adjudicator, I have never heard such a flimsy excuse. You think those of us who didn't go to your vaunted Science Academy are ignoramuses who can be fooled by outlandish talk?"

"Worthy Adjudicator, I—"

"Shut up," said Sard. "Just shut up and sit back down."

Adikor took a deep breath, and held it—just as they'd taught him to those 250-odd months ago when he'd been treated for having punched Ponter. He let the breath out slowly, imagining his fury escaping with it.

"I said sit down!" snapped Sard.

Adikor did so.

"Jasmel Ket!" said the adjudicator, turning her fiery stare now on Ponter's daughter.

"Yes, Adjudicator?" said Jasmel, her voice quavering.

The adjudicator took a deep breath of her own, composing herself. "Child," she said, more calmly, "child, I know you lost your mother recently to leukemia. I can only imagine how unfair that must have seemed to you, and little Megameg." She smiled at Jasmel's sister, new wrinkles piling atop the old ones on her face. "And now, it seems perhaps your father is dead, too—and, again, not the inevitable death that comes eventually to us all, but unexpectedly, without warning, and at a young age. I can understand why you are so reluctant to give up on him, why you might accept an outrageous explanation . . ."

"It's not like that, Adjudicator," said Jasmel.

"Isn't it? You're desperate for something to hold on to, some hope to cling to. Isn't that so?"

"I—I don't think so."

Sard nodded. "It will take time to accept what has happened to your father. I know that." She looked around the chambers, then finally her gaze landed on Adikor. "All right," Sard said. She was quiet for a moment, apparently considering. "All right," she said again. "I'm prepared to rule. I do believe it is just and appropriate to find that a good circumstantial case for the crime of murder has been made, and I therefore order this matter be tried by a trio of adjudicators, assuming anyone still wishes to pursue the issue." She looked now at Bolbay. "Do you wish to press the charge further, on behalf of your minor ward, Mega-meg Bek?"

Bolbay nodded. "I do."

Adikor felt his heart sink.

"Very well," said Sard. She consulted a datapad. "A full tribunal will be convened in this Council hall five days from now, on 148/119/03. Until such time, you, Scholar Huld, will continue to be under judicial scrutiny. Do you understand?"

"Yes, Adjudicator. But if I could only go down to—"

"No buts," snapped Sard. "And one more thing, Scholar Huld. I will be leading the tribunal, and I will be briefing the other two adjudicators. I grant there was a certain drama in having Ponter Boddit's daughter speak for you, but the effect won't last for a second try. I strongly suggest you find someone more appropriate to speak for you next time."

Chapter Twenty-nine

By early afternoon, Reuben Montego had good news to report. He'd been talking by phone and e-mail with various experts at LCDC headquarters and the CDC, as well as the hot lab in Winnipeg. "You've surely noticed that Ponter doesn't seem to like grain or dairy products," said Reuben, sitting now in his living room and drinking the strong-smelling Ethiopian coffee Mary had discovered he liked.

"Yes," said Mary, feeling much more comfortable after her shower, even if she did have to put on the same clothes she'd worn the day before. "He loves meat and fresh fruit. But he doesn't seem to have much interest in traditional from-the-ground crops, bread, or milk."

"Right," said Reuben. "And the people I've been talking to tell me that's very positive for us."

"Why?" asked Mary. She couldn't abide Reuben's coffee—although they'd asked for some Maxwell House, and, yes, some chocolate milk, to be delivered later that day, along with more clothes. For the moment, she was getting her caffeine from one of his cans of Coke.

"Because," said Reuben, "it suggests that Ponter doesn't come from an agricultural society. What I've gathered from Hak more or less confirms that. Ponter's version of Earth seems to have a much lower population than this one. Consequently, they don't practice farming or animal husbandry, at least not on anything like the scales we've been for the last few thousand years."

"I would have thought that you needed those things to support any sort of civilization, no matter what the population," said Mary.

Reuben nodded. "I'm looking forward to when Ponter can answer questions about that. Anyway, I'm told that most serious diseases that affect us started in domesticated animals, and then transferred to people. Measles, tuberculosis, and smallpox all came from cattle; the flu came from pigs and ducks; and whooping cough came from pigs and dogs."

Mary frowned. Out the window, she could see a helicopter flying by; more reporters. "That's right, now that I think about it."

"And," continued Reuben, "plaguelike diseases only evolve in areas of high population density, where there are plenty of potential victims. In areas of low density, such disease germs apparently aren't evolutionarily viable; they kill their own hosts, then have nowhere else to go."

"Yes, I suppose that's right, too," said Mary.

"It's probably too simplistic to say that if Ponter doesn't come from an agricultural society, then he must come from a hunting-and-gathering one," said Reuben. "But, still, that does seem the best model, at least from our world, of what Hak has tried to describe. Hunter-gatherer societies *do* have much lower population densities, and also much less disease."

Mary nodded.

Reuben continued: "I'm told it's the same principle as with the first European explorers and the Natives here in the Americas. The explorers all came from agricultural, high-density societies, and were lousy with plague germs. The natives were all from low-density societies, with little or no animal husbandry; they didn't have plague germs of their own, or any of the diseases that transfer from live-stock to humans. That's why the devastation only went one way."

"I thought syphilis was brought back to the Old World from the New," said Mary.

"Well, yes, there's some evidence for that," said Reuben. "But although syphilis perhaps originated in North America, it wasn't sexually transmitted here. It was only when it got back to Europe that it took up that opportun-istic means of transmission and became a major cause of death. In fact, the endemic, nonvenereal form of syphilis still exists, although now its mostly only found among Bed-ouin tribes."

"Really?"

"Yes. So, rather than syphilis being a counterexample of the generally one-way course of epidemic disease, it con-firms that the development of epidemics requires social conditions typical of overcrowded civilization."

Mary digested this for a moment. "So that means you, Louise, and I are probably going to be okay, right?"

"That seems the most probable interpretation: Ponter is suffering from something he got here, but likely has brought nothing over from his side that we have to worry about."

"But what about him? Is Ponter going to be all right?"

Reuben shrugged. "I don't know," he said. "I've given him enough broad-spectrum antibiotics to kill most known bacterial infections, Gram-negative and Gram-positive. Viral infections don't respond to antibiotics, though, and there's no such thing as a broad-spectrum antiviral. Unless we actually get evidence that he's got a specific viral condition, pumping random antivirals into him will probably do more harm than good." He sounded as frustrated as Mary felt. "There's really nothing else for us to do now but wait and see."

The Exhibitionists swarmed onto the Council-chamber floor, surrounding Adikor Huld and shouting questions at him, like spears being shoved into an ambushed mammoth. "Are you surprised by Adjudicator Sard's ruling?" asked Lulasm.

"Who are you going to have speak on your behalf in front of the tribunal?" demanded Hawst.

"You've got a son from generation 148; is he old enough to understand what might happen to you—and to him?" said an Exhibitionist whose name Adikor didn't know, a 147 who presumably had a younger audience watching him over their Voyeurs.

Exhibitionists shouted questions at poor Jasmel, too. "Jasmel Ket, how are relations between you and Daklar Bolbay now?" "Do you really believe your father might still be alive?" "If the tribunal does hand down a murder conviction against Scholar Huld, how will you feel about having defended a guilty person?"

Adikor felt anger growing within him, but he fought, fought, *fought* to conceal it. He knew the Companion-broadcasts from the Exhibitionists were being monitored by countless people.

For her part, Jasmel was refusing to respond at all, and the Exhibitionists at last left her alone. Eventually, those grilling Adikor had their fill, and they filed out of the chamber, leaving him and Jasmel alone in the vast room. Jasmel met Adikor's eyes for a moment, then looked away. Adikor wasn't sure what to say to her; he'd been adept at reading her father's moods, but Jasmel had much of Klast in her, too. Finally, to fill the silence between them, Adikor said, "I know you did the best you could."

Jasmel looked now at the ceiling, with its painted auroras and centrally mounted timepiece. Then she lowered her gaze, facing Adikor. "Did you do it?" she asked.

"What?" Adikor's heart pounded. "No, of course not. I love your father."

Jasmel closed her eyes. "I never knew it was you who had tried to kill him before."

"I wasn't trying to kill him. I was just angry, that's all. I thought you understood that; I thought—"

"You thought because I continued to speak on your behalf that I wasn't troubled by what I saw? That was my *father!* I saw him spitting out his own teeth!"

"It was long ago," said Adikor, softly. "I, ah, I didn't remember it as quite so . . . so bloody. I *am* sorry you had to see that." He paused. "Jasmel, don't you understand? I *love* your father; I owe everything that I am to him. After that . . . incident . . . he could have pressed charges; he could have had me sterilized. But he didn't. He understood that I had—have—a sickness, an inability sometimes to control my anger. I owe that I am still whole to him; I owe that I have a son, Dab, to him. My overwhelming feeling toward your father is *gratitude*. I would never hurt him. I couldn't."

"Maybe you got tired of being in his debt."

"There was no debt. You're still young, Jasmel, and you haven't yet bonded, but soon you will, I know. There is no debt between people who are in love; there is only total forgiveness, and going forward."

"People don't change," said Jasmel.

"Yes, they do. I did. And your father knew that."

Jasmel was quiet for a long time, then: "Who are you going to have speak for you this time?"

Adikor had just ignored the question when it had been shouted at him by the Exhibitionists. But now he gave it serious thought. "Lurt is the natural choice," he said. "She's a 145, old enough that the adjudicators should respect her. And she said she'd do anything to help."

"I hope . . ." said Jasmel. She continued again a moment later. "I hope she does well for you."

"Thank you. What are you going to do now?"

Jasmel looked directly at Adikor. "For now—for right now—I just need to get away from here . . . and from you."

She turned and walked out of the massive Council chamber, leaving Adikor all alone.

Chapter Thirty

NEWS SEARCH

Keyword(s): *Neanderthal*

An Islamic spiritual leader has denounced the so-called Neanderthal man as clearly the botched product of Western genetic-engineering experiments. The Wilayat al-Faqih in Iran is calling on the Canadian government to admit that Ponter Boddit is the product of a wickedly immoral recombinant-DNA procedure...

Ottawa is being pressured to grant Canadian citizenship to Ponter Boddit—and the request is coming from an unusual source. U.S. president George W. Bush today asked Prime Minister Jean Chrétien to expedite the process by which the Neanderthal is made an official Canadian. Ponter Boddit has indicated that he was born in a location corresponding to Sudbury, Ontario, in his world. "If he was born in Canada," says Bush, "then he's a Canadian."

The U.S. president is pushing for Boddit to be issued a Canadian passport so the Neanderthal can travel freely to the United States once the quarantine is lifted, thereby ending the debate on Capitol Hill about whether he could be allowed through U.S. Customs.

Section 5, Paragraph 4, of the Canadian Citizenship Act gives broad discretion, which Bush is urging be invoked: "In order to alleviate cases of special and unusual hardship or to reward services of an exceptional value to Canada, and notwithstanding any other provision of this Act, the Governor in Council may, in his discretion, direct the Minister to grant citizenship to any person..."

An Internet petition with more than 10,000 names gathered worldwide has been forwarded to Canada's Minister of Health, demanding that Ponter Boddit be permanently quarantined...

Inco shares closed today at a fifty-two-week high...

"It's a media circus," said long-time Sudbury Rotarian Bernie Monks. "Northern Ontario hasn't seen anything like this since the Dionne Quintuplets were born, back in 1934..."

Job offers continue to pour in for Ponter Boddit. Japan's NTT Basic Research Laboratory has offered him a directorship of a new quantum-computing unit. Microsoft and IBM have also offered him contracts, with generous cash/stock packages. MIT, CalTech, and eight other universities have offered him faculty positions. The RAND Corporation has likewise made an overture to him, as has Greenpeace. No word yet from the Neanderthal about whether any of these positions appeal to him...

A coalition of scientists in France has issued a statement saying that although Ponter Boddit's arrival on this Earth did indeed take place on Canadian soil, he clearly was not born in that nation, and no Neanderthaler ever lived in North America. His citizenship, they contend, should therefore be French, since the youngest Neanderthal fossils are found in that country...

Civil-rights advocates on both sides of the border are condemning the forced quarantine of the so-called Neanderthal man, saying there is no evidence he poses a medical threat to anyone...

Blood test after blood test came back negative. Whatever Ponter had been suffering from seemed to have abated, and there was no evidence that he was carrying anything dangerous to the humans of this world. Still, the LCDC wasn't ready to cancel the quarantine yet.

Ponter was wearing his own shirt again today, the one

he'd had on when he arrived here. The RCMP had delivered a small wardrobe of additional clothes for him bought at the local Mark's Work Wearhouse, but they really didn't fit very well; clothing didn't seem to come off the rack for a person who looked like a slightly squished version of Mr. Universe.

Ponter's—or Hak's—English was getting remarkably good. The Companion didn't have the *ee* phoneme in its preprogrammed repertoire, but it had now recorded both Mary and Reuben saying that sound, and would play back the appropriate version as required to render English words it otherwise couldn't articulate. But it sounded funny hearing her name said as "Mare-ee," half in one of Hak's voices and half in either her own or Reuben's, so Mary told the Companion not to bother; people periodically called her "Mare," anyway, and it would be just fine for Hak to continue to do that, too. Louise likewise told Hak it was all right if the Companion went on referring to her as just "Lou."

Finally, Hak announced that it had amassed a sufficient vocabulary for truly meaningful conversations. Yes, it said, there would be gaps and difficulties, but these could be worked out as they went along.

And so, while Reuben was busy going over more test results on the phone with other doctors, and while Louise, the night owl, was sleeping upstairs, having accepted Ponter's offer to use the bed when he wasn't, Mary and Ponter sat in the living room and had their first real chat. Ponter spoke softly, making sounds in his own language, and Hak, using its male voice, provided an English translation: "It is good to talk."

Mary made a small, nervous laugh. She'd been frustrated by her inability to communicate with Ponter, and now that they *could* talk, she didn't know what to say to him. "Yes," she said. "It's good to talk."

"A beautiful day," said Ponter's translated voice, looking out the living room's rear window.

Mary laughed again; heartily, this time. Talking about the weather—a pleasantry that transcended species boundaries. "Yes, it is."

And then she realized that it wasn't that she didn't know what to say to Ponter. Rather, she had so many questions, she didn't know where to begin. Ponter *was* a scientist; he must have some sense of what his people knew about genetics, about the split between genus *Homo* and genus *Pan*, about . . .

But no. No. Ponter was a person—first and foremost, he was a person, and one who had gone through a harrowing ordeal. The science could wait. Right now, they would talk about him, about how he was doing. "How do you feel?" Mary asked.

"I am fine," said the translated voice.

Mary smiled. "I mean really. How are you really doing?"

Ponter seemed to hesitate, and Mary wondered if Neanderthal men shared with males of her kind a reluctance to talk about feelings. But then he exhaled through his mouth, a long, shuddering sigh.

"I am frightened," he said. "And I miss my family."

Mary lifted her eyebrows. "Your family?"

"My daughters," he said. "I have two daughters, Jasmel Ket and Megameg Bek."

Mary's jaw dropped slightly. It hadn't even occurred to

her to think about Ponter's family. "How old are they?"

"The older one," said Ponter, "is—I know in months, but you reckon time mostly in years, do you not? The older one is—Hak?"

Hak's female voice chimed in. "Jasmel is nineteen years old; Megameg is nine."

"My goodness," said Mary. "Will they be okay? What about their mother?"

"Klast died two tenmonths ago," said Ponter.

"Twenty months," added Hak, helpfully. "One-point-eight years."

"I'm sorry," said Mary softly.

Ponter nodded slightly. "Her cells, in her blood, they changed . . ."

"Leukemia," Mary said, providing the word.

"I miss her every month," said Ponter.

Mary wondered for a moment if Hak had translated that just right; surely Ponter meant he missed her every day. "To have lost both parents . . ."

"Yes," said Ponter. "Of course, Jasmel is an adult now, so . . ."

"So she can vote, and so forth?" asked Mary.

"No, no, no. Did Hak do the math incorrectly?"

"I most certainly did not," said Hak's female voice.

"Jasmel is far too young to vote," said Ponter. "*I* am far too young to vote."

"How old do you have to be in your world to vote?"

"You must have seen at least 667 moons—two-thirds of the traditional thousand-month lifetime."

Hak, evidently wanting to dispel the notion that it was mathematically challenged, quickly supplied the conversions: "One can vote at the age of fifty-one years; a traditional lifespan averaged seventy-seven years, although many live much longer than that these days."

"Here, in Ontario, people get to vote when they turn eighteen," said Mary. "Years, that is."

"Eighteen!" exclaimed Ponter. "That is madness."

"I don't know of any place where the voting age is higher than twenty-one years."

"This explains much about your world," says Ponter. "We do not let people shape policy until they have accumulated wisdom and experience."

"But then if Jasmel can't vote, what is it that makes her an adult?"

Ponter lifted his shoulders slightly. "I suppose such distinctions are not as significant on my world as they are here. Still, at 250 months, an individual does take legal responsibility for himself or herself, and usually is on the verge of establishing his or her own home." He shook his head. "I wish I could let Jasmel and Megameg know that I am still alive, and am thinking about them. Even if there is no way I can go home, I would give anything just to get a message to them."

"And is there really no way for you to go home?" asked Mary.

"I cannot see how I could. Oh, perhaps if a quantum computer could be built here, and the conditions that led to my . . . transfer . . . could be precisely duplicated. But I am a theoretical physicist; I have only the vaguest of senses of how one builds a quantum computer. My partner, Adikor, knows how, of course, but I have no way of contacting him."

"It must be very frustrating," said Mary.

"I am sorry," said Ponter. "I did not mean to shift my problems to you."

"That's all right," said Mary. "Is there—is there anything we, any of us, can do to help?"

Ponter said a single, sad-sounding Neanderthal syllable; Hak rendered it as "No."

Mary wanted to cheer him up. "Well, we shouldn't be in quarantine too much longer. Maybe after we're out, you can travel around, see some sights. Sudbury is a small town, but—"

"*Small?*" said Ponter, deep-set eyes wide. "But there are—I do not know how many. Tens of thousands at least."

"The Sudbury metropolitan area has 160,000 people in it," said Mary, having read that in a guidebook in her hotel room.

"One hundred and sixty thousand!" repeated Ponter. "And this is a small town? You, Mare, come from somewhere else, do you not? A different town. How many people live there?"

"The actual city of Toronto is 2.4 million people; greater Toronto—a continuous urban area with Toronto at its heart—is maybe 3.5 million."

"Three and a half million?" said Ponter, incredulously.

"Give or take."

"How many people are there?"

"In the whole world?" asked Mary.

"Yes."

"A little over six billion."

"A billion is . . . a thousand times a million?"

"That's right," said Mary. "At least here in North America. In Britain—no, forget it. Yes, a billion is a thousand million."

Ponter sagged in his chair. "That is a . . . a staggering number of people."

Mary raised her eyebrows. "How many people are there on your world?"

"One hundred and eighty-five million," said Ponter.

"Why so few?" asked Mary.

"Why so many?" asked Ponter.

"I don't know," replied Mary. "I never thought about it."

"Do you not—in my world, we know how to prevent pregnancy. I could perhaps teach you . . ."

Mary smiled. "We have methods, too."

Ponter lifted his eyebrow. "Perhaps ours work better."

Mary laughed. "Perhaps."

"Is there enough food for six billion people?"

"We mostly eat plants. We cultivate"—a *bleep*; Hak's convention upon hearing a word that wasn't yet in its database and that it couldn't figure out from context—"we grow them deliberately. I've noticed you don't seem to like bread"—another *bleep*—"um, food from grain, but bread, or rice, is what most of us eat."

"You manage to comfortably feed six billion people with *plants*?"

"Well, ah, no," said Mary. "About half a billion people don't have enough to eat."

"That is very bad," said Ponter, simply.

Mary could not disagree. Still, she realized with a start that Ponter had, to this point, been exposed only to a sanitized view of Earth. He'd seen a little TV, but not enough to really open his eyes. Nonetheless, it did indeed seem that Ponter was going to spend the rest of his life on this Earth. He needed to be told about war, and the crime rate, and pollution, and slavery—the whole bloody smear across time that was human history.

"Our world is a complex place," said Mary, as if that excused the fact that people were starving.

"So I have seen," said Ponter. "We have only one species of humanity, although there were more in the past. But you seem to have three or four."

Mary shook her head slightly. "What?" she said.

"The different types of human. You are obviously of one species, and Reuben is of another. And the male who helped rescue me, he seemed perhaps to be of a third species."

Mary smiled. "Those aren't different species. There's only one species of humanity here, too: *Homo sapiens.*"

"You can all breed with each other?" asked Ponter.

"Yes," said Mary.

"And the offspring are fertile?"

"Yes."

Ponter frowned. "You are the geneticist," he said, "not I, but . . . but . . . if they can all breed with each other, then why the diversity? Would not over time all humans end up looking similar, a mixture of all the possible traits?"

Mary exhaled noisily. She hadn't quite expected to get into that particular mess so soon. "Well, umm, in the past—not today, you understand, but . . ." She swallowed. "Well, not as *much* today, but in the past, people of one race"—a different bleep; a recognized word that couldn't be translated in this context—"people of one skin color didn't have much to do with people of another color."

"Why?" said Ponter. A simple question, so simple, really . . .

Mary lifted her shoulders slightly. "Well, the coloration differences arose originally because populations were geographically isolated. But after that . . . after that, limited interaction occurred due to ignorance, stupidity, hatred."

"Hatred," repeated Ponter.

"Yes, sad to say." She shrugged a little. "There is much in my species' past that I'm not proud of."

Ponter was quiet for a long moment. "I have," he said at last, "wondered about this world of yours. I was surprised when I saw the images of skulls at the hospital. I have seen such skulls, but on my world they are known only from our fossil record. It startled me to see flesh on what to this point I had only known as bone."

He paused again, looking at Mary as if still disconcerted by her appearance. She shifted slightly in her chair.

"We knew nothing of your skin color," said Ponter, "or the color of your hair. The"—*bleep*; Hak also bleeped as a placeholder when a word was omitted because the English equivalent wasn't yet in the Companion's vocabulary—"of my world would be astonished to learn of the variety."

Mary smiled. "Well, it's not all natural," she said. "I mean, my hair isn't really this color."

Ponter looked astonished. "What color is it really?"

"Kind of a mousy brown."

"Why did you alter it?"

Mary shrugged a little. "Self-expression, and—well, I said it was brown, but, actually, it has a fair bit of gray in it. I—many people, actually—dislike gray hair."

"The hair of my kind turns gray as we age."

"That's what happens to us, too; nobody is born with gray hair."

Ponter frowned again. "In my language, the term for one who has knowledge that comes with experience and for the color hair turns is the same: 'Gray.' I cannot imagine someone wanting to hide that color."

Mary shrugged once more. "We do a lot of things that don't make sense."

"That much is clearly true," said Ponter. He paused, as if considering whether to go on. "We have often wondered what became of your people . . . on our world, that is. Forgive me; I do not wish to sound"—*bleep*—"but you must know that your brains are smaller than ours."

Mary nodded. "About 10 percent smaller, on average, if I remember correctly."

"And you seemed physically weaker. Judging by attachment scars on your bones, your kind was believed to have had only half our muscle mass."

"I'd say that's about right," said Mary, nodding.

"And," continued Ponter, "you have spoken of your inability to get along, even with others of your own kind."

Mary nodded again.

"There is some archeological evidence for this among your kind on my world, too," said Ponter. "A popular theory is that you wiped each other out . . . what with being not all that intelligent, you see . . ." Ponter lowered his head. "I am sorry; again, I do not mean to upset you."

"That's all right," said Mary.

"I am sure there is a better explanation," said Ponter. "We knew so little about you."

"In a way," said Mary, "the knowledge that it could have gone another way—that we didn't necessarily have to end up surviving—is probably all to the good. It will remind my people of how precious life really is."

"This is not obvious to them?" asked Ponter, eyes wide in astonishment.

Chapter Thirty-one

Adikor finally left the Council chamber, walking slowly and sadly out the door. This was all madness—madness! He'd lost Ponter, and, as if that weren't devastating enough, now he would have to face a full tribunal. Whatever confidence he'd once had in the judicial system—an entity of which he'd only been vaguely aware to this point—had been shattered. How could an innocent, grieving person be hounded so?

Adikor headed down a long corridor, its walls lined with square portraits of great adjudicators of the past, men and women who had developed the principles of modern law. Had this—this *travesty*—really been what they'd had in mind? He continued along, not paying much attention to the other people he occasionally passed . . . until a flash of orange caught his eye.

Bolbay, still wearing the color of the accuser, down at the end of the corridor. She'd tarried in the Council building, perhaps to avoid Exhibitionists, and was now making her own way outside.

Before he'd really given it any thought, Adikor found himself running down the corridor toward her, the moss carpet cushioning his footfalls. Just as she stepped out through the door at the end, exiting into the afternoon sun, he caught up with her. "Daklar!"

Daklar Bolbay turned, startled. "Adikor!" she exclaimed, her eyes wide. She raised her voice. "Whoever is monitoring Adikor Huld for his judicial scrutiny, pay attention! He is now confronting me, his accuser!"

Adikor shook his head slowly. "I'm not here to harm you."

"I have seen," said Bolbay, "that your deeds do not always match your intentions."

"That was *years* ago," said Adikor, deliberately using the noun that most emphasized the length of time. "I'd never hit anyone before that, and I've never hit anyone since."

"But you *did* do it then," said Bolbay. "You lost your temper. You lashed out. You tried to kill."

"No! No, I never wanted to hurt Ponter."

"It's inappropriate for us to be speaking," said Bolbay. "You must excuse me." She turned.

Adikor's hand reached out, grabbing hold of Bolbay's shoulder. "No, wait!"

Her face showed panic as it swung back to look at him, but she quickly changed her expression, staring meaningfully at his hand. Adikor removed it. "Please," he said. "Please, just tell me *why*. Why are you going after me with such . . . such *vindictiveness*? In all the time we've known each other, I've never wronged you. You must know that I loved Ponter, and that he loved me. He wouldn't possibly want you to pursue me like this."

"Don't play the innocent with me," said Bolbay.

"But I *am* innocent! Why are you doing this?"

She simply shook her head, turned around, and began walking away.

"Why?" Adikor called after her. "*Why?*"

"Maybe we can talk about your people," Mary said to Ponter. "Until now, we've only had Neanderthal fossils to study. There's been a lot of debate over various things, like, well, for instance, what your prominent browridges are for."

Ponter blinked. "They shield my eyes from the sun."

"Really?" said Mary. "I guess that makes sense. But then why don't my people have them? I mean, Neanderthals evolved in Europe; my ancestors come from Africa, where it's much sunnier."

"We wondered that, too," said Ponter, "when we looked at Gliksin fossils."

"Gliksin?" repeated Mary.

"The type of fossil hominid from my world you most closely resemble. Gliksins didn't have browridges, so we had assumed that they were nocturnal."

Mary smiled. "I guess a lot of what people conclude from looking just at bones is wrong. Tell me: what do you make of this?" She tapped her index finger against her chin.

Ponter looked uncomfortable. "I know now that it is wrong, but . . ."

"Yes?" said Mary.

Ponter used an open hand to smooth down his beard, showing his chinless jaw. "We do not have such projections, so we assumed . . ."

"What?" said Mary.

"We assumed it was a drool guard. You have such tiny mouth cavities, we thought saliva was constantly dribbling out. Also, you *do* have smaller brains than we do, and, well, idiots often drool . . ."

Mary laughed. "Good grief," she said. "But, say, speaking of jaws, what happened to yours?"

"Nothing," said Ponter. "It is the same as it was before."

"I saw the x-rays that were taken of you at the hospital," said Mary. "Your mandible—your jawbone—shows extensive reconstruction."

"Oh, *that*," said Ponter, sounding apologetic. "I got hit in the face a couple of hundred months ago."

"What were you hit with?" asked Mary. "A brick?"

"With a fist," Ponter said.

Mary's own jaw dropped. "I knew Neanderthals were strong, but—*wow*. One punch did that?"

Ponter nodded.

"You're lucky you weren't killed," said Mary.

"We are *both* lucky—the punchee, as you might say, and the puncher."

"Why did someone hit you?"

"A stupid argument," said Ponter. "Certainly, he never should have done it, and he apologized profusely. I chose not to pursue the matter; if I had, he would have been tried for attempted murder."

"Could he have really killed you with one punch?"

"Oh, yes. I had reacted in time and lifted my head; that is why he connected with my jaw instead of the center of my face. Had he punched me there, he could well have caved in my skull."

"Oh, my," said Mary.

"He was angry, but I had provoked him. It was as much my fault as his."

"Could—could *you* kill someone with your bare hands?" asked Mary.

"Certainly," said Ponter. "Especially if I approached them from the rear." He intertwined his fingers, lifted his arms, then pantomimed smashing his interlocked fists down. "I could smash in a person's skull by doing that from behind. From the front, if I could get a good punch or kick into the center of someone's chest, I might crush their heart."

"But . . . but . . . no offense, but apes are very strong, too, and they rarely kill each other in fights."

"That is because in battles within a troop for dominance, ape fighting is ritualized and instinctive, and they simply slap each other—really just a display behavior. But chimpanzees do kill other chimpanzees, although they do it mostly with their teeth. Clenching the fingers into a fist is something only humans can do."

"Oh . . . my." Mary realized she was repeating herself, but couldn't think of anything better to sum up her feelings. "Humans here get into fights all the time. Some even make a sport of it: boxing, wrestling."

"Madness," said Ponter.

"Well, I agree, yes," said Mary. "But they almost never kill each other. I mean, it's almost impossible for a human to kill another human with his bare hands. We just aren't strong enough, I guess."

"In my world," said Ponter, "to hit is to kill. And so we *never* hit each other. Because any violence can be fatal, we simply cannot allow it."

"But you *were* hit," said Mary.

Ponter nodded. "It happened long ago, while I was a student at the Science Academy. I was arguing as only a youth can, as if winning mattered. I could see that the person I was arguing with was growing angry, but I continued to press my point. And he reacted in an . . . unfortunate manner. But I forgave him."

Mary looked at Ponter, imagining him turning the other long, angular cheek toward the person who had hit him.

Adikor had had his Companion summon a travel cube to take him home, and he now was sitting out back, on the deck, alone, researching legal procedures. Someone might indeed be monitoring his Companion's transmissions, but he could still use it to tap into the world's accumulated knowledge, transferring the results to a datapad for easier viewing.

His woman-mate, Lurt, had agreed at once to speak on behalf of Adikor in front of the tribunal. But although she and others—she'd be allowed to call witnesses this time—could attest to Adikor's character and to the stability of his relationship with Ponter, it seemed unlikely that that would be enough to convince Adjudicator Sard and her associates to acquit Adikor. And so Adikor had begun digging into legal history, looking for other cases involving a charge of murder without a body having been found, in hopes of locating a previous judgment that might help him.

The first similar case he uncovered dated way back to generation 17. The accused was a man named Dassta, and he was said to have killed his woman-mate after supposedly sneaking into the Center. But her body was never located; she'd simply disappeared one day. The tribunal had ruled that without a body, no murder could be said to have occurred.

Adikor was thrilled by that discovery—until he read further in the law.

Ponter and Adikor had selected normal deck chairs—indeed, fragile chairs. It had been a sign of Ponter's unshakable belief that Adikor was cured, that his temper would never again erupt into physical violence. But Adikor was so frustrated now that he smashed the armrest off his deck chair with a pounding of his fist, splinters of wood flying up. For prior cases to have legal significance, he read off his datapad, they had to date from within the last ten generations; society always advanced, said the *Code of Civilization*, and what people had done long ago had no bearing on the sensibilities of today.

Adikor continued searching and eventually turned up an intriguing case from generation 140—just eight generations before the current one—in which a man was accused of killing another male during a dispute over whether the latter had grown a home too close to the former's. But, again, no body was ever found. In that case, too, the tribunal had ruled that the lack of the body was enough to dismiss the accusation. That buoyed Adikor, except—

Except . . .

Generation 140. That was the period between—let's see—about 1,100 to 980 months ago; eighty-nine to seventy-nine years past. But the Companions had been introduced just shy of a thousand months ago; celebrations commemorating that were coming up.

Did the case in generation 140 date from before or after the introduction of the Companions? Adikor read further.

From before. *Gristle!* Bolbay would doubtless argue that this rendered it not germane. Sure, she would say, bodies and even living people could easily disappear during the dark times before the great Lonwis Trob had liberated us, but a case in which there *couldn't* have been a record of the accused's activities had no bearing on one in which the accused had contrived a situation specifically to *avoid* having a record made.

Adikor searched some more. He thought briefly that it might have been convenient if there were people who specialized in dealing with legal matters on behalf of others; that, it seemed, would be a useful contribution. He'd have gladly exchanged labor with someone familiar with this field who could do this research for him. But no; it was surely a bad idea. The mere existence of people who worked full-time on things legal would doubtless increase the number of such matters instigated, and—

Suddenly Pabo came tearing out of the house, barking. Adikor looked up, and, as it always did these days, his heart jumped. Could it be? Could it be?

But, no, it wasn't. Of course not. And, yet, it *was* someone Adikor hadn't expected to see: young Jasmel Ket. "Healthy day," she said, once she was within ten paces.

"Healthy day," Adikor replied, trying to keep his tone neutral.

Jasmel sat on the other deck chair, the one that had

been her father's. Pabo knew Jasmel well; the dog had often come into the Center when Two became One, and was clearly pleased to see another familiar face. Pabo nuzzled Jasmel's legs, and Jasmel scratched the reddish brown fur on the top of the dog's head.

"What happened to your chair?" asked Jasmel.

Adikor looked away. "Nothing."

Jasmel evidently decided not to pursue the point; after all, what had happened was obvious. "Did Lurt agree to speak for you?" she asked.

Adikor nodded.

"Good," said Jasmel. "I'm sure she'll do the best she can." She fell silent, for a time, then, glancing again at the damaged chair: "But . . ."

"Yes," said Adikor. "But."

Jasmel looked out at the countryside. Off in the distance, a mammoth was wandering by, stolid, placid. "Now that this matter has been referred to a full tribunal, my father's alibi cube has been moved to the wing of the dead. Daklar spent the afternoon reviewing parts of it, as she prepares to make her full case against you. That's her right, of course, as accuser speaking on behalf of a dead person. But I insisted she let me review Ponter's alibi archive with her. And I've looked at you and my father together, in the days leading up to his disappearance." She brought her gaze back to Adikor. "Bolbay can't see it but, then again, she has been alone for a long time. But—well, I told you I had a young man interested in me. Despite what you said about me not yet being bonded, I *know* what love looks like—and there is no doubt in my mind that you truly loved my father. After seeing you the way he saw you, I can't believe you would do anything to harm him."

"Thank you."

"Is . . . is there anything I can do to help you prepare to appear in front of the tribunal?"

Adikor shook his head sadly. "I'm not sure anything can save me or my relatives now."

Chapter Thirty-two

NEWS SEARCH

Keyword(s): *Neanderthal*

Playgirl has sent a letter to Ponter Boddit, asking him if he'd like to pose nude...

"Does he have a soul?" said Reverend Peter Donaldson of Los Angeles's Church of the Redeemer. "That's the key question. And I say, no, he does not..."

"We believe the rush to grant Ponter Canadian citizenship is calculated to allow him to represent Canada in the next Olympic Games, and we call upon the IOC to specifically bar all but *Homo sapiens sapiens* from competing..."

Get yours now: T-shirts, with Ponter Boddit's face on them. S, M, L, XL, XXL, and Neanderthal sizes available.

The German Skeptics, headquartered in Nuremberg, today announced that there was no good reason to believe that Ponter Boddit comes from a parallel universe. "That would be the last interpretation to accept," said Executive Director Karl von Schlegel, "and should only be adopted after every other simpler alternative has been eliminated..."

Mounties today arrested three men found trying to infiltrate the cordon around Dr. Reuben Montego's home in Lively, a town 14 km southwest of Sudbury, where the Neanderthal man is quarantined...

There were many ways to pass time, and it seemed that Louise and Reuben had found one of the oldest. Mary hadn't really looked at Reuben in that light, but, now that she did take stock of him, she realized he was indeed quite handsome. The shaved head wasn't her thing, but Reuben did have good, sturdy features, a dazzling smile, and intelligent eyes, and he was lean and nicely muscled.

And, of course, he had that wonderful accent—but that wasn't all. It turned out that he was fluent in French, meaning Louise and he could converse in her language. Plus, judging by his home, he obviously made a fair bit of money—not surprising, given he was a doctor.

Quite a find, as Mary's sister might say. Of course, Mary was sophisticated enough to understand that once the quarantine ended, Reuben and Louise's relationship would likely end, too. Still, it made Mary uncomfortable—not because she was a prude; she liked to think, despite her good-girl Catholic upbringing, that she wasn't. But rather because she was afraid Ponter might get the wrong idea about sexuality in this world, that he might think he was now *expected* to pair off with Mary. And the attention of a man was the last thing she wanted right now.

Still, Louise and Reuben's affair did mean that she and Ponter got a lot of time alone together. After a day, it had developed that Reuben and Louise would spend most of their time downstairs, in the basement, watching videos from Reuben's vast collection, while Mary and Ponter were usually together on the ground floor. And since Reuben and Louise were now sleeping together, they had reclaimed the queen-sized bed from Ponter. Mary didn't know quite what Reuben had said to manage the switch, but Ponter's new bed was the couch in Reuben's upstairs office, leaving the living room all to Mary.

Some Sundays, Mary went to Mass. She hadn't gone this week—although she could have, since it wasn't until Sunday evening that the LCDC had ordered the quarantine. But now she was sorry she'd missed it.

Fortunately, there were Masses on TV; Vision showed a Roman Catholic one broadcast from a church in Toronto every day. Reuben had a TV in his upstairs office, in addition to the set he and Louise were using in the basement. Mary went up to the office to watch the service being broadcast. The priest was dressed in opulent green vestments. He had silver hair but black eyebrows, and a face that made Mary think of a scrawny Gene Hackman.

". . . Grace and peace of our Lord, Jesus Christ, the love of God our Father and the fellowship of the Holy Spirit be with you all," pronounced the priest, a Monsignor DeVries, according to the title superimposed on the screen.

Mary, sitting now on the couch that tonight would serve as Ponter's bed, crossed herself. "Jesus was sent here to heal the contrite," announced DeVries. "Lord have mercy."

Mary joined the TV congregation in repeating, "*Lord have mercy.*"

"He came to call sinners," said DeVries. "Christ have mercy."

"*Christ have mercy,*" repeated Mary and the others.

"He pleads for us at the right hand of the Father. Lord have mercy."

"*Lord have mercy.*"

"May Almighty God have mercy on all of us," said

DeVries, "forgive our sins, and bring us to everlasting life."

"*Amen,*" said the congregation.

The reading, by a black woman with short-cropped hair wearing a purple robe, was from the Book of the Prophet Jeremiah. Behind her, a beautiful stained-glass window depicted a haloed Jesus and the twelve Apostles, with the Virgin Mary looking on. Mary wasn't exactly sure why she'd felt the need to hear a Mass today. After all, she wasn't the one who needed forgiveness for sin . . .

Organ music was playing now; a young man sang, "Save me, O Lord, in Your steadfast love . . ."

Mary had done nothing wrong. She was the victim.

The Eucharist continued, with the Monsignor reading from Luke: " 'Declare that these two sons of mine will sit one at Your right hand and one at Your left in Your kingdom . . .' "

Of course, Mary knew the story the priest was reciting of the woman who beseeched Christ on the road to Jerusalem; she knew the context. But the words echoed in her head: *two sons, one at Your right hand and one at Your left* . . .

Could it have been that way? Could two kinds of humanity have lived peacefully side by side? Cain had been an agriculturalist; he grew corn. Abel had been a carnivore, who raised sheep for slaughter. But Cain had slain Abel . . .

The priest was pouring wine now. "Blessed to You, Lord God of all Creation, through Your goodness we have this wine to offer. Fruit of the vine and the work of human hands, it will become a spiritual drink . . .

"Pray, brothers and sisters . . .

"God of power and might, we praise You through Your Son Jesus Christ, who comes in Your name . . .

"God our Father, we have wandered far from You but, through Your Son, You have brought us back . . .

"We ask You to sanctify these gifts through the power of Your spirit . . .

"Take this, all of you, and eat it. This is My body, which will be given up for you . . .

"Take this, all of you, and drink from it. This is the cup of My blood, the blood of the new and everlasting covenant. It will be shed for you and for all so that sins may be forgiven . . ."

Mary wished she could be with the congregation, taking Communion. When the ceremony was done, she crossed herself again and stood up.

And that's when she saw Ponter Boddit, standing quietly in the doorway, watching, his bearded, chinless jaw agape.

Chapter Thirty-three

"What was *that*?" asked Ponter.

"How long have you been there?" demanded Mary.

"A while."

"Why didn't you say anything?"

"I did not wish to disturb you," said Ponter. "You seemed . . . *intent* on what was happening on the screen."

Well, thought Mary, she had, in a way, usurped his room; the couch where he slept was the one she was now sitting on. Ponter came fully into Reuben's office and moved toward the couch, presumably to sit next to her. Mary scooted down to the far end, leaning against one of the couch's padded arms.

"Again," said Ponter, "what was that?"

Mary lifted her shoulders slightly. "A church service."

Ponter's Companion bleeped.

"Church," said Mary. "A, um, a hall of worship."

Another bleep.

"Religion. Worshiping God."

Hak spoke up at this point, using its female voice. "I am sorry, Mare. I do not know the meaning of any of these words."

"God," repeated Mary. "The being who created the universe."

There was a moment during which Ponter's expression remained neutral. But then, presumably upon hearing Hak's translation, his golden eyes went wide. He spoke in his language, and Hak translated, using the male voice: "The universe did not have a creator. It has always existed."

Mary frowned. She suspected Louise—if she ever emerged from the basement—would enjoy explaining big-bang cosmology to Ponter. For her part, Mary simply said, "That's not our belief."

Ponter shook his head, but was evidently willing to let that go. Still: "That man," he said, indicating the TV, "talked of 'everlasting life.' Does your kind have the secret of immortality? We have specialists in life-prolongation, and they have long sought that, but—"

"No," said Mary. "No, no. He's talking about Heaven." She raised her hand, palm out, and successfully forestalled Hak's bleep. "Heaven is a place where we supposedly continue to exist after death."

"That is oxymoronic." Mary marveled briefly at Hak's proficiency. Ponter had actually spoken a dozen words in his own language, presumably saying something like "that's a contradiction in terms," but the Companion had realized that there was a more succinct way to express this in English, even if there wasn't in the Neanderthal tongue.

"Well," replied Mary, "not everyone on Earth—on this Earth, that is—believes in an afterlife."

"Do the majority?"

"Well . . . yes, I guess so."

"Do you?"

Mary frowned, thinking. "Yes, I suppose I do."

"Based on what evidence?" asked Ponter. The tone of his Neanderthal words was neutral; he wasn't trying to be derisive.

"Well, they say that . . ." She trailed off. Why did she believe it? She was a scientist, a rationalist, a logical thinker. But, of course, her religious indoctrination had occurred long before she'd been trained in biology. Finally, she shrugged a little, knowing her answer would be inadequate. "It's in the Bible."

Hak bleeped.

"The Bible," repeated Mary. "Scriptures." *Bleep.* "Holy text." *Bleep.* "A revered book of moral teachings. The first part of it is shared by my people—called Christians—and by another major religion, the Jews. The second part is only believed in by Christians."

"Why?" asked Ponter. "What happens in the second part?"

"It tells the story of Jesus, the son of God."

"Ah, yes. That man spoke of him. So—so this . . . this creator of the universe somehow had a human son? Was God human, then?"

"No. No, he's incorporeal; without a body."

"Then how could he . . . ?"

"Jesus' mother was human, the Virgin Mary." She paused. "In a roundabout way, I'm named after her."

Ponter shook his head slightly. "Sorry; Hak has been doing an admirable job, but clearly is failing here. My Companion interpreted something you said as meaning one who has never had sexual intercourse."

"Virgin, yes," said Mary.

"But how can a virgin also be a mother?" asked Ponter. "That is another—" and Mary heard him speak the same string of words that Hak had rendered before as "oxymoron."

"Jesus was conceived without intercourse. God sort of planted him in her womb."

"And this other faction—Jews, you said?—rejects this story?"

"Yes."

"They seem . . . less credulous, shall we say." He looked at Mary. "Do you believe this? This story of Jesus?"

"I *am* a Christian," Mary said, confirming it as much for herself as for Ponter. "A follower of Jesus."

"I see," said Ponter. "And you also believe in this existence after death?"

"Well, we believe that the real essence of a person is the soul"—*bleep*—"an incorporeal version of the person, and that the soul travels to one of two destinations after death, where that essence will live on. If the person has been good, the soul goes to Heaven—a paradise, in the presence of God. If the person has been bad, the soul goes to Hell"—*bleep*—"and is tortured"—*bleep*—"tormented forever."

Ponter was silent for a long time, and Mary tried to read his broad features. Finally, he said, "We—my people—do not believe in an afterlife."

"What do you think happens after death?" asked Mary.

"For the person who has died, absolutely nothing. He or she ceases to be, totally and completely. All that they were is gone forevermore."

"That's so sad," said Mary.

"Is it?" asked Ponter. "Why?"

"Because you have to go on without them."

"Do you have contact with those who dwell in this afterlife of yours?"

"Well, no. I don't. Some people say they do, but their claims have never been substantiated."

"Color me surprised," said Ponter; Mary wondered where Hak had picked up that expression. "But if you have no way of accessing this afterlife, this realm of the dead, then why give it credence?"

"I've never seen the parallel world you came from," said Mary, "and yet I believe in that. And you can't see it anymore—but you still believe in it, too."

Once again, Hak got full marks. "*Touché,*" it said, neatly summarizing a half dozen words uttered by Ponter.

But Ponter's revelations had intrigued Mary. "We hold that morality comes from religion: from the belief in an absolute good, and from the, well, the fear, I guess, of damnation—of being sent to Hell."

"In other words," said Ponter, "humans of your kind behave properly only because they are threatened if they do not."

Mary tilted her head, conceding the point. "It's Pascal's wager," she said. "See, if you do believe in God, and he doesn't exist, then you've lost very little. But if you don't, and he does, then you risk eternal torment. Given that, it's prudent to be a believer."

"Ah," said Ponter; the interjection was the same in his language as hers, so no rendering of it was made by Hak.

"But, look," said Mary, "you still haven't answered my question about morality. Without a God—without a belief that you will be rewarded or punished after the end of your life—what drives morality among your people? I've spent a fair bit of time with you now, Ponter; I know you're a good person. Where does that goodness come from?"

"I behave as I do because it is right for me to do so."

"By whose standards?"

"By the standards of my people."

"But *where* do those standards come from?"

"From . . ." And here Ponter's eyes went wide, great orbs beneath an undulating shelf of bone, as though he'd had an epiphany—in the secular sense of the word, of course. "From our conviction that there is *no* life after death!" he said triumphantly. "That is why your belief troubles me; I see it now. Our assertion is straightforward and congruent with all observed fact: a person's life is completely finished at death; there is no possibility of reconciling with them, or making amends after they are gone, and no possibility that, because they lived a moral life, they are now in a paradise, with the cares of this existence forgotten." He paused, and his eyes flicked left and right across Mary's face, apparently looking for signs she understood what he was getting at.

"Do you not see?" Ponter went on. "If I wrong someone—if I say something mean to them, or, I do not know, perhaps take something that belongs to them—under your worldview I can console myself with the knowledge that, after they are dead, they can still be contacted; amends can be made. But in my worldview, once a person is gone—which could happen for any of us at any moment, through accident or heart attack or so on—then you who did the wrong must live knowing that that person's entire existence ended without you ever having made peace with him or her."

Mary thought about that. Yes, most slave owners had ignored the issue, but surely some people of conscience, caught up in a society driven by bought-and-sold human beings, must have had qualms . . . and yet had they consoled themselves with the knowledge that the people they were mistreating would be rewarded for their suffering after death? Yes, the Nazi leaders were pure evil, but how many of the rank and file, following orders to exterminate Jews, had managed to sleep at night by believing the freshly dead were now in paradise?

Nor did it have to be anything so grandiose. God was the great compensator: if you were wronged in life, it would be made up for in death—the fundamental principle that had allowed parents to send their children off to die in war after countless war. Indeed, it didn't really matter if you ruined someone else's life, because that person might well go to Heaven. Oh, you yourself might be dispatched to Hell, but nothing you did to anyone else really hurt them in the long run. This existence was mere prologue; eternal life was yet to come.

And, indeed, in that infinite existence, God would make up for whatever had been done to . . . to *her*.

And that bastard, that bastard who had attacked her, would burn.

No, it didn't matter if she never reported the crime; there was no way he could escape his ultimate judge.

But . . . but . . . "But what about your world? What happens to criminals there?"

Bleep.

"People who break laws," said Mary. "People who intentionally hurt others."

"Ah," said Ponter. "We have little problem with that anymore, having cleansed most bad genes from our gene pool generations ago."

"*What?*" exclaimed Mary.

"Serious crimes were punished by sterilization of not just the offender but also anyone who shared fifty percent of the offender's genetic material: brothers and sisters, parents, offspring. The effect was twofold. First, it cleansed those bad genes from our society, and—"

"How would nonagriculturalists stumble onto genetics? I mean, we figured it out through plant cultivation and animal husbandry."

"We may not have bred animals or plants for food, but we did domesticate wolves to help us in hunting. I have a dog named Pabo that I am very fond of. Wolves were quite susceptible to controlled breeding; the results were obvious."

Mary nodded; that sounded reasonable enough. "You said the sterilization had a twofold effect on your society?"

"Oh, yes. Besides directly eliminating the faulty genes, it gave families a strong incentive to make sure none of their own members ran seriously afoul of society."

"I suppose it would at that," said Mary.

"It did indeed," said Ponter. "You, as a geneticist, surely know that the *only* immortality that really exists is genetic. Life is driven by genes wanting to ensure their own reproduction, or to protect existing copies of themselves. So our justice was aimed at genes, not at people. Our society is mostly free of crime now because our justice system directly targeted that which really drives all life: not individuals, not circumstances, but *genes*. We made it so that the best survival strategy for genes is to obey the law."

"Richard Dawkins would approve, I imagine," said Mary. "But you were speaking of this . . . this sterilization practice in the past tense. Has it ended?"

"No, but there is little modern need."

"You were *that* successful? No one commits serious crimes anymore?"

"Hardly anyone does so because of genetic disorders. There are, of course, also biochemical disorders that cause antisocial behavior, but those are eminently treatable with drugs. Only rarely does sterilization still need to be invoked."

"A society without crime," said Mary, shaking her head slowly in amazement. "That must be . . ." She paused, wondering how much she wanted to let her guard down, then: "That must be *fabulous*." But she frowned. "Surely, though, a lot of crime must go unsolved. I mean, if you can't figure out who did something, then the perpetrator must go unpunished—or, if he had a biochemical disorder, untreated."

Ponter blinked. "Unsolved crimes?"

"Yes, you know: crimes for which the police"—*bleep*—"or whatever you have for law enforcement, can't figure out who did it."

"There are no such crimes."

Mary's back stiffened. Like most Canadians, she was against capital punishment—precisely because it was possible to execute the wrong person. All Canadians lived with the shame of the wrongful imprisonment of Guy Paul

Morin, who had spent ten years rotting in jail for a murder he didn't commit; of Donald Marshall, Jr., who spent eleven years incarcerated for a murder he, too, didn't commit; of David Milgaard, who spent twenty-three years jailed for a rape-murder he also was innocent of. Castration was the least of the punishments Mary would like to see her own rapist subjected to—but if, in her quest for vengeance, she had it done to the wrong person, how could she live with herself? And what about the Marshall case? No, it wasn't *all* Canadians who lived with the shame of that; it was *white* Canadians. Marshall was a Mi'kmaq Indian whose protestations of innocence in a white court, it seemed, weren't believed simply because he *was* an Indian.

Still, maybe she was thinking now more like an atheist than a true believer. A believer should hold that Milgaard, Morin, and Marshall were eventually going to receive their just, heavenly reward, making up for whatever they'd endured here on Earth. After all, God's own son had been executed unfairly, even by the standards of Rome; Pontius Pilate didn't think Christ guilty of the crime with which he'd been charged.

But Ponter's world was beginning to sound worse even than Pilate's court: the brutality of forced sterilizations with an absolute belief that you'd always correctly found the guilty party. Mary suppressed a shudder. "How can you be certain you've convicted the right person? More to the point, how can you be sure you *haven't* convicted the wrong person?"

"Because of the alibi archives," said Ponter, as if it were the most natural thing in the world.

"The *what?*" said Mary.

Ponter, still seated next to her on the couch in Reuben's office, held up his left arm and rotated it so that the inside of his wrist faced toward her. The strange digits on the Companion winked at Mary. "The alibi archives," he said again. "Hak constantly transmits information about my location, as well as three-dimensional images of exactly what I am doing. Of course, it has been out of touch with its receiver since I came here."

This time Mary didn't suppress the shudder. "You mean you live in a totalitarian society? You're constantly under surveillance?"

"Surveillance?" said Ponter, his eyebrow climbing over his browridge. "No, no, no. No one is monitoring the transmitted data."

Mary frowned, confused. "Then what's done with it?"

"It is recorded in my alibi archive."

"And what, exactly, is that?"

"A computerized memory archive; a block of material onto whose crystalline lattices we imprint unalterable recordings."

"But if no one is monitoring it, what's it for?"

"Am I misusing your word 'alibi'?" said Hak, in the female voice it used when talking on its own behalf. "I understood an alibi to be proof that one was somewhere else when an act was committed."

"Um, yes," said Mary. "That's an alibi."

"Well, then," continued Hak. "Ponter's archive provides him with an irrefutable alibi for any crime he might be accused of."

Mary felt her stomach flutter. "My God—Ponter, is the onus on *you* to prove your innocence?"

Ponter blinked, and Hak translated his words with the male voice. "Who else should it be on?"

"I mean, here, on this Earth, a person is innocent until proven guilty." As the words came out, Mary realized that there were many places where that, in fact, wasn't true, but she decided not to amend her comment.

"And I take it that you have nothing comparable to our alibi archives?" asked Ponter.

"That's right. Oh, there are security cameras in some places. But they're not everywhere, and almost no one has them in their homes."

"Then how do you ascertain someone's guilt? If there is no record of what actually happened, how can you be sure you are going to deal with the appropriate person?"

"That's what I meant about unsolved crimes," said Mary. "If we're not sure—and often we have no idea at all—then the person gets away with the crime."

"That hardly seems a better system," said Ponter slowly.

"But our *privacy* is protected. No one is constantly looking over our shoulders."

"Nor is anyone in my world—at least, not unless one is a . . . I do not know the word. Somebody who shows all for others to watch."

"An exhibitionist?" said Mary, raising her eyebrows in surprise.

"Yes. Their contribution is to allow others to monitor the transmissions from their Companions. They have enhanced implants that sense at a higher resolution and to a greater distance, and they go to various interesting places so that other people can watch what is happening there."

"But surely, in theory, someone could compromise the

security of anyone's transmissions, not just those of an ex-hibitionist."

"Why would anyone want to do that?" asked Ponter.

"Well—um, I don't know. Because they can?"

"I can drink urine," said Ponter, "but never have I felt the urge to do so."

"We have people here who consider it a challenge to compromise security measures—especially those involving computers."

"That hardly seems a contribution to society."

"Perhaps not," said Mary. "But, look, what if the person who is accused doesn't want to unlock his—what did you call it? His alibi archive?"

"Why would he not?"

"Well, I don't know. Just on general principle?"

Ponter looked perplexed.

"Or," said Mary, "because what they were actually doing at the time of the crime was embarrassing?" *Bleep*. "Embar-rassing. You know, something you are ashamed"—*bleep*—"of."

"Perhaps an example would help me get your mean-ing," said Ponter.

Mary pursed her lips, thinking. "Well, um, okay, say I was—say I was, you know, having, um, sex with someone else's mate; the fact that I was doing that might be my alibi, but I wouldn't want people to know it."

"Why not?"

"Well, because we believe adultery"—*bleep*—"is wrong."

"Wrong?" said Ponter, Hak having apparently guessed the meaning of the untranslated word. "How can it be, unless a claim of false paternity results? Who is hurt by it?"

"Well, um, I don't know; I mean, we, ah, we consider adultery a sin." *Bleep.*

Mary had expected that bleep, at least. If you had no religion, no list of things that didn't actually hurt somebody else but were still proscribed behaviors—recreational drug use, masturbation, adultery, watching porno videos—then you might indeed not be so fanatic about privacy. People insisted on it at least in part because there were things they did that they'd be mortified to have others know about. But in a permissive society, an open society, a society where the only crimes are crimes that have specific victims, perhaps it wouldn't be such a big deal. And, of course, Ponter had shown no nudity taboo—a religious idea, again—and no desire for seclusion while using the bathroom.

Mary shook her head. All the times she'd been embarrassed and ashamed in her life, all the times she was glad no one could see what she was doing: were they uncomfortable simply because of church-imposed edicts? The shame she felt over leaving Colm; the shame that prevented her from getting a divorce; the shame she felt over dealing with her own drives now that she had no man in her life; the shame she felt because of sin . . . Ponter had none of that, it seemed; as long as he was hurting no one else, he never felt uncomfortable over acts that gave him pleasure.

"I suppose your system might work," said Mary dubiously.

"It does," replied Ponter. "And recall that for serious crimes—those involving assaults on another person—there are usually at least *two* alibi archives available: that of the victim, and that of the perpetrator. The victim usually introduces his or her own archive of the event as evidence, and most of the time it clearly shows the perpetrator."

Mary was simultaneously fascinated and repelled. Still . . .

That night at York . . .

If images had been recorded, could she have brought herself to show them to anyone?

Yes, she said to herself firmly. Yes. She had done nothing wrong, nothing to be ashamed of. She was the innocent victim. All the pamphlets Keisha had given her at the rape-crisis center said that, and she really, really, really, really tried to believe it.

But—but even if there were a recording of what she'd seen, could it have been used to catch the monster? He'd been wearing a balaclava; she'd never seen his face—although a thousand different versions of it had haunted her dreams since. Whom would she have accused? Whose alibi archive would the courts have ordered unlocked? Mary had no idea where to begin, no idea whom to suspect.

She felt her stomach flutter. Maybe that was the real problem—the predicament that Ponter's people had avoided: having too many possible suspects, too much crowding, too much anonymity, too many vicious, aggressive . . . *men,* she thought. Men. Every academic of her generation had been sensitized to the issue of gender-neutral language. But violent crimes were indeed overwhelmingly caused by males.

And, yet, she'd spent her life surrounded by good, decent men. Her father; her two brothers; so many supportive colleagues; Father Caldicott, and Father Belfontaine before him; many good friends; a handful of lovers.

What proportion of men really were the problem? What fraction were violent, angry, unable to control their emotions, unable to resist their impulses? Was it so vast a group that it couldn't have been—"cleansed" was Ponter's word, a nurturing word, a hopeful word—from the gene pool generations ago?

No matter how large or how small the population of violent males was, thought Mary, there were too many. Even one such beast would be too many, and—

And here she was, thinking like Ponter's people. The gene pool *could* indeed use a good cleansing, a therapeutic purging.

Yes, it surely could.

Chapter Thirty-four

Adikor Huld lay in his bed, flush with the ground, staring up at the timepiece mounted on the ceiling. The sun had been up for several daytenths now, but he couldn't see any reason to rise.

What had happened that day, down in the quantum-computing lab? What had gone wrong?

Ponter hadn't been vaporized; he wasn't consumed by flame; he didn't explode. All those things would have left abundant traces.

No, if he was right, Ponter had been *transferred* to another universe . . . but . . .

But that sounded outlandish even to him; he understood how outrageous it must have seemed to Adjudicator Sard. And yet, what other explanation was there?

Ponter had disappeared.

And a large quantity of heavy water had appeared in his place.

Presumably, thought Adikor, it had been an even exchange—identical *masses* transposed, but radically different *volumes*. After all, it wasn't just Ponter that had disappeared; Adikor had heard the air rushing out of the quantum-computing chamber, as if all of it, too, had been shunted to another place. But even a room's worth of air had little mass, whereas liquid water—even liquid *heavy* water—was in the most dense state of that substance, more dense even than the solid, frozen variety.

So: a large volume of air and one man had disappeared from this universe, and an identical mass, but much smaller volume, of heavy water had come through to replace it from . . . from *the other side*; it was the phraseology that kept coming to Adikor's mind.

But . . .

But then that meant that there was heavy water at this location in the other universe. And pure heavy water did *not* occur naturally.

Which meant the . . . the *portal,* another word that came unbidden . . . must have opened into a storage tank for heavy water. And if heavy water was transferred from there to here, then Ponter was transferred from here to there, meaning . . .

Meaning he'd quite likely drowned.

Tears filled Adikor's deep eye sockets, like rainwater gathering in wells.

Ponter shifted on the couch and looked again at Mary. "The alibi archives do not just solve crimes," he said. "They have many other uses. For instance, I saw on television yesterday that two campers were lost in Algonquin Park."

Mary nodded.

"Being lost like that is impossible in my world. Your Companion triangulates on signals from various mountaintop transmitters to pinpoint your position, and if you are injured or trapped by a rockfall or something, it is easy for the rescue teams to home in on your Companion." He raised a hand, copying what Mary had done earlier, forestalling the objection he presumably saw coming. "Of course, only an adjudicator can order that you be tracked like that, and only when you request it by sending an emergency signal, or when a family member asks for it."

Headlines she'd seen all too frequently swirled through Mary's mind. "Police abandon search." "Hunt for missing girl called off." "Avalanche victims presumed dead."

"I guess an emergency signal like that *would* be useful," Mary said.

"It is," replied Ponter firmly. "And the Companion can issue the signal automatically, if you yourself are unable to. It monitors vital signs, and if you have a heart attack—or even are about to have a heart attack—it can summon aid."

Mary felt a twinge. Her own father had died of a heart attack, alone, when Mary had been eighteen. She'd found his body upon arriving home from school one day.

Ponter evidently mistook the sadness on Mary's face for continuing dubiousness. "And just a month before I came here, I misplaced a rain shield that I was very fond of; it had been a gift from Jasmel. I would have been"— *bleep*; devastated?—"had it been lost for good. But I simply visited the archive pavilion where my recordings are stored, and reviewed the last day's events. I saw exactly where I lost the shield and was able to retrieve it."

Mary certainly resented the countless hours she'd spent looking for misplaced books and student papers and business cards and house keys and coupons that were about to expire. Maybe you'd resent that even more if you were sure your existence was finite; maybe that knowledge would drive you to do something to avoid such wastes of time. "A personal black box," Mary said, really to herself, but Ponter responded.

"Actually, the recording material is mostly pink. We use reprocessed granite."

Mary smiled. "No, no. A black box is what we call a flight recorder: a device aboard an airplane that keeps track of telemetry and cockpit chatter, in case there's a crash. But the idea of having my own black box had never occurred to me." She paused. "How are the pictures taken, then?" Mary glanced down at Ponter's wrist. "Is there a lens on your Companion?"

"Yes, but it is only used to zoom in on things outside the Companion's normal recording space. The Companion uses sensor fields to record everything surrounding the person, and the person himself, as well." Ponter made the deep sound that was his chuckle. "After all, it would not be much good if we only recorded what was visible from the Companion's lens: lots of images of my left thigh or the inside of my hip pouch. This way, when playing back my archive, I can actually view myself from a short distance away."

"Amazing," said Mary. "We have *nothing* like that."

"But I have seen products of your science, your industry," said Ponter. "Surely, if you had made it a priority to develop such technology . . ."

Mary frowned. "Well, I suppose. I mean, we went from putting the first object in space to the first man on the moon in less than twelve years, and—"

"*Say that again.*"

"I said, when we wanted badly enough to put somebody on the moon—"

"The moon," repeated Ponter. "You mean *Earth's* moon?"

Mary blinked. "Uh-huh."

"But . . . but . . . that is fantastic," Ponter said. "We have never done such a thing."

"You've never been to the moon? I don't mean you personally; I mean your people. No Neanderthal has ever been to the moon?"

Ponter's eyes were wide. "No."

"What about Mars or the other planets?"

"No."

"Do you have satellites?"

"No, just one, like here."

"No, I mean *artificial* satellites. Unmanned mechanisms you put into orbit, you know, to help in predicting the weather, for communications, and so on."

"No," said Ponter. "We have nothing like that."

Mary thought for a moment. Without the legacy of the V-2, without the missiles of the Second World War, would humans here have been able to send anything into orbit? "We've launched—well, I don't know—many hundreds of things into space."

Ponter looked up, as if trying to visualize Luna's scowling face through the ceiling of Reuben's house. "How many live on the moon now?"

"None," said Mary, surprised.

"You do not have a permanent settlement there?"

"No."

"So people simply go to see the moon, then return to

Earth. How many go each month? Is it a popular thing to do?"

"Umm, nobody goes. Nobody has gone for—well, I guess it's thirty years now. We only ever sent twelve people to the moon's surface. Six groups of two."

"Why did you stop?"

"Well, it's complicated. Money was certainly one factor."

"I can imagine," said Ponter.

"And, well, there was the political situation. See, we—" She paused for a moment. "Gee, this is hard to explain. We called it *The Cold War*. There was no actual fighting going on, but the United States and another large nation, the Soviet Union, were in a severe ideological conflict."

"Over what?"

"Umm, over economic systems, I suppose."

"Hardly sounds worth fighting about," said Ponter.

"It seemed very important at the time. But, anyway, the president of the United States, he set the goal in—when was it?—in 1961, I guess, to put a man on the moon by the end of that decade. See, the Russians—the people from the Soviet Union—they'd put the first artificial satellite in space, and then the first man in space, and the U.S. was lagging behind, so, well, it set out to beat them."

"And did it?"

"Oh, yes. The Russians never managed to put anyone on the moon. But, well, once we'd beaten the Russians, the public pretty much lost interest."

"That is ridiculous—" began Ponter, but then he stopped. "No, I must apologize. Going to the moon is a magnificent feat, and whether you did it once or a thousand times, it is still praiseworthy." He paused. "I guess it is simply a question of different priorities."

Chapter Thirty-five

Mary and Ponter headed downstairs, looking for something to eat. Just after they got to the kitchen, Reuben Montego and Louise Benoît finally emerged from the basement. Reuben grinned at Ponter. "More barbecue?"

Ponter smiled back at him. "Please. But you must let me help."

"I'll show you how," said Louise. She patted Ponter on the forearm. "Come on, big fella."

Suddenly, Mary found herself objecting. "I thought you were a vegetarian."

"I am," said Louise. "For five years now. But I know how to barbecue."

Mary had an urge to go with them, as Ponter and Louise headed out through the sliding glass doors onto the deck. But . . . but . . . no, that was silly.

Louise slid the glass doors shut behind them, keeping the cooled air inside the house.

Reuben was clearing off the kitchen table. He faked the voice of an old Jewish yenta. "So, vhat have you two kids been talking about?"

Mary was still looking out through the glass, at Louise, laughing and tossing her hair as she explained how the barbecue worked, and at Ponter, hanging on her every word.

"Umm, mostly religion," said Mary.

Reuben's voice immediately switched back to normal. "Really?"

"Uh-huh," said Mary. She tore her eyes away from what was going on outside, and looked at Reuben. "Or more precisely, Neanderthals' lack of religion."

"But I thought Neanderthals *did* have religion," said Reuben, now getting some plain white Corelle plates from a cupboard. "The cult of the cave bear, and all that."

Mary shook her head. "You've been reading old books, Reuben. No one takes that seriously anymore."

"Really?"

"Yeah. Oh, some cave-bear skulls were found in one cave that had indeed been occupied by Neanderthals. But it now looks like the bears had simply died in the cave, probably during hibernation, and the Neanderthals had moved in afterwards."

"But weren't the skulls all arranged in patterns?"

"Well," said Mary, getting a handful of cutlery and laying it out, "the guy who first found them claimed they were in a stone crib or coffin. But no photos were taken, workers supposedly destroyed the coffin, and the only two sketches made by the archeologist—a guy named Bächler—completely contradict each other. No, it seems Bächler simply saw what he wanted to see."

"Oh," said Reuben, now rummaging in the fridge for things to make a salad. "But what about Neanderthals burying their dead with stuff the dear departed might need in the afterlife? Surely that's a sign of religion."

"Well, it *would* be," said Mary, "if Neanderthals had really done that. But sites occupied for generations accumulate garbage: bones, old stone tools, and so on. The few examples we thought we had of grave goods at Neanderthal burials turned out to be stuff that had just accidentally been buried with the corpse."

Reuben was pulling leaves off a head of iceberg lettuce now. "Ah, but doesn't burial in and of itself imply a belief in the afterlife?"

Mary looked around for something else she could do to help, but there really didn't seem to be anything. "It might," she said, "or it might just be a case of trying to keep things neat. Lots of Neanderthal corpses are found in tightly wrapped fetal positions. That *could* be ceremony, or it could just be a desire on the part of the poor slob who had to dig the grave to make the hole as small as possible. Dead bodies attract scavengers, after all, and they get to stinking if you leave them out in the sun."

Reuben was now chopping up celery. "But . . . but I read about Neanderthals being, well, the first flower children."

Mary laughed. "Ah, yes. Shanidar Cave, in Iraq—where Neanderthal bodies were found covered with fossil pollen."

"That's right," said Reuben, nodding. "As if they'd been buried wearing flower garlands, or something."

"Sorry, but that's been discredited, too. The pollen was just an accidental intrusion into the grave, brought there by burrowing rodents or groundwater percolating through the sediment."

"But—wait a minute! What about the Neanderthal flute! That was front-page news all over the world."

"Yeah," said Mary. "Ivan Turk found that in Slovenia: a hollowed-out bear bone with four holes in it."

"Right, right. A flute!"

" 'Fraid not," said Mary, leaning against the side-by-side fridge now. "It turns out that the bone was pierced by carnivore gnawing—probably by a wolf. And, yes, in typical newspaper fashion, that revelation did *not* make the front page."

"That's for sure. This is the first I've heard of it."

"I was there at the Paleoanthropology Society meeting in Seattle in '98, when Nowell and Chase presented their paper discrediting the flute." Mary paused. "No, it really does look like right until the very end, Neanderthals—at least on this version of Earth—had nothing that we'd call *religion,* or even culture for that matter. Oh, some of the very last specimens show a little variety in the things they did, but most paleoanthropologists think they were just imitating Cro-Magnons who lived nearby; Cro-Magnons were indisputably our direct ancestors."

"Speaking of Cro-Magnons," said Reuben, "what about crossbreeding between Neanderthals and Cro-Magnons? Didn't I read that fossils of a hybrid child had been found in, what, oh, maybe 1998?"

"Yeah, Erik Trinkaus is big on that specimen; it's from Portugal. But, look, he's a physical anthropologist, and I'm a geneticist. He bases his case entirely on the skeleton of a child that, to him, shows hybrid characteristics. But he doesn't have the skull—and the skull is the only truly diagnostic part of a Neanderthal. To me, it just looks like a stocky kid."

"Hmm," said Reuben. "But, you know, I've seen guys

who look a fair bit like Ponter, in features if not in coloring. Some Eastern Europeans, for instance, have big noses and prominent browridges. Are you saying those guys don't have Neanderthal genes in them?"

Mary shrugged. "I know some paleoanthropologists who would argue that they do. But, really, the jury is still out on whether our kind of humans and Neanderthals even could crossbreed."

"Well," said Reuben, "if you keep spending so much time with Ponter, maybe you'll answer that one for us someday."

Reuben was close enough that she was able to swat him on the arm with an open hand. "Stop that!" she said. She looked into the living room, so that Reuben wouldn't see the grin growing across her face.

Jasmel Ket showed up at Adikor's house around noon. Adikor was surprised but pleased to see her. "Healthy day," he said.

"The same to you," replied Jasmel, bending down to scratch Pabo's head.

"Will you have food?" asked Adikor. "Meat? Juice?"

"No, I'm fine," said Jasmel. "But I've been reading more of the law. Have you considered a counterclaim?"

"A counterclaim?" repeated Adikor. "Against whom?"

"Daklar Bolbay."

Adikor ushered Jasmel into the living room. He took a chair, and she took another. "On what possible charge?" said Adikor. "She has done nothing to me."

"She has interfered with your grieving for the loss of your man-mate . . ."

"Yes," said Adikor. "But surely that is not a crime."

"Isn't it?" said Jasmel. "What does the *Code of Civilization* say about disturbing the life of another?"

"It says a lot of things," said Adikor.

"The part I'm thinking of is, 'Frivolous actions against another cannot be countenanced; civilization works because we only invoke its power over the individual in egregious cases.' "

"Well, she's accused me of murder. There's no more egregious crime."

"But she has no real evidence against you," said Jasmel. "That makes her action frivolous—or, at least, it might in the eyes of an adjudicator."

Adikor shook his head. "I can't see Sard being impressed by that argument."

"Ah, but Sard cannot hear the counterclaim; that's the law. You'd speak in front of a different adjudicator."

"Really? Maybe it *is* worth trying. But . . . but my goal isn't to prolong these proceedings. It's to get them over with, to get this rotting judicial scrutiny lifted so I can get back down to the lab."

"Oh, I agree you shouldn't really pursue a counterclaim. But the suggestion that you might could perhaps help you get your answer."

"Answer? About what?"

"About why Daklar is pursuing you like this."

"Do *you* know why?" asked Adikor.

Jasmel looked down. "I didn't, not until today, but . . ."

"But what?"

"It's not for me to say. If you're going to hear it at all, it will have to be directly from Daklar."

Chapter Thirty-six

Reuben, Louise, Ponter, and Mary sat around the table in Reuben's kitchen. Everyone but Louise was eating hamburgers; Louise was picking at a plate of salad.

Apparently, in Ponter's world, people ate with gloved hands. Ponter didn't like using cutlery, but the hamburger seemed a good compromise. He didn't eat the bun, but instead used it to manipulate the meat, constantly squeezing the patty forward and biting off the part that protruded from the disks of bread.

"So, Ponter," said Louise, making conversation, "do you live alone? Back in your world, I mean."

Ponter shook his head. "No. I lived with Adikor."

"Adikor," repeated Mary. "I thought he was the person you worked with?"

"Yes," said Ponter. "But he is also my partner."

"Your business partner, you mean," said Mary.

"Well, that too, I suppose. But he is my 'partner'; that is the word we use. We share a home."

"Ah," said Mary. "A roommate."

"Yes."

"You share household expenses and chores."

"Yes. And meals and a bed and . . ."

Mary was angry with herself for the way her heart fluttered. She knew lots of gay men; she was just used to them coming out of the closet, not popping through a transdimensional portal.

"You're gay!" said Louise. "How cool is that!"

"Actually, I was happier at home," said Ponter.

"No, no, no," said Louise. "Not happy. *Gay*. Homosexual." *Bleep*. "Having sexual relations with one's own gender: men who have sex with other men, or women who have sex with other women."

Ponter looked more confused than ever. "It is impossible to have sex with a member of the same gender. Sex is the act of potential procreation and it requires a male and a female."

"Well, all right, not sex as in sexual intercourse," said Louise. "Sex as in intimate contact, as in—you know—um, affectionate touching of . . . of the genitals."

"Oh," said Ponter. "Yes, Adikor and I did that."

"That's what we call being homosexual," supplied Reuben. "Having such contact only with members of your own gender."

"Only?" said Ponter, startled. "You mean exclusively? No, no, no. Adikor and I kept each other company when Two were separate, but when Two became One, we of course had—what did you call it, Lou?—'affectionate touching of the genitals' with our respective females . . . or, at least I did until Klast, my woman-mate, died."

"Ah," said Mary. "You're bisexual." *Bleep*. "You have genital contact with men and women."

"Yes."

"Is everyone like that in your world?" asked Louise,

stabbing some lettuce with her fork. "Bisexual?"

"Just about." Ponter blinked, getting it at last. "You mean it is different here?"

"Oh, yes," said Reuben. "Well, for most people, anyway. I mean, sure, there are some bisexual people, and lots and lots of gay—homosexual—people. But the vast majority are heterosexual. That means they have affectionate contact only with members of the opposite gender."

"How boring," said Ponter.

Louise actually giggled. Then, composing herself, she said, "So, do you have any children?"

"Two daughters," said Ponter, nodding. "Jasmel and Megameg."

"Lovely names," said Louise.

Ponter looked sad, obviously thinking of the fact that he'd likely never see them again.

Reuben clearly saw this, too, and sought to move the conversation to something less personal. "So, um, so what's this 'Two become One' you mentioned? What's that all about?"

"Well, on my world, males and females live mostly apart, so—"

"Binford!" exclaimed Mary.

"No, it is true," said Ponter.

"That wasn't a swear word," said Mary. "It's a man's name. Lewis Binford is an anthropologist who argues the same thing: that Neanderthal men and women lived largely separate lives on this Earth. He bases it on sites at Combe Grenal, in France."

"He is correct," said Ponter. "Women live in the Centers of our territories; males at the Rims. But once a month, we males come into the Center and spend four days with the females; we say that 'Two become One' during this time."

"*Par-tay!*" said Louise, grinning.

"Fascinating," said Mary.

"It is necessary. We do not produce food the way you do, so the population size must be kept in check."

Reuben frowned. "So this 'Two becoming One' business is for birth control?"

Ponter nodded. "In part. The High Gray Council—the governing body of elders—sets the dates on which we come together, and Two normally become One when the women are incapable of conceiving. But if it is time to produce a new generation, then the dates are changed, and we come together when the women are most fertile."

"Goodness," said Mary. "A whole planet on the rhythm method. The Pope would like you guys. But—but how can that work? I mean, surely your women don't all have their periods—undergo menstruation—at once?"

Ponter blinked. "Of course they do."

"But how could—oh, wait. I see." Mary smiled. "That nose of yours: it's very sensitive, isn't it?"

"I do not think of it as being so."

"But it is—compared to ours I mean. Compared to the noses we have."

"Well, your noses *are* very small," said Ponter. "They are, ah, rather disconcerting to look at. I keep thinking you will suffocate—although I have noticed many of you breathe through your mouths, presumably to avoid that."

"We've always assumed that Neanderthals evolved in response to Ice Age conditions," said Mary. "And our best guess was that your large noses allowed you to humidify frigid air before drawing it into your lungs."

"Our—the scientists who study ancient humans—believe the same thing," said Ponter.

"The climate has warmed up a great deal, though, since your big noses evolved," said Mary. "But you've retained that feature perhaps because it has the beneficial side effect of giving you a much better sense of smell than you would have had otherwise."

"Does it?" said Ponter. "I mean, I can smell all of you, and all the different foods in the kitchen, and the flowers out back, and whatever acrid thing Reuben and Lou have been burning downstairs, but—"

"Ponter," said Reuben, quickly, "we can't smell you at all."

"Really?"

"Yes. Oh, if I stuck my nose right into your armpit, I might smell something. But normally we humans can't smell each other."

"How do you find one another in the dark?"

"By voice," said Mary.

"Very strange," said Ponter.

"But you can do more than just detect a person's presence, can't you?" said Mary. "That time you looked at me. You could . . ." She swallowed but, well, Louise was another woman, and Reuben was a doctor. "You could tell I was having my period, couldn't you?"

"Yes."

Mary nodded. "Even women of Louise and my kind, if they live together long enough in the same house, can get their menstrual cycles synchronized—and we have lousy senses of smell. I guess it makes sense that whole cities of your women would be on the same cycle."

"It never occurred to me that it might be another way," said Ponter. "I thought it odd that you were menstruating but Lou was not."

Louise frowned but said nothing.

"Look," said Reuben, "does anybody want anything else? Ponter, another Coke?"

"Yes," said Ponter. "Thank you."

Reuben got up.

"You know that stuff's got caffeine in it?" said Mary. "It's addictive."

"Do not worry," said Ponter. "I am only drinking seven or eight cans a day."

Louise laughed and went back to eating her salad.

Mary took another bite of her hamburger, circles of onion crunching beneath her teeth. "Wait a minute," she said, once she'd swallowed. "That means your females don't have hidden ovulation."

"Well, it is hidden from *view*," Ponter said.

"Yes, but . . . well, you know, I used to team-teach a course with the Women's Studies department: The Biology of Sexual Power Relationships. We'd assumed that hidden ovulation was the key to females gaining constant protection and provisioning by males. You know: if you can't tell when your female is fertile, you better be attentive all the time, lest you be cuckolded."

Hak bleeped.

"Cuckolded," repeated Mary. "That's when a man is investing his energies providing for children that aren't biologically his. But with hidden ovulation—"

Ponter's laugh split the air; his massive chest and deep mouth gave him a deep, thunderous guffaw.

Mary and Louise looked at him, astonished. "What's so funny?" said Reuben, depositing another Coke in front of Ponter.

Ponter held up a hand; he was trying to stop laughing, but wasn't succeeding yet. Tears had appeared at the corners of his sunken eyes, and his normally pale skin was looking quite red.

Mary, still seated at the table, put her hands on her hips—but immediately became self-conscious of her body language; hands on hips increased one's apparent size, in order to intimidate. But Ponter was so much stouter and better muscled than any woman—or just about any man— that it was a ridiculous thing to be doing. Still, she demanded, "Well?"

"I am sorry," said Ponter, regaining his control. He used his long thumb to wipe the tears from his eyes. "It is just that sometimes your people do have ridiculous ideas." He smiled. "When you talk about hidden ovulation, you mean that human females do not have genital swelling when they are in heat, right?"

Mary nodded. "Chimps and bonobos do; so do gorillas and most other primates."

"But humans did not stop having such swelling in order to hide ovulation," said Ponter. "Genital swelling disappeared when it was no longer an effective signal. It disappeared when the climate got colder and humans started wearing clothing. That sort of visual display, based on engorging tissues with fluid, is energetically expensive; there was no value in maintaining it once we were covering our bodies with animal hides. But, at least for my people, ovulation was still obvious due to smell."

"You can smell ovulation, as well as menstruation?" asked Reuben.

"The . . . chemicals . . . associated with them, yes."

"Pheromones," supplied Reuben.

Mary nodded slowly. "And so," she said, as much to Ponter as to herself, "males could go off for weeks at a time without worrying about their females being impregnated by somebody else."

"That is right," said Ponter. "But there is more to it than that."

"Yes?" said Mary.

"We say now that the reason our male ancestors—I think you have the same metaphor—'headed for the hills' was because of the, ah, unpleasantness of females during Last Five."

"Last Five?" said Louise.

"The last five days of the month; the time leading up to the beginning of their periods."

"Oh," said Reuben. "PMS. Premenstrual syndrome."

"Yes," said Ponter. "But, of course, that is not the real reason." He shrugged a little. "My daughter Jasmel is studying pre-generation-one history; she explained it to me. What really happened was that men used to fight constantly over access to women. But, as Mare has noted, the only time access to women is evolutionarily important is during the part of each month when they might become pregnant. Since all women's cycles were synchronized, men got along much better for most of the month if they retreated from females, only to return as a group when it was reproductively important that they do so. It was not female unpleasantness that led to the split; it was male violence."

Mary nodded. It had been years since she'd co-taught that course on Sexual Power Relationships, but it seemed downright typical: men causing the problem and blaming women for it. Mary doubted she'd ever meet a female from Ponter's world, but, at that moment, she felt real affinity with her Neanderthal sisters.

Chapter Thirty-seven

"Healthy day, Daklar," said Jasmel, coming through the door to the house. Although Jasmel Ket and Daklar Bolbay still shared a home, they had not spoken much since the *dooslarm basadlarm*.

"Healthy day," repeated Bolbay, without warmth. "If you—" Her nostrils dilated. "You're not alone."

Adikor came through the door as well. "Healthy day," he said.

Bolbay looked at Jasmel. "More treachery, child?"

"It's not treachery," Jasmel said. "It's concern—for you, and for my father."

"What do you want of me?" said Bolbay, looking through narrowed eyes at Adikor.

"The truth," he said. "Just the truth."

"About what?"

"About *you*. About why you are pursuing me."

"I'm not the one under investigation," said Bolbay.

"No," agreed Adikor. "Not yet. But that may change."

"What are you talking about?"

"I am prepared to have you served with documents of my own," said Adikor.

"On what basis?"

"On the basis that you are unlawfully interfering with my life."

"That's ridiculous."

"Is it?" Adikor shrugged. "We'll let an adjudicator decide that."

"It's a transparent attempt to stall the process that will lead to your sterilization," said Bolbay. "Anyone can see that."

"If it is—if it is *that* transparent, that flimsy—then an adjudicator will dismiss the matter . . . but not before I have had a chance to question you."

"Question me? About what?"

"About your motive. About why you are doing this to me."

Bolbay looked at Jasmel. "This was your idea, wasn't it?"

"It was also," said Jasmel, "my idea that we come here first, before Adikor proceeded with the accusation. This is a family matter: you, Daklar, were my mother's woman-mate, and Adikor here is my father's man-mate. You have been through a lot, Daklar—we all have—with the loss of my mother."

"This has nothing to do with Klast!" snapped Bolbay. "*Nothing.*" She looked at Adikor. "It's about *him.*"

"Why?" said Adikor. "Why is it about me?"

Bolbay shook her head again. "We don't have anything to talk about."

"Yes, we do," said Adikor. "And you will answer my questions here, or you will answer them in front of an adjudicator. But you *will* answer them."

"You're bluffing," said Bolbay.

Adikor raised his left arm, with his wrist facing toward her. "Is your name Daklar Bolbay, and do you reside here in Saldak Center?"

"I won't accept documents from you."

"You're just delaying the inevitable," said Adikor. "I will get a judicial server—who can upload to your implant whether you pull out the control bud or not." A pause. "I say again, Are you Daklar Bolbay, and do you reside here in Saldak Center?"

"You would really do this?" said Bolbay. "You would really drag me before an adjudicator?"

"As you have dragged me," said Adikor.

"Please," said Jasmel. "Just tell him. It's better this way—better for you."

Adikor crossed his arms in front of his chest. "Well?"

"I've nothing to say," Bolbay replied.

Jasmel let out a great, long sigh. "Ask her," she said softly when it was done, "about *her* man-mate."

"You don't know anything about that," snapped Bolbay.

"Don't I?" said Jasmel. "How did you learn that Adikor was the one who had hit my father?"

Bolbay said nothing.

"Obviously, Klast told you," said Jasmel.

"Klast was my woman-mate," said Bolbay, defiantly. "She didn't keep secrets from me."

"And she was my mother," said Jasmel. "Neither did she keep them from me."

"But . . . she . . . I . . ." Bolbay trailed off.

"Tell me about your man-mate," said Adikor. "I—I don't think I've ever met him, have I?"

Bolbay shook her head slowly. "No. He's been gone for a long time; we separated long ago."

"And that's why you don't have children of your own?" asked Adikor, gently.

"You're so *smug*," replied Bolbay. "You think it's that simple? I couldn't keep a mate, and so I never reproduced? Is *that* what you think?"

"I don't think anything," said Adikor.

"I would have been a good mother," said Bolbay, perhaps as much to herself as to Adikor. "Ask Jasmel. Ask Megameg. Since Klast died, I've looked after them *wonderfully*. Isn't that so, Jasmel? Isn't that so?"

Jasmel nodded. "But you're a 145, just like Ponter and Klast. Just like Adikor. You might still be able to have a child of your own. The dates for Two becoming One will be shifted again next year; you could . . ."

Adikor's eyebrow rolled up. "It would be your last chance, wouldn't it? You'll be 520 months old—forty years—next year, just like me. You might have a child then, as part of generation 149, but certainly not ten years later, when generation 150 will be born."

There was a sneer in Bolbay's voice. "Did you need your fancy quantum computer to figure that out?"

"And Ponter," said Adikor, nodding slowly, "Ponter was without a woman-mate. You and he had loved the same woman, after all, and you were already *tabant* for his two children, so you thought . . ."

"You and my father?" said Jasmel. She didn't sound shocked by the notion, merely surprised.

"And why not?" said Bolbay, defiantly. "I'd known him almost as long as you had, Adikor, and he and I had always gotten along."

"But now he's gone, too," said Adikor. "That *was* my

first thought, you know: that you were simply inconsolable over the loss of him, and so were snapping teeth at me. But you must see, Daklar, that you're wrong to be doing that. I loved Ponter, and certainly wouldn't have interfered with his choice of a new woman-mate, so—"

"That has *nothing* to do with it," said Bolbay, shaking her head. "Nothing."

"Then why do you hate me so?"

"I don't hate you because of what happened to Ponter," she said.

"But you *do* hate me."

Bolbay was silent. Jasmel was looking at the floor.

"Why?" said Adikor. "I've never done anything to you."

"But you hit Ponter," snapped Bolbay.

"Ages ago. And he forgave me."

"And so you got to stay whole," she said. "You got to have a child of your own. You *got away* with it."

"With what?"

"With your crime! With trying to kill Ponter!"

"I *wasn't* trying to kill him."

"You were violent, a monster. You *should* have been sterilized. But my Pelbon . . ."

"Who is Pelbon?" said Adikor.

Bolbay fell silent again.

"Her man-mate," said Jasmel, softly.

"What happened to Pelbon?" asked Adikor.

"You don't know what it's like," said Bolbay, looking away. "You have no idea. You wake up one morning to find two enforcers waiting for you, and they take your man-mate away, and—"

"And what?" said Adikor.

"And they castrate him," said Bolbay.

"Why?" asked Adikor. "What did he do?"

"He didn't do *anything*," said Bolbay. "He didn't do a single thing."

"Then why . . ." started Adikor. But then it hit him. "Oh. One of his relatives . . ."

Bolbay nodded but didn't meet Adikor's eyes. "His brother had assaulted someone, and so his brother was ordered sterilized along with—"

"Along with everyone who shared fifty percent of his genetic material," finished Adikor.

"He didn't do *anything*, my Pelbon," said Bolbay. "He didn't do anything to anyone, and he was punished. *I* was punished. But you! You almost killed a man, and you got away with it! They should have castrated you, not my poor Pelbon!"

"Daklar," said Adikor. "I'm sorry. I'm so sorry . . ."

"Get out," said Bolbay firmly. "Just leave me alone."

"I—"

"*Get out!*"

Chapter Thirty-eight

Ponter finished his hamburger, then looked at Louise, Reuben, and Mary in turn. "I do not wish to complain," he said, "but I am getting tired of this—this *cow*, do you call it? Is there a chance we might ask the people outside to bring us something else for tonight?"

"Like what?" asked Reuben.

"Oh, anything," said Ponter. "Maybe some mammoth steaks."

"*What?*" said Reuben.

"*Mammoth?*" said Mary, stunned.

"Is Hak incorrectly rendering what I am saying?" asked Ponter. "Mammoth. You know—a hairy elephant of northern climes."

"Yes, yes, yes," said Mary. "We *know* what a mammoth is, but . . ."

"But what?" asked Ponter, eyebrow lifted.

"But, well, I mean . . . mammoths are extinct," said Mary.

"Extinct?" repeated Ponter, surprised. "Come to think of it, I have not seen any here, but, well, I assumed they did not like coming close to this massive city."

"No, no, they're extinct," said Louise. "All over the

world. They've been extinct for thousands of years."

"Why?" asked Ponter. "Was it illness?"

Everyone fell silent. Mary slowly exhaled the air in her lungs, trying to decide how to present this. "No, that's not why," she said, at last. "Umm, you see, we—our kind, our ancestors—we hunted mammoths to extinction."

Ponter's eyes went wide. "You did what?"

Mary felt nauseous; she hated having her version of humanity come up so short. "We killed them for food, and, well, we kept on killing them until there were none left."

"Oh," said Ponter, softly. He looked out the window, at the large backyard to Reuben's house. "I am fond of mammoths," he said. "Not just their meat—which is delicious—but as animals, as part of the landscape. There is a small herd of them that lives near my home. I enjoy seeing them."

"We have their skeletons," said Mary, "and their tusks, and every once in a while a frozen one is found in Siberia, but . . ."

"All of them," said Ponter, shaking his head back and forth slowly, sadly. "You killed all of them . . ."

Mary felt like protesting, "Not me personally," but that would be disingenuous; the blood of the mammoths was indeed on her house. Still, she needed to make some defense, feeble though it was: "It happened a long time ago."

Ponter looked queasy. "I am almost afraid to ask," said Ponter, "but there are other large animals I am used to seeing in this part of the world on my version of Earth. Again, I had assumed they were just avoiding this city of yours, but . . ."

Reuben shook his shaven head. "No, that's not it."

Mary closed her eyes briefly. "I'm sorry, Ponter. We wiped out just about all the megafauna—here, and in Europe . . . and in Australia"—she felt a knot in her stomach as the litany grew—"and in New Zealand, and in South America. The only continent that has many really big animals left is Africa, and most of those are endangered."

Bleep.

"On the verge of extinction," said Louise.

Ponter's tone was one of betrayal. "But you said this had all happened long ago."

Mary looked down at her empty plate. "We stopped killing mammoths long ago, because, well, we ran out of mammoths to kill. And we stopped killing Irish elk, and the big cats that used to populate North America, and woolly rhinoceroses, and all the others, because there were none left to kill."

"To kill every member of a species . . ." said Ponter. He shook his massive head slowly back and forth.

"We've learned better," Mary said. "We now have programs to protect endangered species, and we've had some real successes. The whooping crane was once almost gone; so was the bald eagle. And the buffalo. They've all come back."

Ponter's voice was cold. "Because you stopped hunting them to extremes."

Mary thought about protesting that it wasn't all the result of hunting; much of it had to do with the destruction by humans of the natural habitats of these creatures—but somehow that didn't seem any better.

"What . . . what other species are still endangered?" asked Ponter.

Mary shrugged a little. "Lots of kinds of birds. Giant tortoises. Panda bears. Sperm whales. Chim . . ."

"Chim?" said Ponter. "What are—?" He tilted his head, perhaps listening to Hak providing its best guess at the word Mary had started to say. "Oh, no. No. *Chimpanzees?* But . . . but these are our *cousins.* You hunt our cousins?"

Mary felt all of two feet tall. How could she tell him that chimps were killed for food, that gorillas were murdered so their hands could be made into exotic ashtrays?

"They are *invaluable,*" continued Ponter. "Surely you, as a geneticist, must know that. They are the only close living relatives we have; we can learn much about ourselves by studying them in the wild, by examining their DNA."

"I know," said Mary, softly. "I know."

Ponter looked at Reuben, then at Louise, and then at Mary, sizing them up, it seemed, as if he were seeing them—*really* seeing them—for the first time.

"You kill with abandon," he said. "You kill entire species. You even kill other primates." He paused and looked from face to face again, as if giving them a chance to forestall what he was about to say, to come up with a logical explanation, a mitigating factor. But Mary said nothing, and neither did the other two, and so Ponter went on. "And, on this world, my kind is extinct."

"Yes," said Mary, very softly. She knew what had happened. Although not every paleoanthropologist agreed, many shared her view that between 40,000 and 27,000 years ago, *Homo sapiens*—anatomically modern humans—completed the first of what would be many deliberate or inadvertent genocides, wiping the planet free of the only other extant member of the same genus, a separate, more gentle species that perhaps had been better entitled to the double meaning of the word humanity.

"Did you kill us?" asked Ponter.

"That's a much-debated question," said Mary. "Not everyone agrees on the answer."

"What do *you* think happened?" asked Ponter, golden eyes locked on Mary's own.

Mary took a deep breath. "I—yes, yes, that's what I think happened."

"You wiped us out," said Ponter, his own tone, and Hak's rendition of it, clearly being controlled with difficulty.

Mary nodded. "I'm sorry," she said. "Really, I am. It happened long ago. We were savages then. We—"

Just then, the phone rang. Reuben, looking relieved at the interruption, jumped up from the table and lifted a handset. "Hello?" he said.

Mary looked up as Reuben's voice became more excited. "But that's terrific!" continued the doctor. "That's wonderful! Yes, no—yes, yes, that's fine. Thank you! Right. Bye."

"Well?" said Louise.

Reuben was clearly suppressing a grin. "Ponter has distemper," he said, replacing the phone's handset.

"Distemper?" repeated Mary. "But humans don't get distemper."

"That's right," said Reuben. "We're naturally immune. But Ponter isn't, because his kind hasn't lived with our domesticated animals for generations. To be precise, he's got the horse version of distemper; vets call it *strangles* when it happens to a young horse. It's caused by a bacterium, *Streptococcus equii*. Fortunately, penicillin is the usual treatment given to horses, and that's one of the antibiotics I've been giving Ponter. He should be fine."

"So we don't have to worry about getting sick?" asked Louise.

"Not only that," said Reuben, smiling broadly now, "but they're lifting the quarantine! Assuming the final set of cultures—due later tonight—comes back negative, we can leave here tomorrow morning!"

Louise clapped her hands together. Mary was delighted, too. She looked over at Ponter, but he had his head bowed, presumably still thinking about the extinction of his kind on this world.

Mary reached over and touched his arm. "Hey, Ponter," she said gently. "Isn't that great news? Tomorrow, you'll get to go out and see our world!"

Ponter lifted his head slowly and looked at Mary. She was still learning to read the subtleties of his expressions, but the words, "Do I have to?" seemed to fit with his widened eyes and slightly open mouth.

But finally he just nodded, as if in resignation.

Chapter Thirty-nine

Ponter spent most of the evening alone, just staring out the kitchen window at Reuben's large backyard, a sad look on his large face.

Louise and Mary were both sitting in the living room. Mary was sorry she'd left her current book down in Toronto. She'd been in the middle of Scott Turow's latest and really wanted to get back to it, but had to content herself with leafing through the current *Time*. President Bush was on the cover this week; Mary thought it possible that Ponter might be on the cover of the next issue. She preferred *The Economist* herself, but Reuben didn't subscribe to it. Still, Mary did always enjoy Richard Corliss's film reviews, even if she had no one to go to the movies with these days.

Louise, in the adjacent armchair, was writing a letter—in French, Mary had noted—in longhand on a yellow pad. Louise wore track shorts and an INXS T-shirt, her long legs tucked sideways beneath her body.

Reuben came into the room and crouched down between the two women, addressing them both in hushed tones. "I'm concerned about our boy Ponter," he said.

Louise set down her yellow pad. Mary closed her magazine. "Me, too," said Mary. "He didn't seem to take that news about the extinction of his kind very well."

"No, he didn't," said Reuben. "And he's been under a lot of stress, which is just going to get worse tomorrow. The media will be all over him, not to mention government officials, religious kooks, and more."

Louise nodded. "I suppose that's true."

"What can we do about it?" asked Mary.

Reuben frowned for a time, as if thinking about how to express something. Finally, he said, "There aren't many people of my color here in Sudbury. Things are better down in Toronto, I'm told, but even there, black men get hassled by the police from time to time. 'What are you doing here?' 'Is this your car?' 'Can we see some ID?'" Reuben shook his head. "You learn something going through that. You learn you've got rights. Ponter isn't a criminal, and he isn't a threat to anyone. He's not at a border station, so no one can legally demand that he prove he should be allowed to be in Canada. The government may *want* to control him, the police may *want* to keep him under surveillance—but that doesn't matter. Ponter's got rights."

"I certainly agree with that," said Mary.

"Either of you ever been to Japan?" asked Reuben.

Mary shook her head. So did Louise.

"It's a wonderful country, but there're almost no non-Japanese there," said Reuben. "You can go all day without seeing a white face, let alone a black one—I saw precisely two other blacks during the entire week I was there. But I remember walking through downtown Tokyo one day: I must have passed 10,000 people that morning, and they were all Japanese. Then, as I'm walking along, I see this white guy coming toward me. And he smiles at me—he doesn't know me from Adam, but he sees that I'm a fellow Westerner. And he gives me this smile, like to say I'm so glad to see a brother—a brother! And I suddenly realize that I'm smiling at him, too, and thinking the same thing. I've never forgotten that moment." He looked at Louise, then at Mary. "Well, old Ponter can search all he wants, all over the world, and he's not going to see a single face that he recognizes as being like him. That white guy and I— and all those Japanese and me—we have much more in common than Ponter does with any of the six billion people on this globe."

Mary glanced into the kitchen at Ponter, who was still staring out the window, a balled hand under the middle of his long jaw, propping it up. "What can we do about it?" she asked.

"He's been almost a prisoner since he arrived," said Reuben, "first in the hospital, then here, quarantined. I'm sure he needs time to think, to get some mental equilibrium." He paused. "Gillian Ricci tipped me off in an e-mail. Apparently the same thought I had earlier has now occurred to the brass—or should I say the nickel?—at Inco. They want to question Ponter at length about any other mining sites in his world that he might know about. I'm sure he'll be glad to help, but he still needs more time to adjust."

"I agree," said Mary. "But how can we make sure he gets it?"

"They're lifting the quarantine tomorrow morning, right?" said Reuben. "Well, Gillian says I can hold another press conference here at 10:00 A.M. Of course, the media will be expecting Ponter to be there—so I think we should get him out before then."

"How?" asked Louise. "The RCMP has the place surrounded—supposedly to keep us safe from people who might try to break in, but probably just as much to keep an eye on Ponter."

Reuben nodded. "One of us should take him away, out into the country. I'm his doctor; that's what I prescribe. Rest and relaxation. And that's what I'll tell anyone who asks—that he's on a medical rest leave, ordered by me. We can probably only get away with that for a day or so before suits from Ottawa descend on us, but I really do think Ponter needs it."

"I'll do it," said Mary, surprising herself. "I'll take him away."

Reuben looked at Louise to see if she wanted to stake a claim herself, but she simply nodded.

"If we tell the media that the press conference will be at ten, they'll start showing up at nine," said Reuben. "But if you and Ponter head out, through my backyard, at, say, eight, you'll beat them all. There's a fence at the back, behind all those trees, but you should have no trouble hopping it. Just make sure no one sees you go."

"And then what?" said Mary. "We just go walkabout?"

"You'll need a car," said Louise.

"Well, mine's back at the Creighton Mine," said Mary. "But I can't take yours or Reuben's. The cops will surely stop us if we try to drive off. As Reuben said, we've got to sneak away."

"No problem," said Louise. "I can have a friend meet you tomorrow morning on whatever country road is behind Reuben's place here. He can drive you to the mine, and you can pick up your car there."

Mary blinked. "Really?"

Louise shrugged a little. "Sure."

"I—I don't know this area at all," said Mary. "We'll need some maps."

"Oooh!" said Louise. "I know exactly who to call, then—Garth. He's got one of those Handspring Visor thingies with a GPS module. It'll give you directions to any place, and keep you from getting lost."

"And he'd loan that to me?" said Mary, incredulous. "Aren't those things expensive?"

"Well—it'd really be me he'd be doing the favor for," said Louise. "Here, let me call him and set everything up." She rose to her feet and headed upstairs. Mary watched her go, fascinated and stunned. She wondered what it was like to be so beautiful that you could ask men to do just about anything and know that they'd almost certainly say yes.

Ponter, she realized, wasn't the only one feeling out of place.

Jasmel and Adikor took a travel cube back out to the Rim, back to the house Adikor had shared with Ponter. They didn't say much to each other on the trip back, partly, of course, because Adikor was lost in thought about Daklar Bolbay's revelation, and partly because neither he nor Jas-

mel liked the idea that someone at the alibi-archive pavilion was monitoring every word they said and everything
they did.

Still, they had a vexing problem. Adikor *had* to get back
down to his subterranean lab; whatever minuscule chance
there was that Ponter might be rescued—or, thought Adikor, although he hadn't shared this thought with Jasmel,
that at least his drowned body might be recovered, exon-
erating Adikor—depended on him getting down there.
But how to do that? He looked at his Companion, on the
inside of his left wrist. He could gouge it out, he supposed—being careful not to clip his radial artery as he did
so. But not only did the Companion rely on Adikor's own
body for its power, it also transmitted his vital signs—and
it wouldn't be able to do that if it were separated from
him. Nor could he do a quick transplant onto Jasmel or
somebody else; the implant was keyed to Adikor's particular biometrics.

The travel cube let them off at the house, and Adikor
and Jasmel went inside. Jasmel wandered into the kitchen
to find Pabo something to eat, and Adikor sat down, staring across the room at the empty chair that had been Ponter's favorite spot for reading.

Getting around the judicial scrutiny was a problem—a
problem, Adikor realized, in science. There *must* be a way
to circumvent it, a way to fool his Companion—and whoever was monitoring its output.

Adikor knew the life story of Lonwis Trob, the creator
of the Companion technology; he'd studied his many in-
ventions at the Academy. But that had been long ago, and
he remembered few details. Of course, he could simply *ask*

his Companion for the facts he needed; it would access the required information and display it on its little screen or any wall monitor or datapad Adikor selected. But such a request would doubtless catch the attention of the person watching over him.

Adikor felt himself becoming angry, muscles tensing, heart rate increasing, breathing growing deeper. He thought about trying to mask it, but no—he'd let the person who was watching him know how upset they were making him.

As clever as Lonwis Trob had been, there had to be a way to accomplish what he wanted—what he *needed*—to do. And what precisely was that? Define your problem exactly; that was what they'd taught him all those months ago at the Academy. Precisely what needs to be done?

No, he didn't have to defeat the Companions—which was a good thing, because he hadn't come up with a single workable idea for doing so. Indeed, it wasn't *all* the Companions he needed to disable—in fact, to do so would be unconscionable; the implants ensured the safety of everyone. He only needed to disable his own Companion, but . . .

But no, that wasn't right, either. Disabling it would do no good; Gaskdol Dut and the other enforcers might not be able to track him if the Companion stopped working, but they'd immediately know by its lack of transmissions that something was afoot. And it wouldn't take a Lonwis to figure out that Adikor would be heading for the mine, since he'd already been thwarted once before in trying to go there.

No, no, the real problem wasn't that his Companion

was working. Rather, it was that someone was *watching* the transmissions from his Companion. That's what needed to stop—and not just for a moment or two, but for several daytenths, and—

And suddenly it came to him: the perfect answer.

But he couldn't arrange it himself; it would only work if the enforcers had no idea that Adikor was involved. Jasmel could perhaps take care of doing it, though; Adikor had to believe that it really was only his Companion being monitored. Anything beyond that would be outrageous. But how to communicate privately to Jasmel?

He rose and headed into the kitchen. "Come on, Jasmel," he said. "Let's take Pabo for a walk."

Jasmel's expression conveyed that this should be the least of their priorities just now, but she got up and went with Adikor to the back door. Pabo needed no prodding to join them; she bounded after Jasmel.

They walked out onto the deck, out into the summer heat, cicadas making their shrill whine. The humidity was high. Adikor stepped off the deck, and Jasmel followed. Pabo ran ahead, barking loudly. After a few hundred paces, they came to the brook that ran behind the house. The sound of fast-running water drowned out the insect noises. There was a large boulder—one of countless glacial erratics that dotted the landscape—in the middle of the brook. Adikor stepped on smaller rocks to get over to it, and motioned for Jasmel to follow, which she did. Pabo was now running up the riverbank.

When Jasmel reached the boulder, Adikor patted the mossy spot next to where he was sitting, indicating that she should join him. She did so, and he leaned toward her and started whispering, his words all but inaudible against the water crashing around the boulder. There was no way, he felt sure, that the Companion could pick up what he was saying. And, as he told Jasmel his plan, he saw a mischievous grin grow on her face.

Ponter sat on the couch in Reuben's office. Everyone else had gone to bed—although Reuben and Louise, next door, clearly weren't sleeping.

Ponter was sad. The sounds and smells they were making reminded him of himself and Klast, of Two becoming One, of everything he'd lost before coming to this Earth, and all the rest of it he'd lost since.

He'd had the TV on, watching a channel devoted to this thing called *religion*. There seemed to be many variations, but all of them proposed a *God*—that outlandish notion again—and a universe that was of a finite, and often ridiculously young, age, plus some sort of after-death existence for the . . . there was no Neanderthal word for it, but "soul" had been the term Mare had used. It turned out the symbol Mare wore around her neck was a sign of the particular religion she subscribed to, and the fabric that had been wrapped around Dr. Singh's head was a sign of his somewhat different religion.

Ponter had turned the sound on the TV way down—it had been simple enough to find the appropriate control, although he doubted anything he might do would disturb the couple in the adjacent room.

"How are you feeling?" asked Klast's voice, and Ponter felt his heart leaping.

Klast!

Darling Klast, contacting him from . . .

From an *afterlife!*

But no.

No, of course it wasn't.

It was just Hak talking to him. Ponter was presumably stuck now with Hak speaking forevermore with Klast's voice, if he wanted anything other than that droning default male persona the device had come preprogrammed with; certainly there was no way to access the equipment needed to reprogram the implant.

Ponter let out a long sigh, then answered Hak's question. "I'm sad."

"But are you adjusting? You were quite shaky when we first got here."

Ponter shrugged a bit. "I don't know. I'm still confused and disoriented, but . . ."

Ponter could almost imagine Hak nodding sympathetically somewhere. "It will take time," said the Companion, still in Klast's voice.

"I know," said Ponter. "I know. But I *have* to get used to it, don't I? It looks like I—like *we*—are going to spend the rest of our lives here, doesn't it?"

"I'm afraid so," said Hak gently.

Ponter was quiet for a while, and Hak let him be so. Finally, Ponter said, "I guess I'd better face facts. I better start planning for a life here."

Chapter Forty

NEWS SEARCH

Keyword(s): *Neanderthal*

Opposition MP Marissa Crothers charged today in the House of Commons that the clearly fake Neanderthal was a flimsy attempt by the governing Liberal party to cover up the abject failure of the 73-million-dollar Sudbury Neutrino Observatory project . . .

"Stop hogging the caveman!" That was the sentiment on a placard worn by one American protester during a large demonstration outside the Canadian embassy in Washington today. "Share Ponter with the World!" said another . . .

Invitations sent to Ponter Boddit for all-expense-paid visits received c/o the *Sudbury Star*: Disneyland; the Anchor Bar and Grill, home of the original chicken wing, in Buffalo, New York; Buckingham Palace; the Kennedy Space Center; Science North; the UFO museum in Roswell, New Mexico; Toronto's Zanzibar Tavern strip club; Microsoft headquarters; next year's World Science Fiction Convention; The Neanderthal Museum in Mettmann, Germany; Yankee Stadium. Also submitted: offers of meetings with the French and Mexican presidents; the Japanese prime minister and royal family; the Pope; the Dalai Lama; Nelson Mandela; Stephen Hawking, and Anna Nicole Smith.

Question: How many Neanderthals does it take to change a light bulb? Answer: All of them.

. . . and so this columnist urges that the Creighton Mine be filled in, to prevent an army of Neanderthals invading our world via the gateway in its bowels. The last time our kind did battle with them, we won. This time, the outcome could be quite different . . .

Preliminary call for papers: Memetics and the epistemological disjuncture between *H. neanderthalensis* and *H. sapiens* . . .

A spokeswoman for the Centers for Disease Control and Prevention in Atlanta, Georgia, today praised the Canadian government's rapid response to the arrival of a potential plague vector. "We think they acted properly," said Dr. Ramona Keitel. "However, we've found no pathogens in the specimens they've sent us for analysis . . ."

Everything came off flawlessly. Ponter and Mary left Reuben's at just after 8:00 A.M., making it through the trees at the back of his property and over the fence without being seen; Ponter's sense of smell helped them avoid the RCMP officer patrolling the back area on foot.

Louise's friend was indeed waiting for them. Garth turned out to be a handsome, well-muscled Native Canadian about twenty-five years old. He was extremely polite, calling Mary—to her chagrin—"ma'am," and Ponter "sir." He drove them the short distance to the Creighton Mine. The security guards recognized Mary—and Ponter, too, of course—and let them in. There, Mary and Ponter switched into her rented red Neon, which had acquired a patina of dust and bird droppings while sitting in the parking lot.

Mary knew where to head. The night before, she had said to Ponter, "Is there anywhere in particular you'd like to go tomorrow?"

Ponter had nodded. "Home," he'd said. "Take me home."

Mary had felt so very sad for him. "Ponter, I would if

I could, but there's no way. You know that; we don't have the technology."

"No, no," Ponter had said. "I don't mean my home in my world. I mean my home in *this* world: the place on this version of Earth that corresponds to where my house is."

Mary had blinked. She'd never even thought of doing that. "Um, yeah. Sure. If you'd like to see it. But how will we find it? I mean, what landmarks will you recognize?"

"If you can show me a detailed map of this area, I can find the spot, and then we can go there."

Reuben's password had gotten them into a private Inco website containing geological maps of the entire Sudbury basin. Ponter had no trouble recognizing the contours of the land and finding the spot he wanted, about twenty kilometers from Reuben's house.

Then Mary drove Ponter as close as she could get to the place he'd indicated. Most of the land surrounding the city of Sudbury was covered with Canadian shield outcrops, forest, and low brush. It took them hours to hike through it all, and, although Mary wasn't much of an athlete—she played an occasional mediocre game of tennis—she actually enjoyed the exercise, at least for a while, after having been cooped up for so long at Reuben's place.

Finally, they came over a ridge, and Ponter let out a delighted yelp. "There!" he said. "Right there! That is where my house was—I mean, where my house *is*."

Mary looked around, taking in the location: on one side, there were large aspens mixed in with thin birch trees, covered with papery white bark; on the other, a lake. Mallard ducks were floating on the lake, and a black squirrel scampered across the ground. Running into the lake was a babbling brook.

"It's beautiful," said Mary.

"Yes," said Ponter, excitedly. "Of course, the vegetation is completely different on my Earth. I mean, the plants are mostly of the same types, but the specific places where they are growing are not the same. But the rock outcrops are very similar—and that boulder in the brook! How I know that boulder! I have often sat atop it reading."

Ponter had run a short distance away from Mary. "Here—right here!—is where our back door is. And over here—this is our eating room." He ran some more. "And the bedroom is right here, right beneath my feet." He made a sweeping motion with his arm. "That is the view we have from the bedroom."

Mary followed his gaze. "And you can see mammoths out there in your world?"

"Oh, yes. And deer. And elk."

Mary was wearing a loose-fitting top and lightweight slacks. "Didn't the mammoths overheat in the summer, what with all that fur?"

"They shed most of their fur in summer," Ponter said, coming over to stand nearer to her. He closed his eyes. "The sounds," he said wistfully. "The rustle of the leaves, the buzz of insects, the brook, and—there!—you hear it? The call of a loon." He shook his head slightly in wonder. "It sounds the same." He opened his eyes, and Mary could see that his golden irises were surrounded now by pink. "So close," he said, his voice trembling a bit. "So very close. If only I could—" He shut his eyes again, hard, and his whole body jerked slightly, as if he were trying by an effort of will to cross the timelines.

Mary felt her heart breaking. It must be awful, she

thought, to be torn from your own world and dumped somewhere else—somewhere so similar, yet so alien. She lifted her hand, not quite sure what she intended to do. He turned to her, and she couldn't say, she didn't know, she wasn't sure which of them had moved first toward the other, but suddenly she had her arms wrapped around his broad torso, and his head was resting against her shoulder, and his, body was shuddering up and down, and he cried and cried and cried, while Mary stroked his long, blond hair.

Mary tried to remember the last time she'd seen a man cry. It had been Colm, she supposed—not over any of the problems with their marriage; no, those had been borne in stony silence. But when Colm's mother had died. Even then, he'd tried to put on a brave face, letting only a few tears trickle out. But Ponter was crying now without shame, crying for the world he'd lost, the lover he'd lost, the children he'd lost, and Mary let him cry until he was good and ready to stop.

When he did, he looked up at her, and opened his mouth. She'd expected Hak to translate his words as, "I am sorry"—isn't that what a man is supposed to say after crying, after letting his guard down, after wallowing in emotion? But no, that's not what came forth. Ponter simply said, "Thank you." Mary smiled warmly at him, and he smiled back.

Jasmel Ket started her day by heading off to find Lurt, Adikor's woman.

Not surprisingly, Lurt was in her chemistry lab, hard at

work. "Healthy day," said Jasmel, coming through the square door.

"Jasmel? What are you doing here?"

"Adikor asked me to come by."

"Is he all right?"

"Oh, yes. He's fine. But he needs a favor."

"For him, anything," said Lurt.

Jasmel smiled. "I was hoping you would say that."

It had taken longer to hike from Mary's car to the location of Ponter's home than Mary had expected, and, of course, just as long to hike back. By the time they did reach her car, it was after 7:00 P.M.

They were both quite hungry after all that walking, and, as they drove along, Mary suggested they get something to eat. When they came to a little country inn, with a sign advertising that it served venison, Mary pulled over. "How does this look?" she asked.

"I am no adjudicator of such things," said Ponter. "What kind of food do they provide?"

"Venison."

Bleep. "What is that?"

"Deer."

"Deer!" exclaimed Ponter. "Yes, deer would be wonderful!"

"I've never had venison myself," Mary said.

"You will enjoy it," said Ponter.

The inn's dining room only had six tables, and no one else was eating just now. Mary and Ponter sat opposite each other, a white candle burning between them. The main course took almost an hour to arrive, but she, at least, enjoyed some buttered pumpernickel bread beforehand. Mary had wanted an appetizer Caesar salad, but she felt self-conscious enough about having garlic breath when eating with regular humans; she certainly didn't want to risk it with Ponter. Instead, she had the house salad, with a sun-dried-tomato vinaigrette. Ponter also had a house salad, and although he left behind the croutons, he seemed to enjoy everything else.

Mary had also ordered a glass of the house red, which turned out to be eminently potable. "May I try that?" Ponter asked when it arrived.

Mary was surprised. He'd declined when offered some of Louise's wine at dinner back at Reuben's house. "Sure," said Mary.

She handed him the glass, and he took a small sip, then winced. "It has a sharp flavor," he said.

Mary nodded. "You get to like it," she said.

Ponter handed the glass back to her. "Perhaps one would," he said. Mary slowly finished the wine, enjoying the rustic, charming inn—and the company of this gentle man.

The balding innkeeper obviously knew who Ponter was; his appearance, after all, was striking, and Ponter was speaking softly in his own language, so that Hak could translate his words. Finally, it clearly got to be too much for the man. "I'm sorry," he said, coming to their table, "but Mr. Ponter, could I have your autograph?"

Mary heard Hak bleep, and Ponter raised his eyebrow. "Autograph," said Mary. "That's your own name, written out. People collect such things from celebrities." Another bleep. "Celebrities," repeated Mary. "Famous people. That's what you are."

Ponter looked at the man, astonished. "I—I would be honored," he said at last.

The man handed Ponter a pen, then flipped over the little pad he used for taking orders, exposing its white cardboard back. He placed it on the table in front of Ponter.

"You usually write a few words in addition to your name," said Mary. " 'Best wishes,' or something like that."

The innkeeper nodded. "Yes, please."

Ponter shrugged, clearly stunned by it all, and then made a series of symbols in his own language. He handed the pad and the pen back to the man, who scurried away, delighted.

"You've made his day," Mary said after he disappeared.

"Made his day?" repeated Ponter, not getting the idiom.

"I mean, he will always remember today because of you."

"Ah," said Ponter, smiling at her over the candle. "And I will always remember this day because of you."

Chapter Forty-one

Assuming Lurt could pull it off, Adikor would have access to the quantum-computing lab tomorrow. But he needed to make some arrangements before then.

Saldak was a big town, but Adikor knew most of the scientists and engineers on its Rim, and a good fraction of those who lived in the Center. In particular, he'd become friends with one of the engineers who maintained the mining robots. Dern Kord was a fat and jolly man—there were those who said he let robots do too much of his work. But a robot was just what this job called for. Adikor set out to see Dern; now that it was evening, Dern should be home from work.

Dern's house was large and rambling; the tree that formed the bulk of its shape must have been a thousand months old, dating to the very beginnings of modern arboriculture.

"Healthy—well, healthy evening," said Adikor as he came up to Dern's home. Dern was seated out on his deck, reading something on an illuminated datapad. A thin mesh between the deck's floor and the awning above it kept out insects.

"Adikor!" said Dern. "Come in, come in—watch the

flap there; don't let the bugs follow. Will you have drink? Some meat?"

Adikor shook his head. "No, thank you."

"So, what brings you here?" asked Dern.

"How are your eyes?" asked Adikor. "Your vision?"

Dern flared his nostrils at the odd question. "Fine. I've got lenses, of course, but I don't need them for reading— at least not on this pad; I just choose larger symbols."

"Go get your lenses," said Adikor. "I have something I want to show you."

Dern looked puzzled, but headed into the house. A moment later, he emerged with a pair of lenses connected to a wide elasticized fabric band. He slipped the band over his head, bringing it down to nestle in the furrow behind his browridge. The lenses were on little hinges; he flipped them down over his eyes and looked at Adikor expectantly.

Adikor reached into the pouch attached to the left hip of his pant and pulled out the sheet of thin plastic he'd written on this afternoon. Adikor had made the symbols as small as he possibly could—he'd had to search for a stylus with a fine-enough point. Scanner resolution had improved since those images of Adikor hitting Ponter had been recorded, but there still was a limit to how much detail could be made out. Adikor had endured cramps in his right hand making ideograms smaller than anyone back at the archive building could possibly read.

"What's this?" said Dern, taking the sheet and peering at it. "Oh!" he exclaimed as he began reading. "Really! Do you think? Well, well . . . I can't let you have a new one, of course—not if there's a good chance you're going to lose

it. But I've got several old ones that are due to be decom-
missioned; one of those should fit the bill."

Adikor nodded. "Thank you."

"Now, where and when do you need this?"

Adikor was about to shush him, but for all his exuber-
ance, Dern was no idiot. He nodded after finding the information he was looking for on the sheet. "Yes, that's fine.
I'll be there, waiting for you."

After dinner, Ponter and Mary got into Mary's car and
started driving back toward Sudbury. "I enjoyed today,"
said Ponter. "I enjoyed getting out of the city. But I suppose
I should now see other places."

Mary smiled. "There's a whole wide world out there
waiting to meet you."

"I understand," said Ponter. "And I must accept my new
life as . . . a curiosity."

Mary opened her mouth to protest, but couldn't think
of anything to say. Ponter *was* a curiosity; in a crueler century, he'd have ended up as a circus freak. Finally, she just
let the comment pass, and said, "Our world has a lot of
variety. I mean, geographically it's no more varied than
yours, I'm sure, but we have many cultures, many kinds of
architecture, many ancient buildings."

"I understand that I must travel; that I must contribute," said Ponter. "I had thought to stay here, to stay near
Sudbury, in case, somehow, the portal reopened, but it has
been so many days now. I am sure Adikor has tried; he
must, therefore, have failed—the conditions must not be

reproducible." Mary could hear reluctant acceptance grow-ing behind his words. "Yes, I will go wherever I am ex-pected to go; I will go far from here."

By then they were well away from the lights of the inn and the small village it had been part of. Mary looked out her side window, noticing the sky.

"My God," she said.

"What?" said Ponter.

"Look at all those stars! I've never seen so many!" Mary pulled the car over to the side of the country road, getting it well up on the shoulder, out of the way of any traffic that might come along. "I've got to have a look." She got out of her car, and Ponter did the same. "It's gorgeous," said Mary, bending her neck backward and looking up.

"I always enjoy the night sky," said Ponter.

"I never get to see it like this," said Mary. "Not in To-ronto." She snorted. "I live on a street called Observatory Lane, but you're lucky if you can see a few dozen stars on even the darkest winter night."

"We do not light up the outside world at night," said Ponter.

Mary shook her head in wonder, imagining not need-ing to have streetlights, not needing to protect yourself from your own kind. But suddenly her heart jumped. "There's something in the bush," she said softly.

She couldn't really see Ponter as anything more than a vague outline, but she could hear him inhale deeply. "Just a raccoon," he said. "Nothing to worry about."

Mary relaxed and tipped her head up to look at the stars some more. Her neck creaked a bit as she did so; it wasn't a comfortable posture. But then a memory came back to her from her teenage years. She stepped over to the Neon's front, and scooted her rear up onto the hood, then worked her way back until she was leaning comfortably against the windshield on the driver's side. She patted the hood next to her and said, "Here, Ponter. Have a seat."

Ponter moved in the dark and made his way up onto the hood as well, the metal groaning as it took his weight. He leaned back against the glass next to Mary.

"We used to do this when I was a kid," Mary said. "When my father took us camping."

"It *is* a great way to look at the sky," said Ponter.

"Isn't it, though?" said Mary. She let out a long contented sigh. "Look at the Milky Way! I've never seen it like that!"

"Milky Way?" said Ponter. "Oh, I see, yes. We call it the Night River."

"It's lovely," said Mary. She looked to her right. Ursa Major sprawled across the sky above the trees.

Ponter turned his head as well. "That pattern there," he said. "What do you call it?"

"The Big Dipper," said Mary. "Well, at least that part— those seven bright stars. That's what we call it here in North America. The Brits call it 'The Plow.' "

Bleep.

"A farming implement."

Ponter laughed. "I should have known. We call it the Head of the Mammoth. See? It is a profile. That is his trunk arching out from the block-shaped head."

"Oh, yeah—I see it. What about that one there? The zigzag shape?"

"We call it the Cracked Ice," said Ponter.

"Yeah. I can see that. We call it Cassiopeia; that's the name of an ancient queen. The shape is supposed to represent her throne."

"Umm, does not that pointy part in the middle hurt her bum?"

Mary laughed. "Now that you mention it . . ." She continued to look at the constellation. "Say, what's that smudge just below it?"

"That is—I do not know what name you give it; it is the closest large galaxy to ours."

"Andromeda!" declared Mary. "I've always wanted to see Andromeda!" She sighed again and continued to look up at the stars. There were more than she'd ever seen in her life. "It's so beautiful," she said, "and—oh, my. Oh, my! What's that?"

Ponter's face was now slightly illuminated. "The night lights," he said.

"Night lights? You mean the *northern* lights?"

"They are associated with the pole, yes."

"Wow," said Mary. "The northern lights! I've never seen them before, either."

There was surprise in Ponter's voice. "You haven't?"

"No. I mean, I live in Toronto. That's farther south than Portland, Oregon." It was a factoid that often astonished Americans, but probably didn't mean a thing to Ponter.

"I have seen them thousands of times," said Ponter. "But I never tire of them." They were both quiet for a time, enjoying the rippling curtains of light. "Is it common for your people to have not seen them?"

"I guess," said Mary. "I mean, there're not many of us

who live in the extreme north—or south, for that matter."

"Perhaps that explains it," said Ponter.

"What?"

"Your people's unawareness of the electromagnetic filaments that shape the universe; Lou and I spoke of this. It was in the night lights that we first identified such filaments; they, rather than this big bang of yours, are our way of explaining the structure of the universe."

"Well," said Mary. "I don't think you're going to convince many people that the big bang didn't happen."

"That is fine. Feeling a need to convince others that you are right also is something that comes from religion, I think; I am simply content to know that I *am* right, even if others do not know it."

Mary smiled in the darkness. A man who cried openly, a man who didn't always have to prove he was right, a man who treated women with respect and as equals. *Quite a find,* as her sister Christine would say.

And, thought Mary, it was clear that Ponter liked her— and, of course, it *had* to be for her mind; she must appear as, well, as homely to him as he did to—no, not to her, not anymore, but to others here on this Earth. Imagine that: a man who really did like her for who she was, not what she looked like.

Quite a find, indeed, but—

Mary's heart skipped a beat. Ponter's left hand had found her right one in the dark, and had begun gently stroking it.

And suddenly she felt every muscle in her body tense up. Yes, she could be alone with a man; yes, she could hug and comfort a man; but—

But, no, it was too soon for that. Too soon. Mary retrieved her hand, hopped off the hood of the car, and opened the door, the dome light stinging her eyes. She got into the driver's seat, and, a moment later, Ponter entered from the passenger's side, his head downcast.

They drove the rest of the way back to Sudbury in silence.

Chapter Forty-two

DAY EIGHT
FRIDAY, AUGUST 9
148/119/02

NEWS SEARCH

Keyword(s): Neanderthal

The environmental group Emerald Dawn has claimed responsibility for the bombing of the Sudbury Neutrino Observatory. SNO Director Bonnie Jean Mah, however, says that no explosion occurred, blaming the destruction of her facility on a rapid infusion of air . . .

X-rays of Ponter Boddit's skull were put up for sale on eBay this morning. Bidding reached $355 before the online auction site pulled the offer, after a spokesperson for the Sudbury Regional Hospital said on CBC Radio that they must be fake . . .

The Canadian dollar dropped more than two-thirds of a cent yesterday as relationships between Canada and the United States continued to show signs of strain over the question of who should be controlling the fate of the interloping caveman . . .

Indications from the Montego encampment in Northern Ontario are that Neanderthals don't share all our scientific beliefs. Indeed, in what's sure to be a boon to creationists, the Neanderthals apparently reject the big bang, science's favorite explanation for the origin of the universe . . .

Unconfirmed rumors today that Russia has targeted Northern

Ontario with ICBMs carrying nuclear weapons. "If a plague has entered our world, somebody needs to stand ready to sterilize the infected area, for the greater good of all mankind," said a person signing himself as Yuri A. Petrov in an Internet newsgroup devoted to crossborder health issues . . .

Ponter Boddit has agreed to throw the first pitch at SkyDome next Thursday, when the Blue Jays face the New York Yankees . . .

"According to our CNN online poll, the top three questions people would like to ask the Neanderthal are: What are women like in your world? What happened to our kind of human in your world? And do you believe in Jesus Christ?"

Lurt, Adikor's woman-mate, had every right to view her own alibi archive whenever she wished. Indeed, she'd had cause to access it just a few months earlier, when a formula she'd written on the wallboard had accidentally been erased by an apprentice. Rather than trying to re-create it, she'd simply come to the archive building, accessed her alibi recording, found a good, clear view of the wallboard, and jotted down the string of symbols.

Because of this recent visit, Lurt knew that her alibi cube was plugged into receptacle 13,997; she told the Keeper of Alibis that, rather than having her look it up on the computer. The keeper accompanied Lurt to the correct niche, and Lurt faced her Companion toward the blue eye. "I, Lurt Fradlo, wish to access my own alibi archive for reasons of personal curiosity. Timestamp."

The eye turned yellow; the cube agreed that Lurt was indeed who she claimed to be.

The archivist held up her Companion. "I, Mabla Dabdalb, Keeper of Alibis, hereby certify that Lurt Fradlo's identity has been confirmed in my presence. Timestamp."

The eye went bloodshot, and a tone emanated from the speaker.

"All set," said the keeper. "You can use the projector in room four." Dabdalb turned to go, and Lurt followed her. She entered room four, which was a small chamber with a single chair. Somewhere, in one of the other rooms, Lurt imagined an enforcer was watching Adikor's transmissions in real time as they were being received and recorded.

But watching as something was recorded was entirely different from trying to record and play back at the same time. Lurt pulled on control buds, selecting a day at random to review, and watched as the holo-bubble in front of her filled with banal pictures of her working in her lab. As the images played on, Lurt left the chamber, ostensibly heading for the washroom. And once she'd passed into a corridor that had no one else in it, she slipped on a pair of dining gloves, fished out the small device she'd brought with her, activated it, and dropped it into a recycling tub. She then removed the gloves.

Bolbay had been wrong, Lurt thought, whistling as she returned to the viewing chamber. Deep underground wasn't the perfect place to commit an unobserved crime. No, the perfect place was right here in the archive pavilion, when no one else was watching you and your own alibi cube was playing back instead of recording . . .

Her first thought had been to use hydrogen sulfide, which surely would have had the desired effect. But concentrations greater than 500 parts per million over even a short period could be fatal. She'd then considered polecat musk, but when she'd looked up the formula, it had been complex: trans-2-Butene-1-thiol, 3-Methyl-1-butanethiol, trans-2-Butenyl thioacetate, and more. Finally, she settled on ammonium sulfide, that favorite of prankster children who hadn't come to grips with the fact that their Companions were recording their actions.

Having a keen olfactory sense certainly had its advantages, although Lurt had heard it said that the reason people ate so few plants, while other primates thrived on them, was that the acute sensitivity to odors made it hard to tolerate the flatulence that went with a diet heavy in vegetation. Anyway, this was just what the doctor had ordered— even if that doctor was a physicist trying to keep from going under the knife.

Lurt thought she smelled it first, before anyone else, even though her viewing room was hardly the closest to the corridor where she'd left the device. Then again, she'd been waiting for it, doubtlessly dilating her nostrils in anticipation. But she refused to be the first one to react. She sat until she heard others running about, then left her room, trying not to gag at the horrendous stench. A big, burly fellow came out of one of the other viewing chambers, holding a hand over his nose. Lurt thought perhaps he was the enforcer monitoring Adikor's transmissions, and that was confirmed when, as she herself exited, she caught sight of the holo-bubble the man had been watching, which showed Jasmel and Adikor leaving Adikor's house.

"What is that awful smell?" said a wincing Dabdalb, the Keeper of Alibis, as Lurt passed her.

"It's horrible!" said another patron, hustling through the lobby.

"Open the windows! Open the windows!" shouted a third.

Lurt joined the small crowd hurrying out into the clean, open air outside the building. It would be at least a quarter of a day, Lurt knew, before the smell would dissipate enough to make going back indoors possible.

She hoped that would be enough time for Adikor to accomplish what he was trying to do.

Mary went to Laurentian University the next morning, having finally managed to get rid of the reporters waiting in the lobby of the Ramada. They'd been disappointed that Ponter hadn't turned out to be staying there, as well. Apparently Reuben had implied to the journalists that he might be—presumably as a way of putting them off Ponter's trail; Mary had returned him to Reuben's house last night, which, as far as she knew, was where he'd stayed.

At 10:30 A.M., Mary was surprised to run into Louise Benoît in the corridor outside the Laurentian genetics lab. Louise was wearing tight-fitting denim cutoffs and a white T-shirt tied in a knot over her flat midriff. Well, thought Mary, it *was* blisteringly hot today, but *really*—she looks like she's *asking* for it . . .

No.

Mary cursed herself; she knew better than that. No matter how a woman dressed, she was entitled to safety, entitled to be able to walk around without being molested.

Mary decided to be friendly and trotted out her few words of French. "*Bonjour,*" she said, as she got closer to Louise. "*Comment ça va?*"

"I'm fine," replied Louise. "And you?"

"Fine. What brings you here?"

Louise pointed down the hall. "I was visiting some guys I know in the physics department. There's not much for me to do at SNO right now. They've finished draining the detector chamber, and a team from the original manufacturer is just beginning work on reassembling the sphere, although that will take weeks. So I thought I'd talk over an idea with a couple of the people here—see if they could shoot any holes in it."

Mary was heading toward the vending machines, looking to get a bag of Miss Vickie's sea-salt-and-malt-vinegar kettle chips—an indulgence she could only afford in a monetary sense, but it had long been traditional for her to start each work week with a 43-gram bag.

"And did they?" Mary asked. "Shoot any holes in it, I mean?"

Louise shook her head and fell in beside Mary as she continued on down to the lounge.

"Well, that's the best kind of idea, isn't it?" Mary said.

"I suppose," said Louise. Once they reached the lounge, Mary fished in her purse for some change. She pulled out a loonie and a quarter, and fed them into one of the vending machines. Louise, meanwhile, got herself a cup of coffee from another machine.

"Remember that meeting we had in the Inco conference room?" said Louise. "Well, as I said then, the many-worlds interpretation of quantum mechanics states that whenever a quantum event can go two ways, it *does* go two ways."

"A splitting of the timeline," said Mary, leaning her

bum against the arm of a vinyl-padded chair in the lounge.

"*Oui,*" said Louise. "Well, I spent some time talking to Ponter about this."

"Ponter mentioned that," said Mary. "I must have missed it."

"It was late at night, and—"

"You went into Ponter's room again after we'd finished the language lessons?" Mary was astonished by the rush of—of, my God, of *jealousy*—she felt.

"Sure. I like to be up at night; you know that. I wanted to learn more about the Neanderthal view of physics."

"And?" said Mary, trying to keep her tone even.

"Well, it's interesting," said Louise. She took a sip of her coffee. "Here in this world, we've got two major interpretations for quantum mechanics: the Copenhagen interpretation and Everett's Many-Worlds interpretation. The former postulates a special role for the observer—that consciousness actually influences reality. Well, that idea makes some physicists very uncomfortable; it's seen as a return to vitalism. Everett's Many-Worlds interpretation was an attempt to work around that. It says that quantum phenomena cause new universes to split off constantly, with each possible outcome of a quantum interaction occurring, but in a separate universe. No observers are required to shape reality; instead, every reality that *can* conceivably exist is automatically created."

"Okay," said Mary, not because she really understood, but because the alternative seemed to be an even longer lecture.

"Well, Ponter's people have a *single* theory of quantum mechanics that's sort of a synthesis of our two theories. It allows for many worlds—that is, for parallel universes—but the creation of such universes doesn't result from random quantum events. Rather, it only happens through the *actions of conscious observers*."

"Why don't we have the same single theory, then?" asked Mary, munching on a particularly large chip.

"Partly because there's a lot of math that seems irreconcilable between the two interpretations," said Louise. "And, of course, there's that old problem of politics in science: those physicists who favor the Copenhagen interpretation have devoted their careers to proving that it's right; same thing for the guys on Everett's side. For them all to sit down and say, 'Maybe we're both partly right—and both partly wrong' just isn't going to happen."

"Ah," said Mary. "It's like the Regional Continuity versus Replacement debate in anthropology."

Louise nodded. "If you say so. But suppose the Neanderthal synthesis of quantum physics is actually correct. It implies that consciousness—human volition—has the power to spin off new universes. Well, that raises a significant question. Presumably in the beginning, at the moment of the big bang, there must have been only *one* universe. Sometime later, it started splitting."

"I thought Ponter didn't believe in the big bang?" said Mary.

"Yes, apparently Neanderthal scientists think the universe has always existed. They believe that on large scales, redshifts—which are our principal evidence for an expanding universe—are proportional to age, rather than distance; that is, that mass varies over time. And they think the gross structure of galaxies and galactic clusters are caused by monopoles and plasma-pinching magnetic vortex filaments. Ponter says the cosmic microwave background—which we take as the residue of the big-bang fireball—is really the result of electrons trapped in these strong magnetic fields absorbing and emitting microwaves. Repeated absorption and emission by billions of galaxies smoothed out the effect, he says, producing the uniform background we detect now."

"Does that seem possible to you?" asked Mary.

Louise shrugged. "I'm going to have to look into it." She took another sip of coffee. "But, you know, after telling me all that, Ponter said the most astonishing thing."

"What?" asked Mary.

"I guess you showed him a church service, right?"

"Yes. On TV."

Louise took a seat on one of the other vinyl-covered chairs. "Well," she said, "apparently he spent some time that night watching Vision TV, soaking up more religious thought. He said our story of the universe having an origin is just a creation myth, like from the Bible. 'In the beginning God created the Heavens and the Earth . . .' and all that. 'Even your science,' Ponter said, 'is contaminated by this error of religion.' "

Mary sat down properly as well. "You know . . . I mean, physics is your field, not mine, but maybe he's right. I mentioned Regional Continuity versus Replacement a moment ago; sometimes that's called Multiregionalism versus Out-of-Africa. Anyway, there are those who've observed that Replacement, which is what I and other geneticists favor, is also basically a biblical position: humanity came full-blown out of Africa, ejected from a garden, and there's a hard-

and-fast line between us and everything else in the animal kingdom, including even other contemporaneous members of the genus *Homo*."

"It's an interesting point of view," said Louise.

"And you can argue that the other side is fighting for a biblical interpretation, too: the parallels between Multiregionalism and the Ten Lost Tribes of Israel are pretty blatant. Beyond that, there's the whole 'mitochondrial Eve' hypothesis—that all modern humans trace their origin to one woman who lived hundreds of thousands of years ago. Even the theory's name—Eve!—screams that it's being pushed more because of biblical resonances than because it's good science." Mary paused. "Anyway, sorry, you were talking about the Neanderthal version of quantum physics . . ."

"Right, right," said Louise. "Well, my thought was, suppose they are correct about how parallel universes are spun off, but wrong about this universe having existed forever. If the universe *did* have a beginning, then when did that first split occur?"

Mary frowned. "Well, umm, I don't know. I guess the first time somebody made a decision."

"Exactly! I think that's exactly right! And when was the first decision made?" Louise paused. "You know, it *is* interesting what Ponter says about how our scientific worldview is always, down deep, trying to say the same things our creation myths say—the big bang and your model of hominid evolution both being modern retellings of Genesis. Well, maybe I'm being guilty of the same kind of thinking here. After all, in the Bible, the first decision made by anyone other than God is when Eve decided to take the

apple—the original sin—and, well, one could think of that
as having split the universe. In one timeline, the one we're
supposedly in, humanity was cast out of paradise. In another, we weren't. In fact, it's even a bit like Ponter's own
case, with a being crossing over from one version of reality
to the other."

Mary was completely lost. "How do you mean?"

"I'm talking about Mary—not you, Professor Vaughan;
Mary, the mother of Jesus. You're a Catholic, aren't you?"

Mary nodded.

"I noticed your crucifix." Mary looked down, self-
conscious. "I'm Catholic, too," continued Louise. "Anyway,
as a Catholic, you probably don't make the same mistake
lots of other people do. The doctrine of the immaculate
conception—a lot of people think that's a fancy term for
Christ's virgin birth, but it isn't, is it?"

"No," said Mary. "No, it refers to the conception of
Mary herself. The reason she was able to give birth to the
son of God was that she herself was conceived devoid of
original sin—it was *her* conception that was immaculate."

"Exactly. Well, how do you get a person without original sin in a world in which everyone is descended from
Adam and Eve?"

"I have no idea," said Mary, truthfully.

"Don't you see?" said Louise. "It's as if Mary was shifted
into this universe from the other timeline, from the one
in which Eve never took the apple, the one in which Man
never fell, the one in which people live without the taint
of original sin."

Mary nodded dubiously. "One *could* argue that."

Louise smiled. "Well, you'll see the parallel between

Ponter and the Virgin Mary in a second. Let me get back to my earlier question: I said if he's right, and the universe does split every time a decision is made, when did the universe first split? And you said the first time someone made a decision. But when was that? Not in the Bible, but, well, in reality . . . ?"

Mary fished out another potato chip. "Gee, I don't know. The first time a trilobite decided to go left instead of right?"

Louise put her cardboard coffee cup down on a little table. "No, I don't think so. Trilobites have no volition; they, and all other primitive forms of life, are just chemical machines. Stephen Jay Gould keeps talking about rewinding the tape of life in his books and getting a different outcome, and when he says that, he thinks he's making an allusion to chaos theory. But he's wrong. No matter how many times you placed a trilobite at the same fork in the road, it will go the same way. A trilobite doesn't think; it doesn't have consciousness. It just processes the inputs of its senses and does what they dictate. No choice is made. Gould is right—sort of—that if the initial conditions were changed, the outcome could be radically different, but rewinding the tape of life and playing it again no more gives a different outcome than rewinding a tape of *Gone with the Wind* and playing it again results in an ending in which Rhett and Scarlett stay together. I don't think real decisions—real choices, real *consciousness*—emerged until much, much later. I think *we—Homo sapiens*—were the first conscious beings on this planet."

"There was lots of sophisticated behavior by earlier forms of humans," said Mary. "*Homo ergaster, Homo erectus,*

Homo habilis, even the australopithecines and *Kenyanthropus.*"

"Well, I realize this is your field, Professor Vaughan—" Had she really in all the time they'd spent quarantined together never volunteered that Louise could call her Mary?—"but I've been reading up on this on the Web. As far as I can tell, those earlier kinds of man didn't really have behavior any more sophisticated than a beaver building a dam."

"They made tools," said Mary.

"*Oui,*" said Louise. "But weren't they repetitive, virtually identical tools, turned out over the centuries by the thousands? All made to the same mental template, the same design?"

Mary nodded. "That's true."

"Surely there has to be some natural variation among stone tools," said Louise, "just based on chance accidents and random differences that occur when implements are chipped from stone. If there *was* consciousness at work, even without coming up with a better idea on their own, early humans should have seen that some tools happened to be better than others. It's like you don't have to think of the round wheel right off the bat; you might start with a five-sided one, then accidentally make a six-sided one— and note that it rolled slightly better. Eventually, you'd come up with the perfectly round one."

Mary nodded.

"But if there's no consciousness at work," said Louise, "you simply toss aside the better version as not fitting your mental template of what was supposed to be produced. Right? And that's what happens with the tools in the archeological record: instead of gradual refinement over time, they just stay the same. And the only explanation I can think of for that is that there was no conscious selection of better variants: the toolmaker simply wasn't *aware*, he couldn't see that *this* particular way of hitting nodules produced something better than *that* way. The design was frozen."

"Interesting take," said Mary, genuinely impressed.

"And when we see complex repetitive behavior in other animals—such as building a dam—we call it instinct, and that's what that kind of toolmaking was. No, until *Homo sapiens*, there was no consciousness, and—here's the kicker—in fact, for the first sixty thousand years that *Homo sapiens* existed, *there was no consciousness.*"

"What are you talking about?" said Mary.

"When did anatomically modern humans first appear?" asked Louise, picking up her coffee cup again.

"About one hundred thousand years ago."

"That's the same figure I saw on the web. Now, do I understand that right? A hundred-K years in the past, creatures that looked exactly like us, that walked exactly like us, first appeared, right? Creatures with brains that were the same size and shape as our brains, judging by their cranial cavities?"

"That's right," said Mary. She'd finished her chips, and got some Kleenex out of her purse so she could wipe her greasy fingers.

"But," said Louise, "according to what I read, for sixty thousand years, they thought no thoughts. For sixty thousand years, they did nothing that wasn't instinctual. But then, forty thousand years ago, everything changed."

Mary's eyes went wide. "The Great Leap Forward."

"Exactly!"

Mary felt her heart pounding. The Great Leap Forward was the term some anthropologists gave to the cultural awakening that occurred 40,000 years ago; others called it the Upper Paleolithic Revolution. As Louise had said, modern-looking human beings had been around for six hundred centuries by that point, but they created no art, they didn't adorn their bodies with jewelry, and they didn't bury their dead with grave goods. But starting simultaneously 40,000 years ago, suddenly humans were painting beautiful pictures on cave walls, humans were wearing necklaces and bracelets, and humans were interring their loved ones with food and tools and other valuable objects that could only have been of use in a presumed afterlife. Art, fashion, and religion all appeared simultaneously; truly, a great leap forward.

"So you're saying that some Cro-Magnon 40,000 years ago suddenly started making choices, and the universe started splitting?"

"Not exactly," said Louise. She'd evidently finished her first coffee; she got up and bought a second one. "Think about this: what *caused* the Great Leap Forward?"

"Nobody knows," said Mary.

"For all intents and purposes, it's a marker, right there in the archeological record, showing the dawn of consciousness, wouldn't you say?"

"I suppose," said Mary.

"But that dawning isn't accompanied by any gross physical change; it's not like a new form of humanity appeared who suddenly started making art. Brains *capable* of consciousness had existed for sixty thousand years, but they *weren't* conscious. And then something happened."

"The Great Leap Forward, yes. But, as I said, no one knows what caused it."

"You ever read Roger Penrose? *The Emperor's New Mind?*"

Mary shook her head.

"Penrose is an Oxford mathematician. He contends that human consciousness is quantum-mechanical in nature."

"Meaning what?"

"Meaning that what we think of as intelligence, as sentience, doesn't arise from some biochemical network of neurons, or anything as crude as that. Rather, it arises from quantum processes. Specifically, he and an anesthesiologist named Hameroff argue that quantum superposition of isolated electrons in the microtubules of brain cells creates the phenomenon of consciousness."

"Ah," said Mary dubiously.

Louise sipped some of her new coffee. "Well, don't you see?" she said. "*That* explains the Great Leap Forward. Sure, our brains had been just as they are today since one hundred thousand years ago, but consciousness didn't begin until a quantum-mechanical event occurred, presumably at random: the one and only spinning off of a new universe that happened the way Everett thinks it does."

Mary nodded; it *was* an interesting notion.

"And quantum events, by their very nature, have *multiple* possible outcomes," said Louise. "Instead of that quantum fluctuation, or whatever it was, creating consciousness in *Homo sapiens*, the same thing might have happened in the other kind of humanity that existed 40,000 years ago—Neanderthal man! The first splitting of the universe was an accident, a quantum fluke. In one branch, thought and cognition arose in our ancestors; in another, it arose in Ponter's ancestors. I read that Neanderthals had been around since maybe 200,000 years ago, right?"

Mary nodded.

"And they had even bigger brains than we did, right?"

Mary nodded again.

"But on this world," said Louise, "in this timeline, those brains never sparked with consciousness. Ours did instead, and the edge that consciousness gave us—cunning and foresight—led to us absolutely triumphing over the Neanderthals, and becoming rulers of the world."

"Ah!" said Mary. "But in Ponter's world—"

Louise nodded. "In Ponter's world, the opposite happened. It was Neanderthals who became conscious, developing art and culture—and cunning; they took the Great Leap Forward while we remained the dumb brutes we'd been for the preceding sixty thousand years."

"I suppose that's possible," said Mary. "You could probably get a good paper out of that."

"More than that," said Louise. She sipped some more coffee. "If I'm right, it means Ponter might get to go home."

Mary's heart fluttered. "What?"

"I'm basing this in part on stuff Ponter told me, and in part on our own world's understanding of physics. Suppose that each time the universe splits, it doesn't do it the way amoebas do—with one amoeba becoming two daughters, and the parent disappearing in the process. Suppose instead it happens more like vertebrates giving birth: the original universe continues on, and a new daughter universe is created."

"Yes?" said Mary. "So?"

"Well, then, you see, universes actually are of different ages. They might *appear* absolutely identical, except for your choice of breakfast this morning, but one of them is twelve billion years old, and the other is"—she looked at her watch—"well, a few hours old now. Of course, the daughter universe would *seem* to be billions of years old, but it wouldn't really be."

Mary frowned. "Umm, Louise, you're not by any chance a creationist, are you?"

"*Quoi?*" But then she laughed. "No, no, no—but I see the parallel you're alluding to. No, I'm talking real physics here."

"If you say so. But how does this get Ponter home?"

"Well, assume this universe, the one you and I are in right now, *is* the original one in which *Homo sapiens* became conscious—the one that initially split from the universe in which Neanderthals became conscious instead. All the other googolplex of universes in which conscious *Homo sapiens* exist are daughters, or granddaughters, or great-great-great-great-granddaughters, of this one."

"That's a huge assumption," said Mary.

"It would be, if we had no other evidence. But we *do* have evidence that this particular universe is special—Ponter's arrival here, out of all the places he might have gone. When Ponter's quantum computer ran out of universes in which other versions of itself existed, what did it do? Why, it reached across to universes in which it *didn't* exist. And, in doing so, it latched first onto the one that had initially split from the entire tree of those in which it did exist, the one that, forty thousand years previously, had started on another path, with another kind of humanity in charge. Of course, as soon as it reached a universe in which a quantum computer didn't exist in the same spot, the factoring process crashed and the contact between the two worlds was broken. But if Ponter's people repeat the exact process that led to him being marooned here, I think there's a real chance that the portal to this specific universe, the one that first split from their timeline, will be re-created."

"That's a lot of ifs," said Mary. "Besides, if they *could* repeat the experiment, why haven't they already?"

"I don't know," said Louise. "But if I'm right, the doorway to Ponter's world may open again."

Mary felt her stomach fluttering—and not just because of the potato chips—as she tried to sort out her feelings about that possibility.

Chapter Forty-three

Adikor Huld stared at the mining robot Dern had provided. It was a sorry-looking contraption: just an arrangement of gears and pulleys and mechanical pincers, vaguely resembling a stubby pine tree denuded of needles. The robot had obviously endured a fire at some point; there had been one in the mine about four months ago, Adikor recalled. Some of the robot's components had fused, some metal parts were extensively fatigued, and the whole thing had a blackened, sooty look to it. Dern had said this unit was to have been sent to the recycling yards, anyway, so no one would mind if it were lost.

It was tricky determining how to control the robot, though. Although there were robots with artificial intelligence, they were very expensive. This one didn't have the smarts to do what needed to be done on its own; it would have to be operated by remote control. They couldn't use radio signals; those would interfere with the quantum registers, ruining the attempt to reproduce the experiment. Dern finally decided to simply run a fiber-optic cable from the robot's torso back into a small control box, which he perched on a console in the quantum-computing control room. He used twin joysticks to move the robot's hands, having the machine press down on the top of register 69 just as Ponter had originally done.

Adikor looked at Dern. "All set?"

Dern nodded.

He looked at Jasmel, who was also present. "Ready?"

"Yes."

"Ten," said Adikor, standing next to his control unit; he shouted the countdown just as he had the first time, even though there was no one out on the computing floor to hear him.

"Nine." He desperately hoped this would work—for Ponter's sake, and for his own.

"Eight. Seven. Six."

He looked at Dern.

"Five. Four. Three."

He smiled encouragingly at Jasmel.

"Two. One. Zero."

"Hey!" shouted Dern. His control box jerked off the desk and clattered to the floor, skittering across it as the fiber-optic cable coming out of its back end was pulled tight.

Adikor felt a great wind swirling about, but his ears didn't pop; there was no significant change in pressure. It was as if air was simply being *exchanged* . . .

Jasmel's mouth formed the words, "I don't believe it," but whatever sound she was making was drowned out by the wind.

Dern, dashing across the room, had stopped the console from being pulled farther by clamping down on its cable with his right foot. Adikor hurried over to the window to look down on the computing floor.

The robot was *gone*, but—

—but the cable was pulled taut, half an armspan above the floor, stretching from the open control-room door to three-quarters of the way across the computing facility, until—

Until it *disappeared*, into thin air, as if through an invisible hole in an invisible wall, right next to register column 69.

Adikor looked at Dern. Dern looked at Jasmel. Jasmel looked at Adikor. They hurried over to the monitor, which should be displaying whatever the robot's camera eye was seeing. But it was just an empty, black square.

"The robot's been destroyed," said Jasmel. "Just like my father."

"Maybe," said Dern. "Or maybe video signals can't travel through that—whatever that is."

"Or else," said Adikor, "maybe it's just emerged into a completely dark room."

"What—what do you suppose we should do?" asked Jasmel.

Dern shrugged his rounded shoulders slightly.

Adikor said, "Let's haul it back in—see if anything can survive going . . . going *through*." He walked out onto the computing floor and gently took hold of the cable, disappearing a few paces away into nothingness at waist height. He added his other hand and began to pull gently.

Jasmel came over to be behind him, and she began to pull gently as well.

The cable was hauling back easily enough, but it was obvious to Adikor, at least, that there was a weight hanging off the end, as if, somewhere on the other side of the hole, the robot was dangling over a precipice.

"How strong are the connectors on the robot's end of the cable?" asked Adikor, shooting a glance at Dern, who, now that he no longer had to hold down his control box, had come out onto the computing floor as well.

"They're just standard *bedonk* plugs."

"Will they come free?"

"If you jerk them hard enough. There are little clips that snap onto the cable's connector to help hold it in place."

Adikor and Jasmel continued to pull gently. "And did you engage the clips?"

"I—I'm not sure," said Dern. "I mean, maybe. I was plugging and unplugging the cable a fair bit as I set the robot up . . ."

Adikor and Jasmel had already hauled in perhaps three armspans' worth of cable, and—

"Look!" said Jasmel.

The robot's squat form was emerging through—well, through *what* they couldn't say. But the machine's base was now visible, as if somehow it were passing through a hole in midair that precisely matched the robot's cross-section.

Dern hurried across the computing chamber, the closed ends of his pant making loud slapping sounds against the polished rock of the floor. He reached out and grabbed one of the robot's spindly arms, now partially protruding from the air. He was just in time, too, for the cable connector did give way, and Adikor and Jasmel went tumbling backwards, him falling on her. They quickly got to their feet and saw Dern finish pulling the robot through from—the phrase came again into Adikor's mind—from the other side.

Adikor and Jasmel ran over to join Dern, who was now sitting on the floor, the robot, toppled over, next to him. It seemed no more damaged than it had been before it had gone through. But Dern was staring at his own left hand, a dumbfounded look on his face.

"Are you all right?" asked Adikor.

"My hand . . ." said Dern.

"What about it? Is it broken?"

Dern looked up. "No, it's fine; it's fine. But—but when I first grabbed hold of the robot . . . when the cable came loose, and the robot fell backward, my hand passed *through*. I saw half of it disappear through . . . through whatever that was."

Jasmel took Dern's hand in hers and peered at it. "It looks all right. What did it feel like?"

"I didn't feel anything. But it looked like it was cut off, right behind the fingers, and the edge was absolutely straight and smooth, but there was no bleeding, and the edge kept moving down my fingers as I pulled my hand back."

Jasmel shuddered.

"You're sure you're all right?" asked Adikor.

Dern nodded.

Adikor took a half step forward, toward where the opening had been. He slowly stretched his right arm out and tentatively swept it back and forth. Whatever door had been open appeared to be closed now.

"Now what?" asked Jasmel.

"Well, I don't know," said Adikor. "Could we get a lamp to put on the robot?"

"Sure," said Dern. "I could take one off a head protector. Do you have extras?"

"On a shelf in the little eating room."

Dern nodded, then held up his hand and rotated it from the wrist, now palm up, now palm down, as if he'd never seen it before. "It was incredible," he said softly. Then, shaking his head slightly to break his own reverie, he headed off to get the lamp.

"You know what happened, of course," said Jasmel, as they waited for Dern to return. "My father went through whatever that was. That's why there's no trace of his body."

"But the other side isn't at ground level," said Adikor. "He must have fallen and—"

Jasmel raised her eyebrow. "And maybe broken his neck. Which . . . which means what we might see on the other side is . . ."

Adikor nodded. "Is his dead body. That thought had occurred to me, I'm sorry to say . . . but, actually, I'd expected to see him drowned in a tank of heavy water." He reflected on this for a moment, then moved over to the robot, which was bone dry. "There was a reservoir of heavy water on the other side when Ponter went through, and— *gristle!*"

"What?"

"We must have connected to a *different* universe, not the one Ponter went to."

Jasmel's lower lip quivered.

Adikor hoisted the robot onto its treads. He checked out the cable connector, but, as far as he could tell, it was in fine shape. Jasmel, meanwhile, had gone off, walking slowly, head down, to get the loose end of the fiber-optic cable; she brought it to Adikor, who snapped it into place. He then brought down the two clamps that clicked into notches on the connector's edge, helping to hold it in position.

At this point, Dern returned with two electric lamps and the spherical battery packs that powered them. He also had a coil of adhesive tape, and he used this to firmly attach the lamps on either side of the robot's camera eye.

They repositioned the robot exactly as it had been before, right beside register 69, and then the three of them headed back into the control room. Adikor got some equipment boxes and stood on them so that he could simultaneously operate his console and look back over his shoulder onto the computing floor.

He called out the countdown once more: "Ten. Nine. Eight. Seven. Six. Five. Four. Three. Two. One. Zero."

This time, Adikor saw the whole thing. The portal opened like an expanding hoop of blue fire. He heard air rushing around again, and the robot, which seemed to be right on the lip of a precipice, tottered over and disappeared. The control cable went taut, and the blue hoop contracted around its perimeter, then disappeared.

The three of them turned as one to the square video monitor. At first it seemed again that there was no video signal at all, but then the light beams must have caught something—glass or plastic—and they briefly saw a reflection bouncing back at them. But that was all; whatever space the robot was dangling into must be huge.

The lights played across something else—intersecting metallic tubes?—as the robot swung back and forth like a pendulum.

And then, suddenly, there was illumination everywhere, as if—

"Someone must have turned on the lights," said Jasmel.

It was now clear that the robot was actually twirling at the end of its tether. They caught glimpses of rocky walls, and more rocky walls, and—

"What's that?" exclaimed Jasmel.

They'd only seen it for an instant: a ladder of some sort, leaning against the curving side of the vast chamber, and, scuttling down the ladder, a slight figure in some sort of blue clothing.

The robot continued to rotate, and they saw that a large geodesic latticework was sitting on the floor, with things like metal flowers at its intersections.

"I've never seen anything like that," said Dern.

"It's beautiful," said Jasmel.

Adikor sucked in his breath. The view was still swinging, and it showed the ladder again, two more figures coming down it, and then, maddeningly, the figures disappeared as the robot turned away.

Its rotation offered two more tantalizing glimpses of figures wearing loose-fitting blue body suits, and sporting bright yellow shells on top of their heads. They were way too narrow-shouldered to be men; Adikor thought perhaps they were women, although they were thin even for females. But their faces, glimpsed ever so briefly, seemed devoid of hair, and—

And the image jerked suddenly, then settled down, the robot no longer rotating. A hand had reached in from the side, briefly dominating the camera's field of view, a strange, weak-looking hand with a short thumb and some sort of metal circle wrapped around one finger. The hand had clearly clamped onto the robot, steadying it. Dern was working frantically with his control box, tipping the camera down as fast as it would go, and they got their first good look at the face of the being now reaching up and clutching the hanging robot.

Dern gasped. Adikor felt his stomach knotting. The creature was *hideous,* deformed, with a lower jaw that protruded as if the bone within were encrusted by growths.

The repulsive being was still holding on to the robot, trying to pull it down, closer to the ground; the robot's treads seemed to be about half a bodylength above the floor of the vast chamber.

As the robot's camera tilted, Adikor could see that there was an opening in the bottom of the geodesic sphere, as if part of it had been disassembled. Lying on the chamber's floor were giant, curved pieces of glass or transparent plastic piled up one atop another; they must have been what had originally caught the robot's lamps. Those curved pieces of glass looked like they might have once formed a huge sphere.

They could now intermittently see three of the same beings, all equally deformed. Two of them were also devoid of facial hair. One was pointing directly at the robot; his arm looked like a twig.

Jasmel placed her hands on her hips and shook her head slowly back and forth. "What *are* they?"

Adikor shook his head in wonder.

"They're primates of some sort," said Jasmel.

"Not chimpanzees or bonobos," said Dern.

"No," said Adikor, "although they're scrawny enough. But they're mostly hairless. They look more like us than like apes."

"It's too bad they're wearing those strange pieces of headgear," said Dern. "I wonder what they're for?"

"Protection?" suggested Adikor.

"Not very efficient, if so," said Dern. "If something fell on their heads, their necks, not their shoulders, would take the weight."

"There's no sign of my father," said Jasmel, sadly.

All three of them were quiet for a time. Then Jasmel spoke again. "You know what they look like? They look like primitive humans—like those fossils you see in *galdarab* halls."

Adikor took a couple of steps backward, literally staggered by the notion. He found a chair, spun it around on its base, and lowered himself into it.

"Gliksin people," he said, the term coming to him; Gliksin was the region in which such fossils—the only primates known without browridges and with those ridiculous protuberances from the lower jaw—had first been found.

Could their experiment have reached across *world lines*, accessing universes that had split from this one long before the creation of the quantum computer? No, no. Adikor shook his head. It was too much, too crazy. After all, the Gliksin people had gone extinct—well, the figure half a million months ago popped into his head, but he wasn't sure if it was correct. Adikor rubbed the edge of his hand back and forth above his browridge. The only sound was the drone of the air-purification equipment; the only smells, their own sweat and pheromones.

"This is huge," Dern said softly. "This is gigantic."

Adikor nodded slowly. "Another version of Earth. Another version of humanity."

"It's talking!" exclaimed Jasmel, pointing at one of the figures visible on the screen. "Turn up the sound!"

Dern reached for a control. "Speech," said Adikor, shaking his head in wonder. "I'd read that Gliksin people were incapable of speech, because their tongues were too short."

They listened to the being talking, although the words made no sense.

"It sounds so strange," said Jasmel. "Like nothing I've ever heard before."

The Gliksin in the foreground had stopped pulling on the robot, evidently realizing that there was no more cable to be payed out. He moved away, and other Gliksins loomed in to have a look. It took Adikor a moment to realize that there were both males and females present; both kinds mostly had naked faces, although a few of the men did have beards. The females generally seemed smaller, but, on a few at least, the breasts were obvious beneath the clothes.

Jasmel looked out at the computing floor. "The gateway seems to be staying open just fine," she said. "I wonder how long it can be maintained?"

Adikor was wondering that, too. The proof, the evidence that would save him, and his son Dab, and his sister Kelon, was right there: an alternative world! But Daklar Bolbay would doubtless claim the pictures, being recorded on video of course, were fake, sophisticated computer-generated imagery. After all, she'd say, Adikor had access to the most powerful computers on the planet.

But if the robot could bring back something—*anything!* A manufactured object, perhaps, or . . .

Different parts of the chamber were selectively revealed as people moved about, briefly opening up views of what was behind them. It was a barrel-shaped cavern, maybe fifteen times as tall as a person, and hewn directly out of the rock.

"They certainly are a varied lot, aren't they?" Jasmel said. "There seem to be several different skin tones—and look at that female, there! She has *orange* hair—just like an orangutan!"

"One of them is running away," said Dern, pointing.

"So he is," said Adikor. "I wonder where he's going?"

"Ponter! *Ponter!*"

Ponter Boddit looked up. He was sitting at a table in the dining hall at Laurentian, with two people from the university's physics department, who were helping him over lunch to work out an itinerary for a tour of physical-science installations worldwide including CERN, the Vatican Observatory, Fermilab, and Japan's Super-Kamiokande, the world's other major neutrino detector, which had recently been damaged in an accident of it's own. A hundred or so summer students were staring at the Neanderthal from a short distance away, in obvious fascination.

"Ponter!" Mary Vaughan shouted again, her voice ragged. She almost collapsed against the table as she came up to it. "Come quickly!"

Ponter started to get up. So did the two physicists. "What is it?" asked one of them.

Mary ignored the man. "*Run!*" she gasped at Ponter. "Run!"

Ponter began to run. Mary grabbed his hand and began running as well. She was still panting for breath; she'd already run all the way from the genetics lab, over in the Science One building, where she'd received the call from SNO.

"What is happening?" asked Ponter.

"A portal!" she said. "A device—some sort of robot or something—has come through. And the portal's still open!"

"Where?" said Ponter.

"Down in the neutrino observatory." She moved her hand to the center of her chest, which was heaving up and down. Ponter, Mary knew, could easily outpace her. Still running, she fumbled open her small purse and fished out her car keys, offering them to him.

Ponter shook his head slightly. For a second, Mary thought he was saying, *Not without you.* But it was surely more basic than that: Ponter Boddit had never driven a car in his life. They continued to run, Mary trying to keep up with him, but his stride was longer, and he'd only just started running, and—

He looked at her, and it was obvious that he also sensed the dilemma: there was no point in beating Mary to the parking lot, since there was nothing he could do there until she arrived.

He stopped running, and she did, too, looking at him with concern.

"May I?" said Ponter.

Mary had no idea what he meant, but she nodded. He reached out with his massive arms and scooped her up from the ground. Mary draped her arms around his thick neck, and Ponter began to run, his legs pounding like pistons against the tiled floor. Mary could feel his muscles surging as he barreled along. Students and faculty stopped and stared at the spectacle.

They came to the bowling alley, and Ponter put all his strength into running, surging forward, the sound of his massive footfalls thundering in the glass-walled corridor. Farther and farther, past the kiosks, past the Tim Hortons, and—

A student was coming through a door from outside. His mouth went wide, but he held the glass door open for Ponter and Mary as they surged into the daylight.

Mary's perspective was to the rear, and she saw divots flying up in Ponter's wake. She squeezed tighter, holding on. Ponter knew her car well enough; he'd have no trouble spotting the red Neon in the tiny lot—one of the advantages of a small university. He continued to run, and Mary heard and felt the change of terrain as he bounded off the grass onto the asphalt of the parking lot.

After a dozen meters, he slowed and swung Mary to the ground. She was dizzy from the wild ride, but managed to quickly cover the short remaining distance to her car, her electronic key out, the doors clicking open.

Mary scrambled into the driver's seat, and Ponter got into the passenger's seat. She put the key into the ignition, and flattened the accelerator to the floor, and off they shot down the road, leaving Laurentian behind. Soon they were out of Sudbury, heading for the Creighton Mine. Mary usually didn't speed—not that there was much opportunity to in Toronto's gridlock—but she was doing 120 km/h along the country roads.

Finally, they came to the mine site, racing past the big Inco sign, through the security gate, and careening down the winding roads to the large building that housed the lift leading down to the mine. Mary skidded the car to a halt, sending a spray of gravel into the air, and Ponter and she both hurried out.

Now, though, there was no further need for Ponter to wait for Mary—and time was still of the essence. Who knew how long the portal would stay open; indeed, who knew if it even still *was* open? Ponter looked at her, then surged forward and grabbed her in a hug. "Thank you," he said. "Thank you for everything."

Mary squeezed him back hard—hard for her, as hard as she could, but presumably nothing like what a Neanderthal woman could have done.

And then she released him.

And he ran off toward the elevator building.

Chapter Forty-four

Adikor, Jasmel, and Dern continued to stare at the monitor, at the scene taking place a few armspans—and an infinity—away.

"They're so fragile-looking," said Jasmel, frowning. "Their arms are like sticks."

"Not that one," said Dern, pointing. "She must be pregnant."

Adikor squinted at the screen. "That's not a woman," he said. "It's a man."

"With a belly like that?" said Dern, incredulously. "And I thought I was fat! Just how much do these Gliksins eat?"

Adikor shrugged. He didn't want to spend time talking; he just wanted to look, to try to soak it all in. Another form of humanity! And a technologically advanced one, at that. It was incredible. He'd love to compare notes with them on physics, on biology, and—

Biology.

Yes, that's what he needed! The robot had been touched by several Gliksins now. Surely some of their cells had rubbed off onto its frame; surely some of their DNA could be recovered from it. That would be proof that Adjudicator Sard would have to accept! Gliksin DNA: proof that the world shown on the screen was real. But—

There was no guarantee that the portal would stay open much longer, or that it could ever be reopened again. But at least he would be exonerated, and Dab and Kelon would be spared mutilation.

"Reel the robot back in," Adikor said.

Dern looked at him. "What? Why?"

"There's probably some Gliksin DNA on it now. We don't want to lose that if the portal closes."

Dern nodded. Adikor watched him walk across the room, take hold of the fiber-optic cable, and give it a gentle tug. Adikor turned back to the square monitor. The Gliksin nearest the robot—a brown-skinned specimen, probably a male—looked startled as the robot jerked upward.

Dern gave another tug. The brown Gliksin was looking back over his shoulder now, presumably at another person. He shouted something, then he nodded as somebody shouted back at him. He then grabbed onto the bottom of the robot's rising frame, now dangling most of the man's height off the ground.

Another male Gliksin ran into the field of view. This one was shorter, with lighter skin—as light as Adikor's own—but his eyes were . . . strange: dark, and half-hidden under unusual lids.

The brown Gliksin looked at the newcomer. The newcomer was shaking his head vigorously—but not at the brown one. No, he was looking directly up into the robot's glass lens, and making a wild motion with his arms, holding both hands flat out, palms down, and swiping them back and forth in front of his chest. And he kept shouting a single syllable over and over again: "*Wayt! Wayt! Wayt!*"

Of course, thought Adikor, they, too, were anxious to have an artifact to prove what they'd seen; doubtless they didn't want to give up the robot. He turned his head and shouted out to Dern. "Keep hoisting!"

Mary Vaughan finally caught up with Ponter at the far end of the elevator building, past the area where miners changed into their work clothes. Ponter was standing on the ramp leading down to the lift entrance—but the metal grating over the lift shaft was closed; the cage could have been anywhere, even down at the lowest drift, 7,400 feet below. Still, Ponter had evidently persuaded the operator to bring it up now—but it could be several minutes before it reached the surface.

Neither Ponter nor Mary had any authority here, and the mine's safety rules were posted *everywhere*; Inco had an enviable record for accident prevention. Ponter had already put on safety boots and a hardhat. Mary walked away from the ramp and put on a hardhat and boots, as well, selected from a vast rack of such supplies. She then moved back to stand next to Ponter, who was tapping his left foot in impatience.

At last the lift cage arrived, and the door was hoisted. There was no one inside. Ponter and Mary entered, the operator here at the top sounded the buzzer five times— express descent with no stops—and the cab lurched into motion.

Now that they were going down, there was no way to communicate with the SNO control room—or anyone else, except the lift operator, and he could only be signaled with a buzzer. Mary had said little to Ponter on the hair-raising drive over, partly because she'd been trying to concentrate on keeping the vehicle under control, and party because her heart had been racing at least as fast as her car's engine.

But now—

Now she had an extended time with nothing to do while the elevator dropped a mile and a quarter straight down. Ponter would probably run off as soon as the cage reached the 6,800-foot level, and she couldn't blame him. Slowing so she could keep up would delay him by crucial minutes as he covered the three-quarters of a mile to the SNO cavity.

Mary watched as level after level flashed by. It was, after all, a fascinating spectacle that she'd never seen before, but . . .

But this might well be her final chance to talk to Ponter. On the one hand, the trip down seemed to be taking an enormous amount of time. On the other, hours, days—or maybe even years—wouldn't be enough to say all the things Mary wanted to say.

She didn't know where to begin, but she was sure she'd never forgive herself if she didn't tell him now, didn't make him understand. It wasn't as if he were disappearing into prehistoric time, after all; he'd be going *sideways*, not backwards. Tomorrow would be tomorrow for him, too, and the tenth anniversary of the day they'd met would be simultaneous on both versions of Earth—although he'd probably note it on the hundredth month, or some such date. Still, Mary had no doubt that he would reflect and wonder and feel sad, trying to piece together his emotions, and hers—trying to understand what had transpired, and, just as importantly, what had failed to transpire between them.

"Ponter," she said. The word was soft, and the clattering of the lift was loud. Perhaps he didn't hear. He was looking out the cage door, absently watching the dark rock speeding by as they plummeted farther and farther.

"Ponter," Mary said again, more loudly.

He turned to her, and his eyebrow rolled up. Mary smiled. She'd found his quizzical expression so disconcerting when she'd first seen it, but now she was used to it. The differences between them were so much less than the similarities.

But, still, all along, all this time, there had been a gulf between them—a gulf caused not by his being a member of a different species, but rather by the simple fact of his sex. And more than that. It wasn't *just* that he was male, but that he was so *overwhelmingly* male: muscled like Arnold Schwarzenegger; hairy all over; bearded; powerful, rough, and clumsy all at the same time.

"Ponter," she said, uttering his name for a third time now. "There's—there's something I have to tell you." She paused. Part of her thought it would be better not to give voice to this, to leave it, as she had so many other things, unspoken, unsaid. And, of course, there was a chance that by the time they reached the SNO chamber—still many minutes away, by lift and by foot—that whatever portal had magically appeared between his world and hers would be closed, and she would continue to see Ponter day in and day out, but with her having laid bare her soul, that ethereal essence that she believed they both had and that he was sure neither of them possessed.

"Yes?" said Ponter.

"You'd assumed," said Mary, "and I'd assumed, that whatever fluke of physics had deposited you here was ir-reproducible—that you were stranded here forever."

He nodded slightly, his large face moving up and down in the semidarkness.

"We thought there was no way you could get back to Jasmel and Megameg," said Mary. "No way to get back to Adikor. And though I know your heart belonged to him, to them, and always would, I also knew that you were re-signing yourself to making a life in this world, on this Earth."

Ponter nodded again, but his eyes shifted away from her. Perhaps he saw where this was going; perhaps he felt nothing more needed to be said.

But it *had* to be said. She had to make him under-stand—make him understand that it wasn't him. It was her.

No, no, no. That was wrong. It wasn't her, either. It was that faceless, evil man, that monster, that demon. *That's* who had come between them.

"Just before we met," said Mary, "on the day you arrived here in Sudbury, I was . . ."

She stopped. Her heart was pounding; she could feel it—but all she could hear was the clattering rumble of the lift.

The elevator passed the 1,200-foot level. She could see a miner out in the drift, waiting for a ride up, his harsh headlight beam lancing into the cage, no doubt briefly playing across her face and Ponter's, a stranger intruding from outside.

Ponter said nothing; he just waited quietly for her to go on. And, at last, she did. "That night," Mary said, "I was . . ."

She'd intended to say the word baldly, to pronounce it dispassionately, but she couldn't even give it voice. "I was . . . hurt," she said.

Ponter tilted his head, puzzled. "An injury? I am sorry."

"No. I mean I was *hurt*—by a man." She took a deep breath. "I was attacked, at York, on the campus, after dark"—pointless details delaying the word she knew she'd have to say. She dropped her gaze to the lift's mud-covered metal floor. "I was raped."

Hak bleeped—the Companion had the sense to do so at a great volume so that the sound could be heard over the noise of the elevator. Mary tried again. "I was assaulted. Sexually assaulted."

She heard Ponter suck in air—even over the rumble of the lift, she heard his gasp. Mary lifted her head and sought out his golden eyes in the semidarkness. Her gaze flickered back and forth, left and right, from one of his eyes to the other, looking for his reaction, trying to gauge his thoughts.

"I am very sorry," said Ponter, gently.

Mary assumed he—or Hak—meant "sorry" in the sense of sympathy, not contrition, but she said, because it was all that occurred to her to say, "It wasn't your fault."

"No," said Ponter. It was now his turn to be at a loss for words. Finally, he said, "Were you hurt—physically, I mean?"

"Roughed up a little. Nothing major. But . . ."

"Yes," said Ponter. "But." He paused. "Do you know who did it?"

Mary shook her head.

"Surely the authorities have reviewed your alibi archive and—" He looked away, back at the rock wall flashing by. "Sorry." He paused again. "So—so he will get away with this?" Ponter was speaking loudly, despite the delicacy of the matter, in order for Hak to pick up his voice over the racket around them. Mary could hear the fury, the outrage, in his words.

She exhaled and nodded slowly, sadly. "Probably." She paused. "I—we didn't talk about this, you and I. Maybe I'm presuming too much. In this world, rape is considered a horrible crime, a terrible crime. I don't know—"

"It is the same on my world," said Ponter. "A few animals do it—orangutans, for instance—but we are people, not animals. Of course, with the alibi archives, few are fool enough to attempt such an act, but when it is done, it is dealt with harshly."

There was silence between them for a few moments. Ponter had his right arm half raised, as if he'd thought to reach out and touch her, to try to console her, but he looked down and, with an expression of surprise on his face, as if he were seeing a stranger's limb, he lowered it.

But then Mary found herself reaching out and touching his thick forearm herself, gently, tentatively. And then her hand slid down the length of his arm and found his fingers, and his hand came up again, and her delicate digits intertwined with his massive ones.

"I wanted you to understand," said Mary. "We grew very close while you were here. We talked about anything and everything. And, well, as I said, you thought you were never going home; you thought you would have to make a new life here." She paused. "You never pushed, you never took advantage. By the end, I think, you were the only man on this entire planet that I was getting comfortable being alone with, but . . ."

Ponter closed his sausagelike fingers gently.

"It was too soon," said Mary. "Don't you see? I—I know you like me, and . . ." She paused. The corners of her eyes were stinging. "I'm sorry," she said. "It hasn't happened often in my life, but there have been times when men were interested in me, but, well—"

"But when that man," Ponter said slowly, "is not like other men . . ."

Mary shook her head and looked up at him. "No, no. It wasn't because of that; it wasn't because of the way you look—"

She saw him stiffen slightly in the strobing light. She didn't find him ugly—not anymore, not now. She found his face kind and thoughtful and compassionate and intelligent and, yes, dammit, yes—attractive. But what she'd said had come out all wrong, and now, in trying to explain so his feelings wouldn't be bruised, so he wouldn't be left wondering forevermore why she'd responded the way she had to his soft touch when they were stargazing, she'd ended up hurting him.

"I mean," said Mary, "that there's nothing wrong with your appearance. In fact, I find you quite"—she hesitated, although not from lack of conviction, but rather because so rarely in her life had she ever been so forward with any man—"handsome."

Ponter made a sad little smile. "I am not, you know. Handsome, I mean. Not by the standards of my people."

"I don't care," said Mary at once. "I don't care at all. I mean, I can't imagine you found me attractive physically, either. I'm . . ." She lowered her voice. "I'm what they call plain, I guess. I don't turn a lot of heads, but—"

"I find you very striking," said Ponter.

"If we'd had more time," said Mary. "If *I'd* had more time, you know, to get over it"—not, Mary was sure, that she ever would—"things . . . things might have been different between us." She lifted her shoulders a bit, a helpless shrug. "That's all. I wanted you to know that. I wanted you to understand that I did—do—like you."

A crazy thought ran through her head. Had things indeed been different—had she come up to Sudbury a whole person, instead of shattered inside, maybe now Ponter wouldn't be rushing as fast as he could to return to his old life, his own world. Maybe . . .

No. No, that was too much. He had Adikor. He had children.

And, anyway, if things *had* been different, maybe *she* would be getting ready to go with him, through the portal, to *his* world. After all, she had no one here, and—

But things were *not* different. Things were precisely as they were.

The lift shuddered to a halt, and the buzzer made its raucous call, signaling the opening of the cage door.

Chapter Forty-five

Suddenly there was considerable commotion among the Gliksins. At first, Adikor couldn't tell what was going on, but then he realized someone was coming down into the barrel-shaped chamber, descending the same long ladder they'd seen before. The person's broad back was facing the robot's eye; presumably, it was a Gliksin leader, come to make an assessment of this strange contraption, that— if the effect was mirrored on the other side—appeared to be attached to a cable that was protruding from thin air.

The Gliksins visible in the foreground were beckoning for the newcomer to approach. And he did, running quite fast. The robot was swinging at the end of its tether, as Dern hauled it higher and higher, but then Adikor caught a glimpse on the monitor of the face of the person who had just arrived.

Yes! Incredibly, wonderfully yes!

Adikor's heart was pounding. It was Ponter! He was clad in the strange clothing of the Gliksins, and wearing one of those plastic turtle shells on top of his head, but there could be no doubt. Ponter Boddit was alive and well!

"Dern!" shouted Adikor. "Stop! Let the robot back down!"

The camera's perspective started lowering on the screen. Jasmel gasped and clapped her hands together with glee. Adikor wiped tears from his eyes.

Ponter hurried over to the robot. He bent his head oddly, and it took Adikor a moment to realize what Ponter was likely doing: looking at the manufacturer's contribution stamp on the robot's frame, confirming for himself that this really was an artifact from his own world. Ponter then looked up into the robot's camera lens, grinning widely.

"Hello," said Ponter—the first word out of the cacophony that Adikor had understood. "Hello, my friends! I'd thought I'd lost you forever! Who's looking at this, I wonder? Adikor, no doubt. How I've missed you!"

He paused, then two of the Gliksins spoke to him: one of the light-skinned ones and the dark-skinned man who had been holding on to the robot earlier.

Ponter turned back to the camera. "I'm not sure what I'm supposed to do now. I see the cable coming out of the air, but is it safe for me to cross back over? Can"—his voice caught for a moment—"can I come home?"

Adikor turned away from the screen and looked at Dern, who had returned to the control room. Dern lifted his shoulders. "The robot seemed to come through just fine."

"You don't know how long you'll be able to keep the gate open," said Jasmel, "or whether you'll ever be able to establish it again if it closes. He should come through right now."

Adikor nodded. "But how do we let him know that?"

Jasmel said decisively, "I know how." She hurried down

the steps onto the computing floor, then strode over to where the cable disappeared into the hole in the air. Jasmel placed her hand on the cable, then slid her grip along the cable's length until her fingertips, then her whole fingers, then her hand, then her forearm disappeared. When everything up to her shoulder was projecting through, she shoved her head over into the other side, and simply shouted out—Adikor and Dern could hear it, but it came entirely from the speaker on the monitor; there was no sound at all coming from the computing floor—"Daddy! Come home!"

"Jasmel, sweetheart!" shouted Ponter, looking up. "I—"

"Come right now!" Jasmel replied. "There's no telling how long we can keep this open. Just follow the cable— use that ladder, there, to get up here. The computing-room floor is about half an armspan below where my head is; you should have no trouble finding it."

Jasmel then pulled her head back over to her side and ran over and up into the control room.

There was a flurry of activity visible on the monitor; it was clear no one was quite prepared for this. Two men went to get the ladder Jasmel had indicated. One of the men gave Ponter a great hug, which Ponter enthusiastically returned—it seemed that he hadn't been mistreated by the Gliksins.

And now a yellow-haired woman had appeared next to Ponter; she hadn't been there before, and she looked quite winded. She stood on her toes and pressed her lips against Ponter's cheek; he smiled broadly in return.

The robot swiveled its camera under Dern's command, and Adikor saw that the problem was more difficult than

Jasmel had thought. Yes, the cable was protruding from a hole—but that hole was nowhere near any part of the cavern's rocky walls. Rather, it was in the middle of the air, several body-lengths above the ground, and at least that far from the closest wall. There was nothing to lean the ladder against.

"Could he climb the cable?" asked Adikor.

Dern shrugged. "He outweighs the robot, I'm sure. It *might* hold him, but . . ."

But if it snapped, Ponter would crash down to the rock floor, possibly breaking his back.

"Can we get a stronger cable through to him?" asked Jasmel.

"If we *had* a stronger cable," said Dern, nodding. "But I've no idea where to get one down here; I'd have to go up to my workshop on the surface, and that'd take too long."

But the Gliksins, puny though they might be, were resourceful. Four of them were now holding the base of the ladder, steadying it with all their strength. It wasn't leaning against anything, but they were shouting at Ponter, presumably urging him to try climbing it anyway.

Ponter ran over to the ladder, and was about to step onto the first rung, even though it was still none too steady. Suddenly, the yellow-haired woman ran up to him, and touched his arm. He turned, and his eyebrow rolled up his browridge in surprise. She pressed something into his other hand and stretched up to place her face against Ponter's cheek again. He smiled once more, then began climbing the ladder the Gliksins were holding on to.

The ladder swung more and more the higher Ponter

got, and Adikor's heart jumped as it looked like it was going to come crashing down, but more Gliksins rushed to help, and the ladder was straightened again, and Ponter started reaching out with his hand, trying to grab the cable just shy of where it protruded from the midair hole. The ladder swung back, forth, left, right, and Ponter grabbed, missed, grabbed again, missed once more, and then—

Dern's control box jerked forward slightly. Ponter had the cable!

Adikor, Jasmel, and Dern rushed down onto the computing floor. Jasmel and Dern had taken positions directly in front of the opening, and Adikor, looking to see if there was something he could do to help, moved *behind* the opening, and—

Adikor gasped.

He saw Ponter's head appear from nowhere, and, from this rear angle, Adikor could see into his neck as if it had been chopped clean through by some massive blade. Dern and Jasmel were helping pull Ponter in now, but Adikor watched, stunned, as more and more of his beloved emerged through the widening hole that hugged his contours—and as the slice through him worked its way down his body, now revealing cross sections through his shoulders; now through his chest with beating heart and inflating lungs; now through his guts; now through his legs; and—

And he was through! All of him was through!

Adikor rushed around to Ponter and hugged him close, and Jasmel hugged her father, too. The three of them laughed and cried, and, finally, disengaging himself, Adikor said, "Welcome back! Welcome back!"

"Thank you," said Ponter, smiling broadly.

Dern had politely moved a short distance away. Adikor caught sight of him. "Forgive us," he said. "Ponter Boddit, this is Dern Kord, an engineer who has been helping us."

"Healthy day," said Ponter to Dern. Ponter began walking toward him, and—

"*No!*" shouted Dern.

But it was too late. Ponter had walked into the taut cable, and it had snapped in two, and the part that projected into the Gliksin world reeled out through the gateway, and the gateway disappeared with an electric blue flash.

The two worlds were separate once more.

Chapter Forty-six

Dern, clearly feeling like a travel cube without a passenger, politely left, heading back up to the surface, letting the family reunion occur in private. Ponter, Adikor, and Jasmel had moved to the small eating room in the quantum-computing lab.

"I never thought I'd see you again," said Ponter, beaming at Adikor, then at Jasmel. "Either of you."

"We thought the same thing," said Adikor.

"You're fine?" asked Ponter. "Everyone is fine?"

"Yes, I'm all right," said Adikor.

"And Megameg? How is darling little Megameg?"

"She's fine," said Jasmel. "She really hasn't understood everything that's been going on."

"I can't wait to see her," said Ponter. "I don't care if it is seventeen days until Two next become One, I'm going to go into the Center tomorrow and give her a great big hug."

Jasmel smiled. "She'd like that, Daddy."

"What about Pabo?"

Adikor grinned. "She missed you awfully. She keeps looking up at every sound, hoping it might be you returning."

"That sweet bag of bones," said Ponter.

"Say, Daddy," said Jasmel, "what was it that female gave you?"

"Oh," said Ponter. "I haven't even looked myself. Let's see . . ."

Ponter reached into the pocket of his strange, alien pant, and pulled out a wad of white tissue. He carefully opened it up. Inside was a gold chain, and attached to it were two simple, perpendicular bars of unequal length, intersecting each other about one-third of the way down the longer of the two pieces.

"It's beautiful!" said Jasmel. "What is it?"

Ponter's eyebrow went up. "It's the symbol of a belief system some of them subscribe to."

"Who was that female?" asked Adikor.

"My friend," said Ponter softly. "Her name—well, I can only say the first syllable of her name: 'Mare.' "

Adikor laughed; "mare" was, of course, the word in their language for "beloved." "I know I told you to find yourself a new woman," he said, his tone joking, "but I didn't think you'd have to go that far to meet one who would put up with you."

Ponter smiled, but it was a forced smile. "She was very kind," he said.

Adikor knew his partner well enough to understand that whatever story there was to tell would come out in its own good time. Still . . .

"Speaking of women," said Adikor. "I, ah, have had some dealings with Klast's woman-mate while you've been away."

"Daklar!" said Ponter. "How is she?"

"Actually," said Adikor, looking now at Jasmel, "she's become rather famous in your absence."

"Really?" said Ponter. "Whatever for?"

"For making and pursuing a murder accusation."

"Murder!" exclaimed Ponter. "Who was killed?"

"You were," said Adikor, deadpan.

Ponter's jaw dropped.

"You went missing, you see," said Adikor, "and Bolbay thought . . ."

"She thought you had *murdered* me?" declared Ponter incredulously.

"Well," said Adikor, "you *had* disappeared, and the mine here is so deep within the rocks that the alibi-archive pavilion couldn't pick up the signals from our Companions. Bolbay made it sound like the perfect crime."

"Incredible," said Ponter, shaking his head. "Who spoke on your behalf?"

"I did," said Jasmel.

"Good girl!" said Ponter, sweeping her up in another hug. He spoke over his daughter's shoulder. "Adikor, I'm sorry you had to go through this."

"Me too, but—" He shrugged. "You'll doubtless hear it soon enough. Bolbay said I resented you; she said that I felt like merely an adjunct to your work."

"Nonsense," said Ponter, releasing Jasmel. "I could have accomplished nothing without you."

Adikor tipped his head. "That's generous of you to say, but . . ." He paused, then spread his arms, palms up. "But there was truth in her words."

Ponter put an arm around Adikor's shoulders. "Perhaps the theories were indeed more mine than yours—but it was you who designed and built the quantum computer, and it is that computer that has opened up a new world to us. Your contribution exceeds mine a hundredfold because of that."

Adikor smiled. "Thank you."

"So what happened?" said Ponter. He grinned. "Your voice doesn't sound any higher, so I assume she didn't succeed."

"Actually," said Jasmel, "the case will be heard by a tribunal, starting tomorrow."

Ponter shook his head in wonder. "Well, obviously, we must have the accusation expunged."

Adikor smiled. "If you'd be so kind," he said.

The next morning, Adjudicator Sard was joined by a wizened male and an even more wizened female, one sitting on each side of her. The Gray Council chamber was packed with spectators and ten or so silver-clad Exhibitionists. Daklar Bolbay was still wearing orange, the color of accusation. But there was considerable whispering among the crowd when Adikor entered, for instead of the accused's blue, he had on a rather jaunty shirt with a floral print, and a light green pant. He made his way to the stool he'd gotten to know so well.

"Scholar Huld," said Adjudicator Sard, "we have traditions, and I expect you to observe them. I think by now you've learned how little patience I have for wasting time, so I won't send you home to change today, but tomorrow, I'll expect you to be wearing blue."

"Of course, Adjudicator," said Adikor. "Forgive me."

Sard nodded. "The final investigation of Adikor Huld of Saldak Rim for the murder of Ponter Boddit of the same locale now begins. Presiding tribunal consists of Farba Dond"—the elderly man nodded—"as well as Kab Jodler, and myself, Komel Sard. The accuser is Daklar Bolbay, on behalf of her late woman-mate's minor child, Megameg Bek." Sard looked around the packed room, and a self-satisfied frown creased Sard's face; she clearly knew this was a case that would be talked about for countless months to come. "We will begin with the initial statement of the accuser. Daklar Bolbay, you may begin."

"With respect, Adjudicator," said Adikor, rising, "I was wondering if the person speaking for me might present my defense first?"

"Scholar Huld," said Dond, sharply, "Adjudicator Sard has already warned you about ignoring traditions. The accuser always goes first, and—"

"Oh, I understand that," said Adikor. "But, well, I *do* know of Adjudicator Sard's desire to speed things along, and I thought this might help."

Bolbay rose, perhaps sensing an opportunity. After all, if she went *after* the defense, she'd be able to pull it apart during her initial statement. "As accuser, I have no problem with the defense being presented first."

"Thank you," said Adikor, bowing magnanimously. "Now, if it—"

"Scholar Huld!" snapped Sard. "It is not up to the accuser to determine protocol. We will proceed as tradition dictates, with Daklar Bolbay speaking first, and—"

"I only thought—" said Adikor.

"Silence!" Sard was getting quite red in the face. "You

shouldn't be talking at all." She faced Jasmel. "Jasmel Ket, only you should speak on Scholar Huld's behalf; please make sure he understands this."

Jasmel rose. "With great respect, Worthy Adjudicator, I am not speaking for Adikor this time. You did, after all, suggest that he find a more appropriate defender."

Sard nodded curtly. "I'm glad to see he can listen at least some of the time." She scanned the crowd. "All right. Who is speaking on Adikor Huld's behalf?"

Ponter Boddit, who had been standing just outside the Council-chamber doors, walked in. "I am," he said.

Some spectators gasped.

"Very well," said Sard, looking down, preparing to make a note. "And your name is?"

"Boddit," said Ponter. Sard's head snapped up. "Ponter Boddit."

Ponter looked across the room. Jasmel had been restraining Megameg, but now she let her younger sister go. Megameg ran across the Council-chamber floor, and Ponter swept her up off the ground, hugging her.

"Order!" shouted Sard. "There will be order!"

Ponter was grinning from ear to ear. Part of him had worried that the authorities might try to keep the existence of the other Earth a secret. After all, it was only at the last moment that Doctors Montego and Singh had prevented Ponter from being taken away by the Gliksin authorities, possibly never to be seen again. But right now, thousands were using their Voyeurs at home to look in on what the Exhibitionists here were seeing, and a room full of regular Companions were transmitting signals to their owners' alibi cubes. The whole world—*this* whole world—would soon hear the truth.

Bolbay was on her feet. "Ponter!"

"Your eagerness to avenge me is laudable, dear Daklar," he said, "but, as you can see, it was premature."

"Where have you been?" Bolbay demanded. Adikor thought she looked more angry than relieved.

"Where have I been?" repeated Ponter, looking out at the silver suits in the audience. "I must say I'm flattered that the trifling matter of the possible murder of an undistinguished physicist has attracted so many Exhibitionists. And, with them all here and with a hundred other Companions sending signals to the archive pavilion, I will be glad to explain." He surveyed the faces—broad, flat faces; faces with proper-sized noses, not those pinched things the Gliksins had; hairy male faces and less-hairy female ones; faces with prominent browridges and streamlined jaws; handsome faces, beautiful faces, the faces of his people, his friends, his species. "But first," he said, "let me just say that there's no place like home."

Chapter forty-seven

SIX DAYS LATER
FRIDAY, AUGUST 16
148/119/09

Adikor and Ponter arrived at the home of Dern, the robotics engineer. Dern ushered them inside, then turned off his Voyeur—he was a fellow Lulasm fan, Ponter saw.

"Gentlemen, gentlemen!" said Dern, "it's good to see you." He pointed at the now-black square of the Voyeur. "Did you look in on Lulasm's visit to the Economics Academy this morning?"

Ponter shook his head; so did Adikor.

"Your friend Sard has stepped down from being an adjudicator. Apparently, her colleagues thought she looked somewhat less than impartial, given the way your trial turned out."

"*Somewhat?*" said Adikor, astonished. "There's an understatement."

"In any event," said Dern, "the Grays decided she'd make a more meaningful contribution by teaching advanced mediation to 146s."

"It probably won't catch any Exhibitionist's eye," said Ponter, "but Daklar Bolbay is getting help now, too. Therapy for grief management, anger management, and so on."

Adikor smiled. "I introduced her to my old personality

sculptor, and he's gotten her hooked up with the right people."

"That's good," said Dern. "Are you going to demand a public apology from her?"

Adikor shook his head. "I have Ponter back," he said simply. "There's nothing else I need."

Dern smiled and told one of his many household robots to fetch beverages. "I thank you both for coming over," he said, lying down on a long couch, ankles crossed, fingers interlaced behind his head, his round belly rising up and down as he breathed.

Ponter and Adikor straddled saddle-seats. "You said you had something important to talk about," said Ponter, prodding gently.

"I do," said Dern, lolling his head so that he could look at them. "I think we need to find a way to make the gateway between the two versions of Earth stay open permanently."

"It seemed to stay open as long as there was a physical object passing through the gateway," said Ponter.

"Well, yes, on short time scales," said Adikor. "We really don't know if it can be maintained indefinitely."

"If it can," said Ponter, "the possibilities are staggering. Tourism. Trade. Cultural and scientific exchange."

"Exactly," said Dern. "Have a look at this." He swung his feet to the floor and placed an object on the polished wooden table. It was a hollow tube, made of wire mesh, a little longer than his longest finger and no thicker than the diameter of his shortest one. "This is a Derkers tube," he said. He used the ends of two fingers to pull on the mouth of the tube, and the tube's opening expanded and expanded, its mesh with an elastic membrane stretched across it growing larger and larger, until it was as wide as Dern's handspan.

He handed the tube to Ponter. "Try to crush it," Dern said.

Ponter wrapped one hand around it as far as it would go, and brought in his other hand and encircled more of the tube. He then squeezed, lightly at first, and then with all his strength. The tube did not collapse.

"That's just a little one," said Dern, "but we've got them here at the mine that expand to three armspans in diameter. We use them to secure tunnels when a cave-in seems likely. Can't afford to lose those mining robots, after all."

"How does it work?" asked Ponter.

"The mesh is actually a series of articulated metal segments, each with ratcheting ends. Once you open it up, the only way to collapse it is to actually go in with tools and undo the locking mechanisms on each piece."

"So you're suggesting," said Ponter, "that we should re-open the gateway to the other universe, and then shove one of these—what did you call it? A 'Derkers tube'? Shove one of these Derkers tubes through the opening, and expand it to its full diameter?"

"That's right," said Dern. "Then people could just walk through from this universe to that one."

"They'd have to build a platform and stairs on the other side, leading up to the tube," said Ponter.

"Easily enough done, I'm sure," said Dern.

"What happens if the gate doesn't stay open indefinitely?" asked Adikor.

"I wouldn't suggest anyone linger in the tunnel," said Dern, "but presumably if the gate did shut down, it would simply sever the tunnel, cutting it into two parts. Either that, or it would draw the tunnel fully into one side or the other."

"There are issues to be concerned about," said Ponter. "I got very sick when I was over there; germs exist on the other side to which we have no immunity."

Adikor nodded. "We'd have to exercise caution. We certainly wouldn't want pathogens moving freely from their universe into ours, and travelers headed there would presumably require a series of immunizations."

"It could be worked out, I'm sure," said Dern. "Although I don't know exactly what the procedures should be."

There was silence between them for a time. Finally, Ponter spoke. "Who makes the decision?" he asked. "Who decides if we should establish permanent contact—or even reestablish temporary contact—with the other world?"

"I'm sure there are no procedures in place," said Adikor. "I doubt anyone has even considered the possibility of a bridge to another Earth."

"If it weren't for the danger of germs traveling here," said Ponter, "I'd say we should just go ahead and open up the gateway, but . . ."

They were all silent, until Adikor spoke. "Are they— are they good people, Ponter? *Should* we be in contact with them?"

"They are *different*," said Ponter, "in many, many ways. But they showed a lot of kindness toward me; I was treated very well." He paused, then nodded. "Yes, I do think we should be in contact with them."

"All right, then," said Adikor. "I suppose the first step

is to make a presentation to the High Gray Council. We should get to work on that."

Ponter had thought a lot about what Mare had said to him in the elevator on the way down to the neutrino observatory. Yes, he had indeed been interested; she had read him correctly. Even across species boundaries, even across timelines, some things were clear.

Ponter's heart was pounding. It seemed he was going to get to see her again.

Who knew what would come of it?

Well, there was only one way to find out. "Yes," said Ponter Boddit, smiling. "Let's get to work."

Usually, one had to wait until September for Toronto to be so heart-stoppingly beautiful, with the sky's complexion clear and flawless, the temperature *perfect*, and the wind a gentle caress—the kind of profound pleasantness that reminded Mary of just why it was that she believed in God.

But September was still two weeks away, and, of course, when Labour Day, that final, abrupt punctuation mark at the end of summer, came around, Mary would have to go back to work, back to her old life of teaching genetics, and having no one special, and eating too much. For now, though, for right now, with the wonderful weather, Toronto seemed like heaven.

While in Northern Ontario, Mary had lost a few of the extra pounds she normally carried around, but she knew they would return. Every diet she'd ever been on reminded her of Crisco oil: it all came back, except for maybe one tablespoon.

Of course, she hadn't been on a concerted diet. She simply hadn't been eating as much as usual. Part of it had been excitement during the time she'd spent in Sudbury, the time she'd spent with Ponter, over all the incredible things that had come and gone.

And part of it—the part that wasn't over, that could never be over—was the aftermath of the rape.

Mary had agreed to come in to York today, a Monday, for a departmental meeting, and so, for the first time since that horrible night—had it really been just seventeen days?—Mary had to walk by the spot on the campus where the attack had taken place, the concrete wall that the rapist, his head sheathed in a black balaclava, had slammed her body against.

But, of course, it wasn't because of the wall that she'd been raped. It was because of *him*—that monster—and the sick society that had produced him. As she passed by, she ran her fingers across the wall, taking care not to chip her red-painted nails—and, as she did so, a crazy thought occurred to her. She remembered another wall from long ago, one she and Colm had carved their initials into.

It was a ridiculous thing for a thirty-eight-year-old woman to contemplate, but maybe she should carve MV+PB here on this wall—although to do it right, she supposed, she should really carve MV plus the symbols in Ponter Boddit's language that represented his name.

Either way, she'd then smile every time she saw the wall, instead of being disgusted by it. To be sure, it would be a rueful smile, for she knew she'd likely never see him again. But, still, a memory of . . . *love*, yes: a memory of love lost was infinitely preferable to one of what had happened here.

Mary Vaughan continued on past the wall, forward, into the future.

Appendix

A GUIDE TO NEANDERTHAL TIMEKEEPING

Earth has three natural timekeeping units: the day (the time it takes the Earth to revolve once on its axis), the month (the time it takes the moon to orbit the Earth), and the year (the time it takes the Earth to orbit the sun).

Because of our agricultural economy, which is based on seasonal sowing and harvesting, we emphasize the year—and corrupt the true lengths of all three units to make them into simple multiples or fractions of each other.

The actual sidereal year (one orbit around the sun, relative to the fixed stars) is 365 days 6 hours 9 minutes 9.54 seconds, but we reckon common years as 365 whole days and leap years as 366 whole days.

The true synodic month (a complete cycle of lunar phases) is 29 days 12 hours 44 minutes 3 seconds, but we have "months" ranging from 28 to 31 whole days long.

And the true sidereal day (a complete revolution of the Earth, measured relative to the fixed stars) is 23 hours 56 minutes 4.09 seconds, but we round that up to 24 hours.

Further, many of our religions obfuscated the calendar to reserve power to the clergy (the secret of how to calculate the date of Easter, for instance, was originally closely guarded).

But with a nonagricultural society and no religion, the Neanderthals have no reason to make timekeeping complex. Because of its importance to their reproductive biology, they never corrupt the length of the synodic month (the time between successive full moons). Of course, anyone can keep track of this time unit just by looking up at the night sky, so this is far more egalitarian than our system.

The smallest common unit of Neanderthal timekeeping is the *beat*, originally defined as the duration of one at-rest heartbeat, but now formally defined as 1/100,000 of a sidereal day.

The rest of Neanderthal timekeeping is mostly based on decimal multiples of the base units. Here are the standard units, in ascending order of duration, and their approximate equivalents in our units:

Neanderthal unit	Equivalent
beat	0.86 seconds
hundredbeat	86 seconds
daytenth	2.39 hours
day	1 sidereal day
month (all of identical length)	29 days 12 hours 44 minutes
tenmonth	295.32 days
year	1 sidereal year
hundredmonth	8.085 sidereal years
generation	10 years (1 decade)
thousandmonth	80.853 years

Appendix

(Very roughly, one can think of a beat as a second, a hundredbeat as a minute, a tenmonth as a year, a hundredmonth as a decade, and a thousandmonth as a century.)

The Month

The Neanderthals divide the month both into its obvious quarters (new moon, waxing half-moon, full moon, waning half-moon), and into specific groupings based on menstrual cycles:

Day	Event
1	*new moon*
1–5	peak menstruation
8	*waxing half-moon* (first quarter)
10–17	pregnancy possible
15	*full moon*
15	peak ovulation
22	*waning half-moon* (last quarter)
25–29	"Last Five"

Generations

Generations are born every ten years. The year is used as the basis for generational calculation because births are timed to always occur in the spring; infant-mortality rates are reduced by giving the child eight months before having to face its first winter.

Calendar dates are designated by three numbers: the generation number, the month within that generation, and the day within that month: 148/118/28 is the 28th day (when the moon is a mere sliver, and about to disappear) of the 118th month (the middle of the ninth year) of the 148th generation since the founding of the modern Neanderthal calendar (which happened in the year we call A.D. 523).

Generation	Year Begun (A.D.)	Current Age Members (years)	Members
148	1993	9	Megameg Bek, Dab
147	1983	19	Jasmel Ket
146	1973	29	
145	1963	39	Ponter, Adikor, Daklar Bolbay
144	1953	49	
143	1943	59	Dabdalb (keeper of alibis)
142	1933	69	Sard (adjudicator)
141	1923	79	

The Companion Era began when Lonwis Trob introduced the implants near the end of generation 140, in the year we call A.D. 1922.

further Reading

In addition to speaking directly with the experts on Neanderthals mentioned in the Acknowledgments, I also consulted hundreds of books, magazine and journal articles, and web sites. For those who might be interested in following up on ideas explored in this novel, I offer this list of some of the books I found particularly stimulating:

General Paleoanthropology

Klein, Richard G. *The Human Career: Human Biological and Cultural Origins,* 2nd ed. Chicago: University of Chicago Press, 1999.

Lieberman, Philip. *Eve Spoke: Human Language and Human Evolution.* New York: W. W. Norton, 1998.

Potts, Rick. *Humanity's Descent: The Consequences of Ecological Instability.* New York: Avon, 1996.

Further Reading

Tattersall, Ian. *Becoming Human: Evolution and Human Uniqueness*. New York: A Harvest Book (Harcourt Brace), 1999.

Tattersall, Ian, and Jeffrey Schwartz. *Extinct Humans*. Boulder, Colorado: Westview Press, 2000.

Tattersall, Ian. *The Fossil Trail: How We Know What We Think We Know about Human Evolution*. New York: Oxford University Press, 1995.

Wolpoff, Milford H. *Paleoanthropology*, 2nd ed. New York: McGraw-Hill, 1999.

Wolpoff, Milford, and Rachel Caspari. *Race and Human Evolution*. Boulder, Colorado: Westview Press, 1997.

Neanderthals

Jordan, Paul. *Neanderthal: Neanderthal Man and the Story of Human Origins*. Gloucestershire: Sutton Publishing, 1999.

Mellars, Paul. *The Neanderthal Legacy: An Archaeological Perspective from Western Europe*. Princeton, New Jersey: Princeton University Press, 1996.

Palmer, Douglas. *Neanderthal*. London: Channel 4 Books (Macmillan), 2000.

Shreeve, James. *The Neandertal Enigma: Solving the Mystery of Modern Human Origins.* New York: William Morrow, 1995.

Stringer, Christopher, and Clive Gamble. *In Search of the Neanderthals: Solving the Puzzle of Human Origins.* New York: Thames and Hudson, 1993.

Tattersall, Ian. *The Last Neanderthal: The Rise, Success, and Mysterious Extinction of Our Closest Human Relatives.* New York: Macmillan, 1995.

Trinkaus, Erik, and Pat Shipman. *The Neandertals: Changing the Image of Mankind.* New York: Alfred A. Knopf, 1993.

Evolutionary Psychology and Primatology

Boyd, Neil. *The Beast Within: Why Men Are Violent.* Vancouver, British Columbia: Greystone Books (Douglas & McIntyre), 2000.

Browne, Kingsley. *Divided Labours: An Evolutionary View of Women at Work*, "Darwinism Today" series. New Haven, Connecticut: Yale University Press, 1998.

de Wall, Frans, and Frans Lanting. *Bonobo: The Forgotten Ape.* Berkeley: University of California Press, 1997.

Further Reading

Diamond, Jared. *The Third Chimpanzee: The Evolution and Future of the Human Animal.* New York: HarperPerennial (HarperCollins), 1992.

Fouts, Roger, with Stephen Tukel Mills. *Next of Kin: What Chimpanzees Have Taught Me About Who We Are.* New York: Morrow, 1997.

Ghiglieri, Michael P. *The Dark Side of Man: Tracing the Origins of Male Violence.* Reading, Massachusetts: Perseus Books, 1999.

Jolly, Alison. *Lucy's Legacy: Sex and Intelligence in Human Evolution.* Cambridge, Massachusetts: Harvard University Press, 1999.

Mithen, Steven. *The Prehistory of the Mind: The Cognitive Origins of Art and Science.* New York: Thames and Hudson, 1996.

Russell, Robert Jay. *The Lemurs' Legacy: The Evolution of Power, Sex, and Love.* New York: A Jeremy P. Tarcher/Putnam Book, 1993.

Thornhill, Randy, and Craig T. Palmer. *A Natural History of Rape: Biological Bases of Sexual Coercion.* Cambridge, Massachusetts: MIT Press, 2000.

Wrangham, Richard, and Dale Peterson. *Demonic Males: Apes and the Origins of Human Violence.* New York: Mariner Books (Houghton Mifflin), 1996.

Wright, Robert. *The Moral Animal: The New Science of Evolutionary Psychology.* New York: Pantheon Books, 1994.

Agricultural vs. Hunter-Gatherer Societies

Brody, Hugh. *The Other Side of Eden: Hunters, Farmers and the Shaping of the World.* Vancouver, British Columbia: Douglas & McIntyre, 2000.

Diamond, Jared. *Guns, Germs, and Steel: The Fates of Human Societies.* W. W. Norton, New York, 1997.

Stanford, Craig B. *The Hunting Apes: Meat Eating and the Origins of Human Behavior.* Princeton, New Jersey: Princeton University Press, 1999.

Tudge, Colin. *Neanderthals, Bandits & Farmers: How Agriculture Really Began,* "Darwinism Today" series. New Haven, Connecticut: Yale University Press, 1998.

Wright, Robert. *Nonzero: The Logic of Human Destiny.* New York: Pantheon Books (Random House), 2000.

About the Author

ROBERT J. SAWYER, a member of The Paleoanthropology Society, is the best-selling author of a dozen previous novels, including *The Terminal Experiment*, which won the Science Fiction and Fantasy Writers of America's Nebula Award for Best Novel of the Year; *Starplex*, which was both a Nebula and Hugo Award finalist; and *Frameshift*, *Factoring Humanity*, and *Calculating God*, all of which were also Hugo Award finalists.

Sawyer has won twenty-five national and international awards for his fiction, including an Arthur Ellis Award from the Crime Writers of Canada, seven Aurora Awards (Canada's top honor in science fiction), the *Science Fiction Chronicle* Reader Award, and the top SF awards in France (*Le Grand Prix de l'Imaginaire*), twice in Japan (*Seiun*), and twice in Spain (*Premio UPC de Ciencia Ficción*); he's also been nominated for the Horror Writers Association's Bram Stoker Award.

Maclean's: Canada's Weekly Newsmagazine says, "By any reckoning Sawyer is among the most successful Canadian authors ever." He is profiled in *Canadian Who's Who*, has been interviewed over 150 times on TV (including on *Rivera Live* with Geraldo Rivera), and has given talks and readings at countless venues including the U.S. Library of Congress and the Canadian Embassy in Tokyo. He lives in Mississauga, Ontario (just west of Toronto), with Carolyn Clink, his wife of seventeen years.

For more about Rob Sawyer and his fiction—including a readers' group discussion guide for this novel, and a preview of *Humans*, the forthcoming sequel—visit his World Wide Web site (called "the largest genre writer's home page in existence" by *Interzone*) at **www.sfwriter.com**.